Richard,

With sincere appreciation

Walter

MUSIC
MAKERS

To Ida

MUSIC MAKERS

The Lives of Harry Freedman & Mary Morrison

WALTER PITMAN

THE DUNDURN GROUP
TORONTO

Copy-editor: Jennifer Gallant
Design: Jennifer Scott
Printer: Friesens

Library and Archives Canada Cataloguing in Publication

Pitman, Walter

   Music makers : the lives of Harry Freedman & Mary Morrison / Walter Pitman.

Includes bibliographical references.

ISBN-10: 1-55002-589-9
ISBN-13: 978-1-55002-589-7

   1. Freedman, Harry, 1922-2005 2. Morrison, Mary, 1926-
3. Composers--Canada--Biography. 4. Singers--Canada--Biography. I. Title.

ML410.F837P68 2006   780'.92'2   C2005-906317-3

1   2   3   4   5   10   09   08   07   06

We acknowledge the support of the **Canada Council for the Arts** and the **Ontario Arts Council** for our publishing program. We also acknowledge the financial support of the **Government of Canada** through the **Book Publishing Industry Development Program** and **The Association for the Export of Canadian Books**, and the **Government of Ontario** through the **Ontario Book Publishers Tax Credit program**, and the **Ontario Media Development Corporation**.

Printed and bound in Canada.
www.dundurn.com

Dundurn Press
3 Church Street, Suite 500
Toronto, Ontario, Canada
M5E 1M2

Gazelle Book Services Limited
White Cross Mills
Hightown, Lancaster, England
LA1 4X5

Dundurn Press
2250 Military Road
Tonawanda, NY
U.S.A. 14150

MUSIC
MAKERS

CONTENTS

PREFACE

MUSIC MAKERS explores the lives of two outstanding Canadian artists who happen to have been a married couple for more than fifty years. Harry Freedman was one of Canada's most prolific and prestigious composers. He produced an extensive repertoire that includes works for symphony orchestra, choir, and instrumental and choral ensemble, large and small. He composed for radio, film, and television. He wrote scores for ballet and live theatre. As a professional musician, he was an English horn player for the Toronto Symphony Orchestra for nearly a quarter of a century.

Mary Morrison has had an extraordinarily versatile career as a solo soprano on stage and on radio, and as a choral ensemble member of the Festival Singers, later to become the Elmer Iseler Singers. As a soloist and as a member of the Lyric Arts Trio, she became Canada's most respected vocal performer of twentieth-century music and, in particular, the works of Canadian composers. Not content with one career, she then came to excel as an outstanding teacher of voice and vocal presentation.

Harry and Mary began to make their contributions in the 1940s, at a time when there was minimal cultural infrastructure in Canada and when the funding for the arts was very fragile and in some situations nonexistent. It was a difficult time to be an artist, particularly if one was dependent mainly on income from the gate at a performance of serious music.

Fees for performance on radio and later television were not generous, but they were more attractive than those for most live performances.

Both Harry and Mary had the courage and determination to build careers in the arts in Canada in spite of these difficult circumstances. Their example encouraged others at a time of national concern over Canadian consciousness and identity. The First World War had ensured Canada's emergence as a sovereign nation. The Second World War had no such dramatic impact. Canada emerged as a major industrial state but very much just another middle power, still perceived to be in the shadow of the fast-declining British Empire but even more beholden to the newly predominant United States.

In the minds of many observers in the 1950s, unless Canadians could perceive and value their own national identity amidst the pressure of sharing a continent with a giant superpower, there would be no country left by the end of the century. It was more than retaining control over the commanding heights of the country's economy, maintaining a continental transportation system, being both bilingual and multicultural, and ensuring that there was a national communication network, including a broadcasting system. Survival and sovereignty demanded the celebration of a distinctive culture. Harry Freedman and Mary Morrison devoted their lives to this cause.

Most important of all, Canada needed to recognize itself as a nation with a purpose and a future. Until there were artists, arts organizations, and cultural institutions and industries, there could be no expression of that nationhood. Mary and Harry were members of that small number of artists, musicians, composers, and performers who explored and expressed what it was to be a Canadian. When it seemed that successive governments of Canada were prepared to sell off Canada's manufacturing capacity and enter into trade agreements that placed the ongoing sovereignty of the country at risk, even putting the future control of the nation's natural resources at threat, it was artists who made it clear that the world would suffer a momentous loss if Canada, with its distinct writers, philosophers, playwrights, and journalists, was allowed to disintegrate or be taken over by another world power. This volume seeks to answer questions that whirl around Harry and Mary, both of whom remained in Canada during all these decades, struggling to create a country that could play a role in moulding a world dedicated to peace and justice.

Such a volume demands the assistance of an enormous number of individuals who gave time and energy to the task of making the stories of Harry Freedman's and Mary Morrison's careers more broadly known. In the course of my research I spoke to Vincent Tovell, Victor Feldbrill, Phil Nimmons, John Weinzweig, Etian Cornfield, John Beckwith, Robert Cooper, Larry Lake, David Jaeger, Elizabeth Bihl, Ezra Schabas, John Gray, Robert Aitken, Jean Ashworth Bartle, and Lorna MacDonald.

The Freedman-Morrison family was most co-operative. Harry and Mary gave many hours of their time providing information and checking details of their lives that they alone could have corroborated. I was also able to speak to all their children — Karen ("Kim"), Cyndie, and Lori, who were most helpful. Harry's brother, Israel ("Doc"), with valued memories of the early years that he and Harry shared, was most supportive.

There were those who read part or all of the manuscript, and I cannot convey with sufficient emphasis my appreciation to Paul Schafer, Jo-Anne Bentley, and my wife, Ida, who spent countless hours poring over the pages of this work.

It is too easy to diminish the splendid role of those who oversee the collections of materials that make such an account possible. My thanks must go in greatest measure to Maureen Nevins and her colleagues at the National Library of Canada, where both Harry and Mary have deposited their papers. However, once again, I must recognize the active involvement of those who direct the various archive collections of the CBC, particularly Barbara Clark (Radio Archives), Randy Barnard (General Manager of CBC Records), and Paulette Bourget (Co-ordinator, CBC Records). I am indebted particularly to Richard Truhlar, who, along with Neil Gardner, who looks after Centrediscs at the Canadian Music Centre, searched for and found examples of Harry's music on disc. Such recordings of Mary's voice were sought but, sadly, with no success.

Even after the book is written there are those whose advice regarding promotion and marketing is most valuable. Janet Stubbs has always been present at the OAC Foundation with wise advice, and Stephen Campbell consistently provides welcome assistance.

In this age of technology, my words would never have reached the printed page without the assistance of Brian Stewart, Allan Thompson, and my sons Wade and Mark. My daughter Anne never failed in her determination to provide support and comfort in the nation's capital, where the Morrison and Freedman papers are to be found.

I cannot adequately thank Kirk Howard, Beth Bruder, Tony Hawke, Barry Jowett, Jennifer Gallant, and their colleagues at The Dundurn Group who have invariably made the role of author one that continues to be pleasurable and satisfying.

While this volume was in preparation, news reports indicated that, for a number of reasons, there were virtually no books published in the 1990s and the early years of the new century on the shelves of our public schools. Dundurn colleagues and I decided to initiate a pilot project to make books available to our young people by providing free copies to secondary schools, in this case to those with music programs. The SOCAN Foundation and the J.P. Bickell Foundation have most generously provided grants that have made this project possible.

Travel, research, and writing costs can be overwhelming; *Music Makers* was made possible by the Ontario Arts Council's Chalmers Arts Foundation.

This account of the practical production of the volume must include a note on what this volume does not purport to be. Musicologists and scholars of music theory and composition will find no analysis of Harry's music compositions in this book. It is fortunate that Gail Dixon's book, *The Music of Harry Freedman*, was "designed primarily as a study of his music," and I have sought to avoid any repetition of its contents.

Arden, 2006.

CHAPTER 1
Crossing an Ocean

"Stay there as a Polish Army officer … and die!" That was the prediction of the extended Freedman family who had already left Lodz in Poland to settle in Western Canada. It was transmitted to Max Freedman, who, along with his wife, Rose, and sons, Israel and Harry, was, in the early 1920s, still living in the family homeland. These relatives believed they understood the danger of Max's unwise decision to remain in the country from which they had fled and were determined to warn him of the unhappy time that Poland faced in the years ahead.

Margaret MacMillan, in her splendid study of the process of peace-making, *Paris, 1919*, has graphically described the situation in Europe after the smoke had cleared and the continent was being refashioned in the wake of the most devastating conflict in world history. "The peace-makers were reaching out hundreds of miles from Paris to impose order on a protean world of shifting allegiances, civil wars, refugees and bandit gangs, where the collapse of old empires had left law and order, trade and communications in shreds." In particular, a major drama was being played out in Eastern Europe as justice was sought for Poles deprived of a homeland for over a century. "The rebirth of Poland was one of the great stories of the Paris Peace Conference. It was also a source of endless difficulties," writes MacMillan.

Indeed, Max Freedman was at some risk. Although the newly established state of Poland had the support of Britain, France, and the U.S.A. in its efforts to secure the land and resources that would make its future as a nation possible, it was obvious that the Polish army would represent a fragile front line in the newly drawn map of Europe. The Allied powers wanted a continent with a strong base in Eastern Europe, one that could be a bulwark against Bolshevik Russia. There was also a need for a nation that could hold back any newly forged German nationalism that might emerge from the outrage over the punishment unleashed by the Treaty of Versailles. A viable state of Poland would at least delay any military action directed at France and Britain.

Unfortunately any defensible and economically workable Poland would leave many hundreds of thousands of angry Germans within its borders. As well, there would be disappointed Ukrainians, Hungarians, Czechs, and even Croats and Slovaks who would resent their inclusion in this reborn nation-state. Many people perceived this peremptory and unrealistic redrawing of boundaries as a work-in-progress that provided hope for a future realignment closer to President Wilson's simplistic view that the principle of self-determination could accommodate all the appropriate expectations of this mix of peoples that had, over many centuries, been held together by the old Austro-Hungarian Empire. The Treaty of Versailles sought peace, but it meant that Poland was faced with enemies on all sides as it struggled to maintain the borders it had been bequeathed.

Max Freedman was in place to be the victim of both real and prospective violence from the Bolsheviks in the new Russia being created by revolution, from a Ukraine now deprived of territory it coveted, from Baltic states all pursuing lands they believed to be theirs, and from the German citizens left in the Danzig Corridor and coveting inclusion in a postwar Germany. Even if the presence of the state of Poland was the pride of those who sought a new Europe based on principles of democracy and self-determination, there was little hope for the peace that might make Max's survival more likely.

As important to his future was the fact that Max's Jewishness was an affront to a large number of people who wanted racial purity in any rebuilding of Eastern Europe and particularly among those who had triumphed in the creation of a new Poland. The military establishment of any country demanded full commitment to national aims and ambitions — a commitment that was perceived to be impossible from representatives of a "Chosen People" with loyalty to a higher cause. The Dreyfus Affair in early twentieth century France had pointed out this dichotomy of conflicting loyalties and had become the *cause célèbre* in that nation's history.

Max and Rose were not practising Jews. They were living in the sophisticated urban setting of Lodz, the second-largest city in Poland but fortunately a community that had, in the past, accepted the broadest range of nonconformity in religious practices, as well as the presence of large numbers of those who, though Jewish, eschewed the synagogue and all its expectations. When the various members of the Freedman family had come to North America, however, they had settled, one by one, in North Winnipeg neighbourhoods close to synagogues to which the more religiously inclined Jews could walk, thereby avoiding the need to break the inconvenient Sabbath observances that restricted travel by mechanized transit. Such practices meant little to the Freedman clan, but the location ensured that there would be other Jews nearby. The culture was very much present, assuring that the typical Jewish love for intellectual confrontation along with a traditional concern for community well-being would be a legacy passed on to future generations.

It was to a recently married couple, Max and Rose Freedman, still living in troubled Poland, that on April 5, 1922, a second son, Harry, was delivered. The first-born, Israel, had arrived two and a half years earlier, in October 1919, coinciding with the very period during which the Allied powers were deciding both the existence of this new country, Poland, and the fate of the area in the Middle East that was to share its name with the welcome first addition to the family.

Max had decided to remain in the army after the Armistice and had achieved officer rank. Previously, he had held a job delivering coal, employment that badly damaged his lungs. Thus, although the economy of Eastern Europe was in a deplorable state in the immediate postwar world, Max Freedman's family was far from destitute. Indeed, their station could be described as middle class — somewhat in contrast to the status that had driven Max's twelve brothers to forsake this part of the Russian Empire and seek opportunity in a faraway land.

Ironically, the most significant influence on Harry's future came from the unusual employment situation that his mother had experienced before her marriage. Although she had trained as a nurse, she had taken a job as a nanny to the son of a distinguished widowed physician who found himself the sole parent of a mentally disadvantaged son who required almost constant attention. This prominent doctor had a very unusual lifestyle. With patients in both Lodz and Berlin, he moved back and forth between the two cities. As the companion of his young child, who was so dependent on her support, Rose moved with him. In the more wealthy and sophisticated society of Berlin, the doctor was a member of a highly artistic community and served as a host to an extraordinary assortment of musicians, artists, and academics. Rose, a young and impressionable girl, was entranced by the animated conversation, the intellectual banter, and the exchange of philosophic positions. Her delight in being included in this setting led her to learn to speak German. Certainly it was a dramatic contrast to the way of life she had previously experienced in a backward sector of the Russian Empire.

Unfortunately, Rose's employer's son died and the doctor no longer had any need of Rose's services. Her employment was peremptorily terminated. This taste of the upper-middle-class life, including the companionship of bright young artists, registered an unforgettable image of the lifestyle Rose desired for both herself and any children she might bear. However, first she had to find a husband, and she chose Max not fully realizing that he did not share her social and intellectual ambitions. She was now consigned to a conventional marriage with a man of her own station, who, at least for now, could provide a decent living. In spite of the limited prospects that her marriage promised, she was determined to do everything she could to ensure that her children were prepared to partake of an enriched way of life like that she had experienced in Berlin.

Max Freedman was a man of limited intellect and even less strength of will. It was a mismatch from the outset, but in the Jewish community of early-twentieth-century Eastern Europe, unwise marriages had to be endured. Nevertheless, Rose had already decided that whatever her own fate might be, she would see that her children were introduced to the kind of society she had so much admired. Of that there would be no doubt, whatever country, community, or continent claimed her presence.

In the face of Rose's determination and domination, Max was most certainly the lesser influence on the lives of his children, Harry, Israel, and finally Dorothy, who was born in Canada and was to be this couple's final offspring. Rose was a beautiful woman, elegant in her carriage, confident in attitude, intelligent and articulate, as well as charming, with an enormous sense of humour that bubbled forth and brought delight to both her children and their friends. There is no doubt that she moulded the character and interests of each child with steel-tipped determination. Without her Harry would never have leaped from the streets of North Winnipeg to the heights of Canadian creative achievement. But there was an underside to this relationship. Harry was constantly aware of her impact on his character well into mid-life. "What she did for me and what she did to me were beyond calculation," he admitted.

Harry spent the first three years of his life in Lodz. However, Rose had become convinced that the only rational solution to Max's threatened life in the Polish army, and the only hope for a better future for her two boys, lay in following the rest of the Freedman family, a clan that included her husband's parents, his many brothers, and other assorted relatives, to North America, and in particular to Western Canada. By 1922, this part of the world was in the midst of a "roaring" economy, while Eastern Europe was still struggling to rebuild a society disrupted by four years of war and still fighting to defeat Bolshevism over the eastern border in the Soviet Union.

Israel, nearly three years older than Harry, remembers the Old World, and has a particular memory of accompanying his mother in a horse and carriage and being terrified by his mother's feigned fear as they forded a fast-rushing stream. There were band concerts in the Lodz parks, and Israel had his first experience of conducting music standing on his chair in the audience, much to the delight of his mother but no doubt also to the discomfort of nearby listeners. The family lived in a quite comfortable, upper-middle-class home with adequate space, gracious furniture, and a courtyard that provided a pleasant playground for the Freedman boys and a white pomeranian dog that had to be left behind when, in 1925, passage was booked for Quebec City on the steamship *Megantic*. Many years later, Harry Freedman was able to find his name, and those of the rest of the family, in the logbook of the

Megantic, archived at the Halifax Immigration Centre, even though the vessel had actually docked in the Port of Quebec City. Harry's only memory of the long voyage was his effort to launch a small toy shaped like a steamer so that he could pull it behind the ship — not behaviour that was appreciated by the *Megantic*'s crew, who were responsible for passenger safety.

Quebec City was but a place to board a train to the family's destination — the city of Winnipeg. It was a long and tiring journey across endless miles of forest. For the boys it was their first experience of the land that was to be their home. The landscape of forest and rock that Harry saw from that train window was the first of many images of Canada to capture his attention. It has been said that he is the "most Canadian" of those serious composers who formed the first phalanx who sought to musically express the sights and sounds of a new nation. He was to direct his eye and his hand, his ear and his musical sensitivity, his intellect and his emotions to the task of interpreting the nature of this land that he first viewed sleepily from a railway coach while journeying to his new home.

The Canadian immigration policy of the time focused on filling the empty prairies with farmers. Foolishly it was perceived that the new immigrants from Europe would be perfect subjects for the experiment in planned settlement. It was not understood that many of these newcomers were being drawn from European elites (such as those who had dwelled in Lodz) and had neither the desire nor the needed skills and knowledge to make farming their vocation.

Max and Rose expected a new life in the city of Winnipeg, where the Freedman clan was already living in considerable numbers. The twelve brothers in Max's family, along with assorted other family members, formed an impressive gathering of "new Canadians" in the still largely empty Canadian West. Max and Rose Freedman and their boys had arrived in the now famous community of North Winnipeg, the very epicentre of left-wing political thought and action in Canada. Harry's first encounter with this particular social milieu was too early to have any influence, but he was to return and live his teens in the years of continuing confrontation that followed the Winnipeg General Strike, certainly the most highly visible and highly publicized example of class struggle in Canadian history. It was to be his philosophic "home base" throughout his life.

At this point, however, Winnipeg was but a way station for Max and Rose Freedman and their boys, who were, a few days later, on a second train destined for the small community of Medicine Hat. The extended family had decided that Max and his family should join two other Freedman brothers, David and Hyman, in an enterprise that they believed would ultimately bring a measure of prosperity to them all. It was a time of growing high fashion in North America, and animal hides and furs were a symbol of new wealth. The West was teeming with creatures whose coats could serve this new market. Medicine Hat was close to valuable sources of furs, and both the natives and Metis who hunted and trapped these animals participated in a vast enterprise that could purchase the results of their efforts. It was the new white arrivals who processed these furs through all the necessary stages before sending them to the lucrative markets of New York or Toronto and other large cities in the United States and Canada. All the extended Freedman family in the West would, of course, make the initial investment that would launch the operation. Thus was born the Winnipeg Hide and Fur Company in Medicine Hat.

The Max Freedman family was now settled in the small frontier town in Western Canada. Harry has vivid memories of his time in that community. For a Jewish boy from a developed city in Eastern Europe, it was a revelation. There were no other Jewish children in the neighbourhood, and when, a couple of years after his arrival, he was enrolled in the local elementary school, he was the only Jewish student in his class, and, except for his brother, Israel, in the entire school. There was no synagogue in the area, and he played with children of every imaginable ethnic background, a good many of them from First Nations and Metis families. Of course, these aboriginal hunters were the main suppliers of the Winnipeg Hide and Fur Company. Harry has clear memories of watching them bringing in stacks of furs for sale to his father and uncles. These hunters and traders were often accompanied by their families, including their children, and Harry has a vivid memory of falling in love at the age of six with a particularly beautiful native maiden "with black shining eyes" who caught his eye and heart. She was the archetype of a boy's first attraction to a member of the opposite sex, and Harry was already an observant young lad.

Israel's interest was captured by the efforts made to inform and attract the attention of the citizenry to the work of the company by filling the shop window with stuffed animals — the beavers, muskrats, and wolves that were the source of the furs so much needed to fulfill the orders that were now pouring in. His and Harry's classmates came to gaze in wonder at this new addition to the Medicine Hat townscape.

There could not have been a commercial experience more "Canadian" than having a father who was a responsible executive in a company dedicated to the trade for, and processing of, furs. It was upon the back of this enterprise that the entire discovery and development of the country had been based. A young lad regularly viewing Canada's First Nations citizens carrying out their traditional functions of centuries-long duration could be permanently influenced by such things, and he, many years later, came to seek out the sounds, both natural and man-made, of that past. The company prospered through the 1920s as the fashion industry in the east of the continent demanded more and more fur in all its variety, colour, and texture. In an effort to make the Winnipeg Hide and Fur Company a central asset to the morale of the city, the Freedmans financed a local hockey team, the Medicine Hat Tigers, still today a force in western Canadian hockey. Israel and Harry were taken to see Canada's national sport — a further indication of the rapid assimilation of immigrants, particularly in isolated communities like Medicine Hat. Harry was conscious that for him and his brother, and soon a young sister, Dorothy, the conversation around the dinner table was not focused on the European past but on the nature of Canadian sport and family prospects in a new land.

Furs, however, are basic to the luxury garment trade, and as the new decade of the 1930s emerged a dramatic change was taking place in the world economy, one that very much influenced the markets the Winnipeg Hide and Fur Company sought to serve. By 1931, two years after the Great Depression struck, the Freedman brothers had a bankrupt company on their hands. It was thus back to Winnipeg for Max Freedman and his family.

Now nearly ten years old, Harry was mature enough to be conscious of the world around him and realized that it was not the prosperous Winnipeg he had first encountered. It was a city trapped in the throes of that Great Depression. He came to realize that he was poor and that "it was really tough being a member of a family with only $35 a month to live on!" Bread may have cost only a nickel a loaf, but the relief cheque of $35 had to pay the rent, buy food and clothing for five, and look after all the medical emergencies that were the typical lot of families in poverty. It was little wonder that in the mid-twentieth century it was from Western Canada that medicare came, fuelled by the memory of collective penury and a determination to provide more generously for those in need, whether they be aged, disabled, or unemployed.

For Max, the failure of the Winnipeg Hide and Fur Company was a personal disaster. In Medicine Hat he had achieved a certain social status as the part owner and operator of a substantial operation engaged in an historic process of some present significance. Back in North Winnipeg, forced to take whatever employment he could find, he lost the prestigious role he had once assumed in the community and initially had no choice but to join many thousands on welfare and accept charity from relatives.

These events taught Harry early in his life that earning an adequate income was a vital role for a husband and father. When he chose to be a composer, a vocation promising no great monetary rewards, he took pains to ensure that the experience of his childhood would not be repeated in the lives of his own daughters. For Harry there was no fantasy that he should create music simply because his talent and genius demanded it. He believed he had every right to be paid for his creativity and for the drudgery as well as the delight that musical composition imposes. Harry Freedman saw at first hand the impact of poverty and its effect on a father who had to cope with failure, and he had no intention of following in his footsteps.

It was Rose who again took over the headship of the family, organizing its finances and ensuring that the new circumstances did not damage the opportunities that might make the lives of her children more satisfying. She was a dynamic leader. Uncomfortable in the role of welfare recipient, she discovered that if she could sign up a coterie of neighbours who might be customers for a milk route, a local dairy would create a job for her husband. It turned out badly. She found the customers, but no job emerged. Max was turned down by the manager of the dairy when he presented Rose's list of potential customers. For Max, it was the last straw. He became a ghostly figure in the family who disappeared presumably chasing various employment opportunities, many outside Winnipeg, but never did find work. In 1944, when Harry was in the armed forces but happened to be stationed for a few months in Winnipeg, his father died of tuberculosis, probably from the coal dust he had inhaled as a young man in Poland.

For all the disaster it represented, Harry's return at the age of nine to Winnipeg was a godsend. It opened doors that did not exist in Medicine Hat. He was now well into his elementary education and would soon be in middle school, the Machray High School, an institution serving young people in grades 7, 8, and 9. He was no longer the only Jewish kid in the class. However, he was not drawn to join any exclusive group of co-religionists — rather he found his way into the multi-ethnic but English-speaking mix of students who formed the mainstream of student life in the Winnipeg educational system. But even more important was the presence of learning institutions beyond the central public school system that were now accessible and available to serve Rose's ambitions for her children.

For Rose, Winnipeg was a veritable paradise. Even in the 1930s Winnipeg was a city with a strong cultural life. In the later years of the century Winnipeg was to stand out across North America as a city uniquely devoted to the work of artists. Most communities of its size would have one major cultural asset. It might be an outstanding symphony orchestra, a distinguished theatre company, or an extraordinary ballet or dance ensemble. Winnipeg, quite uniquely, came to have all three such institutions — an anomaly for communities of this moderate scale, surpassing even cities serving a more prosperous market in the United States. Along with the performing arts, there developed the Winnipeg Art Gallery. By the early 1950s it was in the hands of the Viennese-born Dr. Ferdinand Eckhardt, who soon made it one of the finest visual arts institutions in Canada. Yet even before all this later twentieth century cultural development, Winnipeg signalled the opening of the skies for Rose. Her past experience in Berlin and the exciting times she had experienced in the company of painters, sculptors, poets, novelists, and musicians flooded her mind. It was a world she wanted to ensure her children knew something about.

Winnipeg was responsible for most of the influences that defined Harry's future as a creator. It was then and still is both the geographic and leftist philosophic centre of the nation. It is a western city but it looks east more comfortably than any other major urban centre west of Windsor. Its very isolation is its entree to intense "Canadian-ness." Though it has always had easy transportation through Minneapolis–St. Paul to the rest of the world, its self-image is contained and inwardly based. Unlike Halifax and Saint John, which share a seaboard with the New England states, Montreal, which looks to Vermont and New Hampshire, or Toronto, which is obsessed with New York, Winnipeg self-consciously celebrates its isolated grandeur on the Canadian Prairies. For the Freedmans, it was, as well, a window on the Canadian West, and in spite of the sacrifice it represented in the dark Depression days, Rose insisted on having the family travel to Banff, providing the children with the opportunity to experience the magnificence of the Rockies in the belief that such an experience should be the right of every Canadian child. Even though her own roots and those of her husband lay in Eastern Europe, she was determined that her children would share a knowledgeable appreciation of this new land. She was resolute that they would be both cultured and Canadian.

Rose was single-minded in deciding her children would take music lessons. At that time a piano in the parlour and the kids learning their scales was the mark of a middle-class Canadian family. It was certainly the plan followed for Harry's sister, Dorothy. For Israel, there was a variation — he was to learn the violin. Rose believed the violin, easily carried from place to place, was a paramount route to an artist's life, as it would be the most likely path to employment as a musician in an orchestral ensemble, a direction that promised, in her view, an enriched future for its owner. Much to Rose's disappointment, for Israel, "the violin did not take." Yet, many years later, at a surprise birthday party, the Freedman family greeted his arrival by displaying a huge blow-up of a photograph that depicted him as a youth in short pants playing his violin. The sound of the one piece he ever learned, *Ramona*, was heard in the background, provoking much hilarity and derision.

Israel may have failed his mother's hopes for a career in music, but he played an enormous role in Harry's life. Even though only a couple of years older, he became Harry's father figure. Fortunately Israel was a splendid student, popular, and well-liked — a model of some substance for a shy younger brother to emulate. Israel, though having no contact with the healing arts, became "Doc" to all his friends and colleagues after attending university. He had an enormous influence on Harry's philosophic future. Even as a teenager, Israel was entranced by the politics of North Winnipeg, going off to J.S. Woodsworth's political meetings in the evening at a time when the Cooperative Commonwealth Federation (CCF), Canada's democratic socialist party and precursor of the New Democratic Party (NDP), was being formed. He provided an example of active political involvement that Harry followed throughout his life.

Ironically, for Harry it was the visual arts that his mother perceived as the open door to a full and rewarding life. Even in Medicine Hat, Harry, like many young boys, had become enamoured with the airplane as a miracle machine and had become prolific in sketching representations of airplanes he saw in the skies or in books and magazines. The graceful lines of the design that predicted the powerful thrust into the open sky were a source of delight. His drawings convinced Rose that she had a great artist on her hands. Harry had been enrolled in the local Jewish school, where classes were held in the late afternoon. One of the skills taught was writing Hebrew script, and Harry was so proficient that he became the student who was enlisted whenever there was need for a citation on a document or a sign for public display. A distinguished visitor to the school watched Harry and informed his mother that although her son was not interested in Jewish history, his calligraphy was superb and he would benefit from attending an art school.

At fourteen, Harry was enrolled in the Winnipeg Art School, first in Saturday morning classes, but as his proficiency developed he attended evening classes as well. The school had as its principal and teacher extraordinaire LeMoine Fitzgerald, a distinguished painter whose canvases were even in the 1930s to be found in the major collections across the nation. Harry took his work at the art school very seriously, realizing that this opportunity had come with some sacrifice on the part of his mother, whose insistence had overcome the disapproval of a father for whom these artistic activities had little meaning.

He worked hard seeking to express himself through the form and colour produced by pencil, crayon, and paint-filled brush, moving from an obsession with air technology and design to natural forms and patterns. Fortunately he was mentored by Fitzgerald, whose capacity to make use of muted colours in revealing how the easy flexible lines of the natural world contrasted with the severe images of man-made interventions had become widely appreciated. His paintings differed dramatically from the wild hues that became the trademark of the Group of Seven painters he ultimately joined and who were his contemporaries, but Fitzgerald expressed Canada with comparable integrity.

Harry spent four years at the Winnipeg Art School. Then a deep dissatisfaction enveloped him. He felt his artwork was not effectively mirroring his thoughts or emotions but rather was merely photographically correct. He was now an active teenager with very strong feeling about the world about him. He had experienced nearly a decade of global depression. He had seen the hopes and expectations of his father and his uncles dashed in the wake of the economic collapse that now dominated the planet but in Canada bore down most cruelly on communities beyond the more mature and thus more resilient eastern and far western regions of the country. He saw the dark clouds of war gathering across the ocean on a continent that had once been his home. He needed a voice, and the images on paper and canvas were insufficient.

Harry was a member of an extended family that included literally dozens of uncles and aunts, cousins, and even two Yiddish-speaking grandparents. However, he realized that his particular family unit was dysfunctional. Max, his father, was a prototypical *nubuch*, a pathetic figure unable to provide a model for his sons. He had little in common with his wife, Rose, whose interests were bound up in a future for her children. She had little interest in his well-being. Though she was a splendid keeper of the household and the family's resources, her penchant for ensuring that there were art or music lessons for every child meant that there was little hope of an easier future for him. Indeed his long absences spent seeking to become some kind of entrepreneur in rural Manitoba and Saskatchewan were welcome, keeping him out of the house — removing his negative presence at mealtimes or during the long silent evenings interrupted only by Dorothy's musical efforts.

Fortunately Harry had fashioned strong bonds of affection with his mother. She cared deeply about the quality of his life. She was a constant pressure that made success in high school a top priority. Harry graduated with high marks and could have attended university on a mathematics scholarship. But he passed up the opportunity, not knowing what possible employment that discipline would bring. Thus, another piece of evidence indicating the existence of a connection linking the disciplines of music and mathematics can be found in the scholastic record of the teenage Harry Freedman.

Harry needed more opportunity to find his own path, and, ironically, it came partly through Rose's insistence that music should be an element of his younger sister's preparation to face the world. As he watched Dorothy's progress, Harry found that he was enthralled by the sheer delight that Dorothy displayed as she performed Strauss waltzes. Even more, when Dorothy taught him to play the second part in arrangements for four hands he found that he was intensely excited by the very process of making music. He was hypnotized by the way a few dots on lined paper could translate into sound. It was magic. Years later, he was wise enough to spend a couple of years in formal pianoforte study, enough to be able to make use of the instrument in his music making but, significantly, not long enough to develop any comfort as a player.

On his eighteenth birthday he purchased a clarinet. He had spent four years in the Winnipeg Art School, and though he never lost his enthusiasm for visual art, he was convinced that his work was neither leading to a career nor satisfying his inner need to express his thoughts and feelings. Now he would take another direction.

To some extent, it was an act of rebellion. To that point he had followed his mother's expectations at art school. Now he wanted to follow his own light. This purchase was the most important of his young life. Ultimately it decided what kind of music he would perform and what kind of composer would emerge. Continuing on the pianoforte would undoubtedly have led to other outcomes. In these years, seeking keyboard competence would have directed him into the repertoire dominated by Bach, Beethoven, and Chopin, with a possible foray into the works of Debussy and Ravel. Such limited explorations of the broader span of musical composition might, even at this age, have made less likely the experiences in the popular dance band, jazz combo, and orchestral repertoire that made Harry's preparation as a contemporary classical composer unique.

The clarinet was an entree to the world of popular music and yet not a predictable one. The saxophone was the central core instrument of the twentieth-century "big band." Yet the clarinet in the hands of a superb orchestra leader such as a Benny Goodman or an Artie Shaw was certainly a beacon of ambition for any young clarinet student *hoping* for virtuoso status in the future. At the local level in Winnipeg, it provided a foothold in popular or jazz bands and could also be an opening for a young person aspiring to become an arranger or even a composer. Harry came to realize that the clarinet was also a window on the full range of woodwind instruments that could lead to employment as a musician in several fields of music making he might encounter.

Significantly, the clarinet was of substantial importance to the symphonic orchestra or the brass band, both ensembles capable of playing a broad classical repertoire and, at their best, both involved in contemporary, serious music making. The instrument, a relatively recent addition to the forces of the modern symphony orchestra, introduced its player to the most sublime music written by Mozart, Brahms, and Weber. Indeed, it eventually catapulted its enthusiastic supporter into the repertoire written by American composer Aaron Copland and his contemporaries.

Most important, abandoning the piano for the clarinet helped to decide what process of composing Harry Freedman was to follow. Most music creators work from the piano or, today, the synthesizer keyboard. The themes and harmonies are discovered and then, if it is an orchestral work, the sound is fleshed out as other instruments are orchestrated to suit the ensemble for which the composition has been written. Great composers have overcome the transition from keyboard to the incredible array of sounds and effects that the addition of strings, woodwinds, brass, and percussion brings to the ear. However, some composers never make the leap. For Harry, there was no problem. With minimal keyboard skills, he never conceived his compositions through the medium of the piano sound later to be orchestrated to a broad range of instruments. He heard the composition fully clothed as a work-in-progress, with all the sounds of the sections of the orchestra breaking forth as appropriate. Thus this clarinet that he bought himself as a teenager in Winnipeg became the vehicle for a journey towards becoming a distinctive Canadian composer.

CHAPTER 2
Winnipeg Triumphs

Purchasing a clarinet had not been a thoughtless decision. Harry had been captured by the magic of Dorothy's music making transpiring in his own home. But he was also a radio addict, and the sounds coming to his ear from that source had fired his imagination. Winnipeg, though geographically isolated, was an example of a community that the new communication technologies of the twentieth century were to transform most dramatically. It was only in the 1900s that the sounds of the world's greatest musicians could be accessed by individuals ensconced in the every corner of the country. Listening to the local radio station, Harry heard a broad repertoire, from classical to the most current popular music, and though the momentary "top ten" ballads captured his attention first, it was other selections that overtook that initial enthusiasm. One Saturday night, a program called *Let's Dance* featured the music of the Benny Goodman Band, and for Harry "the whole world opened up. After hearing Goodman my head was filled with questions. How did he do that?"

Benny Goodman was an extraordinary musician who could move from one end of the musical spectrum to the other. Jazz and pop music enthusiasts thought him a god, but he was equally welcome to share the concert stage with the New York Philharmonic Orchestra. Indeed, it was just about the time that Harry first heard Goodman's music that this icon had brought his ensemble to Carnegie Hall, the mountaintop of

classical music performance, for a concert that changed people's attitude to jazz music in America forever. Even serious composers like
Aaron Copland would present him with a clarinet concerto to play. The
quality of his sound and the clarity of his technique were legendary.
Harry's choice of instrument came from his realization that this clear,
warm tone was what he wanted to produce in his playing and encourage in his music composition. He became aware that he could use the
clarinet to play the music in his own head, not unlike the experience of
wielding his paintbrush over an empty canvas. The clarinet became the
first step into a range of instruments that produced the sounds that
pleased his ear, with the oboe and the English horn becoming particular favourites in later years.

His work at the Winnipeg Art School ceased with the intrusion of
his new interest. In an interview with music educator Helen Dahlstrom
in the late 1980s he made the point succinctly: "When I was in art school
in my fourth year I recognized that I could draw anything and it was
photographically accurate — but that's all it was. There was nothing of
me in it. I still marvel that I could recognize this fact at that early age."
Yet he carried his visual arts perceptions of reality throughout his life.

The connection with Goodman opened many questions about
style and presentation, but before long the same bedside radio that had
introduced Harry to Goodman provided him with the sounds of the
Duke Ellington Orchestra. Ellington was now a prestigious composer
as well as a highly respected performer who showed Harry the broad
range of music that could be included in the popular genre. His future
was decided: "After that first listening experience I knew I just wanted
to write music … any kind of music." In that same interview with
Helen Dahlstrom Harry admitted, "He [Ellington] remains to this day
one of my chief influences." Ellington once made the observation that
there are only two kinds of music: "good and the other kind." That has
been Harry's belief as well. He became a rebel in his determination to
include what he felt was the best of his jazz and popular music background in his composition of "serious" music (a term he resented, con-
sidering it an academic nomenclature designed to enhance the
response to contemporary "classical" and to denigrate other forms of
musical composition).

Another experience was equally dramatic — seeing the Walt Disney movie *Fantasia* in Winnipeg in the early 1940s. Harry raced to see it as soon as it arrived on the local screen — and went back again and again. The first segment of the film featured an orchestral arrangement of J.S. Bach's Prelude and Fugue in D Minor conducted by Leopold Stokowski, juxtaposed with abstract images that moved, dissolved, and recreated themselves on the screen. A young Harry Freedman was dazzled. It was beyond anything he had ever witnessed, and all those years at the Winnipeg Art School took on new meaning. He was captivated by the dual impact of sound and image. Suddenly he realized how music could reveal the central essence and meaning of a great painting or sculpture — or, indeed, a great landscape. This focus became the hallmark of Harry's genius. Later this capacity to visualize in sound was to become bound up in his work in the theatre and the film studio. From this revelation he became convinced that his painting and his music could converge, that his visual expression and his musical creation could be one.

First, though, he realized he must begin the long process of personal preparation. Having graduated from high school he had to find a job to pay for this excursion into the mysteries of a new art form. He was hired as a "newsy," selling papers and sweets on the train from Winnipeg to Edmonton. His remuneration came in the form of commission on sales, and he soon found he was making little money. Obviously, he was not aggressive enough to be a salesman. He then took a job in a neighbourhood drug store, employment that provided both income and time to pursue his new obsessions — the clarinet and the secrets of music composition. This position lasted for nearly two years, but in 1940 he moved to a job in a motion picture theatre. This work, though short-term, was perfect, as, though it filled his evenings, it left him the entire day to pursue his new enthusiasm. He soon became the assistant manager, which meant that he could open the theatre at six o'clock and close it at midnight, but in the off hours he had access to a large space in which he could test out the variations in sound production that were possible on his chosen instrument. With incredible speed he mastered the clarinet well enough to join local dance bands at gigs that provided some income and, more important, the inspiration to continue his study.

His clarinet instructor was Arthur Hart, the most proficient performer on the clarinet in Winnipeg at that time. Indeed, he came to occupy the first chair in the clarinet section of the Winnipeg Symphony Orchestra. Hart already had a command of the classical repertoire, playing in a number of ensembles in the city, and was able to provide Harry some insight into the life of the working professional musician — a role that Harry was to fill for a quarter of a century. The hours with Arthur Hart made it possible for Harry to learn at first hand what making music as a vocation was all about!

Very soon he recognized that to be a composer like Ellington he must learn the basics of music creation. He found a place in the studio of Captain J.P. O'Donnell, the most accomplished music theory instructor in Winnipeg. Soon he found that exploring the disciplines of harmony and counterpoint were as exciting as mastering the techniques of sight-reading and sound production that had allowed him to make his way into musical groups and ensembles across the city.

He was drawn to the genre of jazz, which seemed to him a kind of "composing on the spot" experience, and the sounds of that genre were to become recognizable even in the most sombre and restrained classical compositions he wrote throughout his career. Its inevitable rhythm and spontaneous excitement made jazz a favourite genre from which to draw his inspiration. All of this enabled him to become a figure in the musical life of his city scarcely before he had left his teenage years behind. Soon he was not only performing but also taking on the tasks of arranging music for various groups, usually small bands securing "one-night stands" playing intimate public venues or even private affairs of distinguished Winnipeg citizens.

Harry had fallen into a career path, but the events in Europe and around the world put his ambitions, like those of so many others, on hold. He realized that it was time to serve his country in a way that made some sense in terms of his skills and interests, and he initially chose to join the Royal Canadian Air Force (RCAF) as a performer and composer-arranger. He applied for overseas duty, seeking to join the first air force band that was being sent to England. Circumstances conspired to close off that option. Harry was scheduled to be shipped over to the U.K. when he had an attack of chronic appendicitis and was hospitalized. He found that the RCAF was unprepared to take any further chances with his health in such an unpredictable state, at least not on the other side of the Atlantic.

Instead, he was fortunate to be assigned to the RCAF Central Command Band, based in Rockcliffe, near Ottawa, at that time perhaps the most prestigious silver band in the nation, made up of singularly talented, established musicians who had made the same choice as Harry. It was an ensemble that was continually on the move across the country, making appearances at formal military events, recruiting drives, war bond promotions, and even concerts arranged for high school students. In short, it was the most effective public relations arm of the RCAF in the nation. This role meant that a very broad repertoire was necessary, as the ensemble was playing on concert stages of larger communities as well as in the gymnasiums and auditoriums of high schools in smaller places where no concert hall existed. Harry's preparation for writing music soon came into play, as did his penchant for popular music, for the smaller dance bands that formed themselves within the full ensemble. It was a perfect, hothouse experience for a young man yearning to be a professional composer and arranger as well as performer.

Meanwhile, back in the Winnipeg, a young woman was achieving a similar degree of attention during the latter years of the 1930s and the early 1940s as an acclaimed singer. Her name was Mary Morrison, and she was the offspring of a Scottish couple who had come to the New World. In settling in Winnipeg, they were joining generations of Scots who had arrived in the Red River settlement in the late eighteenth century when Lord Selkirk had established a colony and initiated a process of settlement that would ultimately lead to a confrontation with fur-trading Metis seeking to make their life in the Canadian West. The battles that ensued became known as the Riel Rebellion. The descendents of these intrepid Scots settlers were now present to welcome this new twentieth-century infusion from the old country taking their place in the very different context of a growing urban centre.

Mary's mother, Louise MacLeod, had come mainly because she could join an older sister already living in Winnipeg. Like so many immigrants who came from the British Isles in the pre–First World War years, Mary's father, Donald Morrison, had come because there were no prospects on the Isle of Lewis where he lived, whereas the New World offered better opportunities. Louise and Donald met, courted, and married. Like so many recent immigrants, Donald soon returned to the old country in 1914 as a member of the Canadian Armed Forces on a ship filled with fellow countrymen determined to defend King and Empire. And like so many of the men who formed the Canadian contingent, he returned to Canada after years in the trenches with his lungs badly damaged by mustard gas. He was, however, able to gain employment with the Canadian National Railway (CNR), a fortunate choice of employer, as a company policy allowed the employees' families to travel free each year on one of the nation's major railway networks. As a result, a favourite extended excursion for the Morrison family over the years became rail trips to Vancouver, British Columbia, eating packed lunches in transit and camping on Kitsilano Beach, thereby bequeathing a love of the country and an appreciation of its size and beauty in the minds of their daughters, Mary, born on November 9, 1926, and her younger sister, Kathleen, born three years later.

Although they had little money throughout their lives, the Morrison family lived a rich life in the arms of the Scottish culture they refused to abandon no matter how many thousands of miles away their homeland lay. Mary and Kathleen grew up in a home that was saturated with Scottish songs, dances, and oatcakes and scones, one that remained closely connected to a larger community of Winnipeg Scots. Their parents might be far from their place of birth but they were determined to retain their cultural roots. The tradition of the *ceilidh*, a gathering of Gaelic-speaking couples and their children that included an evening of piping, dancing, and singing, was central to the lifestyle of the Morrison household. These distinctive parties were held in one home after another, or on occasion a rented hall, every fortnight, and the Morrisons were delighted hosts even if their abode was too small to contain the overwhelming sound of bagpipes in full flight — except from a distant corner of the cellar. The fact that the Scottish presence had a long and proud history in the Red River Valley over so many decades made this particular cultural enthusiasm quite appropriate in strictly Canadian terms. Mary, referred to in local newspaper coverage of her youthful triumphs as a "fair Scottish lassie," had a platform from which she could move into a variety of musical tastes that ran from popular ballads and folk songs to light opera and eventually to the heights of the grand operatic repertoire and ultimately the mountaintops of the Bach Passions, Mass, and Cantatas.

Mary accompanied her parents to church on Sunday, where even the spoken word was Gaelic. She sang the words of hymns without a shred of understanding of their meaning but came to love the melodies of the Gaelic hymnary. In later life she was to sing in several languages, and there were many occasions when she had to pick up the precise sounds of phrases she had never encountered before. These Sunday morning experiences had prepared her well. She credits her earliest conquest of the Gaelic hymns and Hebridean songs as the first preparation for a career in opera and concert and the conquest of a traditional repertoire that included works in French, Italian, and German. Yet, just as important, the Scottish folk songs remained extremely popular with her audiences, never failing to arouse a fevered ovation at the conclusion of her recital programs. They were to form the last segment and the encore of her concerts decades after her departure from Winnipeg.

At the age of six her strong, sweet soprano voice had become appreciated not only by her parents but by their Scottish friends as well, and although her parents ensured that she learned to play the piano, it was clear that her voice was her treasure. These early pianoforte lessons from teacher Mary Bornoff were important, for she continued to study piano throughout her later studies at the Toronto Conservatory and it meant she was at ease accompanying her own singing and, in later years, that of her students. Indeed, she did so throughout her career, even, on occasion, in public performance, not an expected talent of most singers of serious music that so often has a demanding score that challenges even the most accomplished virtuoso accompanist.

Thus, as a child, she was entered in singing competitions and began at an early age to win prizes, much to the pride of the entire family, who saw to it that she could study with Doris Mills Lewis, a prominent Winnipeg teacher who could be trusted with this magnificent voice. It became apparent that there was a young woman growing up in the south end of Winnipeg who could be an outstanding vocal artist, and she was encouraged on every side. When she reached Kelvin

High School, she came under the influence of Gladys Anderson, a teacher who was to become renowned among arts education instructors across the entire city and beyond. Each year while at Kelvin, Gladys mounted a production of Gilbert and Sullivan, always a favourite choice in a section of the city to which more trainloads of U.K. immigrants had arrived in the 1920s and '30s and now in the '40s. They were pleased that this well-remembered repertoire from the old country was being performed in their new homeland. Mary had leading roles, enlarging her experience and, more importantly, adding the vital skill of acting to her musical experience. Her memories of her childhood in Winnipeg are filled with moments of joy and accomplishment. She had the enormous advantage of loving parents who themselves revelled in the confidence of a secure community, and Mary could carry that confidence into her own life both in her studies and in her chosen field of vocal music.

As she grew older, her accomplishments were fully recognized by a wider community. Her school principal, a devotee who was to follow her career long after he retired and moved far distant from Winnipeg, wrote in 1943, "Your singing has been exceptionally good this spring and your diction was perfect." He commented on her "charming girlish modesty," a trait that was to endear her to audiences long after the adjective "girlish" was appropriate. When she graduated from secondary school a scholarship was made available to her that assisted in meeting the expenses of pursuing a musical education beyond Winnipeg.

Mary's schooling was a flow of singing accomplishments in an educational system dedicated, as few in Canada were, to the study and enjoyment of vocal and instrumental music. The schools of Winnipeg, perhaps because of the greater expectation that they should play an artistic role in the isolated frontier reality of the Canadian West, perhaps because of the strong Mennonite influence, had developed excellent music programs. Whereas there were schools in Toronto, Montreal, and Vancouver whose arts programs played little part in the preparation of a musically sophisticated citizenry, the Winnipeg school system believed it had a unique responsibility to build a culture, one that could be achieved in no other way. Orchestral ensembles, and especially choirs of all sizes and makeup, abounded. Indeed, in 1944 the National Film Board produced a documentary, *A City Sings*, celebrating the outstanding achievements of choirs and soloists in that mid-twentieth-century Canadian city.

However, it was clear as Mary entered her teenage years that she was destined for a career as a singer. By now she was a familiar figure in the community with experience singing in a number of choirs, in Rosedale United Church in particular, as well as distinguishing herself in solo presentation in other places of worship. Even before she had completed her elementary grades, her parents enrolled her at the Bornoff School of Music in Winnipeg, a fine institution with a quite splendid faculty. It was here that she discovered the excitement that awaited her if she worked hard and secured excellent instruction from outstanding teachers like Doris Mills Lewis and Mary Bornoff.

She took summer courses in Winnipeg, and it was in the context of one of these experiences that she met Dr. Ernesto Vinci, a dedicated teacher from the Conservatory in Toronto. She had met other members of the Canadian musical elite who came through her city, usually on the way to somewhere else, but her encounter with Dr. Vinci was of particular importance. He was a medical doctor who had fled Europe in the realization that Hitler would soon create a tornado of violence and disruption. He was equally a fine musician. When Mary came to the Conservatory in Toronto it was to study with Dr. Ernesto Vinci. He became not only a close friend, entrusting his son, Tom, to her care on occasion, but a mentor who was to play an important role in her development as a professional singer.

Having been successful at local competitions, Mary was encouraged to travel to others taking place in western Canadian cities. A competition in Vancouver brought her into contact with Sir Ernest MacMillan, the principal of the Toronto Conservatory of Music, the conductor of the Toronto Symphony and the Mendelssohn Choir, and dean of the Faculty of Music at the University of Toronto. Impressed by her unique talent, he encouraged her to continue her education in Toronto — obviously at his Toronto Conservatory (later to become the Royal Conservatory).

By 1944, she had become a local sensation. In that year, she won both the Rose Bowl and the Tudor Bowl at the Manitoba Music Festival, the pinnacles of success of all the major competitions in Winnipeg vocal music. It was unheard of that one performer should win both these awards in the same year, and in order to encourage a wider allotment of honours in the competitive life of the city, it was never allowed again. One could win one but not two such awards, as Mary had done!

At one competition, the adjudicator was John Goss, a distinguished educator originally from the U.K., described by one of Mary's correspondents as "a crank at that." Uncharacteristically, Goss praised her voice and her musicality with unrestrained enthusiasm, stating openly that he "could find no way to adequately measure the brilliance of her performance. She is very musical, has a lovely voice and excellent breath control. She has a dignified, modest manner, but above all else she possesses that imponderable thing called imagination with which she colours everything she does. One cannot describe it in words except to say she is an artist." He concluded his assessment with an extraordinary comment: "She can have as many marks as she wants." Goss's enthusiasm for her voice led him, at that time, to provide her with lessons in his home in Vancouver when she was able to reach the West Coast. His adjudicating colleague, a Dr. Pirani, supported this appraisal, commenting, "Whenever I hear such singing with its sincerity and simplicity I want to sit in a quiet corner and cry for the very joy."

At seventeen, Mary was an established singer recognized by the people of Winnipeg and able to command remuneration for her singing at various church services, weddings, funerals, and various other occasions. Indeed, at sixteen, she was invited to sing on the program *Just a Song*, produced by the local CBC affiliate radio station, at first in the studio choir (she was very much the youngest, the "baby" of the ensemble), but often as a soloist. This opportunity expanded her repertoire and was followed by her own program, *Sweethearts*, in which this teenage sensation was teamed with a male guest each week to sing ballads that explored musically the intimacy of human relationships. It had an extraordinarily wide and enthusiastic audience. She went from program to program, including a CBC show called *Prairie Schooner* and a local radio station's program called *Music for You*.

She was building an enormous musical reputation and could have remained as a distinguished figure in the cultural life of Winnipeg for the rest of her life. Her sister, Kathleen, had taken up the violin by this point and had also achieved some recognition in the musical community. However, she too, emulating her older sister, partially abandoned her stringed instrument for the development of a beautiful voice. It was possible for the girls to play and sing together at occasional recitals, and a high degree of close musical association replaced what could have been competitive conflict between two gifted sisters. Indeed, several years later, in Toronto, they were invited to appear together on the CBC program *Singing Stars of Tomorrow*.

By the early 1940s, Mary's voice was becoming familiar to Scottish listeners across the ocean as tapes of her singing of Gaelic songs were exchanged with stations in the United Kingdom. Mary quietly concedes that the pressure of weekly performances of a vast variety of unfamiliar music in foreign languages that she could not hope to fully understand and interpret honed her vocal musical skills magnificently, taking her far beyond the Gaelic culture she had come to know so intimately.

In 1945, an important decision was made. Mary wanted to have a professional career as an opera singer, a concert and recital artist, and to do so felt she needed training at a higher level than she could find in Winnipeg. In Canada, only Toronto, for English-speaking vocal students, could provide such an opportunity. It was difficult for her parents, who had given her every support and now saw her on the mountaintop of success in Western Canada, with her own radio programs, her pick of invitations to sing in various churches, and a host of concert series that were built around her performance, to understand her decision. Why would she need to leave home, go to Toronto, and be buried by the enormous mound of competition she would face in that busy marketplace when she was not yet twenty years old?

Very fortunately, Geoffrey Waddington, a man who was to become a legend in the context of CBC musical presentation, playing the many roles of conductor, arranger, administrator, and friend of virtually every musician who came into contact with the CBC during what many would call the golden age of Canadian broadcasting, was leaving the Winnipeg affiliate station for a new position in Toronto. For Mary's parents, he represented a trusted local citizen from whom they could seek advice. He was invited over for tea, and with thoughtful, helpful words he tried to allay the fears of Donald and Louise Morrison. He could see that they were tormented by the thought of their beautiful young daughter going off alone to a big city. It was not a matter of financial pressure; they had already found some of the resources necessary for transportation, accommodation, and instructional fees, and other scholarships and bursaries were promised. But this teenager was already earning what they considered to be splendid remuneration for her singing! The question remained: what was the advantage in continuing to study and learn, even if she had generous scholarships, when she had already "made it"?

Geoffrey Waddington quietly listened to these troubled parents, considered how best to alleviate their concerns, and encouraged them to allow Mary to make the leap that would enhance her career and her life. She could go to London, New York, or Toronto for the kind of educational experience she needed. He realized that letting Mary go off to the United States would be too difficult for her fearful parents. In England, there was the reality that, although the thought of Mary living in the U.K. her parents fondly remembered was reassuring, life in post–Second World War Britain would be hard and demanding. It would not be the best choice. That left Toronto, and it was to this unfamiliar territory with its Conservatory that her parents turned. Mary, with her confidence in Dr. Vinci as her future instructor, was delighted.

There were exciting things happening at the Toronto Conservatory by this time. The University of Toronto, at that point responsible for the institution based in a substantial building on the southwest corner of College Street and University Avenue, had been convinced that it was time to put some attention to the future of opera in Canada. The move towards establishing an appropriate program was in full flight. Arnold Walter, a man with broad operatic experience, had arrived in Toronto as a refugee from the oppression in Europe promised by the rise of Adolph Hitler and had been hired by Upper Canada College. Assuming wrongly that this was a post-secondary institution, he had been disappointed to discover his mistake and was delighted to move to the Toronto Conservatory. A search for another faculty member who could give leadership in vocal studies and who could also conduct produced a young Czech singer who had also developed his skills in the rich expanse of European operatic tradition. His name was Nicholas Goldschmidt, and he was to become a legend, making an incomparable contribution to Canadian music presentation throughout the next six decades. Within a couple of years, Goldschmidt had contacted a colleague he had known back in Czechoslovakia, Herman

Geiger-Torel. It was this trio who can be credited with bringing the experience of grand opera to Canadian singers and audiences. It would be a glorious experiment, and Mary Morrison, arriving in 1945, would be there on the ground floor and would make her own outstanding contribution to this exciting time in the nation's cultural history.

Fortunately, Mary's friend and mentor, Geoffrey Waddington, recognizing the developments taking place at the nearby Conservatory, saw the CBC as a part of this operatic birthing process. There was no true opera company in Canada, even in Toronto — but opera on radio was a possibility. And there were even rumours of a new broadcast technology that was "in the works" and would be perfect for transmitting visual images along with sound — surely the ultimate dream of those who perceived opera as the appropriate culmination of any career in the vocal arts. But for Canada, television was still years away.

Strangely, in spite of their joint occupancy of Winnipeg during the 1930s and early '40s, Mary Morrison and Harry Freedman never actually met. Harry was some four years her senior (and at that age, four years is a significant age difference) and for most of the war had been stationed in Ottawa and Edmonton. But it was more than that. Although they were both participating in the musical life of Winnipeg, particularly at the end of the war, with Harry playing in bands and enjoying the thrill of professional music making while Mary carried off prizes at every level of competition, these two young people were in different worlds. North and South Winnipeg were not simply geographical descriptions. They represented two very different cultures. North Winnipeg, with citizens at the lower levels of income and status, politically represented the demand for social justice and greater equality; South Winnipeg, with more prosperous inhabitants (though the Morrisons certainly did not qualify as "normal" citizens on those grounds), was driven by a commitment to social order and status quo, particularly after the Winnipeg General Strike in 1919. The former was the comfortable base for left-wing politics and union action led in part by intellectually lively Jewish citizens; the latter was the comfortable home of the traditional Anglo-Saxon urban immigrants who sang "Rule Britannia" and "Jerusalem" with the intense fervour of patriotic citizens of a vanishing empire.

There was almost a moment of contact. In 1945, as Mary prepared to move off to Toronto, she was invited to a party given by Gordon Kushner, a respected accompanist, at his own Winnipeg home during a visit of Ernesto Vinci. Indeed it was this visitor who ensured that Mary knew all about the scholarships that were available and aroused her excitement about the future that lay before her in the ensuing months and years at the Conservatory. Harry Freedman, who had been stationed in Winnipeg during the last days of the war, was also invited. Feeling somewhat intimidated by this gathering of singers in the living room, he retreated immediately to the kitchen, discovered there an old friend from his world of popular music, and departed for a local pub before even shaking the hand of the stunning young woman who was ultimately to be his life partner.

CHAPTER 3
Toronto and Its Conservatory

The Toronto Conservatory received its "royal" status within two years of Mary and Harry's arrival. In spite of this impending designation it was not, in 1945, the centre of Canada's musical world. But it was to become so! An initiative had already begun to create an opera school, one that gave a focus to vocal studies and brought Arnold Walter, Nicholas Goldschmidt, and Herman Geiger-Torel to Canada. They were to ignite the firestorm that was to follow. This decision had been made in the context of a new sense of mission that had come from impending royal recognition but even more from the flood of mature, demanding students who arrived in 1945 and 1946, some from the battlefields of Europe and the skies overhead, along with the normal intake of young people from secondary schools aspiring to musical careers.

It had been nearly twenty years since Ernest MacMillan took over as principal of the Toronto Conservatory on the death of A.S. Vogt. Particularly in the early years of his tenure, MacMillan had devoted his enormous energy and musical genius towards making this institution the major music school in the country. From what Ezra Schabas, his biographer, has called "essentially nothing more than a conglomeration of private studios and an effective examination system modelled after Britain's," this school had come some distance. MacMillan had gone on a tour of similar music education institutions and had been impressed by, for example, the New England Conservatory, which had developed an advanced program for the preparation of professional musicians, a splendid symphonic orchestra, a fine choral ensemble, and even an opera department. Within a few years, all these aspects of a fully fleshed out "conservatory" had appeared at the Toronto Conservatory. Indeed, by the end of the 1920s, a Toronto Conservatory Opera Company (TCOC) had been capable of producing quite respectable performances of Humperdinck's *Hansel and Gretel* and Purcell's *Dido and Aeneas* and had even given the North American premiere of Ralph Vaughn Williams's *Hugh the Drover*. On some evenings the TCOC had been successful in filling such venues as Hart House Theatre and the Royal Alexandra Theatre with large and appreciative audiences.

However, the times, the 1930s and '40s, were not with MacMillan. Less than half a decade after his elevation to the post of principal, the Depression, followed by the Second World War, had dashed any hope the young MacMillan could have harboured that dramatic changes were possible at the Toronto Conservatory. Schabas recorded that, in 1936, it was "still the same limited and backward school" it had been when MacMillan took office a decade before. Now, in the mid-1940s, his successor as principal, Ettore Mazzolini, was filled with expectations that the end of the Second World War would bring resources and enrolments that would encourage a great leap forward, one that would make it possible for the Conservatory to support an enlivened Canadian musical culture from coast to coast.

Mary Morrison and Harry Freedman, completely unknown to each other, arrived in the fall of 1945 with contrasting ambitions — Mary, to become a fully professional singer and opera "diva," and Harry, to learn something of performing as a wind player and, when it became possible in Canada, a functioning "serious" composer. Both had left Winnipeg with plans to return to their native city. Mary had already built a considerable career in radio, on the concert stage, and in the church sanctuaries in that city. She knew exactly with whom she wanted to work in Toronto — the esteemed Dr. Ernesto Vinci, a man who could both perform and teach. Although she was to study piano with Myrtle Rose Guerrero and lieder with Emmy Heim and later took lessons from Greta Kraus and Weldon Kilburn, it was Dr. Vinci who was her prime mentor and inspiration.

Many years later Mary would be invited to become a member of the University of Toronto's Faculty of Music, to where by this time Conservatory studies in opera and voice had moved. Mary was to become an internationally recognized teacher of voice, but in spite of the many honours that were heaped on her she never forgot these first months as a Winnipeg girl in a large, forbidding institution. She understood that as a teacher her first task was to find and enhance her students' confidence, assuring them of comfort and caring. She knew what it was like to arrive from a smaller community, where recognition had been almost instant, to the terrifying commanding heights of the musical life in a major city.

She had come from the West with a career already in place and could analyze with considerable sophistication the quality of the teaching and mentoring that she was receiving. It gave her the first vision of a career beyond her performance years — and a respect for that role as more than just something that a retired singer could do later in life. She was able to bring a mature and thoughtful approach, with some distance, to the contribution that Vinci and other instructors were making to the next stage in her singing career.

Mary found that her highest priority was to find a place to live. For two years she stayed at the YWCA, but finally she secured a room in the Orde Street Conservatory residence, one she could share with Betty-Jean Hagen, a very gifted violinist. Although both were full-time students, by the third year they both had flourishing professional careers. These gigs often took them out of town overnight. Unfortunately, one of the house rules that was at the top of some unexplainable list of regulations stated that suitcases were not to be left in student bedrooms. Betty-Jean and Mary, who refused to go through the mindless and time-consuming process of retrieving their suitcases from some distant point in the building every few days, engaged in a subterfuge of hiding their travel bags under beds, behind chests of drawers, and in dark corners of closets, even involving classmates in a variety of strategies that made the suitcases disappear when an unexpected inspection was in full flight.

Harry soon discovered that he had connections with a wide spectrum of friends and associates, all involved with one another in the smaller ensembles that emerged at the Conservatory. He was also confident that by the time he learned to play what was now his new enthusiasm, the oboe, there would be a place for him in the newly established Winnipeg Symphony Orchestra. Perry Bauman, a splendid oboist, had been hired by the Toronto Symphony Orchestra five years earlier and was now teaching at the Conservatory. Harry knew all about him and the extraordinarily beautiful sound he was producing. Besides, beyond the mastery of his instrument he had a single passion — learning from John Weinzweig, already established at the Conservatory as the beacon for composing and teaching the "new" twentieth-century music and well on his way to becoming the spokesperson and dean of Canada's contemporary classical composers. The rest of the activities at the Conservatory were of little interest to him.

Thus, in the fall of 1945, the Conservatory became the new home for both Mary and Harry. It turned out that they were surrounded by a surge of mature students, many, like Harry, who had spent three, four, or five years in the armed forces, but others who had simply delayed their further education until the war was over and there was some sign of life in the red brick building in the centre of Toronto. These students, unlike their predecessors, were impatient and demanding, unwilling to accept the delays and inadequacies that institutions are wont to allow in the name of perceived academic integrity.

There were figures arriving in these years who would occupy the major concert stages in North America and Europe for the rest of the century. Some, like soprano Teresa Stratas and tenor Jon Vickers, were to climb the heights of the operatic world. Ironically, Jon Vickers had been singing in an operetta with Mary in Winnipeg when she remarked to him, "Have you ever heard your voice?" She advised him to make a recording and to follow her own example — head east and take advantage of the Toronto Conservatory program. He agreed, and she took a copy of the audiotape back to that institution, sang his praises, and ensured that an invitation to enroll ensued. Years later, recognizing her role in his success, Vickers, ensconced at Covent Garden in 1957, preparing *Dei Meistersinger von Nüremberg*, *Carmen*, *The Masked Ball*, and *Les Troyens*, wrote to Mary, "There never has been in all my experience greater delight than in our work together." He knew she had been the initiator of a career that was to be unique in the annals of Canadian operatic success.

Others were determined to build a musical culture in their homeland, which by the end of the twentieth century had been transformed by their contributions. There was Phil Nimmons, who was to achieve for jazz in Canada, both as a performer in the 1950s and '60s and as teacher in subsequent decades, the kind of influence that Benny Goodman exerted in the U.S.A. There was Lois Marshall, whose voice and presence in recital, opera, and oratorio became the pride of all knowledgeable citizens, moving even the incomparable Arturo Toscanini to hire her as a performer. There was Mario Bernardi, a conductor whose leadership of the National Arts Centre Orchestra (NACO), founded at the end of the 1960s, was absolutely essential to the future of an ensemble that was moderate in size but outstanding in performance and paved the way for the National Arts Centre (NAC) to someday become the nation's artistic showplace. There was Harry Somers, a close friend of Harry Freedman — the two becoming known as "Weinzweig's two Harrys," the first two Canadian composers to live from the proceeds of their own musical composition. For Mary, the opportunity to work with such singers as Elizabeth Benson Guy and later Margaret Stilwell and Patricia Rideout was reason enough to have sought the richer fields of Toronto's music scene.

As a result of her radio work in Winnipeg, Mary's arrival in Toronto had been heralded by the CBC. A press release announcing the 1945–46 season of the program *Singing Stars of Tomorrow* informed the network's listeners of her Winnipeg triumphs. Interestingly, it was indicated that "her ambition is radio or the concert stage" and that her preference was for light opera. Mary made an impact on the program from the beginning, and for a later program her sister Kathleen came from Winnipeg to join her for a *Singing Stars of Tomorrow* duet. Mary went on to appear on the CBC's *Northern Electric Hour, Startime, Sunday Strings, The Stage,* and *Showtime.* Her immediate experience as a professional performer while still a student was to be a matter of pride for a now "royal" Conservatory desperately seeking its place in post–Second World War Canada.

Ettore Mazzolini, who had replaced MacMillan as principal in the middle of the war years, declared it the most exciting time he ever experienced at the Conservatory — a view that was echoed by virtually every colleague and student who graced the familiar building on a site now occupied by Ontario Hydro. Graduates looked back at the late 1940s as the vintage years, when there was an impatience of delayed personal ambition but also a wider concept of collective mission that compelled intense performance. It resulted in days of experimenting together, arguing and confronting over coffee, and constant reaching out to the community for inspiration and example. Many of the musicians, desperately in need of remuneration, took part-time work as organists and choirmasters and completely changed the musical landscape of the very conservative city of Toronto.

In the light of later years, it was a moment in Canada's cultural history when there was virtually an empty canvas of possibility on which each musician could paint. However, it must be conceded that the entire musical development of almost the first half of the twentieth century had escaped Canadian notice. Schoenberg, Honegger, and Webern were invisible, and even Ravel and Debussy and Richard Strauss were rarely heard. Although Canada's musical heritage was imposing, particularly in the scope of its choral activity, it was nevertheless minuscule in terms of the needs of a people now settled in an urbanized, industrial society. Significantly, these young people were preparing themselves in their own country, rather than in the United States, and there was on the faculty a man who was as close to the edge of new directions in the making of music as could be found anywhere on earth: John Weinzweig. John had been asked to join the faculty before the outbreak of war to the astonishment of all observers of musical style in 1930s Canada. Eschewing the usual pattern of training for Canadian students of music, Weinzweig had gone not to the U.K. but to the U.S.A. and the Eastman Conservatory in Rochester, where, under the ministrations of Howard Hanson and the direct influence of Bernard Rogers, new musical sounds were being encouraged, ones that would change the nature of music making in the twentieth century completely. Ironically, Harry had actually applied to Eastman at that point, just in case he could not secure admission to the Toronto Conservatory. When he asked his old high school office to forward his records, those of another, less academically oriented, Harry Freedman were sent to Eastman by mistake and his application was rejected. Harry was to comment that after listening to some of the music of Eastman's more recent graduates he came to the conclusion that it was not a great tragedy. At the same time he was delighted that, with Weinzweig on board, going to the Toronto Conservatory meant "I wouldn't have to analyze Elgar which was what was studied everywhere else in Canada in those days."

The nearly four years Harry spent in RCAF bands had been a perfect apprenticeship for the challenge of the Conservatory. In Ottawa, he had been playing with first-class musicians in a host of venues and experiencing the sound of massed instruments and learning something of the power of a splendid band that could scale the heights of a symphony orchestra's repertoire. There were opportunities to produce background music for films at the newly created National Film Board, where Louis Applebaum was gathering a coterie of fine composers. There was even an opportunity for a few to participate in a new venture — the beginnings of what would become the Ottawa Philharmonic once hostilities ceased. That Harry, barely twenty, with only two years of study and practice on a clarinet and just an ambition to play the oboe, could have fallen amongst this assembly of splendid musicians was truly miraculous. His instrumental technical skills had been stretched by the expectations of his colleagues. Even his rudimentary learning of harmony and counterpoint was pushed further than could have been expected. Indeed, it was in Ottawa, after Harry had returned west to other postings, that John Weinzweig had turned up, already with a reputation as a composer and a teacher of composition and a fully developed consciousness of what direction he wished to take Canadian music once the war was concluded. And it was there, in the capital, that John Weinzweig and Louis Applebaum had first discussed the need for an organization, a "league of composers" as it was called in the United States, that could attract Harry into its ranks to advocate on behalf of Canadian music and composers. Harry had been in exactly the right place in his role as a performer and arranger in the early months of his recruitment. A half-century later, he would remember it as "a wonderful experience."

On two occasions, his time in the forces could have resulted in a very different life experience. Shortly after he enlisted, he was slated to be sent to the first overseas RCAF band in the U.K., not a life-threatening disadvantage but not an experience that could compare with being part of the Central Command ensemble. When it was discovered that he suffered from chronic appendicitis, however, his overseas transfer fell off the RCAF's agenda and Harry remained at Rockcliffe for the rest of 1942. It was then that he discovered a posting for a clarinet player in an air force band stationed in Winnipeg, and he reluctantly left Ottawa to return home to Winnipeg — to family and friends and even more importantly to the musical world that he knew so well and where at least he could, at off-times, both play and arrange for local civilian groups. By this time, he was sure that he really wanted to play the oboe, an instrument with a piercing, dark, mysterious sound that attracted his ear. While in Ottawa he had journeyed to Montreal and had purchased an instrument and had even begun taking lessons from an oboist in the Central Command Band. Although the Winnipeg RCAF band had an opening for another oboe in its ranks, the recalcitrant bandmaster refused to accommodate Harry's new enthusiasm, and Harry was forced to continue his efforts to master the clarinet while surreptitiously learning to play his second woodwind instrument of choice. After a training stint in Edmonton, he returned to the Winnipeg band as the war wound down and to a new bandmaster who was more flexible. Thus, by the time he reached Perry Bauman at the Conservatory, he had a working knowledge of the next instrument on which he hoped to achieve greater proficiency.

In 1944, discovering that there were exciting openings outside the ranks of musicians, Harry asked for a transfer to active service as a pilot. At that point, with all the losses suffered in air raids over Europe, the RCAF was desperate for replacements for trained pilots and was even prepared to lower vision standards to attract recruits. And so Harry went off to training school in Edmonton, where he found himself in the midst of Aussies and New Zealanders being similarly trained, one of them a concertmaster from the Melbourne Symphony Orchestra, all taking part in the British Commonwealth Air Training Plan into which Harry had now been dropped. It was not the sophisticated crowd of musicians he had come to know at Rockcliffe. Indeed, Harry's attempt to capture and thereby listen to the strains of the New York Philharmonic under the baton of Arturo Toscanini on the single radio in the mess hall — as opposed to the broadcast of a baseball game — had been enough to create a near riot.

The initial training included little about flying or navigation, focusing instead on the identification of enemy aircraft and Morse code, still a method of communication in that era. Harry had but one week of flying instruction when the program suddenly ceased and the training aircraft were taken out of service. The fortunes of war had turned; it appeared the Allies had captured the European skies — no more aircrew were needed. Now stuck in Edmonton with his future as a pilot no longer in view, Harry awaited posting to some other centre. Fortunately, he was picked up as a performer-arranger by a group of RCAF musicians who had been assigned the task of conducting a whirlwind tour of the North, where engineers and military personnel were frantically trying to complete the Alaska Highway. The liberation of Europe might well end the war on the Western Front and bring Germany to its knees, but Japan was still, at that point, very much in control of vast stretches of the Pacific. The morale among those planning and building a military highway to defend the length of the Canadian west coast was flagging, and a sturdy crew of entertainers was seen to be an antidote to the darkness, cold, and boredom of the construction sites stretching north to the Arctic Circle.

Harry, having been recruited as a clarinetist, discovered that he had also been designated stand-up comic as the plane dropped down again and again into every construction camp along the route of the highway. As well, he was the arranger for a small coterie of seven entertainers that included two women, one a singer and the other a dancer, accompanied by five instrumentalists, including Harry. What could have been a terrible trial turned out to be a revelation. Harry had never seen the Canadian North and he was emotionally captured by what he witnessed. He remembered the arctic landscape painting that he had seen every day while he attended the Winnipeg Art School. The image that had intrigued him depicted on canvas absolutely overwhelmed him as he looked down from the cabin of a low-flying aircraft. The limitless expanse of the tundra, the magnificence of the landforms, and the endlessness of the horizon all left him breathless. He could not find the words to express his feelings. Years later, his first major composition, *Tableau*, was an attempt to give musical expression to his awe in the only way he could — through his first mature orchestral composition.

The atomic bomb ended the strategic need for the Alaska Highway's immediate completion and thus Harry's role as an entertainer. In 1945, Harry was sent back to the RCAF band in Winnipeg as an oboe player for the months that remained before demobilization took place. He received his discharge but listed his home as Toronto on his release papers. In that way, he could secure a free rail trip to Ontario's capital and to the classes offered by John Weinzweig at the Conservatory. The Liberal Mackenzie King Government treated its veterans more decently than had the Union Government led by Robert Borden at the end of the 1914–18 engagement. Every veteran was offered free post-secondary education at an accredited institution, and the Conservatory qualified. Harry arrived at Union Station in Toronto and made his way to 7 Spadina Road, a rooming house that soon was filled with other veterans who were determined to take advantage of the rehabilitation plans of the federal government.

Very soon, Harry was attending the classes offered by the object of his quest, John Weinzweig, already a legend among musicians who perceived music as a way of expressing what they had experienced in their lives as unemployed workers or as servicemen and women. Weinzweig's teaching was as novel as the music he was writing. It was not about detailed examination of the classics, but what he called "eye-music," an understanding of music visually rather than aurally. It was a matter of encouraging each student to seek his own direction, based on his or her experiences — surely a wise and appropriate strategy for young composers who had several years of wartime experiences to express. "The composer is … a practical psychologist who translates feeling into tone … carries sensitivity to a higher and finer level, and is more openly and subtlety aware of the relationship between tone and meaning" was Weinzweig's philosophy. Yes, it meant a clear approach to what many referred to as "that twelve-tone thing," a method of building sound with a broader reach across more uninhibited tonal opportunities than composers had accepted in previous centuries — sounds that demanded more careful and thoughtful attention from both composer and audience.

Harry had no hesitation in according his mentor a pre-eminent role in the development of his career. "Weinzweig taught me my craft," and he was a "wonderful teacher," Harry said. He specifically credited Weinzweig with teaching him how to *teach himself*. The great teacher works to make

himself redundant. By the third year of their association Harry was simply bringing his compositions to Weinzweig, and his instruction had
become a discussion of the music that Harry was writing.

Weinzweig had another influence: "You learn from every piece you
compose. If you stop learning, you start dying." Harry never allowed
himself to find a comfortable "rut" — a style of composition that produced a recognizable sound that would identify his music as a
"Freedman piece." Every work was a start-from-scratch exploration of
the architecture of sound, taking into account the context of the commissioned work, particularly the peculiar strengths of the ensemble for
which it was being composed — all the Weinzweig traits that Harry
both consciously and unconsciously inherited from his years of interaction with this incomparable master.

It was not long before Harry became aware of the presence of a fellow Winnipegger, one Mary Morrison. He had never been impressed by
vocal artists. In his mind, they were not really musicians with any deep
commitment to professionalism. With Mary, however, he was intimidated from his first meeting. She was already "virtually a professional"
in his eyes. He knew of her triumphs in radio and in the churches and
performing spaces of Winnipeg. Now in Toronto, she was not only a star
of *Singing Stars of Tomorrow* but also a part of one of CBC's major productions, *Northern Electric Hour*. In the CBC *Times*, April 1948, she
would be extolled as an "accomplished pianist" who was equally comfortable in a vocal repertoire that included opera arias and popular
songs and even "traditional Scottish airs."

All these engagements meant that she could support herself and
thus relieve some of the financial pressure on her parents. A glance at a
partial list of her remuneration indicates the full schedule of a performing star — but reveals as well the minimal payment for vocal services in the 1940s and '50s. It was the CBC Opera Company on radio that
in 1948 gave her $75 for the part of Mimi in *La Bohème*, the same for
the parts of Euridice in *Orpheus and Euridice*, Flora in *La Traviata*, and
for acting as an understudy for Elvira in *Don Giovanni*. Interestingly,
that same year the Kelvin Grads Mixed Glee Club in Winnipeg paid her
$350 for a week of performances of *Naughty Marietta*. Two years later,
the Kelvin Grads Mixed Glee Club paid her $450 for her part in *The*

Vagabond King, leading an observer a half-century later to wonder whether Winnipeg was far ahead of Toronto and Eastern Canada in remunerating its artists.

By 1950 professional fees had risen: the role of Michaela in *Carmen* brought a stipend from the CBC of $150, and there was a leap to $175 for the role of Liu in *Turandot*. By 1951 that same role of Mimi brought in a $175 cheque from the CBC. But the fees were not automatically expanding, as the role of Gretel in a concert performance of *Hansel and Gretel* at a TSO Pops appearance in 1953 brought in only $100, and in that same year she earned the same amount for appearing in a performance of the *St. Matthew Passion* in Carnegie Hall in New York City. Nevertheless, it was apparent that this Conservatory student was successfully finding a place in the musical life of the country and was earning enough to survive.

For students like Harry and Mary, there was no time to waste. A world war had stalled Harry's career during the years that would normally have been given to explorations of various learning and vocational alternatives. Though Mary had surged forward, she soon found herself with students who saw their colleagues not just as competitors but also as collaborators. Pianists needed experience as accompanists, and most vocalists and instrumentalists needed the experience of performance, if not before paid audiences then at least before fellow students. Composers needed instrumentalists who could provide an opportunity for them to hear their own work. On Saturday afternoons, Conservatory students gathered for informal sessions that served all these interests. Harry remembered that Mary was always available for these Saturday gatherings. The postwar 1940s brought these heights of performance excitement that led to the designation of this period as the golden years at the Royal Conservatory, never to be repeated but never to be forgotten.

Harry realized he had met an extraordinary artist in Mary Morrison, a stunning, attractive woman who was both intelligent and, in the light of the accolades she had already received, unexplainably humble. They came into contact continually as a result of their common experience in the extraordinary interactions that pervaded the Conservatory lifestyle. At the outset their relationship was merely an extension of the "jam sessions," of talking incessantly about Canada and the cultural life that could be if only there were resources and encouragement from the government and the private sector.

When there was a moment not occupied by a rehearsal or a gig, there was some social life. One night in 1950, Phil Nimmons, Harry's former rooming house mate, took Mary Morrison on a double date with Harry Freedman, who invited Arlene Meade, the hostess of a jazz radio program on a local station, CJBC. It was to the Palais Royale, the pre-eminent dance emporium on Toronto's waterfront at Sunnyside Beach, they went. Fortuitously, trading partners on the dance floor was quite acceptable, and Mary came to realize that Harry, with his long association with the world of jazz and popular musical idioms, was a splendid dancer who could move with blinding speed and grace across a crowded floor. Harry was, by now, captivated by this beautiful young woman from Winnipeg and quickly moved to secure a second date that would cement their relationship. A round of dates followed, and together they attended a performance of *The Importance of Being Earnest* at the Hart House Theatre that involved the talents of John Beckwith, who was then an actor but was soon to emerge as a composer and who was to become Harry's close colleague in the days ahead. Thus by the middle of the twentieth century, Harry and Mary were an item, and it was only a matter of time before an official ceremony would give legal recognition to their love — one built on a dual commitment to music and its making.

By this time, Harry had become a regular performer, not in the Winnipeg Symphony as expected, but in the Toronto Symphony. In a sequence of events that challenges the imagination, the four years of introduction to and mastery of the oboe that Harry had planned became a year of full-time study with Perry Bauman — and three years of part-time study accompanied by a surprise initiation into the life of a professional player in Canada's major symphonic ensemble.

The circumstances could not have been foreseen. In 1946, an opening, not for an oboist but for an English horn player, suddenly occurred at the TSO, and the frantic conductor, Ernest MacMillan, had to find an immediate replacement. There were not many English horn players about. It was not an instrument that attracted much attention, even though its deep sensuous tones have been appreciated particularly by composers of the late Romantic era.

Bauman, realizing that this was an opportunity not to be missed, informed Harry of the opening. Bauman was sure that he had such an English horn back home in Philadelphia and invited Harry to take possession of it. He was impressed with his mature student and his progress as a fine oboe player, but here was a unique opportunity to join the woodwind section of the most prestigious orchestra in Canada. As well, the auditions were taking place at a time and in circumstances that advantaged Harry's presentation. Ernest MacMillan may have been seen as a rather reluctant supporter of Canadian repertoire in his concert schedule, but he was a supporter of Canadian musicians. He could surely do no less — he was, after all, still the dean of the Faculty of Music at the University of Toronto and had been the principal of the Toronto Conservatory for many years before. Hiring his own students, particularly those who had served their country in war, was imperative if MacMillan was to be considered a loyal Canadian. There was no doubt that now that the war was over he was determined to improve the quality of his TSO, assuring its position as the best in Canada but also reaching a level that would enable it to tour across the continent and beyond. However, the best of all possible worlds in his mind was the inclusion of the finest Canadian musicians that could be found now that the Orchestra was on the verge of a postwar era pregnant with new possibilities. There was also the reality that the Musicians' Union, represented by an aggressive Walter Murdoch, was putting pressure on MacMillan and every other Canadian decision-maker to hire home-grown musicians where at all possible.

Harry worked furiously with Perry Bauman to achieve a credible audition performance on his new instrument, a rather creaky old English horn that had been left unused for some years. However, the time for preparation could be measured in weeks, whereas Harry would claim that to find a place in a professional orchestra, even in the mid-1940s, a period of at least four years of intense training and maturation was required. With much trepidation Harry arrived, played, and was astonished to find himself offered a position by the determined Sir Ernest, who found his tone appealing, just what he wanted in his renewed woodwind section. In November 1946, a little over a year after his arrival in Toronto, Plan A to spend four years full-time at the Conservatory was replaced by Plan B — becoming a member of the TSO, while continuing to work part-time with Bauman, but more importantly, as an aspiring composer, with John Weinzweig.

The circumstances were with Harry in every way. The TSO, even in 1946, had a very limited performance schedule. Members of the orchestra could not survive on their stipend as players but were expected to play for any number of other ensembles associated with theatres and particularly in the studios of the CBC, now increasing its activities in the direction of live music. (Ironically, in the 1950s and '60s the problem for music making in Toronto was not the presence of an army of starving and relatively silent instrumentalists waiting for more work but an inadequate number of able musicians who had to race from one gig to another with insufficient preparation to play anything well. This pressure was even more evident in the next decade, when both the Canadian Opera Company and the National Ballet of Canada arrived on the Toronto scene, each determined to have splendid orchestras in the pit.)

Also working in favour of Harry's composing ambitions was the fact that his instrument did not demand his presence at every rehearsal and concert simply because it did not play a role in the works of many composers. It could not have been a more perfect situation for Harry: he could continue his Conservatory role as a student of composition, explore that role actively from his chair in the woodwind section, have a regular income, and begin the process of planning the next stage of his life as a musician and, more importantly, as a composer.

There was one downside — Harry felt that he had "no business being in a professional orchestra." He never lost the sense that he was in the orchestra by accident. In his first appearance with the TSO, at a Toronto Police Association charity extravaganza at Maple Leaf Gardens, there was, in fact, an English horn solo, and while Harry got through it "with flying colours," in the words of his colleagues, it was a traumatic event. "I completely blanked out … I could not remember a thing," he recalled. However, this feeling of inadequacy as a performer had one advantage: he never perceived his role in music as simply a woodwind player — even though he was still a member of the TSO a quarter of a century later. He saw himself as a composer who could put food on the table by being a competent member of an improving orchestra, a very different position than his full-time Royal Conservatory colleagues felt they occupied as delayed travellers on the path of a career in music making in mid-twentieth-century Canada.

As well, Harry was one of a kind. He saw himself as a working musician with a unique take on the composing of music. These notes on paper had a practical application. He, like Schoenberg, came to see music as written for the moment, rather than for posterity, and written for the particular musical forces and the specific performance event that must be served. Sitting in his place in the woodwind section, surrounded by the massive forces of reverberation, he came to see his role as a musical architect. In a description of composer Ferdinand Hiller, Russell Martin observes that for him "the joy of shaping sound into art remained synonymous with living." So it could be said of Harry Freedman.

Fortunately, he had found a companion in Mary Morrison, who understood and shared his passion for music and was prepared to be patient in dealing with the frustrations of the irregular hours and unplanned crises of show business. Even more fortunately, Harry had a partner who would herself have a career in music that demanded the same understanding on his side. Either it would be a supportive and caring relationship or it would end in tatters, as each demanded the finite space and energy to make a difference in the music marketplace to the exclusion of all else.

CHAPTER 4
Earning a Living, Making a Life

The Toronto Symphony that had hired Harry Freedman in 1945 was emerging from difficult days, but with the Second World War over it was anticipating a brighter future. Ernest MacMillan, now Sir Ernest, had taken over the TSO in 1931, and by the 1940s it had become an asset to the musical life of the city. However, there was a long way to go before it could be perceived a competent, mature symphonic ensemble. It gave less than two dozen concerts a year, mostly "twilight" shows that were held in the early evening before its players were needed for their nightly appearances in movie houses, live theatres, or churches. There were in each season, however, four regular evening subscription performances and three more in the afternoon for children. The quality of the players still left a great deal to be desired.

The onslaught of the Depression in the 1930s had seriously limited any hope of increasing the number of concerts, improving the quality of performance, or raising the level of remuneration available to its members. Ironically, the war years of the 1940s had been kinder to the TSO than had been expected with a global conflict preoccupying the public mind. Indeed, the Second World War had the surprisingly positive effect of raising Toronto's consciousness of the need for great music. The example of the U.K., where good music was used to raise the morale of London's populace in the worst days of the Blitz, was certainly a factor in the turnaround. Even the unexpected use of the opening bars of Beethoven's Fifth Symphony to encourage the spirit of the people in Allied countries supported the awareness of a still largely Anglo-Saxon city that the presence of a symphony orchestra was essential to the war effort.

Yet it was evident that any major improvement in the quality of the ensemble, which might, for example, result in invitations to tour major cities in North America or Europe, had not yet been seriously contemplated. The question of touring was important. Canadian artists still regarded themselves as second-rate colonials until declared competent by American and European critics and audiences. An unexpected increase in the number of concerts performed had occurred simultaneously with Harry's unheralded arrival as a TSO member in 1945. The number of Friday evening popular classics concerts leapt from eight in the 1944–45 season to twenty-four in 1945–46, with four more to be added in 1946–47. As well, the number of subscribers was increasing, enabling an improvement in the per concert payment to the orchestra members. Within two more years, the subscription sales had soared, and it was possible to repeat the programs on a second night instead of adding more single performances.

Harry's successful audition had changed his life substantially. He was now a colleague rather than a student of Perry Bauman's, with, depending on the repertoire, the prospect of dozens of concerts and rehearsals added to his schedule. Even more importantly, he was now drawn into the elite coterie of instrumentalists who were available for orchestral performance dates at CBC Radio, often playing in musical productions or, more likely, providing the background music for the radio dramas for which the CBC was developing an international reputation. There might even be a performance of the CBC Symphony Orchestra or, by 1948, the CBC Opera Company.

Harry found he was very much a part of the CBC's emerging commitment to contemporary composers and their music. Many years later, when John Roberts was asked to write a report on that aspect of the CBC's past, he contacted Harry, who responded most generously. Harry made the point that playing in a CBC Symphony Orchestra that addressed a more modern repertoire than the TSO's had enabled him to discover the techniques of Webern, Schoenberg, Stravinsky, and Richard Strauss, as well as the more avant-garde Canadian composers. Fortunately Harry had his fair share of commissions to do background music for dramas and documentaries — indeed, along with playing his English horn, it was his bread and butter. This period of the CBC's history became remembered as a glorious era, a pinnacle of Canadian radio broadcasting still warmly held in the minds of older citizens. It was a reputation that carried CBC Radio through the rest of the twentieth century.

Harry was studiously practising his English horn, seeking to achieve a higher comfort level as a professional performing musician. He was self-deprecatingly frank about his early inadequacies, confessing to Larry Lake on a special CBC program, *Two New Hours*, celebrating his eightieth birthday, "For the first two or three years I don't know how they tolerated me." Yet he also conceded that for the following ten years and more, he quite enjoyed his role in the TSO. As he neared the end of his playing career, he became increasingly dissatisfied with the tone that he was producing on his English horn. He began debating whether he should step down from his position in the TSO. His playing career seemed at risk in late 1960s when conductor Seiji Ozawa asked another member of the TSO woodwind section to play a solo that would normally have been Harry's to perform. It indicated that Ozawa was conscious of a severe tonal deterioration. That led to Harry's most dramatic life decision — to leave the world of performance and concentrate on composing. Within a few short weeks of making this decision he was in Paris to witness a ballet whose score he had written. He took his English horn to its manufacturer, and it was discovered that the bore of the instrument had shrunk, probably because the wood had been too green at the time of the instrument's production. Once the bore was hollowed and restored, the sound was perfectly in tune. Harry was now mature and confident enough to perceive the irony of his accidental shift from player to composer with no regrets.

At the same time, during the 1950s and '60s, he worked assiduously on improving his performance on the oboe, realizing that repertoire decisions could restrict his income on the English horn, but if he could double on the oboe, he could expand his services and his remuneration. Yet with this waxing and waning of his commitment to his role as a journeyman musician, Harry focused increasingly on music composition rather than performance. He was becoming aware of the musical landscape that he was entering. The Willan-MacMillan nineteenth-century British tradition at the Conservatory and the University of Toronto's Faculty of Music still dominated decades later. True, there were in the late 1930s and early '40s a few prospective modern Canadian composers gathering around John Weinzweig. There was also Godfrey Ridout, who was almost a kind of bridge from the traditionalists to the true modernists, and Louis Applebaum, along with a collection of associates at the National Film Board in Ottawa whose work was largely devoted to documentary film and background radio music. The two Harrys, Freedman and Somers, soon to be followed by John Beckwith and an array of women, including Norma Beecroft and Violet Archer, had also come into some prominence in the 1950s. The time had arrived to bring together this small collection of contemporary classical composers determined to connect Canadian music composition to the developments that were taking place in Europe and even in the United States. Harry was one of the original eight who made this decision. It was very simply the right moment to create a composers' organization that could support the process of Canadian composition. Harry quickly became a central figure in this initiative.

In spite of his busy performing schedule, Harry persisted in writing music, inspired by the presence and example of Weinzweig and goaded in particular by a classmate he met soon after his arrival, Harry Somers. They clicked on their first encounter at the Conservatory, and Somers remained Harry's valued colleague over many years. Indeed, on Somers's death, Harry wrote *Graphic IX* as a tribute to this extraordinary relationship. Somers was a thoughtful and critical admirer who realized that Harry's continuing preoccupation with painting, and with Japanese sumi-e painting in particular, with its sparse brush strokes in black ink, very much reflected the restrained but beautifully crafted work of his musical composition.

When in 1951 the Canadian League of Composers (CLC) was formed, Harry Freedman was very much on the scene and became the League's first secretary. (Weinzweig was, of course, its first president, and Louis Applebaum, an early proponent with considerable experience in the United States, its first vice-president.) Applebaum and Weinzweig both saw the CLC as an extension of the North American example — there was already a League of Composers in the U.S.A. that by the 1950s had even shown interest in having Canadian music performed. Harry, as a North Winnipegger, was immediately drawn to the ranks of the CLC for ideological reasons. He had brought all the baggage of a home-town commitment to social justice and political action that had become honed during war years' discussions, when the struggles of capitalism and communism were surfacing within the Allied war aims that had motivated the support of both the U.S.A. and U.S.S.R.

Ideally, the union movement was more than just a mechanism for collective bargaining; it was about justice — rewarding honest work with appropriate remuneration. Though collective bargaining as found in the industrial sector sense was impossible in dealing with independent com-posers, Harry knew by now that composing was indeed hard work that included the excitement of inspired expression but also the hours of tedi-um that were essential before any manuscript was completed and avail-able for performance. One of the disadvantages in organizing his col-leagues was the fact that nearly all composers had day jobs, which could include being professors, teachers, or church organists and choirmasters, many of whom thought that, like reading, composing had its intrinsic rewards and that remuneration should never be an issue. Harry's sup-port of the CLC came from his roots as a politically aware youth, and he never lost his focus on the difficulties of being a professional composer. He became a member of the Canadian Association of Publishers, Authors, and Composers (CAPAC), the performing rights organization responsible for collecting royalties, and allowed his name to stand for election to the CAPAC executive in the 1980s. There was no doubt of where he stood on the issue of payment for creative work.

In the first stages of establishing its importance, thereby drawing interest from composers from Montreal to Vancouver, the CLC turned to the example of the American League of Composers, which had taken on the task of encouraging the performance of contemporary music. Harry, with his roots in the performing arts, knew that task would be difficult in Canada, where the opportunities to hear and become familiar with contemporary music played by orchestras and chamber ensembles were even less available than they were in the U.S.A. Audiences would have to be found in a country where even the music of Beethoven, Brahms, Bruchner, and Mahler had relatively few enthusiasts and twentieth-century composers like Rachmaninoff, Prokofiev, Sibelius, and Richard Strauss were a considerable stretch. The music of Schoenberg, Stravinsky, Hindemith, and even Ravel and Debussy were rarely attempted by Canadian ensembles, and completely beyond the pale were the works of living Canadian composers. Dedication to the British imperial tradition ensured that Elgar, Vaughn Williams, and later Britten would receive some attention, but that enthusiasm had more to do with appropriate colonial behaviour than it did with music appreciation.

Sir Ernest MacMillan, who dominated Canadian musical life both as a conductor and an arts education administrator and who was a composer himself, was not seen to be an enthusiastic supporter of the "modern" sounds of the serialist and twelve-tone schools to which, worldwide, music creators were leaning in an effort to find a more authentic opportunity to express themselves. To be fair, the many conflicting roles that Sir Ernest was playing made it impossible for him to be a champion of the contemporary composer, as he had to find people who would attend his TSO and Mendelssohn Choir concerts, and they were almost single-minded in their opposition to "tuneless" modern music. It meant that the man, himself a composer, who could have championed the cause of contemporary music was simply not available.

In the 1951–52 performing season, the CLC launched a series of concerts of Canadian contemporary music, the first for small orchestra conducted by Ettore Mazzolini, the Conservatory's principal, and, two years later, another for large orchestra with the CBC's Geoffrey Waddington on the podium. At the second concert, Harry Freedman's *Nocturne* was featured, along with Harry Somers's *North Country* and Alexander Brott's Violin Concerto. Harry had arrived as a composer in the eyes of his colleagues and was now a presence in the ears of a number of people who called themselves supporters of Canadian contemporary music. The playing of *Nocturne* was a coup of some significance for a recently minted Conservatory student. It was well received. However, it was not his first composition. Even in the later 1940s he had composed works that, in retrospect, he came to believe deserved a place as part his life's work. As early as 1947, while mastering the oboe, his first published effort was a Divertimento for Oboe and Strings, followed the next year by a Trio for Two Oboes and English Horn. It might be argued that Harry's Divertimento was influenced, in the first case, by a similar divertimento that John Weinzweig had written in that period. In fact, both the Trio and Divertimento reflect Harry's determination to explore the instruments whose tone and technical limitations he was experiencing in his other role as performer as much as an opportunity to discover his capacity to make music. Both were lean and accessible with themes that were delightfully intertwined. These pieces indicated that Harry's music would follow the Weinzweig path, offering dissonance as well as familiar harmony in an acceptance of traditional forms of contrapuntal writing in his effort to express through sound his impressions of life in mid-century Canada.

In that same year, he composed a Symphonic Suite — his first attempt at confronting larger orchestral forces. Normally, one expects composers to find their way to major works from songs, that is, melodic lines for voice or solo instruments with keyboard accompaniment, to pieces that demand a string quartet or wind quintet, to, finally, much later, compositions that demand a full orchestral response. Harry saw that this was not to be his direction. He had moved from the popular dance or jazz band to the full-size military band to the regular symphony orchestra as a musician. Harry was ready to write "large." His Symphonic Suite was featured at the yearly symposium of major schools of music in northern U.S.A. and Canada's Royal Conservatory, making use of the twelve-tone technique that he was later largely to abandon.

Even more important to his future, Harry had become a master of at least three significant wind instruments. He was physically situated in the very centre of the symphony orchestra, where he could hear every strand that made up the warp and weft of the world's most impressive musical sounds. From the outset, Harry moved to the sounds of the complete orchestral ensemble in his head. Harry realized that he heard his musical ideas fully blown in orchestral sounds. John Beckwith was fascinated by Harry's steps in beginning a work — identifying and placing on paper the words that would portray what his music would eventually express. It was Harry's challenge to see that his architecture of

sound was accurately placed in the score that would be put before conductors and the full range of orchestral instrumentalists.

It meant that Harry had come to know, understand, and appreciate
all the possibilities that master musicians could bring forth from their
instruments. While he spent a good part of the next quarter-century as a
performer, he was simultaneously studying and analyzing the full spectrum of orchestral repertoire that created a rich and never-ending variety of combinations for these instruments. It was an experience that no
lecture hall could replicate. He recognized that the orchestra was indeed
his classroom and that every score of every composer was a lesson from
which he could learn. It became his custom, during a rehearsal break, to
approach the podium and examine the conductor's score and even, on
occasion, engage conductors in discussion on the secrets of how certain
sounds and effects that, in the case of the masters, had moved listeners in
concert halls around the world over some centuries were achieved. Harry
was determined to become an orchestral composer in its full meaning,
and the Conservatory, the Toronto Symphony, and the CBC Symphony
orchestras were the first steps on the ladder to the exalted heights of symphonic compositional achievement. There were many more steps to take,
but the foundation of his repertoire was being laid.

The TSO season ended in the spring and resumed in the fall. In
1949, Harry, as a blossoming composer, was given a scholarship that
enabled him to join other music creators at a Tanglewood summer session. One might have expected that a trip to the summer home of the
Boston Symphony in the early 1950s would be a seminal experience for
Harry. It was not! He had been accepted on the basis of his already small
but impressive repertoire, even though he did not have the post-graduate university music degree that was the expected qualification for
attendance. Tanglewood was, in many ways, the centre of the serious
musical creative force in the U.S.A. and later become the annual
acclaimed summer residence for both Aaron Copland and Leonard
Bernstein, but even in the 1940s they and other composers came to
teach and learn in the beautiful New England Appalachian setting. The
year of Harry's attendance Oliver Messiaen had been invited, and with
French as his first language, it seemed wise to populate his class with any
French-speaking students who might be available. Harry found himself

in this class because it was assumed that any Canadian would be bilingual. Although he later strived to speak French fluently and eventually wrote French quite competently, at that time he was almost as unilingually English as most other Canadians. It made his Tanglewood experience less valuable than it might have been.

Yet Tanglewood connected him to the international context of serious composers. With no performing duties, he was able to learn in association with a phalanx of aspiring young, mostly American, music makers who would be his friends throughout the century. In the classes that Copland and Messiaen contrived to give together, progress was made in perceiving the quality of Copland's simplicity, and tinges of America's greatest composer's influence can be found in Harry's compositions. But Tanglewood was also a place to discover that it was not only Canadian composers who were facing disinterest and indeed hostility in seeking new sounds to express a century of incomparable social havoc. He would remember not just the idyllic setting, the fascinating colleagues, the inspiring examples of Copland and Messiaen, but also the pain of realizing that he faced in Canada the same collective rejection that was being experienced by all young North American contemporary music creators. Harry realized that being a composer also meant bearing the responsibility of taking up the cause of serious music in a world obsessed with military adventures and economic preoccupations rather than cultural achievement. This international debate at Tanglewood would eventually come to influence every element of his life's work.

The year 1946 produced as much drama for Mary as it had for Harry. In the fall of that year, the Conservatory Opera School had been launched — with Arnold Walter, Niki Goldschmidt, and Felix Brentano (soon to be replaced by Herman Geiger-Torel) very much in evidence, working daily with students in classrooms and on the stage of the modest Conservatory auditorium. There had to be an event to announce the arrival of this ambitious initiative, and within eight weeks of the beginning of classes a performance of opera excerpts was presented in Hart House Theatre. With its low ceiling, lack of an orchestra pit, and questionable acoustics, it was not the ideal venue for the introduction of opera to the University of Toronto campus. But the concept of such an event turned out to be a stroke of genius. Niki Goldschmidt recounts with glee the impact of the Soldier's Chorus from *Fidelio* sung by veterans of the campaigns to free Europe, dressed in their own uniforms, singing with deep commitment and understanding that came from personal pain. Goldschmidt later claimed that this was the defining moment of the campaign to establish opera in Canada.

The complete offering of the program was to be scenes from the warhorses of grand opera: *La Bohème, Otello, Faust, La Traviata, Fidelio*, and *Der Rosenkavalier*. The quality of the performance surprised both faculty and the participating students. Perhaps the greatest contribution of these giants, Walter, Geiger-Torel, and Goldschmidt, who had been gathered to launch the new Opera School was convincing colonially minded Canadians that they could be as competent on the opera stage as the aspiring singers to be found in any country, North American or European. They succeeded beyond their expectation. Mary became one of their earliest success stories.

A few months later, in March 1947, the Opera School mounted Smetana's *The Bartered Bride* in Eaton Auditorium and, by the fall of that year, Humperdinck's *Hansel and Gretel*. Early in 1948 a performance of Gluck's *Orpheus and Euridice* took place. In the latter production, with a cast filled largely with students who had no theatre experience, the presence in the leading role of Mary Morrison, with all her teenage encounters with public performance, was an enormous advantage. A year later, the CBC brought Gluck's masterpiece to radio audiences, and Mary was even more at the centre. When, a couple of years later, the School decided to attempt *La Bohème*, there was a splendid Mimi available, and Mary made this her signature role, both with the Conservatory and years later with the newly organized Canadian Opera Company, in a production that was to be the culmination of all this operatic activity of the late 1940s and early '50s. Her operetta experience in Winnipeg gave her the confidence to act as well as sing, and her beauty made the role, which involves the immediate attraction of a lover, Rudolfo, her continued obsession with seeking his love, and her poignant death scene that invariably devastates the audience, perfect for Mary. She was sensational and she became Canada's own Mimi!

It had been particularly fortunate in terms of her own confidence that before striding on stage in the Conservatory and later the COC productions, she had sometimes already sung the roles on CBC Radio in the Toronto studio. Recognizing the presence of all the talent that had been gathered at the Conservatory, in 1948 the CBC decided that it should take advantage of this opportunity to reincarnate its own initiative, one that had once been a prominent broadcasting institution: the CBC Opera Company. As it turned out, this fortuitous move by the CBC assisted the coming of staged opera performances beyond the expectations of those who pushed this kind of "elite" programming.

In 1996, the CBC organized a diamond jubilee celebration of public broadcasting in Canada. A major element was a recognition of the work of the CBC Opera Company. A live four-and-a-half-hour broadcast on a Saturday afternoon from the Glenn Gould studio featured tapes that had been transferred from some fifty-year-old hard discs of CBC Opera Company performances. Executive producer for CBC Music Robert Cooper had found these treasures, and they included the voices of featured soloists such as Mary Morrison, Lois Marshall, Glenn Gardiner, and Jon Vickers, who were assembled for interviews as representative stars of those radio opera performances. One was of the very first *La Bohème* that included Mary's portrayal of Mimi. Cooper couldn't believe the quality of her voice and the intensity of her performance. Stuart Hamilton, Canada's "Mr. Opera," whose weekly appearances on "Opera Quiz" (a feature that filled space between broadcast acts "on site"), whether from Toronto or New York, have enhanced his reputation as a voice coach and an accompanist and who was also the incomparable founder of Opera in Concert (a Toronto series of concert performances of lesser known operas with mainly piano accompaniment), was given the task of chatting with these figures from the past. When the sound of Mary's Mimi came through his earphones he was so visibly shaken, so emotionally moved, that he could scarcely conduct the programmed interview. In fact, he recovered his poise by telling the old story that every young opera enthusiast falls in love with his first Mimi and that he had indeed fallen in love with Mary some fifty years before. Mary's Mimi had been superb in his memory and the recording now confirmed it!

The idea behind this CBC opera initiative was that popular operas could be rehearsed by Canadians singers, coached by Conservatory Opera School staff, and then broadcast on the national network. Mary's *La*

Bohème efforts were followed by the lead role in Gluck's *Orpheus and Euridice.* With all her time spent in Winnipeg radio studios, Mary was comfortable in the most demanding roles offered by the CBC Opera Company. When, in 1949, she was invited to sing radio performances of Bizet's *Carmen* in the role of Michaela, she excelled once again. Here was another role in which all her love of family and community could be marshalled and brought to bear upon the text of two of the most appealing arias in all opera. One French-language CBC critic put it most beautifully, "*Vous étiez une Michaela dèliciuse.*" By the 1950s it was becoming evident that her voice was maturing and strengthening as a result of her focus on the opera repertoire and the excellent teaching of the Conservatory staff.

Indeed, it could be said that this radio work gave an enormous strength through all Mary's years both as performer and later as a voice coach and teacher. She became experienced in the use of the microphone, refusing to let it become her enemy as it was for many singers in the early years of unforgiving radio broadcast technology. In an article expounding on the reasons for her success in this medium she responded to questions with wise advice. She had realized that inappropriate technique with a microphone "can make or break a voice" and that she must not allow her voice to become "smaller" as some singers had done. She was determined that her voice would not be "lost behind the mike." Her analysis and relevant strategies were an indication of her intelligence and artistry, and she provided many other young performers with valuable counsel that enhanced their on-air careers.

In short, Mary was among the first flow of vocalists whose names and voices signalled that opera had finally arrived in Canada and was in good hands. Today, as the new millennium begins, as Canada builds its first state-of-the-art opera house in Toronto, as Canadian singers such as Valdene Anderson, Russell Braun, Measha Brüggergosman, Richard Margison, Wendy Neilsen, and Michael Schade can be found on the stages of opera houses around the world, it is hard to imagine the risk that young artists like Mary took in charting a course that would lead to the competitive path of an opera career. There were others: Gilles Lamontagne, Patricia Snell, Andrew MacMillan, Jean Patterson, Joan Hall, Elizabeth Benson-Guy, Pierre Boutet, James Shields, Glenn Gardiner, Ernest Adams, Patricia Rideout, and Louise Roy, to name only a few. Jan Rubes was certainly the stalwart member of this first flight of postwar singers, even though he had trained and performed in Europe before coming to Canada. These were indeed the pioneers who bore the implications of arts penury that bedevilled every opera production in Canada. Opera is the most expensive of all the performing arts to mount effectively, demanding elaborate costumes and sets, a full orchestra in the pit, a chorus of fine voices, and, in some productions, a bevy of dancers, and, most difficult of all, as many as a dozen outstanding vocal artists before the footlights. Yet amidst all the "making do" with inadequate venues and staging there was the thrill of the honeymoon period of English-Canadian artistic development, and there are many opera enthusiasts alive today who remember with special warmth the evenings spent in the "Royal Alec" and Eaton Auditorium.

It was not until 1951 that the Massey Commission completed its report, lamenting the sad state of the arts in Canada and posing the solution of a funding body, a Canada Council modelled on the British Arts Council, that would indeed provide funding to artists and arts organizations. Several years went by before dollars flowed, and it was in those years that steps were taken that made possible first the Stratford and later the Shaw festivals, the National Ballet, and in the mid-1950s the Canadian Opera Company. It was the Mary Morrisons who put enormous energy and musical intelligence into productions that were characterized in some cases by inadequate accompaniment (one piano, four hands, rather than even a minimal orchestral ensemble), endured unattractive, even fragile and dangerous sets, and costumes that were rented and badly fitted, and it is they who deserve the accolades of a nation that saw its vocal arts blossom in the later decades of the twentieth century.

Indeed, Mary's prominence as a particularly attractive vocalist in these early years of the late 1940s can be gauged by the efforts that were made by one of the strongest supporters of this burgeoning opera development, philanthropist Floyd Chalmers. He wished to give Mary an instant experience of European opera houses in Milan, Paris, Rome, and London, and did so by arranging for her to tour these establishments in June 1950 in the company of the fashion editor of *Chatelaine* magazine, Mildred Spicer. Chalmers, the publisher of that highly popular women's magazine, provided this magnificent Canadian "Mimi" with a once-in-a-lifetime opportunity to visit the shrines of grand opera on the budget of his publication by arranging to have her photographed at each venue in clothes featuring the new textiles — DuPont Nylon, in particular — that were coming forward from the chemical industry and needed promotion. He simultaneously ensured that she was provided with a wardrobe that showed off her beauty and the impact that she would have in the productions of the newly formed Canadian Opera Company.

As a generous benefactor of the COC, Chalmers saw all the possibilities present in providing such publicity for opera in a major publication. It was described as "a Cinderella story." For Mary, it was a magnificent promotion of her career. As well as the *Chatelaine* feature story, she appeared on the cover of *Imperial Oilways* — a trade publication with a wide distribution. While *Chatelaine* ran pages of Mary "outfitted in a nylon travel trousseau" and even one shot of her cavorting in the hotel pool in a "royal blue nylon velvet bathing suit," it also made the point that her main focus was on hearing "her first Wagnerian opera and … Kirsten Flagstad." Mary for the first time was able to see productions of opera at the giddiest heights of performance excellence. She saw a production of *Turandot* at the Royal Opera House in Rome that made it her favourite Puccini opera and influenced her own splendid performance as Liu in a CBC Opera effort on radio a few years later.

Although the project gave an enormous boost to Mary's career as both an opera singer and a concert performer, it also revealed the status of the artist in the early years of Canada's cultural awakening. Shortly after her return to Canada she received a letter from an executive of the company whose line of clothing she had been wearing informing her that she would be allowed to keep the suit and the blue dress. She was led to hope that Keyser Lingerie would also be writing to invite her to retain the undergarments!

The adventure to Europe's greatest stages had a great deal to do with the fact that grand opera gained in her favour in comparison to the light opera that had been her preference previously, though this change of view did not prevent her from returning to Winnipeg in November 1951 in the opera off-season to sing in Victor Herbert's *The Vagabond King*.

But opera was only one aspect of the frantic pace that was Mary's lot in these Conservatory years. She was singing on Sundays and rehearsing on Thursdays in order to fulfill her obligations as a soloist at Trinity

United, St. George's United Church, or the First Christian Science Church in Toronto and at Friday evening special services at the various synagogues that enhanced the religious landscape of Toronto. Again, her Winnipeg background in the Gaelic places of worship and the many invitations she received to sing in churches of associated denominational affiliations were her calling card to an extraordinarily busy but effective ministry of music in Toronto. She quickly became a familiar figure whose voice and inter- pretative intelligence could be drawn upon by the city's leading organists and choir masters, like Lloyd Bradshaw, John Lynd, and Richard Tattersall, who played and conducted in the city's largest churches.

There were countless other services to render beyond those associat- ed with faith communities. There was, for example, the CNE Grandstand Show, featuring such notable figures as Danny Kaye and Victor Borge, as well as local productions of Victor Herbert and Gilbert and Sullivan, all calling on this extremely talented soprano who could be depended upon to deliver an exceptional performance.

Mary was also making contacts with the choral community far beyond familiar places of worship. Mid-century Toronto, in part because of the presence of the ubiquitous Healey Willan and in part because of Sir Ernest and the prestigious Mendelssohn Choir, was the centre of Canada's choral world. Indeed, by the mid-1950s Canada's first professional choral ensem- ble, Elmer Iseler's Festival Singers, was to be formed and put on the stage, with Mary Morrison a central figure in its ranks. In becoming involved, Mary was participating in the beginnings of the country's most famous the- atrical development of the 1950s, the Stratford Shakespearian Festival.

Elmer Iseler, a North York high school music teacher, had been rehearsing a group of singers, including Mary, in a room in a downtown secondary school when Ezra Schabas, a member of the faculty and later principal of the Conservatory, and Louis Applebaum, a Toronto compos- er and arts administrator, turned up one evening to assess their efforts. Both were impressed. Applebaum had accepted an appointment as music director of the Shakespearian Festival being planned in a western Ontario railway town called Stratford. The initiator of the festival, Tom Patterson, a Stratford-born journalist, had attracted Tyrone Guthrie, one of Britain's greatest theatre directors, to provide leadership. Guthrie was a musician himself and wanted music as part of the richness of his productions.

Applebaum saw the presence of music as an opportunity to advance both Canadian musicians and Canadian composers. Within weeks he saw to it that the ensemble he had heard in Toronto had formed a professional organization, the Festival Singers, and that it would play a major role in his Stratford Shakespearian Festival that summer. Mary had now added to her rainbow of choral activities membership in Canada's major ensemble. It meant that she would spend the summer months travelling back and forth from Toronto to Stratford engaged in a plethora of performances that came to make up the programme of the expanding Stratford Festival.

Mary remembers these performances with mixed emotions. The first venue in 1953, a tent, was devastatingly hot and humid. Performers collapsed, and those who survived were covered with sweat and totally exhausted. By 1955, conditions had improved, and the Festival Singers under Iseler became the country's pre-eminent professional choir, noted not only for its quality of performance but also for its commitment to contemporary Canadian music, and was to commission her husband, Harry, for some of his most popular contributions to choral literature.

For Mary, it was employment but much more a learning exercise. Elmer Iseler developed a concept of choral sound that influenced his colleagues across the country. Mary found she could sing straight tones with none of the vibrato, that trilling of the voice that enhances its quality in solo performance, and thereby mix her voice in a web of sound that made individual contributions invisible yet strangely essential to the choral musical expression being sought. She did this while simultaneously making use of a vibrato in her operatic and concert work that moved audiences, both live and over the radio.

Stratford became the summer experience for both Harry and Mary as the Festival progressed through the 1950s. Harry played in various ensembles that accompanied recitals of famous artists, operatic performances, and even Gilbert and Sullivan. He also participated in a major project designed to improve orchestral proficiency by engaging first chair players in orchestras across Canada to perform as a pit orchestra for dramatic productions in the evening and play chamber music with each other throughout the day.

For fourteen years, with some interruptions in the mid-1950s to allow for the birth of her children, Mary sang in the Festival Singers, later to be called the Elmer Iseler Singers. She had to leave this choir, largely because late in the 1950s she found another enthusiasm, the Lyric Arts Trio, which addressed an exciting repertoire she could not resist. Her absences on tour were more than Iseler could tolerate. It was time for her to move on! An indication of her understanding of the importance of the development of Canada's first professional choral ensemble is the fact that even now, fifty years later, Mary returns to Iseler Singers' social events and fundraisers — even joining the current choristers, led after Iseler's death by Lydia Adams, in presenting well-remembered selections from a popular repertoire that needs no rehearsal and is enhanced by the larger vocal forces provided by alumnae.

In those days of the 1940s and early 1950s one could question the sanity of any singer, especially a soprano, who believed that the church sanctuary, the concert hall, the opera stage, the recital venue, and the radio studio could provide the basis for financial survival. It was only later, in the late 1960s, '70s, and '80s, when the explosion of the arts and arts industries provided the fastest growing area of employment in Canada, that music became a road to possible prosperity. In the 1940s and '50s, parents and school guidance counsellors warned young people of the life of deprivation that awaited any star-struck student who was foolish enough to consider a career in music. Those driven in the direction of serious classical music were told with even more intensity that such a career choice would lead to both frustration and penury. For Mary, these multiple incomes allowed for sufficient revenue to make a vocal career possible in Canada, just as in the 1970s these many performance opportunities made it possible for Harry to leave the TSO and become a full-time composer.

These were the days when radio was supreme, the insatiable exploiter of musical talent, before it was dwarfed by television, an invention whose commercial development was delayed by the Second World War. The CBC's reputation was built on drama and public affairs in these years. But there had to be high-quality music of a more popular nature, containing ballads rendered by good voices of artists who understood the secrets of radio projection. Singers like Gisèle Mackenzie and "Juliette" Cavazzi made careers on such programs. Mary Morrison was one of the splendid contributors to this genre of broadcasting — using her Winnipeg reputation and a continuing capacity to sing somewhat mundane lyrics with style and class, ensuring a healthy audience that could be dissuaded from seeking its entertainment from the American stations flooding Canada with their signals. Coming to Toronto, Mary had been forced to abandon *Sweethearts*, but now quality family entertainment shows such as *Startime*, *The General Electric Show*, and *Northern Electric Hour* continued to provide a place for her. Although the opera house, the concert stage, and the church sanctuary continued to beckon, she told Joseph So, the associate editor of the publication *Opera Canada*, that in the 1940s and '50s "radio was how I made my living." Indeed, in her broadcasting career, which was more focused on popular music fare, she was singing with Joyce Sullivan and with Robert Goulet — many years before his sensational performance as a handsome Launcelot in a state of tension with Richard Burton's King Arthur in Rodgers and Hammerstein's *Camelot* launched his career in the United States.

Both Mary and Harry had found a new home at the Royal Conservatory, as did dozens of other music students in the 1940s and '50s. Mary's family remained an "at a distance" support in Winnipeg. Harry's family had, by this time, dispersed. When his father died in the early 1940s, his mother, Rose, ever resilient, had found the work she craved as a costume designer. His sister, Dorothy, had met and married a doctor and had moved to Montreal. His brother, Israel, still planning a career in law, had left Winnipeg to work in war industry and was slowly finding his way into legal studies. Even after graduating with a law degree he spent years giving advice and performing legal services for public service unions in Ontario. For Harry, who had come to Toronto with the intention of returning west and finding employment with the Winnipeg Symphony, home was now a Toronto that included Massey Hall for rehearsals and concerts, the Conservatory for classes, and the upstairs studio on Shuter Street across from the Hall for sessions with his colleagues and friends, and for beer and conversation.

But these years brought international influences to the attention of the two handsome young people, Harry Freedman and Mary Morrison, who were, by this time, discovering each other. The Harry who had not found vocalists to be very interesting people was finding his stereotype challenged. In Mary he had found a totally professional musician. She had all the commitment to fine music that his closest instrumentalist colleagues exhibited. Whereas most singers tended to be caught up in a very narrow repertoire, Mary was unique in the breadth of her enthusiasm. She was intelligent and articulate. She was supporting herself and was perceived by student composers as the finest colleague one could find to premiere a new work and simultaneously provide a critical analysis.

One of the events that brought them together was the annual conference of the International Federation of Music Students, a body made up of those studying at first-rate music schools in the northeast of the continent, including Julliard, Eastman, the New England Conservatory, Yale, Curtis, and the Royal Conservatory. It was an extraordinary opportunity to meet young, mature, aspiring artists preparing themselves for a life in music. They had come from all over North American and beyond and shared not only their ideas but their music as well. There were many concerts presented by the participants. Phil Nimmons wrote a piano sonata for Noreen Spencer, the lady who was to be his life mate, to perform at this conference. These were magic opportunities for Canadians aspiring to be musicians, a career path that can take its followers to every part of the world. It emphasized the fact that music was a universal phenomenon, unencumbered by language or cultural differences.

These were the giddy, idealistic years that emerged from years of war and holocaust, and there was every expectation that music could be a strong element in the struggle for peace and social justice, indeed, that it was an antidote to the triumph of militarism and economic exploitation that, in a new atomic and soon-to-be nuclear age, threatened the very existence of the human species. Harry, Mary, and their friends were caught up in this thread of human compassion that gave greater meaning to the career they had chosen. In later years the appearance of Glenn Gould in Russia seemed to be Canada's great contribution to the containment of the Cold War by providing living proof that Canada was not simply an extension of American or even NATO power but also a cultural entity that could reach out to the world at large.

In the 1950s, the efforts of the Canadian League of Composers to bring Russian and East European composers to Canada were perceived to be part of an anti-war agenda. The McCarthy period in the United States had erupted amidst the disappointment that surrounded the final months of the Second World War, when it seemed that Soviet Communism had stolen the march on the western democracies in Eastern Europe, and that, along with the triumph of Mao in China, was the ultimate proof of something having gone wrong.

Canada was implicated in all this most dramatically through the Gouzenko case, which revealed that a Soviet spy ring was operating out of the Russian Embassy just down the street from the Canadian houses of Parliament. As Senator McCarthy struck out at academics, writers, artists, and particularly those associated with film in the United States, John Weinzweig was targeted as the radical left-wing composer of a work called *The Red Ear of Corn*. He had composed the piece at a time when the adjective "red" had political connotations that had nothing to do with the work itself. His colleague, composer Louis Applebaum, found it very difficult to move back and forth across the border as a result of his association with John Grierson at the NFB, who was most certainly a dangerous "fellow traveller." Harry's immediate involvement with the Canadian League of Composers from its early years indicated a social activism that was also expressed in his compositions, reflecting a pride of country and a determination that it should be independent of the excesses that had come to characterize the American political scene.

Mary, as a performer, did not overtly express a political disposition. She had not experienced the North Winnipeg political atmosphere that had surrounded the Freedman clan. But they were spending time together, much of it in spirited conversation. One could conclude that Mary's extraordinary championing of new music and her determination to explore new sounds that were the battleground for modern interpretations of basic social questions were also marks of an artist seeking meaning in her work. She was not willing to be a conventional vocalist, content to include only the familiar works of the masters in her concert repertoire, nor an opera singer comfortable with the "dinosaurs" that attracted large audiences. She wanted a career that contained much, much more.

In these years immediately following the Second World War, even an interest in radical contemporary music could be considered an attack on conventional social behaviour. It was certainly enough to be perceived as "subversive" south of the Canadian border. Both Harry and Mary were by the 1950s and '60s no longer comfortable in the mainstream traditional thinking about life or politics — or musical expression.

CHAPTER 5
Marriage and Family

On September 15, 1951, Harry and Mary were married in Trinity United Church in Toronto, where Mary herself had spent some time as soprano soloist. A prominent figure in the United Church of Canada, the Reverend Crossley Hunter, who had become a friend of the couple, officiated. Mary's voice teacher, Ernesto Vinci, sang, and Gordon Kushner, a close colleague, played the organ. The groom's best man was Phil Nimmons, a companion with whom Harry had boarded after leaving 7 Spadina Road. Mary and Harry had carried on a courtship for some years and they had watched friends, like Phil and Noreen, take on the responsibility of married life. It was time to join them.

In the beginning of their relationship, Mary had, in Harry's mind, been just a very obviously attractive young woman from his hometown of Winnipeg. In these few Conservatory years she had graduated cum laude with an Artist Diploma from the Senior School of the Royal Conservatory of Music; she had simultaneously achieved a presence as one of Toronto's most sought after soloists, for both live and radio performances.

Harry was not blind and recognized what a prize companion he had found among the student body of the RCM and determined to make her his wife. Fortunately, with a steady job with the TSO, further opportunities with the CBC Symphony, and a window on the performing arts scene of Toronto, he could now consider supporting a wife, particularly one with a professional career of her own.

Mary realized that in Harry she had a bright, witty, but driven man on her hands. He would not be content in the role of a participant in a large ensemble. He was handsome, a physically impressive figure, solid and powerfully built, and he had finely honed intelligence that powered an intense commitment to social justice. He had recently taken on the major role of secretary of the newly created Canadian League of Composers and had become involved as a TSO representative on the executive of the Toronto Musicians' Association. She could recognize and admire that his ambition went far beyond a seat in the woodwind section of the city's symphony orchestra.

Their marriage began happily with a honeymoon trip to New York — what more appropriate destination for two people preparing to devote their lives to the arts and culture? They recognized that their future together held both positive and negative potential. There has always been a tension between the performer and the creator. The music world has made wealthy heroes of individual artists whose combination of great voice or technical skill on an instrument along with musical intelligence can attract audiences willing to pay handsomely for an evening's entertainment. However, these riches rarely spill over into the pockets of the composer. The grossest injustice in the contrast of riches and penury to be found in the arts is most evident in the popular music field — but it most certainly exists in the genre of serious music as well. Harry had a commitment to the day-to-day activity of music perform-ance and could understand the pressures and frustrations of the per-former's role, even though in his case it was a comparatively obscure one as a chair in the woodwind section of a large orchestra. He had always enjoyed the lights, the moments of anticipation and triumph of great collective presentations, even though these had to be shared with eighty or ninety and sometimes almost a hundred other musicians on the stage. However, increasingly, as he moved toward the more intense satisfaction of being a composer, he came to resent the total obsession of those "in charge of our concert business" who simply want to present "musical celebrities." In an interview after his retirement from active performance, he stated categorically that "there has never been a performer and never will be a performer who is as important as the music that is performed." The health of the Freedman marriage depended upon Harry's capacity to keep that view under control in the midst of Mary's enormously successful performing career.

By the year of her marriage Mary was moving on to the heights of her life work. It was plain that happiness could be secured only through the deep love and respect that each brought to the union — and a spirit of accommodation that would meet the demanding and conflicting time restraints that characterized the careers these two people had chosen. They each had very different schedules. This was to be especially true when, within two years, the first of three children, Karen (who became "Kim" to her family), arrived to enhance the lives of this extraordinary couple.

Indeed, the question of family had become central to the nature of the union they were determined to honour, respect, and enjoy. It may be almost a given that a heterosexual couple who want to share their lives for eternity would wish to express that love through the creation and nurturing of offspring, but two artistically creative individuals have another commitment — their own need to perform and craft experiences that will inspire and inform others in a world desperate for such artistic expression. With these two musicians and artists, the desire had been instilled by family experiences that had contained a high consciousness of social responsibility. Both their lives had included a strong sense of family and had been influenced by faiths and cultures that had not emphasized the celebrating of art for art's sake or, even less, art for the making of lots of money. Rather, with little sermonizing or moralizing, both had come to a decision that they would certainly engage in music making, but the dominant theme of their productive lives would be music as the expression of cultural inspiration. Both had already found some success in the more lucrative genre of popular music. They chose instead to pursue contemporary classical music, both choosing paths to what could be claimed to be the inaccessible and even the "unpopular" genre — one as a performer, the other as a composer. Whether this decision could allow them to live abstemiously but decently, would allow them the joy of family hand in hand with the thrill of creative activity, was a question that could be answered only in the doing!

There was another important decision. Each had come to Toronto with a determination to learn in their own country, at the pre-eminent institution that could be found in the Canada of that day. However, in the 1950s in particular, it was obvious that the centre of the music industry would be below the border. That was where Canadians were pursuing careers of some distinction, more likely in the popular genres of music creation to be sure, but funding, largely through private sources and massive audiences, was to be found for contemporary classical music as well. The mindset of many Canadians in the 1950s was very clear — go south to fame and fortune! It was assumed that only the second best stayed in this country. It was the expression of a colonial frame of mind that had permeated the thinking of Canadians who came to believe that being part of a great empire meant being on the perimeter, never at the centre. It was a mindset that dictated that all great books were written, great paintings and sculpture were produced, and great plays were crafted by people who lived somewhere else. The works of people in other lands were the basic subjects of study in the Canadian classroom, the print media gave foreign performers attention when they visited, and every day, now that radio, film, and the output of the recording industry flooded across the border, the best of Canada's artists were believed to be ensconced in another country. This colonialism dominated the arts throughout the twentieth century — long after complete Canadian sovereignty had been achieved after the First World War with the exception of such minor details as the acquisition of a distinctive Canadian flag and an internal process to revise its own constitution.

Harry and Mary, as a couple, were faced with the option of going south, as were many other Canadians determined to pursue their art as a lifetime career. For both of them to stay in Canada was, in so many ways, a questionable choice. Their careers in music had to that point been built around Canadian public institutions, CBC Radio in Mary's case and the Canadian Armed Forces in Harry's. Their comparable childhood and teenage experiences in Winnipeg, a city at the heart of the country with a commitment to cultural development second to none, were calling them to stay north of the border. But could they resist the promise of riches abroad?

The author posed the question to Mary: "Surely you must have realized that with all your success in Toronto, you could have seized an operatic and concert career in the United States and Europe? Do you have no regrets about the fact you remained in Canada?" Her answer was direct: "I would have had to leave Harry and the girls and I couldn't do that!" It was a matter of priority. Her love for Harry and their children was too important to abandon. But along with that personal commitment to each other was the decision that both had made that they wanted to be part of a Canadian cultural awakening. The signs were already apparent and they believed the full blossoming was imminent.

There was another decision to be made. What kind of marriage was it to be? For obvious reasons, it is very difficult for those engaged in the arts to have a normal, successful marriage. Irregular schedules that demand work in the evenings and, in many cases, long periods of absence place long-term relationships at some risk. Most damaging of all, though, was that the total focus demanded by an art form so often makes marriage an exercise in despondency for one partner or the other. With both partners equally possessed by a need to create and perform, the chances for a successful long-term partnership are even slimmer. Mary and Harry had to determine the extent of their commitment to make a qualitative family experience and to make their marriage something more than a legal arrangement.

Perhaps the most significant aspect of that decision was the question of children. With a biological regularity that indicates a serious commitment, Mary and Harry had three children, who arrived in 1953, 1956, and 1958. Pregnancy and birth transpired at the height of Mary's commitment to the demanding role of an opera diva with the newly created Canadian Opera Company. Unlike many modern artists who know that a solo career will mean tours demanding weeks of travel and nights spent in obscure motels and hotels in out-of-the-way communities, Mary did not hire a nanny to provide twenty-four-hour-a-day attention, nor did she take her children with her on tour, forcing them to face the tiring experiences of travel and the boredom of the hotel room while waiting for her return. Both Harry and Mary wanted to have children — and to spend time with them. Both wanted to ensure that their love and their values were accessible to them. For that reason they modified their artistic roles. For Mary, in particular, this was a major shift in the pattern that was extant for concert artists, one she never referred to as a sacrifice. For Harry, it meant that he could not always expect the peace and quiet that authors and composers often require when they work. Both were determined from the outset that they would live in an ordinary neighbourhood where other families had children, indeed, some older who could act as babysitters for the Freedmans. They began their married life in an apartment in the High Park neighbourhood, but they stayed for only a short period. They wanted a house and a home for their children and they could afford to buy only in Richmond Hill, some miles north of Toronto but close enough to drive back and forth to the downtown where both spent most of their working lives. As Mary put it with a wry smile, "Harry and I waved to each other on Yonge Street as he drove south to a concert performance as I drove north after a COC rehearsal."

But the early 1950s were dramatic not only from a personal point of view. The most traumatic event in the history of the Toronto Symphony took place in the same year that Mary and Harry were joined in matrimony — and as a TSO representative on the Toronto Musicians' Association, Harry was in the middle of it.

The TSO had increased the number of concerts in Toronto quite exponentially in the 1940s and had consequently been able to improve the quality of its players and the remuneration that could be paid to them. However, there was one area that needed attention. The TSO had still failed to attract invitations to play in the United States or, indeed, any other country. The colonial mind, already examined above, believed that unless there was acceptance, if not accolades, from critics in the cultural centres of foreign lands, particularly in the U.S.A., the quality of the TSO could not be adequately appreciated and its success as a great orchestra would remain in question. Its now experienced conductor, Sir Ernest MacMillan, understood this fully. In 1951, a concert performance was arranged in Detroit, Michigan. There was one problem — certain members of the orchestra could not secure clearance to cross the border. When a second concert invitation came for the 1952 season, it was made apparent that unless these six members of the TSO were replaced, the invitation would be withdrawn.

As we proceed through the twenty-first century and the politics of fear that has followed 9/11, it is perhaps easier to understand what was transpiring in the late 1940s and early '50s. The era of Senator Joseph McCarthy had arrived. It was a time of apprehension about the power and influence of Communism and its political success in the Far East that seized the United States with particular intensity. The infamous senator was successful in creating a belief that the ideology of Communism had triumphed in China and in other parts of the world because there were traitors to be found in the entertainment industry, in the halls of academe, in the very offices of the government of the United States, and even in its armed forces. McCarthy made it his task to root out these conspirators, and the U.S. government became both his enemy and his ally, at least to the extent of its willingness to close the border to any people who might have been associated with perceived Communist or Communist front organizations in the past.

For Canadians, this was a real problem. Russia was by 1941 an Allied nation, and friendship organizations had sprung up that had recognized the enormous sacrifice of the Soviet Union during the remaining war years. Certainly there were organizations that were sympathetic to the ideological position of the Soviet government, but most were simply offering support and, in some cases, aid that would relieve the dreadful hardships faced by the Russian people. Six of the symphony members had been associated quite openly with one or more of these organizations, essentially in the spirit of artistic collegiality rather than from any desire to forward the Marxist-Leninist theory of world revolution. However, all their protestations were ignored and their guilt was assumed to be undeniable.

In the spring of 1952, when contracts for the 1952–53 season were being signed with TSO musicians, it became plain that these "Symphony Six" were not going to be hired, as this would jeopardize the TSO's efforts to achieve international recognition through its touring program. It was bad luck that the "Symphony Six" were not dispersed in the various sections of the orchestra in a balanced manner and that they were not among the less visible TSO members. If that had been the case, more private and informal arrangements might have been made. But that was not to be. Two of the six were violinists; one of them, Steven

Staryk, perhaps the most distinguished ever to play in TSO ranks, was to return to the TSO as its concertmaster decades later, after a successful international career. Another one was principal flute, Dirk Keetbaas, a splendid musician who subsequently had a fine career in other orchestras commencing with the position of first chair in the Winnipeg Symphony Orchestra. There were three double bass players on the list; one of them, Ruth Budd, would return to the TSO a decade later and become one of the most beloved members of the orchestra, founding on her retirement the Senior Strings, a fine ensemble made up of retired TSO members with a permanent conductor in Victor Feldbrill. It could not have been worse in terms of any hope of handling this unfortunate affair confidentially and with quiet decorum.

Even though a member of only seven years' standing, Harry had been elected to the executive of the Toronto Musicians' Association, an affiliate of the American Federation of Musicians, an organization determined to become as strong as any industrial union on the continent. The American union movement was at its wit's end trying to avoid any suspicions that it had Communist leanings. In order to prove the fact, the federation had kept every known Communist or fellow traveller out of its ranks. When the "Symphony Six" appealed to their own Association for support, their appeal was rejected. Harry remembered the events of the day and his failing effort to seek backing for his beleaguered colleagues. He knew something about the rights of employees, even those on short-term contracts, and even though that impermanence, along with the inability of the "Symphony Six" to fulfill touring obligations, had been used to justify their treatment, the fact remained that, because of the policies of another government, these fine musicians would be deprived of work in their own country. This outraged Harry's North Winnipeg sense of justice. He argued the case for Association support but was outvoted. It was Ruth Budd, the most articulate of the "Symphony Six," who declared that Harry was "a lone voice." He refused to give his assent, the only one required to make the Association's decision unanimous. He feels now that he should have taken even more direct action, but he was relatively new to the TSO, and Walter Murdoch, the powerful force behind the union efforts of musicians, was dead against any action that might be perceived as being soft on Communism or in defiance of the tough anti-Communist stand of the American Federation of Musicians. Murdoch wanted a unanimous vote and Harry denied him that triumph.

Most disappointing of all, Harry found himself attacked by his own TSO colleagues, who were anxious to secure the financial advantages of touring as well as the enhanced status that such touring might bring. Thus, a thoroughly unjust outcome was assured. The "Symphony Six" were not rehired for the 1952–53 Toronto Symphony Orchestra concert season.

The firing, or, more accurately, the non-hiring, of the "Symphony Six" created an uproar on the TSO Board, with resignations taking place and a fierce debate on the editorial pages of Toronto newspapers. Sir Ernest's reputation was damaged, even though many of the orchestra members supported his position that the well-being of the whole orchestra should be put ahead of the handful of member musicians whose careers were under siege. Ironically, as Ezra Schabas points out in his biography of MacMillan, the removal of the "Symphony Six" did not result in an active touring program for the orchestra. Indeed, the next four years brought invitations to appear in American cities on only seven occasions (an eighth occasion was aborted by a snowstorm), and all of the venues were in the state of Michigan — not the centre of musical influence in North America. The crisis did play a role in the subsequent career of Harry Freedman. He became aware that the more radical "civil liberty" stance that he had adopted was not one that moved his colleagues in the orchestra. His commitment to the orchestral musician's role became less intense. Even by the early 1950s he was looking forward to the day when he could leave his place in the midst of the TSO and spend his time at his desk writing *for*, rather than playing *in*, a symphony orchestra — preferably one that could be trusted to defend the rights of its members.

In the midst of a marriage, the uproar surrounding the "Symphony Six" debacle, and the impending creation of the Canadian League of Composers, Harry continued his efforts to be a composer, along with what has been inappropriately called his "day job" as an English horn player. Indeed, in 1950 he had written a piece for violin and piano called *Six French-Canadian Folk Songs*, which was received particularly well. It was the beginning of his attraction to the folk song as a veritable feast of source material for his composing focus throughout his life.

Harry's most popular vocal composition from the early 1950s was *Two Vocalises*, for soprano, clarinet, and piano. Though the work was commissioned by TSO first clarinetist Avrahm Galper, it became a much-loved item in Mary's concert repertoire over several decades. It was a perfect piece for her voice, and in some ways it was the first step on her path to becoming Canada's premier vocal interpreter of Canadian contemporary music. When, many years later, Harry was asked for a program note for the School of Music of the Northeast Louisiana University, he quoted a John Beckwith article in the *University of Toronto Quarterly*: "Freedman is basically an instrumental composer — his *Two Vocalises* for soprano, clarinet and piano is pure chamber music where the voice performs as an instrumental partici-pant, without text." Beckwith stressed Freedman's enthusiasm for jazz — "He instinctively expresses himself in snatches of melody which echo the vocabulary of jazz" — and perceived that the first vocalise has "something of the same quality of fancy in the free, cadenza-like pas-sages for voice and clarinet" that was characteristic of Harry's work. Harry had made use of his knowledge of the woodwind instrument and his loving delight in the sound of Mary's lilting soprano voice and had produced a classic in modern Canadian composition that reflected his wide musical experience beyond strictly classical forms of expression.

However, by far the most successful of his early works that came forth in the 1950s was called *Tableau*, written in 1952. It is a work that has been played in Canada and around the world now for some fifty years, and it was the first composition featured on the CBC–Canadian Music Centre series of CDs that featured the works of five Canadian composers, including Harry, produced in 2002. Professor Gail Dixon of the University of Western Ontario, who has made Harry Freedman's music her research study for two and a half decades, regards *Tableau* as evidence that Harry had come of age as a composer. She states in her book *The Music of Harry Freedman*, "This piece represents the apex of his early and rather self-conscious exploration of the twelve-tone tech-nique." It was one of Harry's favourite selections, as it marked the point when he felt he was no longer a student but a real composer, capable of exploring what was perceived to be the mainstream direction of mod-ern music making, and of doing so for a full string orchestra.

More important, it was the first composition built around Harry's personal experience as a visual artist, based as it was both on the mood of a painting he saw hanging in the Winnipeg School of Art and on his observation of his own country during his air trip to the North during the war. The opening, with its single strand of strings, initiates the sense of awe and wonder. As more and more lower strings are added, the forces of grandeur and mystery increase, and the program note about the images of landscape are entirely unnecessary. It is a most dramatic musical depiction, not of the form, the texture, or the colours of an Arctic landscape, but of the repeated impact of the North on a young student artist searching for his own language to express his intense reaction to this magnificent image. John Beckwith refers to *Tableau* as an "intended evocation of a northern landscape" that may have signalled a short-term preoccupation with the twelve-tone technique and thereby the kind of composer Harry was to become, but it was most certainly the introduction to a series of works that express a thoughtful, reflective mind fascinated by the natural world and determined to recreate it in the thoughts and feelings of his listeners.

In 1957, he added *Images* to his repertoire, a work he called "the second [after *Tableau*] in a series of six compositions related to my art background," essentially "a suite of three pieces, each of which is a musical description [or translation] of a painting by a Canadian artist: *Lake and Mountains* [Lawren Harris], *Structure at Dusk* [Kazuo Nakamura], *Landscape* [Jean-Paul Riopelle]." Harry made it quite plain that "there was no effort to describe the subject matter," that, indeed, two of the three were abstracts but seek "a musical parallel of line, colour, texture and mood." It was also a piece that illustrated the composer's continuing determination to revise and improve, even to the point of seeking different ensembles of instruments. Although *Images* was first composed for string orchestra, it was later revised and then recorded as a work for full orchestra, in this case by the TSO with Seiji Ozawa as conductor. Closely tied to his place in the TSO was Quintet for Winds, written in 1962 for five first chair colleagues in the woodwind section of that orchestra. The last movement, Harry notes, "is based on five short fragments of jazz." Though written for friends, it has been played by virtually every wind quintet on the recital circuit.

By the 1960s Harry had come to know Elmer Iseler and the Festival Singers, an ensemble that Mary had joined at its formation in the early 1950s. Harry's major work in 1964 was *The Tokaido*, a work for choir and wind quintet, the text drawn from an edition of poems associated with the Japanese sumi-e paintings that Mary had brought back from a concert tour in Japan. However, Harry conceded, "The music does not attempt to be Japanese either in content or spirit. ... Rather it is the most strictly serial work I have ever written." John Beckwith, writing in the *Encyclopedia of Canadian Music*, declared that *The Tokaido* had become "the cornerstone of Freedman's language." Beckwith contends, "Though he wrote no more strict serial works, he did use elements of serialism — at will, easily and purposefully in most of his music." In that same year Harry wrote *Fantasy and Allegro*, a piece for strings commissioned by the Boyd Neel Orchestra for a performance sponsored by the Brantford Musical Club. It, too, approached a serial construction being based on a tone-row that was used as a source of material for the work. These and other works came from Harry's pen in these years and convinced him that his true role was that of composer.

For Mary, these were to be the most intense years of her life. Her presentation of opera, which had begun at the Conservatory school and had been enhanced through CBC opera productions on radio and television, had become focused on the most ambitious initiative of all — the creation of the Royal Conservatory Opera Company Festival (RCOCF), which would engage the people of Toronto for eight days in February 1950. The whole affair would be in the hands of Conservatory staff members Geiger-Torel and Goldschmidt. Three operas would be presented for a total of ten performances. Once again *La Bohème* was featured, and once again Mary's characterization of Mimi excelled. Filled with the confidence of her previous conquests in this role, she captured the stage with dramatic movement and a glorious sound, bringing tears to the eyes of countless members of the audience at every performance. Her voice filled the Royal Alexandra Theatre with profound impact, warm and expansive when required, restrained and fragile in the final death scene. The festival was a success, both artistically and financially, and Mary could feel that she had participated in that triumph.

Later that same year Mary was one of the handful of singers, essentially the stars of the RCOCF, who participated in a cross-country tour of a production called *Opera Backstage*, joining such splendid singers as Jan Rubes, Andrew MacMillan, Ernest Adams, Joanne Ivey, and Patricia Snell. It was not an opera experience they were presenting but rather a thematic "operatic caricature-burlesque" involving the staging of certain scenes from familiar operas depicting a variety of human emotions and experiences. It was more of a genre spoof than a sincere attempt to examine the thrill of operatic performance, but as Carl Morey and Ezra Schabas point out in their history of the Canadian Opera Company, the production went well and was toured across the land, becoming the first stage in a program designed to produce "runouts" of Conservatory presentations for communities outside Toronto. Mary not only excelled as a member of the ensemble but also quickly mastered a significant spectrum of roles with very different voice expectations and successfully met the challenge of conquering the styles of a wide variety of composers. As well, she discovered she had a capacity to engage in broad but tasteful comedy, enjoying the experience of joining others in sending up some of the great arias of the repertoire. Her comedy roles would become her forte when, a decade later, she became the voice of the Lyric Arts Trio.

While Mary was fully engaged in performance on stage, the trio of Goldschmidt, Geiger-Torel, and Walter were conspiring to outwit the University of Toronto, which was determined to frustrate the Conservatory's plans to mount yet another opera festival. They had decided that the only way of breaking free from the University's domination of the plans and finances of the Conservatory was to create an independent opera company that would raise money from both government sources and the private sector and be responsible for its own affairs. An Opera Festival Association was formed, a financial base secured, and incorporation successfully acquired. Thus armed, it was possible to announce a 1951 season for the Opera Festival.

Along with three other operas, the new company, later to be named the Canadian Opera Company, would present a production of the great favourite of audiences around the world, Charles Gounod's *Faust*. Mary would play the main female role — the beautiful, virginal Marguerite, who is seduced by Faust — in this production sung by Pierre Boutet, a fine young tenor who would enjoy a career that took him to many opera stages. However, the central figure of the opera is Mephistopheles, the devil incarnate, sung by the man who was to make this part his very own, the Czech-Canadian baritone and mainstay of the company Jan Rubes. The performer who takes on Marguerite is faced with portraying the signal purity of character that rings out in a musical expression that captures both Faust and the entire audience. At the same time, she must exhibit the human characteristics of an innocent girl quickly becoming a passionate woman in love, ready to forsake her virtue and reputation for the man who has traded his soul for her affection. It is a demanding role, but Mary Morrison was now an experienced performer with a confident stage presence. It was a major challenge for a young woman who just months before had completed her requirements for graduation from the Conservatory and was planning her marriage that very year.

In 1952, the Conservatory Opera Festival, now in the first stages of becoming the Canadian Opera Company, was prepared to put on Mozart's *The Magic Flute*, along with Smetana's *The Bartered Bride* and Massanet's *Manon*. Mary had been chosen for a role in *The Bartered Bride*, but the one that became her favourite was Pamina in *The Magic Flute*. It was the box-office success of the festival, with a 94 percent attendance record at the Royal Alexandra Theatre. Her performance had all the brightness, sparkling sound, and endearing warmth that the role demanded. It was clear that with the differing styles of Puccini, Gounod, and Mozart successfully mastered, Mary's career in opera was assured. However, at this point she was forced to make a clear decision: Was she going to have her first-born child in the midst of all this excitement and activity?

As perhaps no other performer, an opera singer's life is one of constant travel and concomitant loneliness. The COC could provide only a few weeks of performance each year, even including the plans that had already been made to move to a season of light opera (*The Merry Widow*, *Carousel*, and *Die Fledermaus*), creating fall productions to go along with its regular winter season in February of that same year. An opera singer must be prepared to spend many weeks in a strange city in order to participate in the plethora of rehearsals leading up to the two or three weeks of presentation. And then it is on to another city for a repeat of the same experience. In contrast, a recitalist can arrive on the same day and even the soloist with full symphony orchestra can expect only one or two days of rehearsal before the performance. As well, the opera singer cannot select a repertoire that might be less strenuous and demanding when, for example, going through the pressures of pregnancy or postnatal recovery. The performer is at the mercy of the composer, the director, the conductor, and even the set and costume designers — ultimately the entire cast on stage. For Mary, the decision of whether to have a family early in her married life was the most important one she could have faced at the very height of her early triumphs when she might well have launched a major international career.

In CBC program releases in 1952 she was described as "one of Toronto's busiest sopranos," performing "opera, oratorio and orchestral concert and song recital." By this point she had become, along with Lois Marshall, one of Sir Ernest MacMillan's favourite soloists, and he had made use of her voice in his Bach presentations with his Mendelssohn Choir of the *St. Matthew Passion*, the *Peasant Cantata*, and the prodigious Mass in B Minor. Even educational authorities had taken notice, and she began touring in schools, bringing her voice to children who knew little or nothing of opera, along with an easy manner and articulation that made them want to learn. However, her time of decision had arrived, and it was one that would determine the nature of her artistic career. She chose in favour of a child and ultimately of a family that she and Harry would come to treasure. It was Sir Ernest who spoke for Toronto opera and great religious music lovers in a note to Mary that stated he was "glad and sorry to hear" her news: "glad for your sake and Harry's — sorry we shall not have you singing with us."

In the 1953 season she sang only two performances of one role, Fiordiligi in Mozart's *Cosi fan tutte*, with Louise Roy singing the other three performances. The reason was very clear. Mary was pregnant with Kim, and two performances were the most she could safely accept. Fiordiligi is a difficult role for any vocalist, but to be diverted by the expectation of a first child made Mary's conquest of the character quite breathtaking. The arrival of a healthy little girl certainly gave confidence to Mary that she could indeed participate in local opera productions and at the same time bring forth children and care for them in those demanding first years. In 1953 Christopher Helleiner, writing in the University of Toronto's *Varsity* newspaper of her Mozart role, commented, "Her particular strength is in her versatility: she turns her hand to many styles and sings them with taste and almost uncanny accuracy … Miss Morrison is the sort of singer that one can listen to for years without tiring for she is not just a technician but an artist." It was an accolade that could only give self-assurance to a singer now straddling the world of family creation and high artistic expectation as a performer.

In the 1954 season, Mary sang Felicia in Ermanno Wolf-Ferrari's *I quatro rusteghi* and was vigorously applauded, but in February of 1955 she sang one of the most appealing roles of her career, Countess Almaviva in Mozart's *Le nozze di Figaro*. With enormous restraint and poise, Mary conceived the part perfectly. Her voice had taken on a maturity and grace that gave her a presence that dominated the stage. The *Opera News Report* spoke of the "superlative *Figaro* in Toronto" and went on to say, "Outstanding in an excellent cast was Mary Morrison's Countess, who struck a nice balance between wistful gaiety and quiet dignity." If Mimi was Mary's initial triumph, the Countess was the peak of her middle years as an opera diva. As Hugh Thomson commented in the *Toronto Daily Star*, "Mary Morrison was the lovely, melancholy Countess in love with her faithless spouse. She gave the part a regal bearing and yet a gentle humanity; and her singing was excellent." Rita Ubraico, writing in *Varsity*, summed up her career to that point: "Mary Morrison, whose Mozart performances have always had true elegance and grace of style, surpassed even her own high standard as the Countess. She combined the mischievous glint and youthfulness of Rosina with a quiet dignity that made her wholly sympathetic." Not to be outdone, the *Globe and Mail* included in its coverage of the opera a feature article on Mary, titled "OPERA STAR VINTAGE '55 — SLIM, NON-TEMPERAMENTAL," that focused on her opera career, expressing surprise that a Canadian could actually make "a substantial living by her voice."

Unfortunately such accolades invite the attention of strange and bizarre characters. In 1955 an Indiana philanthropist, Leland S. Hamilton, who had heard Mary's voice over the CBC's Vancouver station, declared, "I calculate and reckon you as the potentially top soprano of the past half century." He was anxious to arrange a tour, to organize supporters and "exploit" her talent in the U.S. Indeed, he even saw Mary Morrison as a force for cohesion that would unite Canada and the United States. It came to naught when Hamilton realized her association with the Canadian Opera Company had implications of collusion with the University of Toronto, an institution he accused of graduating Communists. Alas, he was but a mentally unstable carryover from the days of McCarthy. Needless to say, Mary took no action on that invitation, and as one would expect Mr. Hamilton quickly lost interest in sponsoring her operatic career.

In 1956, Mary Morrison disappeared from the Canadian Opera Company stage entirely, even though the operas presented included parts that she could have performed with flair and style. She had sung Michaela brilliantly in a radio broadcast of Bizet's *Carmen* and had appeared with obvious capacity in both Puccini and Mozart operas in the past. However, 1956 was dominated not by opera but by the arrival of a second child, Cyndie. To have a two-year-old and a new baby to look after and appear on stage in the full panoply of operatic roles was more than even Mary could contemplate.

The year 1957 was one of great expectation and disappointment for the COC. Geiger-Torel had convinced himself some years before that Toronto audiences would react positively to light operas in the fall. These would be tuneful, with comedy very much in place, and not as demanding for either the performers or the technical staff. For Mary the opportunity was golden. She, of all the Canadian graduates of the Conservatory program, had extensive experience in more popular music. One could imagine her in *Carousel*, for example, as a perfect exponent of the melodies of Rodgers and Hammerstein. It was not to be — her role as mother of a burgeoning family prevented that opportunity for triumph. (As it turned out, the season of light opera did not turn out well in terms of audience acceptance and was never attempted by the COC again.) But in the fall of 1957 she was expecting once again, and she did not appear on stage even in the 1957 winter season. The domestic pressures were overwhelming as the arrival of their third daughter, Lori, completed the Freedman family. The regular season included Puccini and Mozart, but there was no Mary Morrison. Indeed, for three years Mary did not appear on stage, and the role that she had dominated from the outset of opera in Canada, Mimi in *La Bohème*, was taken over by Teresa Stratas. At this point Mary found it necessary to take a formal leave of absence from the Canadian Opera Company. It was granted, accompanied by the heartfelt expression of hope that she would return in later years.

Mary's work with the COC was truly outstanding. She had become, in these years, not only a star in her new hometown firmament, but a figure to be emulated by other Canadian soloists faced with similar dilemmas — whether to follow their ambitions to be opera singers in a country with fewer opportunities or to move on to the stages of other countries. Mary was proving that working in opera, as well as in the church sanctuary and concert hall, could provide at least modest remuneration, quiet satisfaction, and personal delight for the artist remaining in Canada. Even more important for her own life experience, she was gently entering the role of exemplar and teacher. Younger members of the chorus, particularly those who found joy in smaller solo parts, sought her advice and counsel. A second major life role was coming into place.

However, the opera stage had one more triumph reserved for Mary Morrison. In the 1960s there was some realization that in the Centennial Year, 1967, a Canadian opera should be the centrepiece of the Canadian Opera Company season. In a rush of nationalistic enthusiasm, two works were commissioned. The first, *The Luck of Ginger Coffey*, based on a popular Canadian novel, the music composed by Raymond Pannell, with librettist Ronald Hambleton, was mounted in the 1967 season. It was, however, the second opera, commissioned from composer Harry Somers and librettists Mavor Moore and Jacques Languirand, that turned out to be the sensation of the musical year. *Louis Riel*, which placed the nation's foremost traitor at the centre of a Centennial Year presentation, was a controversial choice, one that put the COC at some risk. Thankfully, perhaps because of the inclusive euphoria of the Centennial Year, it caught the hearts and minds of Canadians. The music was lyrical and accessible, but it was the dramatic impact of the libretto and the staging that impressed audiences, enough to ensure that it joined *Aida*, *Tosca*, *Salome*, and the inevitable *La Bohème* on the program for the following year. In 1967, Mary, after some years of absence from the opera stage, returned to play Sara Riel, Louis' sister, and did so with palpable dignity and calm presence. Her voice was becoming even more expressive, and though hers was not a leading role, her contribution was significant. It was to be her final offering with the COC, but over these years, both on stage and, in the case of *Louis Riel*, on television, her influence had been paramount.

It should be realized that although being an opera star in 1950s Toronto may have been a road to fame, it was certainly not a path to wealth. The opera stage, with its limited season, could be sustained as only a minor aspect of making a living. The Freedman family needed two incomes from a variety of sources if it was to be possible for two artists, even at this level of Canadian music making, to cover the costs of a growing family.

Thus, by the 1960s they had become an established married couple whose work as well as their lives would become increasingly entwined. In these years Harry came to compose works for a voice he had come to know with joyous familiarity, and Mary could interpret those works with a confidence and intimacy that was beyond questioning. Yet, even with the pressure of three children, they had also become comfortable in accepting the presence of two separate careers, both demanding time and intense commitment, both containing the possibility of disrupting their life together, yet both providing strong reasons for a productive and loving relationship.

CHAPTER 6

The Decisive Decade

For Mary and Harry the 1960s were years of decisions that fashioned the rest of their lives. They now had a family of three bright, talented, and wilful young girls. By the end of the decade all except Lori, named in honour of Herman Geiger-Torel's wife, would be teenagers and would demand both attention and the increased financial support that would make post-secondary education an option.

In 1954, the suburb of Richmond Hill, with its considerably lower prices for homes, had allowed the young couple to purchase a house, but it had also made travel demands that eventually became impossible. It often took an hour to drive from north of Toronto to Massey Hall or a CBC studio. With both Mary and Harry involved almost every day with the music community, they were scarcely seeing each other. The reality was that the music action was in the centre of the city. Mary had the reputation among her carless singing colleagues as the generous friend who would pick them up in her little Volkswagen and deliver them to whatever distant venue had been chosen for a rehearsal. It was time for Harry and Mary to reduce this dependence on the automobile. As well, the family needed to be nearer to the University of Toronto, a possible learning destination for any one of their daughters. Thus, at the beginning of the 1960s it was to Lowther Avenue, just north of Bloor Street in central Toronto, that the family made its way.

It was a splendid choice. Mary and Harry could walk to the major halls, studios, and rehearsal salons that had become their places of work. Harry discovered that he had a couple of additional hours free each day and used the extra time to resume painting, while Mary found she had more time with her children. The change to new schools was not entirely problem-free, but all three girls found both new teachers and new friends without evident tragic results.

In the mid-1960s it was to a large house on St. Andrews Gardens that the family made its way. There was no doubt that two Freedman incomes would be essential to support the family's educational and recreational activities. Being closer to downtown made it less an insurmountable problem. Harry continued his work as a member of both the TSO and the CBC Symphony Orchestra while continuing to write music for small ensembles. He was also establishing himself as a composer of background music for film and television and was welcome on radio and television as a host or a commentator, a role that would increase in the 1970s and '80s. He was a welcome member of the orchestral ensemble at the Stratford Festival, where music as well as theatre was receiving accolades for its quality and the presentation of a unique and distinguished repertoire.

Mary was earning money from her radio work both in opera and in the popular field. As well, in the mid-1950s she was a regular member of the Festival Singers under Elmer Iseler, and this, along with her work in various venues, religious and otherwise, brought income.

The time had come when they could be more selective in doing what most excited them artistically and consider new directions that would be even more professionally satisfying. Mary had begun the decade as a very popular opera singer and was still the soprano of choice for the great classical works of Bach, Haydn, and Mozart, but her repertoire was perceptively changing. Even at the Conservatory she had been the most courageous student in addressing contemporary music. In 1960 she excelled in the TSO–Toronto Mendelssohn Choir's performance of Gabriel Pierné's *The Children's Crusade*; in 1962 she was the "surprising" addition of a soprano in the Toronto Chamber Orchestra's rendition of Schoenberg's String Quartet no. 2; and a year later, in what was the first University of Toronto concert of electronic music, she was the soloist in Murray Schafer's *Five Studies of Texts by Prudentius* for four flutes (on a tape pre-recorded by Robert Aitken) and a soprano.

By mid-decade she was being approached by young music makers desperate for a quality performance and was singing the new compositions at a Symposium for Student Composers in Toronto. Thomas Pasatieri's *From the Song of Solomon* and John Félice's *Five Songs for Soprano and Clarinet* were her contributions to that event. When the Toronto Mendelssohn Choir addressed Benjamin Britten's demanding *Spring Symphony*, it was to Mary they looked as a soprano soloist, and when the Bach-Elgar Choir in Hamilton took on the works of both Britten and Alan Hovhaness, Mary was brought into the lists once more.

The Festival Singers, now the most prestigious professional choral ensemble in the country, was seeking out unconquered musical horizons and finding them particularly in the works of Igor Stravinsky, who had come to realize that his works received their most sympathetic performances in Canada rather than the U.S.A. or Europe. Mary was accompanying the Festival Singers in his Mass, and in that same year of 1966 she sang with the same ensemble the Vaughn Williams Mass in G Minor and Canadian composer Godfrey Ridout's *In Memoriam Anne Frank*. In 1967, the same year she was to sing in Harry Somers's opera *Louis Riel*, she also performed a new Somers composition, *Twelve Miniatures*, to an audience in Montreal. Her crowning moment of that year was singing Arthur Honegger's dramatic *Joan of Arc at the Stake* at the Lincoln Center in New York City. Before the end of Canada's Centennial Year Mary was a soloist in Britten's *Cantata Academica*, once again with the Toronto Mendelssohn Choir. By the end of the 1960s she had performed Canadian Bruce Mather's *Orphée* and *Madrigal II*, Toru Takemitsu's *Coral Island* with the Toronto Symphony Orchestra, and by the first year of the next decade, she had presented George Crumb's *Night Music I* and *Ancient Voices of Children.*

In the meantime, Harry was wrestling with the ultimate career decision: should he take the leap to full-time composing? By 1960 he had been playing English horn in the TSO for a decade and a half. During those years he had continued his efforts to improve both his technique and tone. He had never lost the feeling of inadequacy that had surrounded his selection as a member of the TSO, which in turn gave him a sense that not only he but also some of his colleagues in the orchestra were not of the highest calibre. And this was the best orchestral ensemble in Canada! From the outset he became engaged in efforts to improve the quality of orchestral presentation, not only in Toronto, but across the country. He believed that more competent players would produce more appreciative audiences, increase the attendance at concerts, and thereby serve the interests of good music. It would also serve his other agenda — broadening the repertoire of the TSO and other Canadian orchestras to include the works of contemporary, and more particularly contemporary *Canadian*, composers. A higher level of instrumental proficiency would raise the sense of confidence that orchestral players brought to their work, particularly to the more demanding expectations of modern music makers.

There were, and still are, many reasons why contemporary music receives little attention from symphony orchestras that seem destined to play works from the eighteenth- and nineteenth-century repertoire for eternity. First, audiences do not demand modern works; indeed, they seek to avoid them by coming late or leaving early depending upon when the composition is programmed on any particular evening. Second, new repertoire demands greater rehearsal time and every minute is expensive when up to eighty or ninety instrumentalists must be remunerated. Third, the works of modern composers have to be prepared for perhaps a single performance, in contrast to the relatively easy preparation for yet another playing of a Beethoven symphony. Orchestras develop a collective negativism towards modern music that must be overcome. As well, live composers may make demands on instrumentalists that may indeed be resented, asking the players to extend themselves far beyond the techniques they learned to conquer in their preparatory training. It has been said that scheduling too much contemporary music is a road to revolt even in the most accomplished ensemble.

Harry was convinced that more capable, confident orchestral personnel would address all those issues. In the late 1950s he had participated in a Stratford Festival experiment to raise the quality of instrumental performance by hiring high-calibre players from Canadian orchestras to spend their evenings playing Gilbert and Sullivan or Offenbach operettas in the Festival Theatre but having the luxury of rehearsing demanding chamber music all day and performing it in special concerts to appreciative audiences when no theatre offerings were scheduled.

In 1963, Harry was one of the signatories, along with oboist Perry Bauman, bassoonist Nicholas Kilburn, French horn player Eugene Rittich, violinist Harry Bergart, and cellist Isaac Mamott, of a letter addressed to Sir John Barbirolli, the eminent British conductor, inviting him to come to Canada and lead a two-week summer workshop. Its purpose for the participants would be "to examine the problem of orchestral playing, subject ourselves to the most intensive criticism and training and thus build ensemble proficiency." It was a splendid idea that came crashing down when Barbirolli found that he could not break out of his schedule of responsibilities and had to decline the invitation. However, even in this failed effort, Harry had shown his support for an improved orchestra even after the shadow of the "Symphony Six" uproar had disabused him of the notion that orchestral players were any less selfish in their behaviour than the rest of mankind.

In spite of all this commitment to orchestral improvement, by the 1960s he knew he was losing interest in orchestra membership. Playing Beethoven's *Eroica* Symphony for the twenty-fifth time had exhausted his patience. He now had a track record as a composer, mostly for compositions commissioned by smaller instrumental ensembles. He had developed a recognizable and most appealing style, drawing from his background of jazz and popular music writing and, of course, several years of work with John Weinzweig, along with his own private study of the music that had been the product of serious composers of the early twentieth century. Now he was realizing that this was what he truly wished to spend his life doing — not performing but composing music. These thoughts could not have come at a better time, as Canada's centennial celebrations loomed as an opportunity for creative artists to participate in joyous event of all kinds.

The 1960s opened with an extraordinary opportunity. The CBC commissioned Harry to produce a symphony. As John Beckwith points out in the *Encyclopedia of Canadian Music*, the composition had been begun in 1953, when Harry was studying at the Royal Conservatory with Ernst Krenek, but it was too early in his personal development for him to achieve an "opus" of this magnitude. In 1960, Harry could scarcely turn down what every Canadian composer at that time was salivating to do but could find little chance — write an extended piece of music. CBC Radio was by far the most lucrative source of commissions but was perceived to serve the short attention span of the normal listener. To be able to write a piece that allowed for the full development of theme, to state ideas that deserved repetition and variation and could capture a listener long enough to have an impact, was a luxury open to few Canadian composers indeed. His Symphony no. 1 was described by one unsophisticated listener unflatteringly as "rather atonal … not exactly catchy," but, in fact, as John Beckwith points out, Harry had turned away from the twelve-tone technique, "having found it inhibiting focused as it was on the manipulation of twelve-tone patterns while his instincts dictated expansive melodies and expressive orchestral disclosure." However, it showed that Canada now had a composer who could deliver such a piece of music, one in which he could reach into his memory of Duke Ellington's contribution to a broad range of popular music. The symphony was premiered by the CBC Symphony in Washington, D.C., under the baton of Geoffrey Waddington. Years later Harry withdrew the work from his repertoire, feeling it was no longer representative of the nature and quality of composition he wished to have associated with his name.

He was developing an enviable reputation for including humour in his music. He was to become a recognized figure in the composing of send-ups, music that revealed pretentiousness or downright dishonesty in modern music composition that deserved ridicule. A small piece composed at this time, *Parodies and Paraphrases*, was described by the *CBC Times* as "an illustrated essay on plagiarism … an example of intentional cribbing." In Harry's view, fun and laughter were as much strands in the human fabric as the more humourless themes of pain, death, and broken relationships. It was an element of his compositional life that emerged on occasion and shocked those who believed that serious music should indeed be *serious*. This perceived aberration resulted in a number of compositions, such as *Pan*, written in 1972 for the Lyric Arts Trio, in which the performers made any number of unusual sounds with instruments and voice, quite startling audiences more comfortable with staid and stately interpretations of the mainstream repertoire.

It was in the 1960s that Harry launched his career as one of Canada's most prominent writers of scores for ballet performance. Brian Macdonald, working at that time as a choreographer for the Royal Winnipeg Ballet (RWB), had found a most beguiling story that he wished to transform through dance. Macdonald had heard Harry's music and had recognized the attention that Harry gave to rhythm. It is true that the great ballets of Tchaikovsky and Prokofiev are noted for the wondrous melodies that issue forth from the orchestra pit. But Macdonald knew that the essential element of music for the ballet was a variety of exciting rhythms and contrasting sounds, and these were already a hallmark of Harry's music.

Harry met Macdonald and was enormously impressed by his understanding and appreciation of the composer's art. Outside of his full-time colleagues among professional instrumentalists and composers, Macdonald was "the most musical person I had ever met." Macdonald described the theme of *Rose Latulippe* as a legend that revealed the tensions of French Canada's colonial times in such terms as "family devotions versus the headstrong impulse of youth, respect for the seigniorial aristocratic class coupled with a fear of corruption by it, a strong predilection for the supernatural and belief in miracles and a love of dancing tinged with apprehension of the licence it can induce." Harry could not resist the opportunity, and it became his first of several commissions from the RWB. Macdonald had set out the confrontations that Harry sought to reveal in his score, and his music reached new heights of lyricism and a rhythmic dynamic that inspired both dancers and their delighted audiences.

Rose Latulippe was the first new full-length ballet ever commissioned by the RWB and it placed enormous pressure on Harry, who was faced with a seemingly impossible deadline. He had to place the score in Brian Macdonald's hands by the beginning of June, allowing a mere two months of writing time, as he could not start until after the TSO season was finished in early April. It was absolutely frantic, but Harry considered the experience a turning point in his understanding of his own capacity. He found he could write music with extraordinary speed if given a clear indication of the project and the timelines that were in place. He timed his work schedule to that of a construction site near his home, rising with the hammering carpenters at 7:30 a.m. and working along with them most of the day, taking a little nap in the afternoon and resuming his work in the evening until close to midnight. It was a work pattern he came to follow throughout his life.

Harry's hurriedly composed score fared better than the ballet, according to one *Globe and Mail* critic, who wrote of the first performance in Stratford in 1966 under the heading "Rose Latulippe Needs Judicious Pruning": "The ballet has a strong backbone in the score of Harry Freedman which often supplied the drama the dancers missed. It is strong rhythmically, and makes limited and effective use of sleigh bells, whip-cracks. The musical fabric is atmospheric without descending to quotations from French songs. In short, the sound is right, tightly woven into the period and style of Macdonald's work." Kenneth Winters also felt the ballet was too long, and the headline to his *Toronto Telegram* review, "A Kind of Success," projected his mild enthusiasm. Yet his comments on Harry's music, which he described as working "beautifully — when it is dispensing drama through the strict rhythmic means of traditional dance as through nearly all of Act II," were essentially positive. It turned out to be one of the most compelling and endearing scores Harry ever produced. He revised the work as an orchestral suite many years later, and it has been included in the programs of major orchestras ever since. *Rose Latulippe* is most certainly one of the highlights of Harry's composing career.

It was followed by two more ballets commissioned by the RWB in the later 1960s — *Five over Thirteen* and *The Shining People of Leonard Cohen* (in which Mary contributed the vocal addition to the score, as she did later in 1973 when Harry's music for the ballet *Romeo and Juliette* was performed). These ballets had an international life, with the Dutch Ballet Theatre securing the rights to perform *The Shining People* in 1970. That ballet became one of two that the Grands Ballets Canadiens presented in an evening of dancing entitled *Lovers*. This combination received an honorary mention in the 1976 Italia Prize competition. On a single night in March of that year came the announcement of the Italia Prize recognition, the playing of Harry's *Tangents* by the TSO Youth Orchestra, and a performance of his *Tapestry* by the NAC Orchestra at

Brock University. Harry's music was achieving moments of extraordinary popularity in a decade that was exhibiting a new societal acceptance of the less familiar and the more challenging.

It is a surprising footnote to Harry's decade-long concentration on dance that Mary and her soprano colleague Elizabeth Elliot were engaged during that same decade to sing with the orchestra of the New York City Ballet touring *Midsummer Night's Dream* to the O'Keefe Centre in Toronto and using Mendelssohn's familiar music. It was not the last time that Mary performed in a score for ballet. Years later, she sang to the music being provided for a Toronto Dance Theatre performance at their Winchester Street Studio in the Cabbagetown area of the city.

The next phase of Harry's enthusiasm for dance came with his commitment to the National Ballet of Canada. It was, however, not before he had expressed his disapproval of the manner in which Canada's major dance company had conducted its affairs. He had been invited in November 1976 to join a panel brought together to address the topic "Ballet — Classical and Contemporary — The Next 25 Years." Harry wanted to deal first with the previous twenty-five years, a period in which virtually no original Canadian score had been commissioned by a company that proudly designated itself the country's "namesake" dance ensemble. In his view, this was an appalling situation. He pointed out that the heights of the discipline's impact on society had occurred in the Diaghilev era, but it had come not only by the presence of great dancers. It had involved an outstanding creative visual artist like Picasso and, even more, Harry pointed out, composer Igor Stravinsky. It was new music that could excite dancers and create a dance community committed to the best opportunities for expressive movement that made a difference in people's thinking about important societal problems. The National Ballet Company felt castigated but not resentful. In a few years Harry would write his most popular ballet score for that very company.

The 1960s are remembered by older composers as the vintage years, when commissions were numerous and generous in the celebratory anticipation of Canada's Centennial Year. For Harry, one of these commissions was *Tangents*, a piece that has become one of the most played orchestral works that Harry has written. The National Youth Orchestra, formed only a handful of years before, had matured as an institution and was now perceived as an important training ground for Canadian orchestral musicians. If Canadian ensembles were to be more than collections of imports from other countries, this institution had to be encouraged. For an orchestra made up entirely of young Canadian instrumentalists to play a composition by a Canadian composer was an appropriate way to celebrate the nation's birthday.

The result of this commission, unique in the fact that it was the first time that a Canadian work had been written for and played by the National Youth Orchestra, was that there now existed an orchestral piece of some significance available for presentation by Canadian and international orchestras. The drama of the work, the moments of forceful statement and quiet reflection, the recognizable themes that thread their way through the bars of this popular item in the Canadian orchestral repertoire were milestones in the composing career of Harry Freedman. John Beckwith described *Tangents* many years later as a composition that "illustrates the command of orchestral resources of a long-time orchestral performer and a composer with exceptional aural imagination." There was a confidence in its presentation that reflected the new consciousness of a country now realizing that it had a history of its own to cherish and celebrate.

Tangents was not the only composition of Harry's for which Canada's centennial celebration could claim credit. In 1966, the Saskatoon Symphony Orchestra had commissioned what became *A Little Symphony*. It was a work in three movements but it was to be played without interruption. The *Saskatoon Star Phoenix* reviewer commented on Harry's drawing on "serial technique" and, realizing that such a description might be perceived a criticism, conceded that "the work displayed imaginative use of the various orchestral sections with the strings and percussion having especially effective passages." Harry had followed his path towards a mode of modern music that made sense in the 1960s but had nevertheless served his audience well.

The year of the Centennial, the artistic community felt the pinch of a predicted federal shift to matters of state other than celebration, and composers were perhaps the hardest hit. However, Harry was commissioned by the CBC to write *Armana*, another orchestral composition that had a title with no relevant meaning except that it was an Eskimo word. Fellow composer Srul Irving Glick called it "a really swinging piece, extremely vital, with a great deal of percussion writing in it." The short description in the *CBC Times* states that *Armana* is in two movements: "The first is a free fantasia ... moody, many textured, using effects almost electronic in feeling, with brass, wind harp and vibraphone colours fading in and out of each other in weird effect. The second movement ... is a very strange mixture, part Latin American rhythms and part French-Canadian fiddle tunes with a chorale in the middle." It was another leap forward in Harry's capacity to address the full symphony orchestra with increasing effectiveness.

However, by 1970 Harry had ended his long soul-searching and, partly as a result of his dissatisfaction with his English horn performance, decided to seek a different form of association with the TSO. Managing Director Walter Homburger stated in his letter outlining the conditions of Harry's departure that he wanted "to express our great appreciation for your excellent contribution and for the great interest you have always shown in the affairs and well-being of our orchestra." Harry's reward was to be appointed the TSO's first composer-in-residence, an arrangement that had the support of both the Canada Council and the Ontario Arts Council and provided a single transitional salary of $5,000.

The letter's kind words were more than what is normally conveyed in any formal leave-taking. There was substance to Homburger's comment of which Harry had every reason to be proud. He had served the orchestra well. In becoming the first composer-in-residence in Toronto, and indeed in Canada, Harry was making more than merely a financial transition from active orchestra member to an invisible severed retiree. He considered it a chance to play a part in dealing with the ongoing problems of orchestral quality and narrow repertoire. He was deeply aware that, unlike writers or painters, composers were at the mercy of the performers who convey their creations to a listening audience. A composer's self-interest was in the direction of better players in better ensembles. He was also aware that Canada in the 1960s, now with more generous funding for the arts, was witnessing an explosion of new orchestras from coast to coast, and that this trend, hand in hand with the growing professionalization of these ensembles, would exponentially increase the need for excellent performers. Thus, orchestral development, along with the expansion of music faculties and conservatories, would be a critical factor in the health of music creation and performance in Canada. Perhaps as composer-in-residence he would be in a position to make a difference.

Harry also felt strongly that more Canadian composers' music needed to be played by his TSO. Perhaps he could act as an advisor to conductors on the best orchestral works of his colleagues and encourage a commitment to the expression of Canadian themes given such attention in Canada's Centennial Year.

However, Harry was too much the friend and confidant of the TSO players and administration. He could make little impact on his old orchestra — its performance or its repertoire selection. As it turned out, the most important contribution that Harry made in his year as composer-in-residence was the presentation of a composition dedicated to the fiftieth anniversary of the TSO, *Graphic I: Out of Silence.*

Nevertheless, this composer-in-residence relationship turned out better than another, just three years later, when the Hamilton Philharmonic approached Harry with a similar proposition. He would spend seven months as composer-in-residence with the orchestra and be "on the spot" for a minimum of thirty days at $100 per day. It did not work well. It was the first such appointment for the Hamilton orchestra and was announced with great fanfare, but there was no clarity on what the orchestra and its conductor, Boris Brott, expected of Harry, and the whole project collapsed. At the end, it was found that the expected thirty days of association had not taken place, and thus Harry was not paid any significant amount on the per diem basis. Once again, an opportunity was missed, and the issue of Harry's lack of remuneration was settled by the Philharmonic's commissioning of an orchestral work for $2,000, scarcely the ideal basis for such a mutual commitment to contemporary music writing and performance. Thankfully, the composer-in-residence concept, partly through Harry's early trials, has in recent years become a valuable addition to the strategies of expanding the Canadian-composed repertoire of the country's symphony orchestras.

Just about the time of all this dislocation in his working role, he received a helpful note from Harry Somers, who knew all about the problems of surviving as a composer. "We've heard rumours that you, Harry, are a very happy composer these days what with awards [the Etrog for film music writing], recognition, time to write and so on. Now you know that is a very unhappy state of affairs." Somers was alluding to the accepted stereotype that great music can come only from a suffering composer. He himself had become Canada's most famous taxi driver in the lean years when he was trying to survive on the fruits of his musical talent. Of this advice, Harry took no notice. He was now a full-time composer and determined to overcome this expectation of relative penury, come hell or high water.

Mary was also going through mental anguish, in her case, that of a performer in transition. Normally this kind of change would come in mid-career, but Mary had risen to prominence very early, becoming a major figure in the first years of Canadian opera, from the initial presentations of major radio productions by the CBC to the first staged operas by the Conservatory Opera School. She had also established herself as the most versatile soloist in Toronto, a favourite of Sir Ernest MacMillan for the great Bach Passions and Mass, yet comfortable performing light opera and solo recitals, and as a member of both professional choral ensembles and various church choirs. But in the 1960s she made a move to a much more concentrated commitment to a contemporary repertoire.

The opera stage was obsessed with the traditional alphabetic French and Italian warhorses of *Aida*, *La Bohème*, and *Carmen*, and the programs of Canadian choirs were dominated by the familiar choral works of German and British nineteenth-century composers. Mary had discovered an extension to her repertoire that stretched her vocal capacities, made demands on her considerable theatrical training and experience, and, most of all, challenged her intellectual and interpretative skills. This new direction had focused on the creativity of Canadian contemporary composers and their works, and, in many cases, she had become the inspiration for their compositions. The interaction of composer and performing artist often resulted in a first performance that set the level of future presentations. Mary had chosen the right period for such a transition — the 1960s. Even though she never abandoned the central concert and recital repertoire of the masters, in 1970 she was able to say, "I left opera because it is almost obsolete"; she said the Lyric Arts Trio, established in 1964, had a more interesting repertoire.

Recognizing her own need for more understanding of contemporary music, in the fall of 1968 she spent three months in Europe attending the major European festivals devoted to this genre. She had been awarded a grant by the Canada Council to cover expenses, and as expected she visited music festivals in Sweden, Poland, Germany, France, and Austria. She listened to the contemporary music of various nations and was interviewed on European radio for her reactions. She also interviewed a broad range of composers, musicians, and arts administrators. She was thrilled by some of what she heard and distracted by other listening experiences. "I wondered what the gimmicks used had to do with music except to provoke audience reaction," she mused in response to one rather lame composition.

Her report to the Canada Council began, "At the outset, I must tell you that in talking to composers and performers, I was shocked to learn that almost no one knew anything by our Canadian composers. I cannot recommend strongly enough that something be done about this situation." She challenged the Canadian League of Composers; the Canadian Association of Publishers, Authors and Composers, Canada's performing rights organization; and the Canadian Music Centre to become "more organized and aggressive about the wealth of talent here." She sought out European singers to discuss contemporary Canadian vocal works but found, with one exception, that they knew nothing — yet all wanted her to send them Canadian compositions. "It became a personal crusade on my part to 'sell' not myself as a performer, but our music." At the end of her trip she took a "coaching lesson" from the famous teacher Jeanne Hericard in Paris, "a composer and singer of 'avant-garde' music." She drew on those experiences for the rest of her life.

Canadian composers now had a champion, and very quickly she was in constant touch with the most prolific creators who now saw her as a colleague. R. Murray Schafer, Bruce Mather, and Serge Garant were seeking her advice, and soon she would be in a position to commission work and would find herself the performer to whom works were being dedicated. It was a distinct change in the relationship of performer and creator, or, perhaps, the role of a co-creator, that she found most appealing.

Moreover, she was achieving a new level of professional recognition. Kenneth Winters provided the most extraordinary assessment of her new role. In his review of a 1968 Lyric Arts Trio concert presented by the Women's Musical Club of Toronto, he commented on Mary's efforts to bring a contemporary song cycle to life. "Even the enchanting Mary Morrison could not emancipate them and what Mary Morrison cannot do with songs of this kind may reasonably be considered beyond doing." In opening this door to a modern repertoire, there were risks, but Mary had the courage to face the challenges of singing compositions that were disasters.

As the 1960s progressed, Harry and Mary saw that their children were now getting older — they no longer had to cope with nursing schedules. All three girls were in school now, and when Harry was at home and neighbours and family were available, Mary could travel for a few days at a time. The supportive family became a paramount advantage, as not only was Harry's mother, Rose, often present, but after Mary's father died in 1955, her mother, Louise, moved to Toronto from Winnipeg. It meant that in the early 1960s Mary could accompany the Montreal Bach Choir Society to Japan, and this tour gave her an inkling of the thrill that could come from bringing great Western choral music to people of another culture. Also in these years, she had become a favourite soloist for the Hamilton Bach-Elgar Choir, one of the oldest choral groups in Canada, and had performed Bach's *St. John Passion* in that distinguished ensemble's 1964 season. It was this performance that produced an accolade in the *Hamilton Spectator* that deserved framing: "And it was this factor, 'musicianship' that made soprano Mary Morrison stand head and shoulders over other soloists." "Her opening phrases," the review continued, "gave full measure of her artistry, shapeliness of line and rhythmic vitality."

Mary began to accept an increasing number of engagements beyond Toronto, and one in particular gave her reputation for flexibility and daring a lift. Elmer Iseler was presenting Vivaldi's *Gloria* and

the much lesser known Buxtehude *Magnificat* at the 1963 Stratford
Choral Workshop, a part of the Festival's music program. It was a conductor's worst nightmare when Iseler discovered on the Thursday
night that his soprano soloist was unable to perform on the next
afternoon. Close to midnight he called Mary, who agreed to perform
both pieces, even though she had never seen the Buxtehude work and
would not have time for an adequate rehearsal. In spite of these
circumstances she sang, as one critic put it, "with confidence and
musicianship." There could not have been a choirmaster in Ontario
who did not put her name down for future reference in case a comparable occasion should arise.

As well as going further afield geographically, Mary was welcoming
a broader repertoire by composers whose music was rarely heard by
choral audiences. However, in spite of glowing reviews like those of
Kenneth Winters, Mary never allowed the quality of her work to stag-
nate. Could she achieve in this new endeavour the level of excellence
that she had achieved on the traditional opera and concert stages?
Contemporary composition demanded another set of skills, as well as
enormous energy and commitment. As it turned out, the critics gave
greater attention to her performances of twentieth-century works, and
the accolades were uniformly enthusiastic.

In November 1961 she took the soprano role in John Reeves and
Norm Symonds's Opera for Six Voices. Though a difficult work, Dr.
Leslie Bell, the major commentator on choral music at that time, wrote
in the *Toronto Daily Star* that Mary Morrison "does a superlatively effi-
cient job." She was perceived to be at the height of her career trajectory,
and the critics could not pour enough accolades upon her head. Udo
Kasemets commented on a performance of Schoenberg with the
Toronto Chamber Choir in 1962: "Mary Morrison did a beautiful job.
Her voice had enough unforced physical and emotional power and clarity to ring convincingly through the orchestral complexity."

Particularly at home in Toronto her performance of contemporary
music was receiving an extraordinarily warm reception. A 1964 recital
at the First Unitarian Church in Toronto brought a review of enormous
support from *Globe and Mail* critic John Kraglund, who recognized her
unquestionable ability to conquer the traditional repertoire but was

"bowled over" by her singing of Roussel's *Deux Poèmes*, which he found "vocally and interpretively flawless," adding that it "approached the superb." Then he made a comment that was stunning in its implications. Toronto by the 1960s was "on the circuit" for most of the internationally known and widely applauded sopranos. The solo recital as a music presentation was still very much in vogue, and week by week these vocal celebrities appeared at Eaton Auditorium, Massey Hall, and a host of smaller venues throughout the fall, winter, and early spring. Kraglund's conclusion on the basis of that First Unitarian Church program was bluntly stated: "I would like to say that of all the singers, in opera or concert, who appeared in Toronto this season, only one may have equalled Mary Morrison."

It was Kraglund who first identified her particular strength in addressing contemporary Canadian works. In March 1965 she stood out in Godfey Ridout's deeply passionate work *In Memoriam Anne Frank*. Though the composer was, in the judgement of Harry and his colleagues, of the old nineteenth-century school in style and pattern, Mary brought life to his moving but conflicting message of despair and hope. Kraglund's *Globe and Mail* review spoke of Mary's "secure, bright vocal clarity that makes her an ideal performer of contemporary music." His assessment was echoed a year later when Patricia Ashley commented in an article in the prestigious American periodical *Saturday Review* on Mary's contribution to the recording of pieces by Harry Somers and Serge Garant in a series called "Music and Musicians of Canada": "The recording uses the voice of Mary Morrison and here again is a soprano for whom a composer can write works of immense difficulty and hear them performed with liquid ease."

It was little wonder that when the Canadian League of Composers wished, in 1968, to honour a Canadian who had made a unique contribution to Canadian composition and its performance, they chose Mary Morrison to receive the Canadian Music Citation. Srul Irving Glick, a prestigious composer in his own right and the president that year of the CLC, said succinctly that she was "not only a musician, but the kind of singer who looks forward to the adventure of creating a new work — a composer's singer." The honour was well deserved and widely applauded. June Marks, a prominent politician and respected member of

Toronto's Board of Control, spoke for her fellow citizens when she observed, "You have enlarged Canada's cultural standing with your musical contribution and we are proud of you." This honour confirmed that Mary had become a contemporary music performing icon. The year before, Victor Feldbrill, the country's most committed orchestral conductor of Canadian music, had received the citation, and in 1969 flutist, composer, and arts administrator Robert Aitken was the recipient. Then the citation award was retired and given no longer. The irony was to be that all three had scarcely begun their work in being the most determined exponents of Canadian contemporary music. It was a cause that led them to dominate that field of endeavour for the rest of Canada's twentieth century.

Mary was now at the height of her singing career. However, it was more the ascending of a range of mountains than of a single snow-covered pinnacle. In October 1963 she had been asked to be one of the judges for the Richard Tucker Competition, and the CBC, without any fear of questioning, could describe Mary as "one of the most gifted and respected singers Canada has produced" who was "anxious to do her part in bringing a new singer to the public."

The 1960s had merely defined the next stage of her working life as a proud and determined performer of music that had little audience anywhere in the world but nowhere less than in Canada. She was prepared to face sparse audiences, criticism, and ridicule. It would not be an easy task, but at least she had the support of a composer husband who fully comprehended her commitment. Margot Christie, an actress who knew much about the tension between married artists, wrote Mary in 1965 with a heartwarming anecdote. Margot had met Harry at a reception and reported to Mary that "he said the most secure husband-wife relationship 'thing' the other day." Realizing Margot didn't recognize him Harry had exclaimed, "I expect you don't remember me. I'm Harry Freedman … Mary Morrison's husband." Margot's comment to Mary was that "most ordinary men would have said so-and-so is my wife. Congratulations!"

These 1960s years of decision about the nature of career were central to the role that Mary and Harry were to play in Canada's musical life. But the decade was crucial to the cultural life of the entire country. It was during those years that there was a growing awareness that the country was no longer a frontier. Cities like Toronto, Montreal, Winnipeg, and Vancouver had already developed a cultural scene before the Second World War. Now communities like Halifax, Ottawa, London, Thunder Bay, Windsor, Hamilton and the Niagara Peninsula, Saskatoon, Regina, Victoria, and Edmonton began to express a need for the arts, arts organizations, and venues both for performance and for exhibition. Although the upcoming celebration of Canada's centennial certainly precipitated both federal money and attention to cultural events, as virtually all such celebrations do, there was already a momentum in place that could give new strength and sustainability to such efforts.

Certainly these new frontiers of artistic development had been encouraged by the Massey Commission, which had reported in the mid-1950s and had proposed that the federal government provide resources to support the arts through a new federal agency, the Canada Council. There was also the long-term demography of a burgeoning population from both a soaring birth rate and increased immigration following the war. Both played a part in enlarging cities from coast to coast. When federal funds are being distributed, there tends to be an expectation of equal treatment in both rural and urban communities, but the fact is that artistic development tends to occur in urban centres. Artists need collective inspiration and interchange as much as they need audiences and viewers, and the concentration of people in a city makes both possible. Thus, for music and music makers, whether composers or performers, the presence of a substantial gathering of people is essential. Individual artists — writers, painters, and sculptors — can sometimes operate in garrets and studios in less populated areas, but music demands interaction between creator and singer/instrumentalist as well as the possibility of reaching an audience.

Although there have always been composers and performers to be found among those who inhabited the French and British colonies that came to make up the Dominion of Canada, they were hard to find in any great numbers before the Second World War. The reasons were obvious: there is little reason to compose if there are not gifted performers to translate the notes sketched on the page into sound, and there were few orchestral and choral ensembles that could carry out the function with any pleasing result in most communities in Canada. Thus composers were organists or teachers and composing was essentially done for personal enjoyment. These observations form the argument for the importance of the decision that Harry made to become a full-time composer in this decade. It was more than a personal response to his own need to be creative — it was a vote of confidence in the cultural capacity of a developing nation.

Did it matter then, in the last decades of the twentieth century? Does it matter now, as the new millennium is launched? It was a question that Harry and Mary asked themselves and each other in reflective moments during the disturbing decade of the 1960s. Thankfully, the answers to these questions were in the affirmative. At a time when Canada was playing a more independent role internationally, one could argue there was a necessity for that positive response to be seen and heard through the expressions of its artists in sound, word, movement, form, and colour. This was particularly true if the country was ever to find its way towards a national purpose that included a global contribution to the goals of environmental well-being and an end to violence and economic exploitation. With its universality in mind, having a Canadian musical voice was a necessary element in any strategy to give the country a role in the search for world peace, environmental sustainability, and greater human security based on ideals of economic justice. That was the case then and it is the case today.

Harry and Mary arrived on the cultural scene at exactly the right moment. In spite of the personal economic pressure that these early years of stunted support for the arts placed on their shoulders, they were to make the argument and provide the evidence that Canadians needed a musical expression that proved its presence as a unique society, music that expressed its values, its hopes and dreams.

Even more obvious, from the outset, was the realization that a basic infrastructure was needed, one that would make possible a transition from colony to nation, from an obsession with economic matters to lifestyles that included aesthetic and intellectual joys as well as spiritual journeys. This led both Harry and Mary to become involved with most of the contemporary music organizations in Central Canada, serving on boards and acting as spokespersons as well as writing music for them and performing in their programs.

There needed to be opportunities to learn the arts in formal educational institutions. Harry, in particular, became a pioneer in the classroom. He realized that schools, colleges, and universities needed to be convinced that the artistic was linked to the intellectual, that, indeed, the delights of eye and ear had a connection with the cultivated mind. As well, attention to educational institutions would ultimately support and nurture artistic institutions, including venues such as concert halls, opera houses, art galleries and museums, or performing arts organizations devoted to providing dance, opera, and choral, chamber, and orchestral music.

But most important was the presence of individual singers and musicians capable of interpreting the music of a contemporary repertoire that speaks to the beauty, the loneliness, the intense feelings of acceptance and rejection — all the attributes of a demographic that stuns the world through its dynamic and difference. Certainly, there needed to be a realization that creativity is a seamless web, one that links the great ideas that emerge within every sector of activity, from music to politics to business — indeed, to every aspect of civilization. The composer and the thoughtful co-creative performer had to be seen as a part of that garment of human decency that emerges from a context of cultural integrity. Mary and Harry were to put their attention to these matters throughout the final decades of the century and into the new millennium.

These were the issues that confronted these two Canadians as they launched their careers in the late 1940s and developed their crafts to extraordinary heights in the '50s and '60s. Harry and Mary were members of a coterie of Canadians who refused to accept the status quo of colonial subservience to the cultural forces of other states. They believed that their fellow Canadians could be brought to support a new age of nationhood, cultural self-reliance, and significant world leadership. In adopting this cause they faced personal economic hardship and unexpected hurdles that demanded unrewarding activity that had less to do with creativity than with producing the infrastructure necessary to make any creative outcome possible.

However, it must be said that without the sacrifice, the enormous contribution of artistic intelligence, and the ability of such pioneers there would not have been the cultural explosion that characterized the late 1960s, '70s, and '80s across the nation. The dedication, energy, commitment, and talent of these two artists was an inspiration to countless singers, instrumentalists, conductors, and, yes, composers and performers.

CHAPTER 7
Pioneers and Advocates

Being a member of Canada's major symphony orchestra made Harry aware that as the nation approached its centennial, not only had many music lovers heard very little contemporary music, but many were unaware of the existence of a considerable coterie of Canadian composers producing sounds that he believed to be uniquely Canadian. The lack of response to serious contemporary music was not just a Canadian phenomenon. In the period after the Second World War, recently composed music faced both disinterest and hostility around the world. The concept of music as essentially melody and simple rhythm, along with the capacity of modern technology to bring the familiar music of the ages to listeners in a constant stream of sound, provided a seemingly hopeless context in which to write contemporary music. There was no understanding that a world of violence, destruction, war, death, and holocaust had created a milieu in which the creative mind could find integrity only by including expressions that were sometimes dissonant and awkward. In doing so, composers appeared to forsake the patterns of musical form that had dominated a society seen as more orderly and predictable.

However, these less accessible musical expressions were changing. Looking back from the early 1970s, William Littler, the music critic for the *Toronto Star*, described the state of contemporary music with some greater hope of public acceptance: "If the '50s pushed 12-tone writing to mathematical extremes and brought electronic music out of its stone age, the '60s surely witnessed an increasing freedom along all exploratory fronts." Surely there would develop an audience who would delight in these innovations.

In the 1950s it had been clear to Harry, John Weinzweig, Lou Applebaum, Harry Somers, Sam Dolin, and John Beckwith, all founding members of the Canadian League of Composers, that only by their direct intervention would they ever hear their own work played. Indeed, without that intervention there was no way to overcome the complete ignorance of the music-loving public that there actually were Canadian composers creating original works. It was, in the 1960s, equally evident to a new generation of composers — Keith Bissell, R. Murray Schafer, Srul Irving Glick, Robert Aitken, Norma Beecroft, Bruce Mather, Serge Garant, Gustav Ciamaga, and William McCauley — that being a composer would involve not just writing music but also promoting its performance. That had been the case when the CLC was organized, and its first role had been to ensure that individual concerts and, later, series of concerts were presented each year. It was even more necessary a decade later.

It meant that composers like Harry would have to be proactive advocates, indeed, would have to become entrepreneurs and arts administrators. Instead of writing more string quartets, they would have to carry out the administrative tasks of hiring the hall and employing the instrumentalists and vocalists who would perform, seeing to the printing of tickets and posters, setting up a box office and selling subscriptions, and even ensuring that the piano was tuned and the chairs both on stage and in the hall were in place. Answering to staff of the Faculty of Music's Edward Johnson Building about scratches on the resident piano after a concert and dealing with the fact that "due to janitorial problems of the liquid variety" access to Walter Hall was denied for a rehearsal became functions of that organizing committee of composers. These were not popular tasks.

Even less attractive was the responsibility of approaching the corporate world for dollars to subsidize the expenses of presentations that cost as much to produce as regular concerts but could attract only a significantly smaller audience. Even the composers' spouses were dragooned into service — just as they had been years before by the CLC — and Mary found herself on the Women's Committee, which included the partners of Keith Bissell, John Weinzweig, and John Adaskin, as well as those of conductor Ettore Mazzolini, modern music enthusiast Michael Koerner, French horn virtuoso Eugene Rittich, and philosophy professor, author, organist, and choir conductor Geoffrey Payzant. The role of the Women's Committee was to take on the drudgery of the mundane and unappealing tasks left uncompleted by their composer spouses and friends.

In 1962, Harry and his colleagues created an organization whose mandate was to produce concerts of "unusual but important works." They called the enterprise the Ten Centuries Concerts, hoping to open the gate for more inclusive programming than that allowed by the CLC's concerts. Playing only Canadian contemporary or even just contemporary music was placing too great a challenge before any substantial number of music lovers. Harry realized that the object must be to emphasize the "ten centuries of music that was being largely ignored" by a music community obsessed with compositions of the seventeenth, eighteenth, and nineteenth centuries but prepared to neglect what had been composed both before and after. This new enterprise allowed programming to range across a wide spectrum of unfamiliar music while at the same time providing a context for the presentation of music by Canadian composers, music that was being totally overlooked. It was to this cause that Harry gave his time, even though he was criticized and ridiculed for it by some of his musician colleagues in the TSO, caught up as they were in the very traditional programming that Sir Ernest MacMillan and his successors as conductors felt would bring people to the regular concert season at Massey Hall.

Into the ears of at least a few Torontonians came programming that reflected not only the conflict of mid-century Europe and the Americas but also the introduction of new technologies resulting in electronic music. From the presence of Phil Nimmons, Norm Symonds, and Harry Freedman came the influences of jazz and a host of musical styles from the popular field. Over a decade later, Harry tried to convince Robert Sunter, head of the Serious Music Department of CBC, that a Ten Centuries program series would be a winner on his network. In doing so, Harry described the concept warmly: "Each program was entirely built around some central idea. For instance, one program was entirely for plucked instruments — ancient and contemporary music for lute, clavichord, guitar, harp, spinet, etc. Another program had the Festival Singers contributing a choral piece followed by the Toronto Wind Quintet doing a contrasting work. After intermission the two groups joined forces in a work especially written for the series. The success of the Ten Centuries series was due entirely to imaginative and innovative programming."

Ten Centuries began in sensational form. The first concert season, 1963–64, was completely sold out. The programming was exciting and relevant. At a fall concert, the Toronto Wind Quartet was featured, and the ensemble, with an additional instrumentalist, played Harry's Quintet for Winds, an early work written when he was particularly comfortable writing for familiar instruments and for friends with whom he played. Attractive themes encouraged virtuoso performance, and the work has continued to be particularly popular at festivals celebrating woodwind repertoire.

In the April concert, Ten Centuries included modern works by Stravinsky followed by a major work, the *Geography of Eros*, by R. Murray Schafer. George Kidd, in his *Toronto Telegram* review, was overwhelmed by Mary's vocal contribution. "If awards are to be given, they should go to Mary Morrison who was forced to sing, speak, moan and sigh her way through the vocal line and at times battle with herself on a tape recording.… Miss Morrison was brilliant and Elmer Iseler and his ensemble frequently matched her." These concerts enhanced Mary's reputation and had an ongoing effect on her entire career. She was still discovering that with her true sense of pitch, she was able to cope especially well with the unusual leaps and descents that seemed to distinguish the modern idiom. She found that she was not only good at it but was perceived by her peers to be outstanding. The music was challenging, especially to audiences. Journalist Susan Cohen, soon to become an arts administrator at the Ontario Arts Council, searched Mary's memory of the excitement of these concerts. "I was involved in some Ten Centuries concerts where people actually got up, walked out and slammed the doors in disgust," Mary recalled. There was no casual or disinterested listening at these events.

In 1965 the series' opening concert premiered John Beckwith's *Trumpets of Summer* and a delightful spoof, *So You Want to Write a*

Fugue, a light and tuneful exploration of that musical form by Canada's most internationally celebrated concert pianist and recording artist, Glenn Gould. The programs were varied, with contrasting styles of music evident and yet with the central strategy of including at least one work by a Canadian composer faithfully sustained.

However, even two years into its mandate, the organizing committee was under criticism by those who believed that Ten Centuries had strayed too far from its original intent and was choosing nice things to hear and then finding musicians to play them. On the other hand, a contrary opinion was expressed that too much avant-garde stuff was being presented. From both sides of the repertoire exchange came the charge that quality was slipping and that missionary zeal was wearing off. More criticisms abounded: the program notes were too long and, on the other side, the program notes were too vague. Astonishingly, in the light of the original mandate and the makeup of the organizing committee, some subscribers charged that too many works by modern composers were being programmed. There was a shot of renewed energy in 1966 when Hugh Davidson, then a federal arts bureaucrat, arrived from Ottawa with the news that programming at Expo '67, the celebration of Canada's centennial in Montreal, would include Canadian music. It was to Ten Centuries Concerts that Davidson turned in order to present four fifty-minute programs on the main stage of the Canadian Pavilion, two of which would contain music exclusively by Canadian composers.

However, it was questionable whether Ten Centuries could survive until 1967. Harry was commissioned to secure donations from the corporate sector. He was not met with wild enthusiasm, though Arthur Gelber, a respected Toronto arts philanthropist, sent him a modest contribution. It soon became clear that financial stability could be based only on a closer relationship with the CBC and its willingness to pay for the recording and broadcasting of such programming. The CBC had producers willing to move the mountains of administrative conservatism to make that happen. More and more often, Ten Centuries Concerts were recorded and partially paid for by the CBC and broadcast on radio a few nights later.

In 1967, programs offered in Toronto were indeed exported to Montreal, including the January concert, which presented a survey of music by Toronto composers and included music by Harry Somers and Barbara Pentland in particular. In April the music of Bach, both C.P.E. and J.S., was contrasted with a jazz segment provided by the Bert Niosi Ensemble along with the music of Bruce Mather and Gilles Tremblay and international composers like Berio and Ligeti. One could scarcely imagine a more eclectic presentation, and visitors to Expo '67, whether from Canada or other lands, must have been both dazzled and impressed.

It was sharply downhill for Ten Centuries from that point. By 1970 there was no longer a women's committee, and audiences for the regular concerts had dwindled. Franz Kramer, who was to be the major Toronto chamber music entrepreneur for the next decade, put it succinctly: "Money problems, erroneous ideas concerning the cost of music, programs that for one reason or another will not attract enough of the 'right kind' of audience are at the bottom of past troubles."

More than anything else, the energy and the resources of the composing community were finite. The enormous expansion of commissions occasioned by the coming of the Centennial Year had occupied composers, and this diversion, along with the diminishing energy and commitment of the organizers, ensured a collapse. A few more colleagues had joined the lists, but there was no rush of new composers to take up the reins. Other arts organizations had to fill the gap in the presentation of Canadian contemporary compositions, in every case involving Harry and Mary.

In Harry and Mary's view, the Ten Centuries experiment had broadened the horizon for a number of Canadians who were to influence the future of music in Canada. The names Szymanovsky, Schutz, Devienne, Biber, Weill, and Milhaud aroused no sign of recognition among even the more sophisticated music audiences — yet they were featured in just three concerts in October, November, and December of 1966. Canadian composers were given a very considerable hearing, and these performances made it clear that, in Toronto, at least, the making of contemporary music was in good hands. Ten Centuries had given confidence to the composers and wider acceptance by thoughtful listeners. It had also encouraged the rise of other organizations in the 1970s, such as Norma Beecroft and Robert Aitken's New Music Concerts, also devoted to contemporary music in a wide variety of forms. By 1976,

New Music Concerts had included presentations to contemporary music groups in Sweden, Norway, Switzerland, France, Belgium, England, and Iceland. Yet it was always a challenge to keep alive an organization devoted to the struggle of learning about Canada and its people and the current world by means of the musical expressions of living composers. Harry and Mary were tireless in their support of every effort, but the rewards seemed particularly meagre.

In an interview with Helen Dahlstrom for a publication devoted to the celebration of the 1988 Music Week by the Canadian Federation of Music Teachers' Associations, Harry expounded at some length on the theme of the challenge that modern composers face in getting attention for their music in the twentieth century. Beethoven had certainly faced resistance to his music composition a century and a half before, but how much more difficult it was when a modern composer had to face the flood of music that permeated every aspect of life. "We value what is rare, we take for granted that which is easily come by," Harry argued. "Today we press a button — and music pours into our ears. It has become the background sound for everything we do and usually it comes at no cost. The recording has become the basic sound on most radio stations and we have become hearers rather than listeners."

Harry kept up a continuous crusade against the pervasive presence of non-requested and, often, unwanted music. This led logically to a commitment to the preciousness of silence. Indeed, it was a statement on that issue that led Harry to compose *Graphic I: Out of Silence* as his major contribution as composer-in-residence during the 1970–71 season, encompassing as it did the TSO's fiftieth anniversary. The orchestra begins with bars of conducted silence, and the composition ends with bars of silence while the conductor continues to indicate the time with the movement of his or her baton. The piece, except for a few accents, was very quiet and made its point dramatically.

William Littler, music critic for the *Toronto Star*, noted that Harry's inspiration was a book by Max Picard, *The World of Silence*, which suggested, "Silence ought to be thought of as a positive quality — not something negative, not an absence, but something with its own role to play." Littler described the work as "growing imperceptibly from a near sonic vacuum to explore a variety of textures before returning once more to the realm of quiet." A day or two later, Littler wrote to Harry, "Thought you might like to know that *Graphic I* generated more mail than any other Toronto Symphony premiere in the last five years. The enclosed letter indicates the tenor of much of the negative comment; perhaps you don't mind sharing a few lumps with Ludwig." The enclosed letter from "a music lover" opened with a complaint about the "horrendous final choral movement" of Beethoven's Ninth and then went on to savage Harry's *Graphic I* as "a new low" and concluded with the observation that "musically Canada is a no-no. Tubby the Tuba is strictly our speed." However, a more sensitive and thoughtful note from another music lover reached Harry thanking him for *Graphic I* and expressing a valid point: "I felt that it would have been more appropriate for the audience to remain silent at the end of your composition. Somehow, the applause, while expressing appreciation, destroyed the peaceful atmosphere that you (& the TSO) created."

However, for Harry the role of promoter extended far beyond organizing a concert series and writing music that encouraged thoughtful and reflective response to contemporary music. He was convinced that composers must be visible, articulate, and interventionist. There was one thesis that Harry held to throughout the many decades he played the role of promoter: effective musical composition depended upon individuals prepared not just to hear but to *listen* to music. There had to be some realization that listening to music — all music — demanded focus and attention. Harry was aware that music had become a kind of continuous backdrop to activities that might include reading, conversing, playing games, eating, making love — all serving perfectly legitimate needs, but all diluting the process of music listening, a process that demanded full concentration on sound and its meanings. Harry became the most provocative critic of the pervasive background music that was being used for purposes that served commercial interests and destroyed any chance to enjoy the silence that he considered a necessary element in life, one that aroused a hunger for music that could only be satisfied by focused musical presentation.

Of course most of the muzak that permeated elevators, hallways, and restaurants was simply sound designed to distract listeners from any critical or analytical thoughts that might restrain their consumerism, or, if effectively programmed, to excite them to buy more and more products.

Whatever its purpose, such ever-present musical sound produced an approach to all music that emphasized only partial attention and trivialized both the writing of serious music and its presentation. For Harry, this was unacceptable and had to be confronted — even before the question of the effective presentation of contemporary music could be adequately addressed. His own family bore the brunt of this magnificent obsession. His children were not allowed to have the radio on while they were doing their homework. It was not just the fact that he, like most composers, could not work with competing musical sounds around him; he was determined that they should bring the single-minded attention to their homework that he brought to his composing. As well, he was anxious that they learn to focus on listening to music as a demanding activity that must command full attention.

This cause was to impel his energy and curt comment throughout a lifetime, as music became increasingly an aural backdrop that imposed itself on every occasion, in both public and private venues. In 1972 Harry wrote a letter to Al Martin, the public relations officer for Air Canada, complaining bitterly about the music he was forced to endure on that airline's flights. He answered the argument that most people like it by pointing out that he was as fussy about the music he listened to as the food he ate, and yet Air Canada would not force him to eat the meals on their flights. He offered a solution, which was eventually adopted: "If Air Canada feels that providing transportation is not enough and that it must get into the entertainment business, then let it provide earphones for those who like that kind of entertainment."

In 1973, he contacted the Canadian Civil Liberties Association (CCLA), an organization he supported throughout his life, asking them to consider the "serious invasion of privacy" that muzak and "other forms of wired music" represented. He declared that, "like the plague, it's everywhere. In supermarkets, restaurants, trains, planes, hotels — everywhere." He called upon the CCLA to recognize a resolution passed by the General Assembly of the International Music Council of UNESCO in 1969 that began: "We denounce unanimously the intolerable infringement of individual freedom and of the right of everyone to silence, because of the abusive use, in private and public places, of recorded or broadcast music."

Harry believed that music should be the object of a precious and sacred moment of private listening and reflection — not an imposed background to the ordinary activities of daily life. Then and then only would people come to value this form of joy and contemplation. He was active with Pollution Probe, a volunteer organization protecting citizens from the dangers of air, water, and food filled with pollutants, but Harry's enthusiasm was in dealing with noise pollution — and mindless musical sound wafting through the atmosphere was nothing more than that! He assisted Probe in devising radio announcements for the purpose of raising people's awareness of this "unfortunate development in urban living"!

He was in every way the perfect spokesperson on such issues. He had an analytical mind that could dissect what his opponents referred to as the totally harmless presentation of "pleasing" music for the public to enjoy and point out the consumer agendas that were being played out in the department stores and malls that were flooded by such sounds.

In the 1960s Harry became a familiar figure on television and radio. His burly masculine form gave him the appearance of a well-dressed truck driver. There was nothing effete about his image. He used common language, eschewing the murky terminology of the academic music instructor for the blunt, plain-speaking language of a man with a cause. He could speak knowledgeably, concisely, and compellingly. Besides a commanding loquacity, he had developed from his experiences in film a familiarity with the techniques demanded by technological communication. He knew how to address both the microphone and the camera. He enjoyed lecturing and even more the free-for-all that often emerged in the subsequent question and answer period.

Harry was one of the first to be asked by the Canadian Music Centre in 1972 to be a "potential lecturer" in a series of tours addressing the total ignorance of Canadian music, mostly in the U.S.A., and was offered a modest travel allowance and per diem as well as a fee for his services. It was to Harry that CMC Director John Peter Lee Roberts turned when he learned that William Littler, a comparatively young and impressionable critic for the *Toronto Star*, was about to write an article about the CMC. The solution was a lunch at which Harry, a bona fide composer, would "give a clear view of the CMC's past" and "where we are going in the future." The lunch went splendidly and Littler has been a composer's friend and a CMC supporter throughout his career.

Mary by the 1960s had become one of the few performers who were obviously open and comfortable with the kind of music that her husband and his colleagues were writing. Even while she was attending the Conservatory she had begun to sing the songs of Oscar Morawetz and John Beckwith and found she was enjoying their contemporary sounds. As Harry's main interest was writing not for voice but for the orchestra or smaller instrumental ensembles, Mary could not be accused of musical nepotism — the Canadian composers she incorporated in her programs in the 1950s and early '60s were Harry's colleagues, men and women who had become family friends, although *Two Vocalises*, one of Harry's early works for soprano, woodwind instrument, and piano was obviously inspired by Mary's voice. There were no lyrics but there could not have been a more custom-built creation for a beloved than these celebrations of the soaring soprano voice. *Two Vocalises* has become a standard in the programs of several young performers since the 1960s, many of them coached by Mary herself. By the end of the decade, Mary had become one of contemporary music's most effective advocates simply by the quality of her performances of the Canadian music that was becoming an increasingly important aspect of her recital presentations.

In the early 1960s, an extraordinary coincidence occurred when two musical families found they dwelt a moment's walk from each other. Scarcely a block distant from the Freedmans on Lowther Avenue was Robert Aitken, an outstanding flutist, a colleague of Harry's in the woodwind section of the TSO, and his wife, concert pianist Marion Ross. Mary became friends with Marion and discovered that the couple shared her enthusiasm for performing contemporary music. Robert was himself a composer and, in 1964, with Marion and Mary established a trio that began making music together for the enjoyment of its members but simultaneously discovered that the sounds of flute, piano, and voice could be thoroughly pleasing as well as infinitely flexible in accommodating the unfamiliar harmonies and dynamics of modern composers. However, they discovered that few composers made use of these forces in their compositions. The Lyric Arts Trio, which began as a self-indulgent opportunity for its members to play music together, became in a few short years the most internationally recognized chamber ensemble in Canadian musical history. They did so by programming the music they enjoyed playing most and by playing most effectively in their concerts the works of contemporary composers, particularly those who were Canadian.

The name "Lyric Arts Trio" promised music to enjoy as well as to be challenged by. They exhibited an energy and excitement that was quite unique. Here were three very attractive young people who performed as though they were delighting themselves with their virtuosity, who smiled and reached out to audiences, who found humour and fun in music as well as serious ideas that demanded attention. The ensemble found a special niche beyond all doubt, one that was theirs alone. Across the country small bands of music lovers were forming, like the Ten Centuries Concerts group in Toronto, who wanted to discover the modern repertoire but also needed instrumentalists and vocalists who wanted to play and sing contemporary music and were courageous enough to face the consequences — very often small and sometimes hostile audiences.

There were times when the criticism included thoughtful comment that commanded Mary's attention. Eustace Jackson, writing in the *Ottawa Journal* about a National Arts Centre concert, said, "One is doubtful whether these serious experiments, in what amounts to a new form of art, are really worthwhile. Are they truly advancing the banner of true art in a materialistic world or are they only another strange sociological phenomena and no symbol of progress?" Throughout a decade and a half of performing together, such questions plagued the minds of Aitken, Ross, and Morrison, making them aware of the need for careful selection of repertoire from the pens of the best composers and for the highest standards of performance. They were described accurately as true musical missionaries facing all the doubts of those daring to displace the familiar and beloved music of past centuries with dissonance and the most shocking sounds that instruments and human voice were capable of producing.

In practical terms, there was always the struggle to administer the schedules of three busy musicians, and Mary took on a great deal of that task. There was another role, one Mary enjoyed beyond measure — dealing with composers who were either commissioned to write works for the group or who were so enthusiastically moved by the ensemble's quality that they insisted on presenting the Trio with pieces, often dedicated to individual members described in the most laudatory terms.

The Trio's first concerts were in Ontario, mostly near Toronto. Their initial appearance took place in 1965 in Brantford at a concert presented by its Music Club, but in 1968 the Trio was featured in a Ten Centuries Concert. It was this concert that led Kenneth Winters to write in the *Toronto Telegram* that the Canadian works were among "the chief delights." The last selection included Norma Beecroft's Elegy and Harry Freedman's Toccata, both for soprano and flute. "Mr. Freedman may well have landed square in the middle of his natural métier," Winters proclaimed. The concert concluded with Harry Somers's *Kuyas* for piano, flute, and soprano. Mr. Winters commented most emphatically, "It is a beautiful piece of work, and I shall be surprised if it is ever heard to better advantage than it was yesterday. Miss Morrison, Mr. Aitken and Miss Ross met it on its own level, carried it through its own beauty with a perception and a personal commitment that went well beyond the responsibilities of ordinary professional music making. Though they did it superbly, they didn't just do it. They meant it. They created it." No words could have validated more accurately the central expectation of the Trio — to be co-creators with composers of new and exciting works that spoke to people living in the latter decades of the twentieth century.

The Trio had begun very modestly, giving only two or three concerts a year in 1966 and 1967. There were so many government-funded concerts going on across the country in the Centennial Year that a new addition to the circuit seemed superfluous. However, it was soon obvious that there was another gathering of appropriate venues awaiting the Trio's attention, one that could be expected to be most attracted by its repertoire — the campuses of universities that were burgeoning in the 1960s, particularly those that had music faculties with at least one contemporary music fanatic. Happily, there were several — the result of the work of John Weinzweig, whose former students were now taking academic appointments in music faculties in universities from coast to coast.

In the first years, it was in Hart House at the University of Toronto, at Queen's University in Kingston, and at Waterloo Lutheran University that the Trio found its most enthusiastic audiences. Within another two years Carleton, the University of Western Ontario, McMaster University, the University of Ottawa, and, in Western Canada, campuses in Saskatoon, Regina, Edmonton, Calgary, Lethbridge, and Brandon were all visited. In 1971 the Trio was a collective artist-in-residence at Simon Fraser University, giving seminar classes but also a series of nine concerts between September and November. The Lyric Arts Trio could now be introduced as an ensemble that "has been garnering rave reviews from critics for several years." Kenneth Winters was again quoted in the Trio's promotional literature: "These three by now are more than just a first-rate singer and two first-rate players. They are musicians whose tender and vital concern with the stuff of their art gives their choice of programs significance, so that composers can be glad of their favour and the rest of us can be grateful for their selectivity."

At Simon Fraser, the Trio discovered the enormous satisfaction of spending several weeks with student music lovers, allowing time to examine a broad spectrum of contrasting compositions. It became the format whereby the Trio could influence the promising composers and performers who represented the country's musical future. In spite of the inconvenience and difficulty in handling family matters while she was on extended visits to a distant university campus, Mary found she enjoyed lecturing and participating in seminars, and indeed everything about the teaching role. She found she was good at it. Paul McIntyre at the University of Windsor put it to Mary that "your visit will represent the beginning of an important emphasis on Canadian music at the U. of W." These experiences were to have an impact on her life work decisions for the rest of career.

Soon the Trio caught the attention of the CBC, with regional centres like Halifax picking up their concert when they reached the Maritimes in 1969. The CBC recognized the Trio's value when deciding to organize a Festival of Contemporary Music in Toronto, and in the spring of 1970 the Lyric Arts Trio was featured prominently in promotional literature designed to capture the interest and approval of both the public and the critics. Then, shortly after, the Trio became the centrepiece of a "Music Today" program that was offered as an adjunct to the Shaw Festival in Niagara-on-the-Lake. It was a three-day affair, surprising in its determination to present contemporary music at a festival devoted to Bernard Shaw and his contemporaries.

Though Shaw had been a ferociously perceptive music critic as well as a prolific playwright, the Shaw Festival had not, like its predecessor in Stratford, placed much emphasis on music. Now, in July, in St. Mark's Church, just a stone's throw from the Shaw Festival's main stage, came extraordinary concerts featuring a Lyric Arts Trio determined to stretch the minds and hearts of those who were prepared to stray beyond the theatre venue and who thought themselves sufficiently brave to venture into the realm of a more modern repertoire. For these patrons, the Lyric Arts Trio provided a revelation of just how far contemporary composers could take them. "Music Today" was such a success at Niagara-on-the-Lake that another series of "Music Today" concerts was organized for the following summer.

However, before that Niagara-on-the-Lake series occurred, the Trio was invited by Toro Takemitsu, Japan's most prestigious composer, to participate in another series of presentations also called "Music Today," this time at Expo '70 in Osaka, Japan. The Trio was the single Canadian ensemble invited to perform at a special Japanese forum — all the other Canadian artists performed at the Canadian pavilion. The Trio scored a major triumph. The local press proclaimed, "These ensemble members are all experts of Music To-day. The technical virtuosity of these players can creatively convey the meaning of today's music." They had now arrived on the international scene.

On their return to the Shaw Festival in 1971 with an even more ambitious program, William Littler described the extent of the emotional range in one concert that "was able to run the gamut from something as wilfully slight and humourous as Charles Eakins's *Tonight I Am* which had the versatile Mary Morrison impersonating a pinball machine, to something as sincerely spiritual as Egil Hovland's *Magnificat*."

It was 1973 when the Trio scaled the heights. They had been invited to the International Society for Contemporary Music Festival (ISCMF) in Reykjavik, Iceland, perhaps the most prestigious gathering of ensembles addressing the music of twentieth-century composers. The society was holding its annual conference, and the Lyric Arts Trio found itself feted by its adoring peers. After pointing out with pride that

Mary was singing "better than ever" in a letter to a close friend, Harry observed, "When the Trio performed at the ISCMF in Iceland last June, three things happened: 1) the Trio received invitations from Iceland [to return], France, Israel and Sweden, and was obviously the hit of the Festival, 2) composers representing several countries announced they were going to write pieces for the Trio, and 3) there were a dozen requests for the music of the Toccata." It had been the first composition that Harry had written for the Trio and a highlight of his composing career. Another selection, *Pan*, was written just a few years later for the Trio and was also celebrated as a favourite of audiences. Although it would be a trivialization to call Harry and Mary a team, these years saw them reach the pinnacle of their collaborations as composer and performer complementing each other's roles.

By the mid-1970s, illustrious composers were providing opportunities for theatrical presentations that were delighting audiences. In his *A Tea Symphony*, Gabriel Charpentier had Mary arrive on stage in a bright blond wig carrying a cello (with a secret compartment designed to carry a bottle of liquor) and a battered bow. Lauretta Thistle, writing in the *Ottawa Citizen*, described her as "a wonderful clown as well as a skilful vocalist," and concluded, "Mr. Charpentier deserves thanks not only for contributing to the gaiety of nations, but for helping to make Canada aware that it has a unique treasure in this trio which is as adept at comedy as at serious music." The Trio had brought joy and laughter to a contemporary music audience, and though its members may not have been whistling any tunes, they were leaving the hall with wide grins on their faces, and their success was repeated in Oslo, Stockholm, Brussels, and London.

Another comic delight written in this period was R. Murray Schafer's *La Testa d'Adriane*. It was commissioned by Joe Macerollo, a fine accordionist, one of those who joined the Trio on occasion when extra instruments were required. The scene included a table with only Mary's sleeping head visible. After a lengthy introduction by a circus huckster, the "head" performs an extraordinary aria moving from the dramatic to the hysterical until sheer exhaustion returns the disembodied part to its original state of slumber. It was a vocal treat that included theatrical effects and proved that hilarity and musical excellence could go hand in hand. At one performance in a Bulgarian marketplace, Mary looked out to see women who were absolutely transfixed by this singing head, soberly crossing themselves as a defence against what seemed to them a most distressing, life-threatening scenario.

In 1978, at the height of its reputation for performing excellence, the Trio disbanded. (The Trio appeared for the final time at a celebration for John Weinzweig's seventieth birthday in 1983.) All three of its members had flourishing solo careers and the demands of travel were becoming overwhelming. Even in 1973 Bruce Mather warned Mary that the Trio was "far from the high standard you are capable of" and that although Mary's contributions were unassailable — "Your ability, your vocal colour, your musicality and warmth of expression are a precious gift" — these, he believed, could not carry the entire ensemble. His solution was that Mary demand that Robert Aitken give twelve hours a week to the Trio. Although Robert had certainly spread himself thinly across the musical life of Toronto and beyond, the breakup had other causes. Fourteen years was a long time for such a performing ensemble to keep a focus on a particular genre of music composition, and all its members were looking for other roles that would lead them to even more opportunities to discover new vistas of performance. It was time to stop, while they were at their peak and enjoying the challenges the work of the Trio presented.

As it transpired, Robert, Marion, and Mary were joined by Harry in a close friendship that never wavered over the decades that followed, though their collaborative music making remained in abeyance. Their times together were spiced with stories of the bizarre happenings that took place in the many cities they visited. There were hotel registration desks that could not get straight who of the Trio needed a room for double or single occupancy. Invariably Mary was given the worst accommodation, often in the hotel basement, while Robert and Marion might be looking out on a glorious vista of ocean, sand, and palm trees.

There were the inevitable misunderstandings on the part of organizers around the unusual performance needs of a Trio emphasizing contemporary music. A particular piece might require taped instrumental interventions demanding that the onstage piano have the same pitch as that found on the tape. On one occasion, the rehearsal revealed a major distance between taped instrument and on-site piano. The problem was resolved by the arrival of a second grand piano on a small stage that then could not accommodate the Trio members. A commission by Gabriel Charpentier called for the participation of liveried grooms played by four male actors on stage. The stagehands were puzzled by what they interpreted as a request for four *brooms*.

On another occasion, a tape of the sound of a raging forest fire was introduced into the performance of a quiet selection, completely baffling the audience and astounding the Trio members. At another concert, Robert was to begin playing a composition that commenced with a flute solo. The score indicated that the flute was to be joined by the piano and voice parts after Marion and Mary entered the concert hall a few minutes later. Disaster struck when the auditorium stage door was unexplainably locked, with both Mary and Marion left outside. The building caretaker had to be found while a confused and impatient Robert provided variations to occupy the unexpected time lapse.

Then, thankfully on very few occasions, there were recalcitrant composers who arrived at the rehearsal to advise on the appropriate interpretation of their precious scores. At one such rehearsal, Mary's soprano line was interrupted by one demanding music maker with various suggestions that changed the very nature of the composition. Mary's response of "That's not what you wrote" became an ongoing litany. Finally the normally even-tempered Mary Morrison threw down the music, marched out of the hall, and took the subway back to the hotel.

Yet throughout all the chaos, the Trio had remained a charming, cohesive ensemble devoted to contemporary music that mattered. Robert Aitken's assessment of her conduct throughout the Trio's existence: "Mary was a saint!"

Larry Lake, eventually to become the host of the CBC's prestigious Sunday night program *Two New Hours*, devoted to Canadian contemporary composition, wrote in the September 1984 periodical *Music Canada* an article called "Growth and Tradition, Composition in Ontario."

Recognizing the Trio's role from 1964 to 1978, he concluded, "The succeeding years have produced many fine groups across the country but few if any with a record approaching that of the Lyric Arts Trio." The statement would be valid even if it had been written in 2006. The Trio was sorely missed by composers who had experienced the thrill of hearing their music superbly and sensitively performed. Over the years, the Trio had played new works by one hundred composers, both Canadian and from other countries. Along with Harry's *Toccata* and *Pan*, Brian Cherney's *Eclipse*, Harry Somers's *Kuyas*, John Beckwith's *Shivaree*, and R. Murray Schafer's *Enchantress* were premiered. Indeed, Anhalt, Kasemets, Morel, Garant, and Papineau-Couture — all major Canadian composers — wrote compositions for this extraordinary group.

It was staggering to realize that during the highest point in the Trio's activities in the 1970s, Mary was balancing her own career as a soprano soloist and incidentally keeping a boisterous family in place. It was not just economics that drove Mary to keep up this exhausting schedule. Ironically, only by proving herself as an interpreter of the finest music of past ages could she be perceived a valid advocate of contemporary music either on stage or at the lecture podium, and only by constant efforts to be with Harry and the girls could she fulfil her desire to be an effective parent.

Mary's voice and presentation skills were very much in demand throughout the 1970s. In May 1973, she performed in a Vancouver production of George Crumb's *Ancient Voices of Children*. It was described by Max Wyman as "a work of surpassing beauty that captures the timeless innocence and the extreme sadness at its inevitable loss." Wyman praised Mary Morrison's solo role: "[She is] superbly flexible of voice and style, able both to answer all technical demands and inject into the music a full measure of involvement and character and feeling." Later that same year she was invited by Seiji Ozawa, who had come to admire Mary's work while he was conductor of the TSO, to sing the Bach *Magnificat* with the San Francisco Symphony Orchestra. A critic commented, "Among the five soloists, Canadian soprano Mary Morrison excelled because of the lucid, soaring quality and intelligence of her singing."

In 1975 she was back on the opera stage in a production at the National Arts Centre in Benjamin Britten's *Turn of the Screw*. Her singing and characterization was summed up in one word by the *Ottawa Citizen*'s Maureen Peterson: "Superb." When Kingston composer István Anhalt's *La Tourangelle* was premiered in Toronto, Harry's creative colleague Louis Applebaum sent back to the local newspaper, the *Whig-Standard*, an accolade that included Mary along with Phyllis Mailing and Roxolana Roslak as "three of the country's finest sopranos who had sung with remarkable intensity." A year later Mary visited the Algoma Festival, where Applebaum's musical description of the Algoma Central Railway (ACR) was appropriately given its first production with Mary as soloist. The headline in the *Sault Star* concentrated on Mary's role: "Soprano hisses, clucks, howls her way through the ACR commercial." A further comment on her more serious contribution to the Festival program enthused, "Miss Morrison, from her Telemann cantata to her haunting Eriskay Love Lilt, was what singing is all about."

In 1979 even the world of film received her attention when she was offered a part in an operatic dramatization of one of the decade's most horrific events. In Wales, a landslide in the mining town of Aberfan had buried the school and dozens of the children who were in its classrooms. The horror, the pain, and the sense of injustice that permeated the event brought upon this Welsh village the sympathy of the world. The documentary was presented with the Media Award for the best serious music telecast by the Canadian Music Centre, but even more prestigious was the fact that the film with Mary, along with Canadian singers Gary Relyea and Glyn Evans, received the TV Opera Prize of the City of Salzburg as well as the CBC's Anik Award for the most outstanding musical program televised that year.

The promotion of Canadian composition continued in the 1970s. The demise of Ten Centuries had opened the way for another concert series, and New Music Concerts filled the gap admirably. This time, though Robert Aitken and Norma Beecroft were the central figures, the emphasis was on the contemporary both Canadian and worldwide, and the organization was to be fuelled by a long-term commitment that came to be measured in decades. Mary was once again involved deeply, being chair of the board at one point, and continues her support of its activities to this day.

As the new century opens it could be said that Canada has stunned the world with the depth and quality of its creative and artistic leadership. Canadian writers dominate the English-language world of letters. The country's dance and theatre have thrilled audiences abroad. Although they receive less publicity and general recognition, it could be said that Canadian composers are also making their presence felt on the international stage. This would not have happened if the first flight of Canadian music makers had not descended into the marketplace, found their way to the media opportunities that were available, spent time in the nation's classrooms, and searched out opportunities for the performance of their work. These composers and their performing colleagues, like Mary, cajoled and harassed arts organizations to play and audiences to listen and evaluate the works of Canadian music makers.

A cultural millennium appears to be launching itself in the wake of a planetary despair that the social injustice and the savagery of war that characterized the twentieth century might well escalate in the twenty-first. The presence of a Canadian musical expression gives hope that Canada has the creative strength and vitality to make a difference in the promotion of planetary values and behaviours that will ultimately lead to the triumph of peace and justice. The reality of a body of twentieth-century Canadian music and the continuing contribution of Canadian composers, singers, and musicians in the twenty-first century will be essential if Canada is to play an active and positive role.

CHAPTER 8
The Artist as Educator

The arts and music in particular have been an aspect of learning from the very beginning of our understanding of how, as human beings, we come to know ourselves and the world around us. We can trace the role that music has played back to the earliest civilizations, and certainly, through many centuries and in most jurisdictions, music has come to hold a central place in any civilized community's education system.

In Canada, teachers of the early grades were once drawn from a social class level that ensured children were able to play the piano and therefore had the basic skills necessary to encourage the making of music. Many prospective teachers were "daughters of the manse," where the presence of a piano or foot-pedal organ could be expected and where hymns were the main parlour repertoire. At the end of the nineteenth century and well into the twentieth century it was expected that every middle-class home had a keyboard instrument, and a major employment opportunity for young women was the provision of music instruction to children in the neighbourhood. Teacher education in colleges across the country put little emphasis on the learning of music, as this was the one area that had been addressed in the lives of these candidates before they arrived to prepare themselves to occupy the province's classrooms.

The twentieth century saw the enormous effect of modern technology on music instruction, first through the presence of the radio and the record player, to be followed later in the century by the tape, the CD, and most recently the DVD, to say nothing of the most pervasive technology of all, the television set. It has led to a decrease in the making of music in the home and of music skills across a broad population. Although there might be a keyboard to be found somewhere in the average abode and even perhaps an electric guitar, the piano no longer has an honoured place in the parlour, if indeed there is such a room in modern residences. The changing nature of the personnel pool from which elementary teachers were drawn, the absence of private music education as an expected attribute of growing up, along with an understandable reluctance on the part of prospective teachers to compete with the polished performances every child witnesses on the television set, reduced the commitment of the schooling system to music education.

When, in the twentieth century, young people were expected to attend at least a grade or two at the secondary level and the public system in Canada was appropriately expanded to Grade 12, music took its place in the curriculum and, even more important, it became a major aspect of extracurricular activities. Many schools had choirs and orchestras, going well beyond the military band that accompanied the school cadet corps. Specialist teachers of music were prepared by the Ontario College of Education, which trained the province's secondary school teachers at the University of Toronto. However, the ideal of a first-rate music program was not assured, especially in communities some distance from major centres.

The goal of public education has shifted from developing children as citizens to providing them with vocational skills, an influence that trickled down from the secondary schools to the earliest grades. Because of this shift, music increasingly became an extracurricular activity in high schools and played a reduced role in elementary classrooms. This generalization does not adequately explain the fact that in certain jurisdictions, in particular schools and in some classrooms, music was given both attention and prominence. It depended on the teacher, and there were music missionaries to be found at all levels, sometimes in the most remote communities. Indeed, *Laurentian Moods*, which Harry wrote in 1957, was specifically commissioned by Barrie Collegiate, a secondary school whose band had a provincial reputation for performance superiority. But for every Barrie Collegiate approaching excellence there were many other

Mary Morrison at the age of eight, with a cup she had just won for her singing in the Winnipeg Kiwanis Festival, 1934.

Harry Freedman, in RCAF uniform, in front of the Peace Tower, Parliament Hill, Ottawa, in 1942.

Mary, a frequent performer on CBC Radio in Toronto, 1947.

Harry, relaxing on a Toronto beach, 1947.

Mary as Mimi in *La Bohème*, 1948.

Harry and Mary on their wedding day, September 15, 1951.

Mary in the role of Marguerita in a Canadian Opera Company production of Charles Gounod's *Faust*, with Jan Rubes as Mephistopholes, 1951.

Mary as the Countess in a Canadian Opera Company production of Mozart's *The Marriage of Figaro*, 1954.

Annual meeting of the Canadian League of Composers, 1955. Standing: Udo Kazemets, Sam Dolin, John Weinzweig, Harry Freedman, Andy Twa, Jean Papineau-Couture, Barbara Pentland, Louis Applebaum, John Beckwith. Sitting and kneeling: Helmut Kalman, Leslie Mann, Harry Somers.

The Freedman family at home, 1959 (left to right): Lori, Mary, Harry, Cyndie, and Kim.

Harry with English horn and daughters Cyndie (with flute), Kim (with clarinet), and Lori (with guitar), 1965.

Harry in conversation with Canadian music legend Sir Ernest MacMillan and Toronto Symphony Orchestra conductor Seiji Ozawa, 1965.

Mary with the
Canadian League of
Composers' citation
for her contribution to
the performance of
music by Canadian
composers, 1968.

Mary Morrison and Harry Freedman, January 1969.

Harry Freedman, composer, 1970.

The Lyric Arts Trio: Mary Morrison, Robert Aitken, and Marion Ross, 1970.

Harry, a member of the Toronto Symphony Orchestra, as
portrayed by artist Adrian Dingle, 1970.

Harry participating in the "Artists in the Classroom" project, instructing young instrumentalists in North York schools, 1972.

The Lyric Arts Trio: Mary playing the role of Zara Nelsova, with her reconstructed cello, in a performance of Gabriel Charpentier's *A Tea Symphony*, 1972.

Mary and Harry in front of their home on St. Andrews Gardens on the occasion of their twenty-fifth wedding anniversary, 1976.

The Lyric Arts Trio: Mary performing R. Murray Schafer's *La Testa d'Adriane* with accordionist Joe Macerollo, 1977.

Harry with Robert Creech, director of the Courtenay Music Camp, 1978.

Harry in conversation with Toronto Symphony Orchestra colleague and instructor Perry Bauman, circa 1980.

Harry in conversation with composer Harry Somers, 1980.

Mary receiving her designation as Officer of the Order of Canada from Governor General Edward Schreyer, 1983.

Harry shaking hands with Governor General Jeanne Sauvé in the receiving line on the occasion of the presentation of his Order of Canada, Rideau Hall, Ottawa, 1984. Mary can be seen next in line.

Harry receiving his designation as Officer of the Order of Canada from Governor General Jeanne Sauvé at Rideau Hall, Ottawa, 1984.

Mary receiving the City of Toronto's medal of service from Mayor Art Eggleton, 1985.

Mary, a member of the
Faculty of Music,
University of Toronto, 1988.

Mary Morrison, 2002.

Mary with Measha Brüggergosman on the occasion of Measha's Carnegie Hall debut, 2004.

schools mired in musical inadequacy and ineptitude, in the classroom and beyond — in the gymnatorium, the cafetorium, and the auditorium.

On the whole, the neglect of music instruction in the last decades of the twentieth century carried on, and those who realized the effect that a complete musical education could have on children were appalled. The impact of this shift is made evident by the results of various research studies. We now know that the enthusiasm for sound and rhythm and the excitement of musical expression open windows in the minds of young children that make the acquisition of other skills possible and in doing so provide a positive influence on the attitudes and behaviour of children toward each other and toward the community as a whole. Yet, in the rush to save costs in the education system and to place mathematics, science, and technology at the forefront, it has been the arts in general and music in particular that have been sacrificed. In many cases, the entire support infrastructure has disappeared, while in other jurisdictions there is the reality that teachers are incapable of providing instruction that effectively addresses the published provincial music curriculum.

Even by the middle of the twentieth century those concerned with the arts in our education system realized that these trends could be reversed only through the direct intervention of the professional artistic community. Otherwise, school graduates would be doomed to live in a society with a very narrow and inadequate appreciation of music expression, one that comprehended only the various forms of pop styles available on radio stations obsessed with the "top 40" or television networks devoted to the latest pop stars. It was apparent that the presence of able performing artists, both vocal and on a wide spectrum of instruments, could be replaced by a narrow track of untrained singers and incompetent musicians capable of providing sound only on the electronic keyboard and the electronically enhanced guitar. Even more likely, there would be a dearth of people who could appreciate the ageless musical expression of our civilization as well as contemporary treasures of our own time, thereby providing meagre audiences to support the solo performers and orchestral ensembles emerging from conservatories and music faculties across the land. The great music through which thoughtful and aware people have expressed their faith and belief, demonstrated their joy and delight, mourned their losses, and coped with pain could be lost to future generations.

It was only in the last decades of the twentieth century that Canada became aware of the need to support the arts in the community. Ironically this change in public policy took place while arts education in the schools continued to diminish. The creation of the Canada Council and through it the provision of financial support to arts organizations in the late 1950s was a turning point in expanding the presence of the arts in Canadian society. Various provinces emulated the federal example and organized art councils with similar mandates, making possible an even more dramatic shift in the direction of arts education, which was the responsibility of the provincial governments as set out in Canada's Constitution. Thus it would be through municipal and provincial funding bodies that the arts community could participate in improving the musical schooling of the young. Performing artists and composers saw the importance of a crusade to change the learning of music in schools, and, in practical terms, of finding a new source of personal income by participating in the process.

Ontario, where Harry and Mary spent their lives after they moved from Manitoba, was one of the earliest provinces to create an arts council. At first, the Province of Ontario Council for the Arts (POCA), later to be renamed the Ontario Arts Council (OAC), was seen as simply a mechanism to channel resources to the Canadian Opera Company, the National Ballet, and the Toronto Symphony Orchestra, but soon artists and arts bureaucrats devised ways to use the annual budget in more diverse programs across the full spectrum of arts disciplines. A major addition became supporting arts education, and Paul Schafer, a young economist at the time, with an intense enthusiasm for the arts in general and music in particular, was hired by the OAC in 1966 to write a report on the economics of the arts. He was soon diverted by a crisis in the Ontario theatre community, but the totality of his work resulted in a focus on arts education as a critical area of concern.

The Ontario Music Conference in 1966 was one of the first projects the OAC initiated. The plan of the OAC's first director, Milton Carman, was to arouse some pressure in the music community that might result in more generous provincial grants to the OAC, thereby allowing it to give greater support to the various choirs, orchestras, smaller ensembles, and solo artists who could now be found across the province. As one might expect, it was the inadequacies of music education that received most of the attention at that event, which had attracted virtually every major Ontario voice in the field. When quite ambitious recommendations were taken to the Ministry of Education, a pervasive territoriality raised its ugly head. The bureaucrats of the Ministry of Education, responsible for all music instruction in the classrooms of the province, were not disposed to allow the OAC to encroach on their role and were quick to make that quite clear.

The OAC's counter-strategy was to set up the Centre for Research in Arts Education, with Paul Schafer at its head, hoping to allay the fears of the ministry while at the same time pursuing the long-term goal of making a difference in the province's schools. Under the aegis of this centre, a training program for arts administrators was devised and, most significantly, a Creative Artists in the Schools program was launched. Schafer hired Linda Zwicker, who gave enormous energy and intelligent leadership over several years to a program that brought hundreds of artists into Ontario schools. It was into this program that Harry was invited, along with fellow composer R. Murray Schafer, poet sean o huigin, and actress Araby Lockhart, to become actively involved with teachers and students in provincial classrooms. The idea was simple. School boards and individual schools would be encouraged by extra funding to invite such people to spend a few days working with students in music, painting, theatre, literature, or crafts. The children would be inspired by their presence and example to pursue their studies in these fields, and, it was hoped, their teachers would also learn something of the arts that they could use in their own instructional methods for many years after.

Fortunately, it was in just such a program that Harry Freedman had already participated over several years. He had been drawn to the classroom at least in part as a result of his own experience. At his high school in Winnipeg, his principal had been a devotee of a learning technique called the Dalton method. It encouraged students to be self-motivated, to engage in projects over a series of weeks. There were compulsory classes, but many were optional. Young people were taught to organize their own learning. It was a unique experience for able students and an introduction to the adult workplace. It did not spread to very many schools, as the less able were simply left behind, and thus for the average classroom it was not politically feasible. For Harry, however, it was a godsend. Students were encouraged to follow their own curiosity and to delve deeply rather than superficially into areas that excited them. They were taught to look to their own devices rather than be dependent on teachers and textbooks. Harry's path to becoming a composer and his success in pursuing a composer's working life followed the precepts learned in his high school experience.

In 1964, three years before the OAC initiative, Harry became involved with the John Adaskin Project, which was funded by a foundation set up to honour the life and contribution of a great Canadian music maker. In that year twenty composers were paid to spend a week working in a Canadian classroom. Harry saw it as more than just a few days of inter-action with aspiring musicians; it was also an opportunity for him to observe the musical experience the student instrumentalists were receiv-ing. "My experience during that week convinced me that if contemporary music is ever going to have an audience, then composers must help create that audience by giving them — during their formative years — an alter-native to the pretty little nothingness with which they are inundated."

Harry's early schooling and his experience with the Adaskin Foundation and its program were enormous advantages that the OAC Creative Artists in the Schools exploited shamelessly in its first tentative efforts to influence teaching and learning in the arts without arousing the opposition of the Ministry of Education. Harry saw his work in the schools as complementary to his role as a composer. As early as 1952 he had writ-ten *March for Small Types*, a small orchestral piece for a children's audience that eventually joined *Caricature* and *Harlem Hoe-down* as movements for his *Matinée Suite*. Each had originally been written for a youth-oriented radio program, *Opportunity Knocks*, which had included a segment that involved performers but came also to feature composers. For three con-secutive years Harry received $50 for composing a short piece that by 1955 could be connected as a single suite suitable for a concert appearance. He realized that working with children and composing went hand in hand, each activity giving meaning and purpose to the other.

Harry could have considered this classroom experience merely an injection of advocacy or a convenient addition to his musician's income, but instead he became engrossed with the energy and excitement of the young people he met and their receptiveness to new ideas and new sounds. It turned out to be a profound learning experience for both him and his students. In 1968, at the CBC Toronto Festival of Contemporary Music, Harry was commissioned by contralto Maureen Forrester to compose pieces to accompany the texts of poems written by young people in his classes. She sang them during a concert that was presented at Toronto's St. James Cathedral. It was a desperately hot night, but Harry's song settings of recent writing of students, simply called *Poems of Young People*, for low voice and piano, were well received, and the young student librettists were understandably thrilled. Harry realized that he could never separate his work with young people from the day-to-day making of music that would move both children and adults.

Even from his chair in the TSO woodwind section, Harry was aware that almost from the beginnings of the Toronto Symphony Orchestra, the Women's Committee had been encouraging not only youth concerts at Massey Hall but also classroom visits by TSO musicians. Indeed, it was this committee that in 1970 commissioned him to write *March!*, a short, lively orchestral offering. It received enthusiastic accolades from young and old alike when it appeared on the TSO's Young Peoples' Concert. It was, as Women's Committee Chair Andrea Alexander noted, a piece that had a "happy, interesting, new and different sound." Inspired by animals to be found in Dr. Seuss's children's books, it was described in John Kraglund's review of its premiere as having "exotic percussion effects — sometimes echoed by the strings — featuring the whole percussion section in a jazz part that permitted their combined efforts to sound like Gene Krupa on a good night." He concluded by congratulating Harry on his "ability to draw forth frequent and enthusiastic giggles." Critic William Littler commented, "It is full of bursts and whizzes, scoops and shivers, not to mention pixilated percussion and an improvised jam session. The youngsters seemed to love it and why not? It's about time someone spoke to them in their own language." From these years of writing for children it was evident that Harry had developed a capacity to introduce the sounds of contemporary music in a manner that held their attention, and, in the case of *March!*, arouse their passion.

A year later, he wrote *Tikki Tikki Tembo* on a commission from the Dundas Library Board and it quickly became a favourite not only for children's programs but also for adult concerts across Canada and the

United States as well. The work was broadcast on CBC and became one of his most popular early works. Thus his determination to engage young people became from the outset an integral aspect of his commitment to the composing of music for all occasions.

Harry was determined that his activities in the classroom would go far beyond a casual appreciation of music and, more particularly, contemporary music. He began to involve himself in the nature and purpose of school instrumental music training programs at every level. During the 1960s, a major injection of money from the federal government made possible a significant development in the music programs of every province, but in none more than Ontario. In order to observe the constitutional niceties that placed education securely under provincial power, the Conservative Diefenbaker Government in 1961 passed the Vocational Training Act, which provided millions of dollars in new buildings and equipment to provincial educational systems all in the name of job training. Significantly, some of this money came into the hands of school boards that were able to provide music rooms and purchase stringed, brass, and woodwind instruments.

A new era of expansion in instrumental music beckoned, but teachers found themselves coping with an unprecedented flood of students expecting to play in bands and orchestras. Unfortunately, there was a dearth of appropriate music for classroom use. What there was available was boring and took no notice of the differences in the difficulties of learning to play each individual instrument. Plentiful unison playing became the strategy to cope with the problems of coping with skill acquisition on specific instruments. Harry saw at once that this practice ensured that students were unable to hear adequately the extent of their faulty intonation. They were simply "playing out of tune until their muscles gathered tone." Harry believed students needed "to hear themselves out of tune," and full orchestral performance, particularly when playing in unison, did not encourage this kind of listening.

Harry had gathered sufficient knowledge of the instruments of the orchestra that he knew, for example, that learning the technique necessary to play in the key of B flat might be easy for the clarinet but would be difficult for the oboe. Avoiding difficult passages in the early weeks of instruction was paramount if students were to become confident on their instruments. As well, he encouraged his students to play in small ensembles and to listen to each other. Most important, he composed pieces that did not make impossible demands upon them, music that took into account the particular challenges of each instrument, that allowed for pleasing harmony in presentation and gave forth feelings of excitement and accomplishment.

His compositions for the classroom exuded what Patricia Shand of the University of Toronto's Faculty of Music called "transparent textures" that "introduce the subtleties of ensemble playing." His music demanded attention to "attacks, releases and conductor's cues," emphasizing the "feeling of playing in a section." During the process of strengthening their capacity to achieve accurate tone and pitch, young people could learn the subtleties of a variety of metres. These attributes of "mixed metres, interesting percussion rhythms and methods of tone production, colourful dynamic contrasts, unusual harmonies, dissonances" all produced exiting sounds that attracted students as they moved towards competence on their instruments. These initial compositions, which Harry called *Little Acorns* for the beginning band, were but an initial step in a massive program of instrumental development that he realized would place Ontario at the forefront of music education in North America.

As his major project, Harry proposed to write a series of original compositions that would take every instrumental student through the elementary, secondary, and advanced levels and deliver a competent, confident performer. He insisted that "the entire series will make use of as many contemporary techniques as possible." The process would produce better musicians as well as better listeners and players of contemporary serious music.

In 1969, Keith Bissell, the co-ordinator of music for the Scarborough Board of Education, contacted the Aid for Cultural Development section of the Rockefeller Foundation, pointing out that Canadian schools had encouraged the interest of musicians and composers in short-term arts education projects and that composer "Harry Freedman became so interested in the entire field of school music that he embarked on a series of pieces for use in the schools." Bissell emphasized that "they were not mere exercises but selections appropriate for concert use." The project for which he was requesting money, some

$45,000 over three years, was for the expansion of the twenty pieces already written to a full complement of seven hundred compositions — in short "a full-fledged, classroom tested series of graded pieces that would take a student from the beginning to the status of a proficient instrumentalist." The pilot project would take at least three years, beginning in September 1970. The application for funding was accompanied by supportive letters from the eminent American composer John Cage and from Seiji Ozawa, now conductor of the San Francisco Symphony Orchestra. The request was rejected.

In 1971, the Canadian Music Council presented a brief to the Canada Council and the Ontario Arts Council requesting a grant to support essentially the same project, only the total number of compositions had been reduced to three hundred. Now it was the North York Board of Education that would provide Harry with the laboratory and the result would be similar, "a classroom tested series of compositions, a milestone in the annals of music education not only in Canada but in the larger world beyond." This effort to find money also failed, as it was outside the jurisdiction of the Canada Council and beyond the funding patterns of OAC programs. In the latter case, Harry was unaware that he was challenging the Government of Ontario's power and the jurisdictional monopoly that was determined to keep him (and his colleagues) out of the arena of music instruction and to ensure that he be kept on the periphery of developing music in the province's schools. It was Ministry of Education territory, and not even Harry Freedman was going to be allowed to invade it.

Years later, in 1977, Harry tried to interest Arnold Edinborough, the director of the Council for Business and the Arts in Canada, hoping that he might be able to point him to a progressive corporation that might pick up the costs of such a project. Edinborough replied that it was "not the time to ask for $75,000 for a school music project," and the matter was dropped. Arts education, buried within the confines of the schooling system, failed to provide the public attention that private donors required. With dogged determination Harry continued his efforts, supported by the OAC Creative Artists in the School program, the North York, Scarborough, and York County boards of education, and enthusiastic board consultants like Laughton Bird and Keith Bissell who were prepared to offer opportunities for him to spend time in their class-rooms with their students. In one local Toronto school, Forest Hill Collegiate, the students voted to carry on with the project even after Harry's presence had been terminated.

During these years it was not only Toronto area schools that received Harry's attention. Early in 1980 he received an invitation from St. Thomas Aquinas High School in the Northern Ontario community of Kenora to spend a day talking to the entire student body of 260 students and then meeting with smaller groups who were especially interested in music. The school flew him up from Toronto, and he enjoyed himself enormously, even though it took a couple of days out of his composing schedule that were scarcely recompensed by the $60 stipend provided by the school's meagre budget.

Although Harry's music and presentation skills benefited from all this contact with students, the account of his larger frustrations represents a tragic public absence of vision and purpose. With all we now know of the positive impact making music has on creative urges, one must wonder what inventions and innovations have been missed as a result of these lost opportunities to incorporate music in the learning process. Even at the level of encouraging amateur music making, the enormous investment in instruments and appropriate space did not substantially change Ontario's cultural landscape in terms of citizen involvement in community bands and orchestras across the province. Nevertheless, a few of Harry's compositions remained in school music libraries and were played year after year.

Throughout the late 1960s and the '70s Harry continued to work with young people in school after school, in classroom after classroom — with warm recognition and appreciation. Jack Gillette, a program director, wrote in July 1973, after Harry had completed another project in North York, "You made a real impact on those students who worked with you, not only by your great skills but also by your tolerant good nature." Harry happened to be the perfect person and the most accomplished composer to carry the message. He realized that not every composer should engage in such activity. In advice to the Canada Council in regard to a Community Musicians Program he stated that a participating professional "must be as gifted as an animateur as much as a musician."

Ironically, during these years he was being courted by universities who wanted to have on their faculty a musician who could serve their instructional needs on woodwinds but could also fulfill an academic role as a member of a music faculty with, by this time, considerable experience in the world of contemporary music. As early as 1963, the dean of the Faculty of Music at the University of British Columbia, G. Welton Marquis, contacted Harry with a proposition that provided little in the way of financial rewards but promised a role that would be most challenging. Harry wrote back that he would not accept being treated as simply another instrumental instructor. He had, by this time, a track record as a composer, and it was this attribute that was of the greatest value to a university seeking some status in the world of music education. Realizing that he was moving on to a different stage, he made it quite clear that he would be a very difficult colleague by announcing that "the academic approach of most university courses is of no interest to me."

In 1971, Paul Pedersen, chair of the Department of Music at McGill University, offered him an associate professorship, just as he was making his break with the TSO and assuming a full-time commitment to composition. It was a dark time of personal financial pressure, and the opportunity to join his composer colleagues who had university faculty positions as a financial fallback was very seductive indeed. However, once again, the offer was met with a negative response. Yet, in 1973, Harry, recognizing that his lack of an undergraduate degree would be a problem if he took on any university faculty employment, was applying for university courses in mathematics.

A few years later, after a year at the Courtenay Music Camp with its leader Robert Creech, Harry was courted to accept a post at the Vancouver City College. Even on the basis of a year's delay and the promise that he would not have any administrative duties and would be involved "essentially as a composer," he turned down the invitation. Despite his history of rejecting offers, he continued to receive invitations to teach at the post-secondary level. In the mid-1980s he was asked by McMaster University to replace a professor in the Faculty of Arts and Science who would be on sabbatical. With considerable hesitation he accepted and was delighted to learn that the objective of the fourth-year course was "to give students an insight into the creative process." He found the students "so alive, so enthusiastic that I may have to reconsider my opinion of the rock generation." Their response even encouraged Harry to suggest an intergenerational interaction around music as a basis for a TVOntario production. Even at the post-secondary level, the one-on-one style of identifying and analyzing creative effort came to make sense to Harry.

Yet, with all his hesitations the fact remains that Harry found great satisfaction and achieved a monumental reputation in working with younger children. Indeed, he had made use of both his quarter-century of experience in orchestral performance and his varied and expanding role as a communicator on radio and television to become an outstanding educator at the elementary and secondary level. Here his lack of formal paper qualifications was not a problem and his skill as a teacher and creator was celebrated by the age groups most comfortable with their own imaginations.

One could say that for students outside the classroom Harry carried out an even more unique informal education role. The students he met in schools, at camps, at lectures, and at workshops were encouraged by his openness and generosity of spirit to write to him for advice. The result was that long before email made it a common occurrence, Harry had built up an extraordinary web of correspondents who sent manuscripts and asked for advice and shared triumphs and defeats. This exchange — surely the most effective form of instruction and inspiration available to the learning spirit — continued throughout his life.

All through the 1970s and into the '80s, Harry was developing a series of graded pieces for elementary and secondary schools. He later described the process to the OAC's arts education officer, Norma Clark: "It is very slow going. First I have to write two or three pieces. Then it is copied and then printed. Then we try them out in class. Then we make whatever changes I feel are needed after getting the various reactions." He had the satisfaction of knowing that the system worked, even if the authorities could not find a way to give his process any kind of universal presence in the educational system.

It was in this role that he could connect his composing with his instrumental instruction, and in 1971 the OAC's Linda Zwicker was able to offer him both fees and expenses to teach a visual arts–music project. Harry's life work was, in a sense, a vindication of the value of integrating the arts disciplines — but few had the knowledge and experience or the courage to follow that path. With young people he could make this connection work to produce greater insight and understanding and he was singular in understanding this reality. His years at the Winnipeg Art School were paying off in a very practical way!

Yet throughout the 1970s and beyond he continued to be invited to lecture at universities across the country. Indeed, it was when, in the mid-1980s, the author of this volume needed a composer to address a post-graduate course he was teaching at the Ontario Institute for Studies in Education that he began a professional relationship with Harry that extended over several years. Harry challenged these students, who would soon be educators themselves, to realize what a precious opportunity they faced teaching young people at the most productive learning moments of their lives. When, in the early 1990s, the Institute organized an international conference on arts education called "Artswork," it was to Harry that the organizing committee turned both to compose a piece, *Alice*, to be performed by Lawrence Cherney and a small group of instrumentalists, and to speak to delegates from around the world about the magic of creativity.

It was in the early 1970s that Harry came in contact with Robert Creech, a fine French horn player in the Vancouver Symphony Orchestra and a splendid arts educator, described by Harry as a man "who cares deeply about the state of music in Canada in all its manifestations." Creech had taken over the Courtenay Music Camp on Vancouver Island, "easily the finest music camp in Canada," in Harry's view. In the fall of 1971 Creech wrote to Harry inviting him to come to Courtenay in the summer of 1972, both as a music instructor and as a composer offering hands-on experience in music creativity. The offer was that he would spend three weeks working with campers and would also compose a new work that would be played at the evening concerts that were very much a part of the program. Harry would be able to exhibit the result of his own creativity. It was a perfect fit for Harry at that time. It enabled him to teach the way he believed all effective instruction should take place. He wrote to Creech outlining his views: "The one thing that is of cardinal importance in any composition course as far as I am concerned is that the students get an opportunity to hear everything they write. There is nothing more useless than the situation that exists in several universities that I know of where the student writes something and then has only his professors' comments to go on. There should be a certain period set aside each week for the performance by students of student compositions. I'm not at all sure that this shouldn't be mandatory." It was agreed that although there would be symposiums to discuss general topics, Harry's students would work with him one-on-one: they would compose, and he would listen and give advice. Even more important, other instrumental students would be found to play the pieces. It was, in a sense, the "Weinzweig-Freedman method," and it would take place in a glorious setting over an intense three-week period.

For the Freedman family Creech's offer was a blessing. These were difficult years financially. Harry was no longer earning a salary as a TSO player. Although he had not been cut off from commissioning revenue in the post–Centennial Year arts funding drought that devastated some of his composer colleagues, with three young and highly intelligent daughters reaching the more costly years of their education he needed money. Even a couple of years later Harry was negotiating with Creech for a more generous stipend. He put it very directly: "It looks as though you will have to get someone else … it's a question of money … I'm going to have to start hustling more work. It also means that what Mary makes, far from being gravy, as it once was, is now indispensable. We simply couldn't get along without it."

Fortunately, Mary's solo career was in full flight, but it was also in these years that she'd had to abandon her role and remuneration as a chorister-soloist with Iseler's Festival Singers. The Lyric Arts Trio was now well established, but in the 1960s they performed only a handful of concerts each year, and the fees they could charge were modest. Indeed, it was not until the early 1970s, when Mary, Robert, and Marion spent several days at St. Mark's Anglican Church in Niagara-on-the-Lake during the Shaw Festival and shared in a warm and deserved reception, that the Trio launched on international tours. Harry had benefited from Mary's involvement with a further CBC commission for a Lyric Arts Trio composition, *Pan*, which became part of the ensemble's more popular repertoire, but such commissions came only sporadically.

In the continuing struggle for survival as a composer, Harry had earned some money adjudicating winds at a talent festival in Winnipeg and had been recruited by the Stratford Festival to write incidental music for three plays, but there was no expectation of future commissions from that source. With the promise of CBC work as a commentator in connection with his Courtenay commission, which was now to be broadcast, Harry accepted Creech's invitation. It represented a chance for his daughters to reach the West Coast and enjoy a few weeks at a venue that would allow them to participate in the music program, to pursue their own instrumental enthusiasms, and to have a good time. Cyndie became an on-site camper but the other two girls shared a cabin with Harry. It turned out well, in spite of Mary's absence.

In an outburst of delight, Harry later exclaimed, "Vancouver Island was a gas." He enjoyed working with students and wrote *Graphic II* as his commissioned work, which was to be played by the Purcell Quartet. Most important, Harry's creative juices had been stirred by the camp experience with young people and the glorious West Coast setting. The New York Times Service described *Graphic II* as "12 minutes of reasonably ingenious if hardly unprecedented coloristic effects." It was hardly an accolade, but the piece received enthusiastic response from the audience and the Purcell Quartet kept it as a selection in its frequently played repertoire for many years. Indeed, years later, the Purcell Quartet asked Harry to write a composition for string quartet and orchestra and caused a minor financial crisis in his life when they lacked the funds to pay him. With expectations of the Quartet's commission Harry turned down other opportunities to compose and worked for months on the Purcell piece — until the spokesman for the Quartet, in a letter of dark humour, informed Harry of a monetary disaster that meant the commission could not go ahead. The spokesman expressed the hope that "you are not too far ahead on the work," and, realizing the impact on the lean income of the composer, concluded, "As a last resort, will you accept wives and children as token recompense?" He promised that the Quartet would "continue to play 'Graphic II' like Angels."

Coming as it did just after his breakup with the TSO, the Courtenay commission turned out to be the beginning of a most productive and satisfying element in Harry's career. For a ten-year period, it was one of the most satisfying aspects of his life. It alleviated, in part, the unsettling task of having to find new sources of revenue in the summer months. In short, it helped prove that he could survive on a composer's income. As well, he was able to indulge himself in the kind of teaching of composition he enjoyed — one-on-one. Despite the pressures, he was writing some of the most important works of his repertoire and was able to catch most of the balls of frantic activity he had thrown in the air in the midst of a frenzy of concern over his family's financial vulnerability in the early 1970s.

In the fall of 1972 Harry began his two-decades-long struggle with a painful back. On the whole, Harry had enjoyed good health throughout his life, but now he faced excruciating back pain that not only focused his mind on his bodily discomfort but also gave him a numb hand that made writing music extremely slow and uncomfortable. For a composer who had no institutional disability plan and was dependent upon writing works on commission, the financial implications of his inability to write were frightening. He became aware of the extent of his vulnerability when he made the point to his insurance company that his inability to produce music had forced him to refuse commissions, resulting in a loss of income for which he felt he should receive compensation. His appeal was met with little understanding and less sympathy. He would receive not a penny.

When Creech invited him to return in the summer of 1973, Harry made it clear that he could not provide a commission in the physical state he was in. He suggested that it might be better for him to "skip a year," that, indeed, the Canada Council that was funding his presence at Courtenay might prefer to spread the opportunity around. Creech was determined to get Harry back, and in a letter to the Council stated, "The success of Harry Freedman's stay exceeded all expectations," and pointed out that he had written other works besides *Graphic II* for student ensembles, including one for eleven French horns, for no compensation whatsoever. Harry, by this time in considerable agony, was driven to reschedule his lecture invitations; in particular, one he was to give to the Hamilton Registered Music Teachers had to be delayed for several months. The full impact of these months can be gauged by the fact that he was forced to sell all his Japanese sumi-e paintings early in 1974. For someone so tied to the visual arts, and to Japanese painting in particular, this was a heartbreaking decision to make.

However, Bob Creech was not prepared to let Harry drift away from the Courtenay Music Camp. He wanted Harry to agree to come to the camp in the summer of 1974. Not only was Harry being courted, but the invitation now included wife Mary and Robert Aitken as well. A commission for Harry to write a violin sonata would also be part of the arrangement. By the late spring, though he conceded that "five weeks at Courtenay had become the highlight of the whole year," Harry still had serious reservations about his health. The pressure was affecting his creative process. In June 1974 he wrote, "I can't get the violin sonata done. I can't get the piece to come together. I keep hearing a particular sound in my head and I can't figure out how to get it on the piano." It was the only occasion when Harry found that his muse was wanting, and he connected it to the ongoing trauma of his back pain. Finally diagnosed as a disc deterioration, the condition would not be resolved until 1993, four operations and twenty years later.

By the late 1970s, the family situation had changed. All the girls would not be coming along to Courtenay every summer. Kim was already looking to Europe and the study of languages at the university level, and the other two wished to remain close to Toronto and programs that were being offered by the Board of Education. Harry and Mary were facing the inevitable experience of seeing their children testing their wings and preparing to fly off into their own separate lives.

Harry failed to complete the violin sonata for Courtenay by the summer of 1974, but eventually it became a piece for violin and piano, *Encounter*, which Steven Staryk premiered two years later. John Kraglund referred to the performance of the work in 1976 as "an impressive exploration of violin sonorities and virtuoso technique beginning with the all but inaudible introduction to the fantastic opening double-stopped passage, and continuing with a dazzling display of trills, harmonics and iron control, until the closing blackout."

When the invitation for the summer of 1975 came, Harry was very tentative in his response and eventually had to turn it down. He was taking a handful of pills each day and his doctor had recommended surgery. In desperation, Harry was ready to experiment with another course and try to improve the condition of his body through the Alexander Technique, a form of healing through movement that had become very popular in the arts community. But in March 1975, Courtenay was far from Harry's mind. He was now down to writing music for only two or three hours a day and he was scheduled to enter hospital on April 9 for an operation. That plan was aborted, however, when the Alexander Technique program emphasizing the carriage of the body, now a part of his daily regimen, appeared to be having a positive effect.

In a moment of madness, Harry, believing that his back was reaching a state of normalcy, took to the golf course. He worsened his condition and was consigned to bed. Once again, an operation was scheduled, but again Harry took the less intrusive path. With careful attention and moderate but consistent exercise and stretching, Harry's back recovered, and in few months he was back to normal with a schedule that made most humans blanch with amazement. However, he realized he could not possibly go to Courtenay that summer. Instead, *Graphic II* was repeated and "was the hit of the evening" at the concert at which it was featured.

It was not the end of Harry's relationship with Courtenay. Bob Creech had an even more ambitious plan for the summer of 1977. He wanted to commission a one-act operetta that would last seventy-five minutes and would engage nine singers and two non-singing actors. He felt he could attract Mavor Moore, by the 1970s an accomplished and many-sided writer, actor, promoter, arts administrator, and broadcaster, to write the libretto. It was based on an Arabian folk tale about a street singer, Dodo, whose mother sells his guitar and sets him up as an astrologer. He is hired to find stolen goods by a somewhat disreputable disco magnate. Dodo is successful and finds the goods, but more importantly he falls in love with the magnate's daughter. The lad is thereby enabled by a thankful father of the bride to remain a singer, happily coupled with a woman who supports his choice of vocation, and is soon on the way to becoming a pop star. It was not a profound work but its humour delighted the Courtenay campers.

Robert Creech thought it could be mounted as an experiment at camp for about $15,000 and that it would have a life beyond. Harry and Mavor completed the operetta, *Abracadabra*, which became the central focus of the 1977 Courtenay Music Camp. The composition did indeed have a further life. Years later, it was revived in Victoria and received considerable popular attention. The music was melodic and perfectly suited the inconsequential plot and limited characterization. Its future was, however, marked by the fact that it had originated at the Courtenay Music Camp, a place that had been a godsend for Harry but was little recognized in the world beyond.

Harry was to visit schools throughout the remainder of the century. His work with young people raised his spirits like nothing else could; he was transported by their energy and delight, so much so that he emerged after hours of conducting and discussion with renewed determination. It resulted in compositions that gave pleasure to both children and adults and gave him hope that the music he wrote for particular occasions would live on to transform future generations of young listeners. It was very much an integral element of his role as a composer and influenced the more prodigious rate of composition for the rest of his life. It was better medicine than any doctor would prescribe. There was healing for countless disturbed young people in the music he composed for them and in the confidence that came from their successful conquest of the challenges these instruments presented. As for Harry, the magic of music kept him sane, capable of overcoming discomfort and pain and pursuing his creative role.

Harry's persistent medical problems were never fully resolved. There were good and bad days, but the music never ceased. It would be simplistic to suggest that there was a cure to his physical woes in the sounds that came from his mind and pen. Yet the fact is that Harry never succumbed. We are learning more about the complexities of mental and physical disease. The work of British composer Nigel Osborne with children in the Balkans after their recent experience of war and violence has revealed new understandings of the impact of making and hearing music on the well-being of children with shattered bodies and dishevelled lives.

Despite the excruciating pain of a back condition that knew no cure, Harry continued to work with children and compose works that revealed truths about the world around him. Learning and healing had transpired over these decades and allowed a life of continued contribution. In place of any medically proven link between these activities there are but muted indications. Nothing more can be expressed; nothing more can be confirmed.

CHAPTER 9

The Artist as Activist

One of the most influential interventions in policy-making of angry Canadian citizens took place in the fall of 1978 on Parliament Hill in front of the Peace Tower in the nation's capital and later in the offices of ministers of the Crown and members of Parliament. The protest was in response to cutbacks to arts organizations and individual artists, and the Canadian Conference of the Arts, led by John Hobday, now director of the Canada Council for the Arts, had organized the event superbly. The participants called themselves the 1812 Committee to remind politicians and the public that it would be the arts that would lead the charge against the overwhelming impact of American domination on Canada's identity and sovereignty. This time, though, the victory for national independence would be achieved through culture rather than through the military strategy and power that had been successfully employed in the War of 1812 by British troops, colonists, and native people. Canada had survived that invasion in the early nineteenth century against impossible odds, and it would be artists who would be the front line of defence in the battle of ideas and for the means of their expression in the twentieth century.

The presence in Ottawa of hundreds of articulate and thoughtful artists had an enormous effect for years to come as successive prime ministers realized how effective a galvanized arts community could be.

Hobday, in a letter to those who had participated, commented on the fact that "in the face of rain, an insane schedule, impossible travel demands and only a ten minute lunch … the dignity and sense of responsibility which the delegates showed were ample proof to the government of our very real concerns about the future of the cultural life of the country." Harry had been there in the front line. His presence and that of the other artists had shaken the nation, and, in doing so, had done something to save it.

The brouhaha around the 1812 Committee surfaced once again a stereotype of the artist — in this case, the composer of music — that persistently reaches the level of the ridiculous. The mindless public imagines that the creation of sound crowds out of the composer's head all consciousness of the issues that decide the kind of society in which the music is to be played or sung. Certainly, if this were true, there would be no expectation that the music would have any impact on the behaviour of that society or, indeed, that the surrounding society would have any influence on the music that is being composed. There are a few oft-repeated anecdotes about Beethoven's outrage over Napoleon's seizure of power in Europe and his subsequent withdrawal of a dedication for the *Eroica* Symphony. Chopin's determination to support the reincarnation of the Polish state, and even, in modern times, Aaron Copland's difficulties with the U.S. House of Representatives Committee on Un-American Activities during the McCarthy period are well known. But these references are seen as mere aberrations. The stereotype remains intact. It can be said without hesitation that no composer negates this irrational perception more completely than Harry Freedman.

To secure a clear image of the values and the ideologies that have gained supremacy in the mind and character of any person, one should examine his or her chequebook. That document reveals the charitable groups and non-governmental organizations that the individual supports. To that piece of evidence must be added the diary that identifies the social and political causes that have commanded the time and energy of the person under examination. Certainly in the case of Harry Freedman such examination reveals that his societal involvement was intense and continuous. Although his early years in Western Canada had introduced him to the democratic left of Winnipeg North, moulding a commitment to a caring and compassionate society, the more conservative-minded community in which he later settled had initially blunted his aggressive stance. The "Symphony Six" incident had thrown him headlong into a fray that challenged his beliefs and his loyalties. By the 1970s all Harry's reticence had disappeared and he had become an activist of the highest order, one who did not just sign petitions or casually join men and women of like mind in one or two voluntary organizations dedicated to the well-being of humankind, but a man who wrote directly to ministers of the Crown, who joined non-governmental organizations and became actively involved in their projects, who made contributions to the coffers of such groups, and who supported candidates in elections who espoused his views. Mary, with a very different background, invariably joined him in these causes, although her schedule provided less opportunity for direct involvement.

The most cursory examination of Harry's charitable giving and active participation in public issues reveals an extraordinary spectrum of support for organizations and causes dedicated to the common good, locally, nationally, and internationally. Some concerned the health and environmental well-being of the community in which he lived or intended to dwell. For example, in the early 1970s Harry ensured that the William Davis Government in Ontario was aware of his complete opposition to the addition of a Pickering Airport to the transportation infrastructure of Toronto, damaging as it would be to the greenbelt and the agricultural community on the eastern fringe of the city. He wrote to Premier Davis and was one of the many who encouraged him to prevent the building of what might have turned out to be as unnecessary a facility as Montreal's Mirabel Airport, today an embarrassment to the government and people of Quebec. The Pickering Airport remains unbuilt, though as circumstances change it appears the opposition may have to be remounted.

When, in 1979, after purchasing land north of Toronto, Harry wrote again to Premier Davis (with a copy to Stuart Smith, leader of the Opposition) about plans to place a hotel complex in the Caledon Hills, Davis replied in some detail, outlining his government's determination to protect valuable farmland and promising to "maintain a permanent secure and economically viable agricultural industry." The hotel complex was never begun. Yet Harry's fears for the area were never at rest, even though the "Caledon retreat" near Creemore was never more than a camping site for the Freedman clan.

With an interest in the countryside north of Toronto much in his mind, in the late 1970s Harry joined those supporting the Elora Gorge Defence Fund. Specifically, it was a group determined to stop the County of Wellington from constructing a bridge across the gorge, thereby threatening the quality of this extraordinary natural beauty spot that revealed much of the land formation of the entire province. The effort failed when the Ontario Municipal Board rejected the arguments put forward and allowed construction. However, Harry accepted the view expressed in a letter to those defeated by official blindness that the campaign did "raise the awareness of the need to protect our heritage" and demonstrated to government agencies that there is "a widespread, sustained support for conservation" and that "heritage and conservation groups can and will fight for long periods and at great cost to protect our environment and that the public is behind these efforts." Harry was engaged in the ecological struggle long before it was fashionable and the results of the deterioration of land, air, and water quality were so apparent.

There seemed to be little interest in the cityscape of Toronto, and Harry, with the eye of an artist, was aware of the importance of great buildings on the minds and imaginations of a seemingly disinterested populace. Thus he joined the campaign to save Toronto's Union Station, a magnificent structure whose dominant presence on a major street near the lakefront of the city was the central landmark that spoke to its railway history. He wrote letters and contacted municipal officials to register his fury that this landmark was in jeopardy. In the twenty-first century, surrounded by glass and metal structures, that building remains as a glorious symbol of a formative era in a great city's development. Coming from a city that the railway had built, Harry was aware of the tragedy the destruction of that building would represent. Even now, the debate around Union Station continues and, one after another, schemes to destroy this landmark have to be turned away.

On a neighbourhood scale, in the mid-1970s Harry became upset over the widening of Wellesley Street, a prominent east-west route joining the University of Toronto and the commercial centre of the city, seeing in this enlargement the loss of a balance of interests and the destruction of yet another viable neighbourhood road enhanced by a healthy mixture of commercial and residential, private and public uses. All were being held hostage to the demands of the motor vehicle. Balance is the constant guide of the creator, especially the composer of music. Appropriate development is but another description of the restraint that allows for an appreciation of heritage and an honouring of the best decisions of that past. It could be said that Harry was a follower of Jane Jacobs, the single greatest force during these years for retaining a balance of interests in Toronto's neighbourhoods in the name of a civil society.

When, in March 1973, the Toronto Arts Foundation at the St. Lawrence Centre, with the help of the Association of Women Electors, wished to bring some attention to the noise pollution that was stifling a vibrant city, Harry was asked to join the panel, along with John Downing, an outspoken journalist who had written extensively on the issue. All panellists brought attention to the physical and psychological damage caused by uncontrolled levels of noise, but Harry contributed his belief in the importance of sound as a cultural feature in a community and explained the impact of the lack of caring about this aspect of the community's health on human communications, both spoken and musical. He favoured a society in which quiet verbal interaction was possible in sidewalk cafés throughout the urban landscape, where the strains of music could be heard as one walked past the Conservatory or the Faculty of Music, and where silence was not unknown in the many parks and open spaces as well as the more remote neighbourhoods that graced the Toronto community.

It was an ongoing cause to which Harry gave time and attention over many years. Listening was the essence for both the appreciation and ultimately the composition of music, and a city in which nothing can be heard but cars, trucks, planes, trains, and industrial activities was not one in which he wished to live. There have been efforts to quiet the noise of the bustling city, but as long as dependence on motor transport is so central to the city's economy and way of life it seems a hopeless struggle. However, the breadth and nature of Harry's commitments are seen as clearly from his support of lost causes as from his efforts on behalf of those battles that resulted in victory.

There were certainly issues that bore upon the health of the creative arts in his country, Canada. In some cases the future of the composer was at stake. Harry kept a watchful eye on national institutions that should have a special interest in Canadian culture. When, in the period of financial restraint that followed the national birthday party called the Centennial Year, which had temporarily expanded government funding of the arts, the National Film Board (NFB) indicated that it did not have money to hire Canadian composers to write music for its films, Harry protested vigorously. He believed that to allow the splendid NFB tradition of commissioning original Canadian music for film backgrounds to be eroded would be a tragedy. In the light of the role that this national institution had played in the development of a Canadian film industry, it was a wise issue to pursue. Although the perpetrators of these negative policies never allow their opponents to claim victory, there is no doubt that the NFB still remains an important player in the production of sound and images that celebrate the essence of the country because individuals like Harry cared enough to protest. It was not just his self-interest as a past and potential composer of film music; indeed, by the late 1970s he had largely lost interest in this kind of composition. However, it was important to his colleagues, and his continuing membership in the Guild of Film Composers and later his presidency of that organization attest to his support of his film score–composing colleagues and, more importantly, the continued presence of an institution devoted to the country's learning about itself, including the nature of its musical composition for film and television.

Harry was interested as well in the quality of the product and the overall influence that music for film could have on the creation of a musical heritage. In June 1972, he wrote to Gerald Pratley, the head of the Canadian Film Development Corporation (CFDC), a body focused on providing financial support for filmmaking, advising him to encourage clients "to hire the finest composers in the country for major film assignments rather than the most commercially successful ones." He suggested that the CFDC make use of the Canadian League of Composers as a source of advisers in setting up a musical advisory board and jurors for panels given the task of making awards for musical excellence in film. The CFDC took his advice, and ultimately Harry found himself on the very committee charged with the task of making awards to Canadian filmmakers.

It was this determination to forward the interests of Canadian film that brought him, in 1980, to send an angry resignation to the Academy of Canadian Cinema, charging that body with accepting standards that were "those of Hollywood," even staging award ceremonies that were "a slavish imitation of the Academy Awards," and charging the leadership with expressing a view that "film that provides a Canadian point of view cannot be a commercial success." Canadian filmmaking has come a long way, but these tendencies remain, and Harry's loss of interest in writing for film came directly from his nationalism, which seemed unfulfilled by that process.

Of all the federal institutions, the one that received the most of Harry's attention, and indeed the attention of the community of music composers, was the CBC. Like all senior Canadian composers who have a nostalgic memory of the CBC's past commitment of resources and broadcast energy to Canadian composition, Harry was a constant critic of a CBC later perceived to be devoid of that commitment and driven to adopt policies that failed to carry out the lofty ideals of the Broadcasting Act.

It is difficult for younger citizens to comprehend the central role that the CBC played in the early stages of Canada's cultural awakening in the late 1940s, '50s, and '60s. It was the CBC that commissioned most of the new works from Canadian composers that came to form the nation's collective repertoire, and without its intervention very little money would have been available for commissioning new music of any kind. There were many local radio stations, but only the CBC recorded recitals and orchestral concerts for broadcast. It had a foreign broadcasting network, which meant that Canadian works were transmitted to other countries. When CBC television finally arrived in Canada in the 1950s, soon to be joined by private networks, the same situation prevailed. That more federal funds went to the CBC than to all the other arts organizations in the country combined could be justified on the basis that broadcasting was the one arts activity that almost every citizen could experience every day. During the last half of the twentieth century, the CBC was the central rock upon which the artistic development of the country depended, not only in music but in theatre as well.

By 1977, the CBC was under fire, with private broadcasters questioning the need for a national citizens' network funded by the taxpayers. The American privatization argument was so pervasive that to many unthinking Canadian citizens it seemed the inevitable future for a corporate free enterprise nation that the private broadcaster should receive support even from agencies originally created to support public broadcasting.

Successful defence of the CBC depended upon gaining the support of those who realized that Canada's nationhood was at stake. If the CBC was to achieve the ratings that would impress the parliamentarians who held the purse strings, more popular programming seemed the only way to go, and those who saw the CBC as the nation's most important purveyor of Canadian culture found themselves at severe risk. The *Globe and Mail*'s Blaik Kirby wrote an article just a few months before Harry took over the presidency of the Canadian League of Composers in the mid-1970s, complaining about the erosion of the arts in the shifting program schedules of CBC Radio. In his public response Harry recognized the problem of maintaining quality programming while in competition for listeners with the less intellectually challenging content of the private sector. This problem had become exacerbated in the scheduling moves occasioned by new technologies that had forced the CBC to create two radio networks, AM and FM. As Harry put it, AM was dead as a medium for serious music and FM had become a network specializing in music for non-listeners, as many Canadians could not even receive FM on their obsolete equipment. He was tough on the CBC administration, now taken over, as he saw it, by the "sausage-makers." While recognizing the pressure on the CBC to secure a large and loyal audience, he argued against what has come to be called the "dumbing down" of programming to appeal to the lowest common denominator. Once again it was a matter of creative balancing that Harry felt the CBC had failed to understand.

The CBC was Canada's last chance culturally, and Harry, along with John Weinzweig, was a continuing critic. Both men saw their role as supporting the fine people, like John Peter Lee Roberts and Srul Irving Glick, who, at the music programming level, were doing their best with reduced resources to keep the light of serious contemporary music burning but were being faced with impossible roadblocks. When Harry became president of the Canadian League of Composers in 1975, putting pressure on the CBC became a central strategy of his tenure in that office. Even a letter from Prime Minister Brian Mulroney congratulating him on his appointment as an Officer of the Order of Canada in 1984 occasioned a somewhat surly reply that demanded appropriate funding for the CBC and, in passing, the Canada Council.

When John Roberts, a popular Toronto politician, was given the responsibility of reviewing the role of the CBC, he wrote to Harry asking for an account of his experience as a composer associated with the CBC. Harry reminded him that, as early as 1967, the CBC had commissioned him to write *Armana*, a piece for full orchestra that Harry admitted has been overshadowed but represented the first time he had tried to incorporate his background as a jazz musician into orchestral work. Harry told Roberts of the scores that he had composed for CBC films and some forty documentaries, including the production of *Rose Latulippe*. "To whatever extent Canadian composers and Canadian music are known throughout the country," he wrote, "we can thank the CBC more than any other organization." He predicted that "unless new music is continually and regularly introduced to audiences, music will die. The concert hall will become a museum." He concluded his letter by explaining that he could speak for all composers in Canada in expressing the hope that the CBC "will be in the vanguard of those efforts" to support contemporary Canadian music and its composers. It was a battle that never ended, and Harry was engaged in a lifetime struggle that has become an element of Canada's determination to remain a sovereign state.

The Roberts exchange brought to Harry's memory just how important the CBC had been to his career. Just three years after *Armana*, the CBC had commissioned a work for alto saxophone, electric bass, and orchestra that was "based entirely on popular idioms." Called *Scenario*, it was ultimately revised for performance on baritone saxophone by Gerry Mulligan, an internationally renowned jazz artist. Harry's contact with Mulligan had occurred when the Dave Brubeck Trio, with whom Mulligan played, arrived in Toronto to collaborate with its symphony orchestra. Mulligan heard a Freedman piece in rehearsal, was impressed, and approached Harry to discuss what ultimately became another CBC commission for a concerto for baritone saxophone and orchestra called *Celebration* to mark Mulligan's fiftieth birthday. Mulligan performed the piece around the world, and a solid bond of friendship between him and Harry and Mary was born.

During one of their several visits, Harry and Gerry Mulligan wondered what might have emerged if the baritone sax had been available to particular great composers of the past, such as Bach and Mozart. As a result, in 1984 Mulligan himself commissioned several composers, Harry included, to write a collection of pieces, *The Sax Chronicles*, that sought to resolve that question, and the piece was performed by Mulligan in Italy, London, Los Angeles, Philadelphia, and particularly at the Lincoln Center in New York City. The Houston Symphony Orchestra recorded *The Sax Chronicles* and the recording received wide distribution among both classical and jazz fans.

Mulligan's influence was crucial. Harry had been somewhat reluctant to emphasize his jazz and popular music past. His association with Mulligan led him to celebrate that heritage. The CBC had been central in its willingness to commission works that crossed the boundaries between serious music and pop. After the Mulligan years, he was not confounded by the purists on either side — the classical music elitists who discounted the view that there could be any true creativity or significant meaning in spontaneous composition, and, at the other end of the spectrum, those who proclaimed that true jazz could not be written down and repeated. Harry believed that the flavour of jazz spontaneity could be retained and its excitement exploited for the most serious purposes. He made use of jazz motifs, harmonies, and rhythms in his most profound compositions. Indeed, one of his most popular works in the twenty-first century was *Duke*, an extraordinary arrangement for symphony orchestra of some of Ellington's most popular music, a piece that is guaranteed to bring enthusiastic audiences to their feet after each performance.

The Canadian Radio Television Commission (CRTC), the regulating body that oversaw broadcasting, both public and private, also demanded Harry's attention. It was this agency that determined the extent of Canadian content on the airwaves, and it would be the CRTC that would provide incentives to both the CBC and private broadcasters to provide theatre, dance, and music "made in Canada." Pierre Juneau, as chair of the CRTC, had encouraged Canadian content, and it was to this dominant figure that Harry launched his letter of support in November 1973: "I can only say that I agree almost entirely with the aims and methods of the Commission. I think the broadcasters should consider themselves fortunate to be dealing with people like you rather than with me, because the idea of turning over the public airwaves to businessmen for their own profit is absolutely insane. The development of radio and television was supposed to herald a new Age of Enlightenment, a new Renaissance in which the arts would flourish as never before. The fact is that this has not happened."

He was not writing for the entire cultural community, as there were colleagues, particularly in the sector of popular music, who looked enviously below the border, where broadcasting was a very lucrative enterprise and very much in the private sector. Understandably Harry's criticisms were resented.

In Harry's view, the "intellectual and spiritual bankruptcy" that threatened the country could be attributed, at least in part, to the commercial policy of serving the lowest common denominator of public appeal. He saw the CRTC as the front line in the struggle to find a way back. Five months later, Juneau received another accolade from Harry when the CRTC's regulations for radio broadcasting demanding specific levels of Canadian content in music and theatre were accepted by the Liberal government. That triumph now having been secured, it was, in Harry's view, time to fight for adequate resources for the CBC to carry out its mandate.

Even educational television fell into the category of public television. When TVOntario (TVO) found itself under attack in 1978 for its programming of *The Jesus Trial*, a modern look at the conviction of Christ as an example of universal intolerance, Harry was adamant that to cancel the program, as some religious groups demanded, would be a restraint of freedom of speech, particularly in the light of TVO's role as a learning channel dependent on public financing. Harry was writing and speaking in support of both the arm's-length principle for a government-sponsored television service and TVO's right to decide upon the programming it should present.

Another object of Harry's concern was Ottawa's National Arts Centre and its responsibility to be a national institution. The building of a cultural centre in the nation's capital within sight of Parliament Hill had been the Centennial Project of the Pearson Government. With all the embarrassments of a massive escalation in the costs of construction and the fact that it was not ready for Centennial Year, the institution had a sour beginning. But it was a splendid structure, with magnificent venues for opera, dance, and theatre addressing both French- and English-speaking audiences. It was expected to be a showplace of Canadian artistic triumph. Significantly, for composers, it had an excellent resident orchestra, not fully symphonic in size but large enough to perform most of the classical repertoire. Even more importantly, it could play nearly all of the Canadian contemporary orchestral works, and the ensemble was small enough to tour with some economy both inside Canada and abroad. For Canadian composers it represented an opportunity to have their works played and noticed.

In 1975, Harry became enmeshed in a controversy when letters to the editor of the *Ottawa Citizen* admonished the NAC Orchestra's conductor, Mario Bernardi, for the lack of programming of Canadian music. Harry had joined the battle in the hope that he could enlarge the debate to include the fact that Canadian symphony orchestras across the country were not playing the works of its own composers. Unfortunately, his particular letter to the editor was construed as an assault on Bernardi and the NAC Orchestra. Harry extricated himself quite effectively, pointing out that Bernardi's defence of his own commissioning and performing policies had been correct, that, indeed, "very few orchestras come close to the NAC Orchestra's record of performance of Canada's music," and apologizing to the NAC Orchestra members and its conductor for any offence that had been given. For a composer to be seen as a critic of orchestras and conductors could be a form of self-annihilation, but Harry had taken on the issue and generalized it, thereby diluting the animosity of both the conductor and the members of the NAC Orchestra in the midst of a nasty controversy, and he had done it in a way that simultaneously made his point regarding the responsibility of Canadian orchestras to play the works of Canadian composers.

In Toronto in the 1960s, Harry was aroused by another fracas involving a public institution. The uproar was caused by the dismissal of its director, Peter Swann, by the Royal Ontario Museum, an institution that, despite its affiliation with the University of Toronto, depended on Ontario government revenues through the Ministry of Colleges and Universities. Swann had been a particularly imaginative director, open and outspoken about his plans, some of which threatened the rather conservative future that the board and its supporters envisioned. Harry believed there was a need for positive and exciting policies that would enhance a stolid operation, too much in the hands of a small, elite clique, and wrote to George Kerr, the Ontario minister of colleges and universities, complaining about Swann's unfair treatment at the hands of the University of Toronto. As would be expected, Kerr simply informed Harry that the government of Ontario had no intention of interfering in the affairs of the University of Toronto and the appointed board of the museum.

Harry's sense of fairness was damaged, as was his belief that government-supported public institutions should be more in the hands of the public they are supposed to serve. In this case, he was drawing on his considerable enthusiasm for the visual elements that enrich our culture and the importance of museums and art galleries as places for celebrating the nation's heritage. For Harry, the magnificent objects designed and produced by former cultures were essential to the inspiration that led him to compose music.

Harry's support went much beyond major museum and art collections. It extended to contemporary painters, sculptors, and filmmakers. He was a continuing supporter of, and contributor to, Three Schools, a Toronto-based avant-garde competitor of the Ontario College of Art, and joined forces with those who supported more generous funding from the Ontario Arts Council and Canada Council. Associated with Three Schools were controversial artists like Michael Snow, whose artistic geese were enhancing the massive, newly built Eaton Centre in Toronto and whose "walking woman" symbol was to be found in a number of public spaces. Snow, a practising visual artist, filmmaker, musician, and outspoken commentator on cultural affairs, was not always popular with arts bureaucrats, nor was the Three Schools institution with which he was linked. Harry was there with Mary when the Three Schools founder iconoclast John Sime finally announced that his institution "was separating from Canada"; in short, the school was clos-ing. For Harry, who considered himself once a visual artist, it was a loss to the community that he resented deeply, and he remained convinced that the lack of public support by funding bodies would result in the tri-umph of "acceptable" arts expression.

But his causes ranged far beyond those that affected the state of the arts. One national issue that greatly concerned Harry was the James Bay Project, the massive development of the power resources of northern Quebec. Harry wrote directly to Donald S. Macdonald, the minister of energy, mines and resources, complaining about the impact of the project on the environment and the way of life of the native people in the region. Aboriginal people had become a concern of Harry's from his earliest contact with the native traders who arrived at his father's fur business in Medicine Hat when he was but a child. Macdonald wrote a "Dear Harry" letter in reply, indicating that by the 1970s the sender had reached a higher status than that of a normal cit-izen. Macdonald pointed out that the federal government was forced to accept the position of the government of Quebec that the James Bay development "appears to be the lowest cost alternative available to meet the increased demand for electrical energy during the period 1979 to 1986." However he assured Harry that "a solution can be developed which will protect the way of life of the native people in this region." As well, his ministry was co-operating with the Province of Quebec to ensure that an extensive environmental assessment took place before the project began. Harry kept up an ongoing monitoring of this development over several years.

In a subsequent exchange with "Don" regarding the well-being of the indigenous people of Canada, Harry concluded his litany of the abuses that were being suffered by Canadian aboriginal peoples with the observation that the "world does not belong to the white races." Harry had seen the seemingly inexorable deterioration of the native people, from the hunters who had proudly exchanged furs for food and neces-sities in Medicine Hat to their humiliating poverty on the streets of Winnipeg and Toronto, and yearned for their restoration both econom-ically and spiritually. The pristine wilderness that so much informed his music included the presence of a proud people.

His concern about Canadian sovereignty was palpable. One would not expect a Canadian composer to have such a highly tuned concern about the erosion of the country's capacity to protect itself against the aggressive takeover of Canadian business and industry. In an October 1976 letter to Macdonald he asserted that the Federal Investment Review Agency (FIRA), which the government had set up to end the full-scale selling-off of Canada's economic power, was virtually useless. It was "not stopping 10 million dollars a day going out of the country … in take-overs, profits, interest payments" to the detriment of present and future generations. "In virtually no case did FIRA prevent ownership of Canadian companies from being transferred to the United States," Harry observed. The minister's reply was innocuous, stressing the fact that it was a free economy and that the government of Canada was, in fact, making efforts to ensure that the process of the Americanization of the Canadian economy would be diverted. Harry's assault on this aspect of the economy was intensified in later years when the Free Trade Agreement negotiated with the United States by the Mulroney Government drew his ire.

In a 1977 exchange of letters with the Committee for an Independent Canada (CIC), a non-governmental organization that Harry had joined, he was informed that the CIC could not afford a pamphlet providing a breakdown of the latest figures on profits and interest being siphoned off by foreign investors. Yet, the letter continued, such statistics were available in regard to "liquor products" handled by the British Columbia and Alberta governments. These statistics confirmed all of Harry's suspicions and he was adamant that this was information that would prove the CIC point that the very future of the nation was at stake.

One of the strongest proponents of a strong nation-state was, of course, Mel Hurtig, the author and publisher who had founded the CIC. The issue came to a head over the cost of oil, and in an exchange of letters with "Don" Macdonald, Harry made his point that provincial greed driven by an oil industry obsessed with corporate profits was undermining the unity of the nation. In his reply, Macdonald criticized Hurtig's calculations of the profits, accompanying his disparaging numbers with a comment that questioned Mel's integrity. "It is regrettable that Mr. Hurtig conveniently forgot to tell his readers how the present average wellhead price of about $6.50 is being divided between governments and industry," Macdonald wrote, and he proceeded to "correct" Hurtig's numbers.

In his reply, Harry informed "Don" that he was unjustly diminishing Hurtig's arguments. "It may be that he [Hurtig] simply assumed that his readers knew what the division was. It's no secret after all. I certainly knew it. I assure you that I am not so ill-informed as to believe that industry was the sole beneficiary of the 13% increase in the wellhead price." Harry then went on to point out that these minor points of detail were of minimal importance. "What I cannot understand is why you feel that this affects, in any way, the gist of Hurtig's argument." The point was that corporate greed was eroding Canadian unity: "Talk about windfall profits!" Harry wrote. Quoting an executive of Imperial Oil who had exclaimed, "We charge whatever the traffic will bear," Harry felt both he and Mel Hurtig had made their points. "Does the government regard such a statement not as an admission but as an expression of perfectly normal, perfectly ethical business practice? Well, I don't. I believe that there is such a thing as excess profits." His solution was that such profits should be taxed as excessive. Yet, at the end of his missive, Harry could congratulate the Liberal government in taxing *Time Magazine* as a foreign publication in spite of that American periodical's proposition that the limited Canadian content allowed it a tax exemption as a Canadian edition and thereby a Canadian publication deserving this advantage.

Harry not only launched his own assessments on the state of the federal government's efforts to support national unity but also joined national organizations and generously supported those whose mandate had similar concerns. The Environmental Law Association, an organization that was focusing on the loopholes in legislation that allowed industries and municipalities to pollute at will, was a recipient of Harry's generosity. His concern for the environment came from an aesthetic rather than a scientific base. His delight in landscape led to a fury over the destruction of the beauty of nature in the interests of short-term profits and private prosperity.

Even though Mary's role as a teacher at universities such as London's University of Western Ontario, Hamilton's McMaster, and the University of Toronto made his dream of living in the country impossible and had resulted in the sale of his beloved Creemore-area property, he continued the fight against any erosion of the Niagara Peninsula as a natural treasure to be protected from private development. Harry's familiarity with the beauty of this part of the province led him to openly congratulate the Ontario government's efforts to contain development on the Niagara Escarpment, even though his own property had been some distance east of that most impressive landform in Southern Ontario and had never been under threat. His fantasy of composing music in the silence of the countryside faded, but his concern for rural Ontario never flagged.

Harry was equally concerned about the environmental hazards produced by cities unwilling or financially unable to ensure that its liquid waste was disposed of in a safe and responsible fashion. He wrote to the Ontario Ministry of the Environment in April 1987 expressing his concern over the "dumping of contaminants into municipal sewers" when the ultimate destination of this waste was the waterways of the province. Though the environment minister of the day, Jim Bradley, assured him that the province's Municipal/Industrial Strategy for Abatement would alleviate the problem, Harry had made it clear that as things stood the provincially owned and operated sewage treatment plants were above the law. Bradley insisted that new legislation passed in 1986, an amending Bill 112 to the Act respecting the Enforcement of Statutes related to the Environment, would mean that these operations could be charged if they violated the provincial regulations for pollution control.

Once again, Harry was pushing a province to bring legislation up to the level of the rhetoric. It was another issue that Harry was unwilling to let go of. If there was one area of public concern that was unpopular as the twentieth century closed, it was the whole matter of waste, both solid and liquid, whether toxic or comparatively harmless. Musicians, and particularly Harry, were mindful that they were composing music for a civil society and for a long-term future. The environment, with all its side issues of global warming and the gradual planetary deterioration of water, land, and air, very much coincided with the time frame of a composer of music who believes his work is destined for eternity. Harry never lost sight of his love of the landscape and his perception of the fragility of the world for which he was writing his music.

The Canadian Civil Liberties Association (CCLA) was the nation's premier organization devoted to protecting the rights of citizens against injustices perpetrated by governments at all levels. It was a difficult time for Canada, as the demand for sovereignty in the province of Quebec initiated responses by the RCMP, including the indiscriminate opening of mail and even the burning of a barn in one corner of the province. It was the CCLA that demanded responsible restraint from the nation's police force. Eventually the organization found itself under severe attack when it opposed interventions allowed by the imposition of the War Measures Act after Pierre Laporte's murder, and CCLA members like journalist June Callwood and NDP Leader Tommy Douglas were badly abused in the public press. Throughout the 1970s the CCLA stood very much alone in questioning this basic abandoning of individual rights, but people like Harry maintained their membership at a time when it could have led to various forms of informal punishment as a composer reliant upon so many public institutions for commissions. The twenty-first century and its obsession with security from terrorist attacks has revealed how close to the abandonment of citizens' rights even the most democratic society finds itself and how relevant Harry's preoccupation was to become.

Harry's compassion was aroused not only by issues and organizations working for the common good but also by individuals. It 1980, Mr. J. Pomelau wrote from his jail cell asking for Harry's help in beginning a career as a songwriter and singer, à la Dylan, Jagger, and Hendrix. Harry wrote back congratulating him on his interest in planning such a future but suggesting Pomelau's sights might fasten on a higher level of musical attainment than that represented by his examples of success and expressing his own view that the achievements of the aforementioned figures "is due entirely to the effects of hype on juvenile tastes." Harry concluded his reply, "In spite of all that I would help you if I could — I just don't know how."

There were even candidates for election that captured Harry's open support and financial contribution as well as his active participation in the election process. At the municipal level, Harry supported William Kilbourn, a York University history professor whose study of William Lyon Mackenzie, the leader of the 1837 Rebellion of Upper Canada, had roused him to seek election to the Toronto City Council, seen to be in the hands of private interests, a modern equivalent of a Family Compact.

Once elected, Kilbourn became the most consistent spokesperson for liberal causes and also espoused support for the arts in a city that was, by the early 1970s, burgeoning with new Canadian theatre, a phalanx of contemporary visual artists, and a plethora of musical organizations. Money for the arts was not a popular cause, but Harry saw in Kilbourn's willingness to forsake the scholarly path for the intense thrust of electoral politics a hope that a more generous approach to strengthening the cultural community would emerge. He was right, and during these years the newly formed Toronto Arts Council, an agency to which both Harry and Mary gave many years of their time, played a major role in the expansion of the arts. Kilbourn received a contribution from Harry and Mary each time he ran for public office.

At the federal level, it was Gordon Cressy, campaigning for the NDP in the St. David's riding, who gained Harry's approval. The NDP had been formed from the fragments of the CCF, Canada's democratic socialist party of the 1930s, '40s, and '50's, and the Canadian Labour Congress, the umbrella body of the trade union movement. During subsequent years, the NDP struggled to end the apparent willingness of Liberal governments to allow American control of the Canadian economy to expand exponentially. It was a cause that Harry had no hesitation in supporting, and Gordon Cressy was a bright young academic who could articulate the demands of the workers seeking to achieve social justice and particularly the need to grasp control of Canada's resources and industrial productive capacity. Cressy's constituency was not NDP territory, but in the 1970s Harry gave time and money nonetheless.

But it was at the international level of political action that Harry was most actively engaged. The 1960s had seen the height of optimism that the idealism permeating Western society at the end of the Second World War might break through and lead towards a more just division of the planet's wealth. The last decades of the twentieth century demanded a response to Pearson's initiatives to see a major shift of financial resources to lesser developed countries. Harry was a contributor to voluntary efforts such as OXFAM, an organization dedicated to an intervention on behalf of the world's poorest of people, particularly children.

But the 1960s and '70s was also a time when consideration of the dangers of the Cold War surfaced along with the realization that the nuclear arsenal in the hands of the Soviet Union and the United States threatened the future of humankind. Dr. Norman Alcock, a distinguished Canadian nuclear scientist deeply concerned about the possibility of a war that would annihilate human life, was driven to make the planet a safer place for its inhabitants. Alcock's training led him to consider the fact that decision-making processes depended on research, and only through the gathering of factual material could there be found alternatives to arms races and war. The reality was that over 90 percent of national resources were spent on making war, and only a miniscule amount had ever been devoted to finding peaceful solutions. The creation of a Peace Research Institute became his cause, and it was one that Harry found attractive and logical. He joined the Toronto chapter of the institute and became its treasurer for a short time, giving his energy to a full-scale campaign to secure both attention and resources. The campaign failed. There were not enough people who were prepared to put their faith in anything but weapons and a strategy of nuclear deterrent against those perceived as enemies.

However, for Harry it was an opportunity to become a member of the "peace" community made up of organizations seeking common security based on disarmament and policies of social and economic justice. His music never directly reflected this passion. There is no War Requiem in Harry's repertoire accosting the madness that leads to death, pain, and the destruction of a world in conflict. Yet there is in nearly all his work, particularly in his larger works like his symphonies and the Concerto for Orchestra, tension and confrontation that is resolved in the sounds of mutuality and inclusiveness, sometimes by the ultimate common bond — silence. It was part of Harry's expectation that his country would lead the world in this quest for world peace.

Throughout these years, the one abiding hope of the internationalist seeking peace with freedom has been the presence of the United Nations. Even with all its faults — the total dependence on the nation-state as the basis of its polity, the predominant influence of the United States, the unwieldy size of the assembly, and the much-resented power of the permanent members of the Security Council, to name a few — the United Nations stood as humankind's only hope. All supporters would seek to initiate reform, but no sane observer of the world scene could imagine a termination of this institution.

Harry was convinced that Canada could play a larger role, and he continually made the point that this country's foreign policies must be in the direction of strengthening the UN. In 1972 he wrote to Mitchell Sharp, the minister of external affairs, demanding that the Canadian government "press for fundamental reform that will make the UN a truly effective world organization." Sharp replied that Canada was supporting a review of the UN and would co-operate in any process that resulted in a reform and strengthening of this agency. Harry was also a member of the World Federalists, an organization devoted to reforming the UN to make it a more democratic and effective agency for peace. In short, Harry was a member of the army of Canadians that continued to expect its government to put its reliance on common security through this frail and often ineffective organization, recognizing, even in a new century, that it was the only sane alternative to general conflagration that would end human existence.

Is the prominence of Canadian themes and arts personages in Harry Freedman's music the result of his preoccupation with supporting causes that have an element of idealism, justice, compassion, and national survival? Surely, the answer must be yes, but these societal concerns influenced the very nature of his composition. Although Harry could never be seen as a minimalist composer, there is a sparseness in his music, a consciousness that eschews overblown musical works of any kind. There is the environmentalist's style in the absence of excess that speaks of a mind attracted to justifiable needs rather than luxurious expansiveness. There is humour in his music, particularly in the rich, rhythmic elements, that recognizes the irony of history as well as the absurdity of contemporary human failings. Yet, in his determination to honour his artist colleagues, there is a commendable recognition of the greatness of spirit that can make a difference in the lives of others. His music exudes a focused attention to the essential matters of body, mind, and spirit. In short, his composing and his social action were of a piece.

He also gave time to providing leadership to colleagues confronted with the fundamental issues of justice that diminished their roles as composers. He is an example of a man who sees the composer's commitment to a life of creativity as a single garment of concern for the well-being of society and as a struggle against the greed and power-mongering that diminish and dehumanize the people for whom he composes.

CHAPTER 10
The Challenge of the Mass Media

Harry recognized that radio broadcasting was more than a source of personal income. It was a major lever in transmitting not only music performance but also an understanding of the nature of modern composition. It could be the significant mechanism by which music could reach out to a general public far beyond the narrow confines of the small serious contemporary classical music community that attended Canadian League of Composer or Ten Centuries or New Music concerts. Harry had no reticence in flaunting his capacity to be witty and articulate. His broadcasting work of the 1950s and '60s meant that by the mid-'70s he was a familiar voice on radio, as both a performer and a commentator. He was well prepared to address the challenges of television.

Harry was encouraged by the experience of his partner, Mary, who had been successful on Winnipeg's radio stations and who had made such an easy transition to the studios in Toronto soon after she had arrived. She had the attention of the CBC, whether it was for opera or popular fare, and it was a major source of her survival income while she studied at the Conservatory. In the late 1950s, Harry was contracted to do the music segment for a youth-oriented television program called *Junior Round-up*, and he enjoyed the task of researching material, writing scripts, and acting as a host before the camera. He was amazed by the number of letters he received from mothers who watched the program with their children

and expressed appreciation for the clarity and integrity of his performance. It was another opportunity to reach a future generation who might
come to understand his music and its meaning.

He was also encouraged by the responses he received from friends
and listeners to his appearances on adult programs. Composer R.
Murray Schafer's wife, Jean, commented on one CBC program to
which Harry had been invited to contribute: "I just have to write you a
note. I'm listening to you doing the program 'New Records'. Anyway I
wish they would get you to do things more often. You have a real way
with broadcasting. Such a nice straightforward style — clear in meaning yet never pretentious or stuffy! After all those canned and processed
CBC fellows you're wonderful. You wave the flag too! (Maple Leaf of
course) … but that's fine."

Jean's note included a postscript from Murray indicating that Harry
was becoming another Milton Cross, a reference to the ubiquitous commentator on the weekly Metropolitan Opera radio broadcasts whose
voice was all too familiar and whose style was self-consciously unique.
Murray's advice was that he should eschew the temptations of broadcasting and get on with his composing.

In the early 1960s, CBC Radio had launched a weekly program called
The Learning Stage, and by 1963 Harry had become a regular performer.
It was a time when Canada's national network was still under the influence of those who saw an educational role for the broadcast media. From
the outset, the strongest supporters of the CBC's mission were the members of the Canadian Association for Adult Education (CAAE), galvanized by Roby Kidd and Alan Thomas and a body of nationalists, many
of whom had been members of the Canadian Broadcast League, led by
Alan Plaunt and Graham Spry. Both organizations had been instrumental in galvanizing support for the creation of a public broadcasting system in the 1930s. Harry had precisely the same view of radio broadcasting as the CAAE — that it should be a force for spreading knowledge and
understanding and also a source of cultural enhancement. In a way that
television has never been, radio in the 1940s and '50s was very much a
binding force for a country that dwelt on the border of the most powerful nation in world history. In short, for Harry, radio and television
broadcasting were not competing technologies synonymous with enter-

tainment. For each there was a much larger and more serious agenda. This ideological congruence was even more important when, in 1975, he became president of the Canadian League of Composers and was expected to be the spokesperson for composers from coast to coast.

As far as the technical demands of the medium went, Harry was already comfortable with the presence of the microphone from his days of playing with dance bands in Winnipeg. He had developed from a shy, withdrawn teenager to an easygoing commentator on stages while in the armed forces and particularly on the morale-building tour of the northern building sites of the Alaska Highway towards the end of the war. It was only a matter of time in the 1940s and '50s before he would find his way from performing in the CBC Symphony and with small ensembles playing the accompaniment both for drama and variety programs to the spoken word. Harry had come to realize that music composed for symphonic and chamber music ensembles in the post–Second World War decades was not receiving acceptance by a broad audience in the concert hall. There was a need to explain the strategies of contemporary composers and to give some pre-eminence to the names of the pioneer creators of this music if it was to have any audience in what was becoming a very unreceptive world to thoughtful reflection and purposeful listening.

Also, he realized that it was only through this reaching out that the composer could come to appreciate the reactions of people who were seeking to understand these modern musical idioms. Thus radio became an essential mechanism in these mid-century years, whether it engaged or enraged individual listeners. In the case of the CBC, not only Canadian listeners were being reached. A solid audience had developed in the northern states of the America Union. On *The Learning Stage*, a series that had become a CBC Radio cultural feast, Harry was asked to do a program on Bela Bartok, a creator for whom he had a particular enthusiasm, having spent an entire summer in the early 1950s studying every published composition that the troubled composer had written. He used Bartok's music as a bridge to explain the sounds that listeners to contemporary classical music were seeking to understand.

Helen Brown of Hamburg, New York, responded perhaps on behalf of many listeners when she wrote, "I have a quarrel with you — and many others — about learning to understand modern music by much listening." She felt she simply became "more and more bewildered or irritated because I don't for the life of me see where the music is going. It's all a jumble of disconnected sounds — not even pleasant sounds, I may add. The instruments shriek and squeal and never, never, sing." She wanted specifics. "How about some examples of tone and how composers use it? How is harmony used? Or is it? Examples, please!" Even with these questions revealing intense antagonism, this avid listener promised to be at her radio the following week!

Not all responses to Harry's interest in twentieth-century composition were negative. When Harry appeared in a segment of an ongoing series called *Soundings*, another American woman, Miss Elsa Hoffman, wrote to him: "When you turned up on a recent 'Soundings' I felt the pleasure of unexpectedly meeting an old friend. Furthermore, I listened with better understanding and, therefore more enjoyment than if I had not met you before on 'The Learning Stage.' When you placed Beethoven, my favourite composer, on the summit and yet discussed with authority and ease entirely different modes of musical expression, I really paid attention. Neither antagonized by over-simplification, nor confused by boring ever-emphasis on esoteric detail, I was fascinated at being given clues to sorting out what had seemed meaningless cacophony."

Harry was discovering that the absence of a blatant scholarly approach to contemporary music had ironically fashioned him into an effective communicator. CBC programmers realized that they had a treasure in their midst, and Harry became a regular guest on programs devoted to modern music and its composition. In 1967 he received a contract to appear on CBC Radio's Thursday music program, a contract that continued through 1968 and 1969. For these segments he received $105 per program, a payment that included his research efforts and preparation of script material. It was not generous but it made it more possible for Harry to consider abandoning the TSO and the English horn.

By the 1970s, the new technology of television beckoned. However, his approach to media attention was not one that thrilled all of his colleagues. The positive negotiations between CAPAC and the Canadian Association of Broadcasters (CAB) had resulted in a release of money that could be devoted to the production of a thirteen-week series on the work of Canadian composers. It was to TVOntario that the CAPAC–CAB Committee turned. The first program was to examine the career of Healey Willan, at that time considered Canada's single internationally recognized creative icon in the field of musical composition. Instead of offering a paean of praise, Harry took a different approach. While appreciating Willan's undoubted genius as a splendid church musician, Harry also saw him as very much connected to nineteenth-century English music.

Harry's program was criticized as being too full of personal references, too popular in tone, and lacking in the dignity such a figure should command. At a preview of this first production, it was felt that the program should be re-edited, and CAPAC was prepared to cover the cost. Indeed, the committee began to question the very concept of an hour-long program, and the decision was taken to reduce the programs to half an hour, obviously long enough to outline the strengths and the contributions of a selection of Canadian composers but not long enough to engage in controversial questions surrounding the particular composer being featured.

Harry had probed the kind of television that might attract the attention of a significant segment of the watching audience and had discovered that the very people he sought to assist, the representatives of Canadian composers, were not prepared to take any risks or threaten the reputations of their colleagues. It was a lesson that Harry was not willing to learn. However, producers who wanted a solid, no-nonsense, often controversial commentary continued throughout the century to draw on his broadcasting skills.

Harry took very seriously the fact that he had been elected president of the Canadian League of Composers in 1975. He had been one of the founders, the first secretary, and had served on the executive at certain points over the two decades of the CLC's existence. John Weinzweig saw in him the kind of determined figure who would support his colleagues and take the opportunity as president to identify and confront the injustices that composers felt they were collectively facing. Such opportunities came soon after his election. The new technologies of broadcasting and recording were disrupting the comfortable hold that serious music had achieved in the programming of the national network. As Canadian composers depended so much on the CBC for commissions, the very livelihood of composers as well as their main mechanism for reaching the public with their music was in danger. Confronting the CBC became Harry's major role as CLC president. His understanding of the workings of CBC decision-making from all his years of professional contact made him an effective opponent.

Harry also had a broad view of the societal pressures the CBC faced. In 1976, he was in constant communication with other groups who opposed the changes that were being proposed. The most consistent confrontation with the CBC came from a British Columbia organization centred in Vancouver calling itself the B.C. Committee for CBC Reform. Within his first few months as president of the CLC Harry could report to them that he had met twice with the head of English-speaking radio, William Armstrong, who had assured him that there would be no overall change in the amount of serious music being broadcast. However, Harry had to warn this committee that in the long run, "the CBC was falling into the hands of people whose values seem to have originated with the Madison Avenue boys." He recognized that radio and particularly television broadcasting was tied to "the ratings game." The CBC that had been created in the 1930s to ward off the loss of a Canadian identity then being swamped by a flood of American radio signals was in the 1970s falling into the hands of the same commercial forces that had motivated its creation. In Harry's view, these powerful influences could weaken the CBC's capacity to play either its unifying or its educational role!

Harry found himself in an embarrassing dichotomy of relationship with the mighty CBC. At the same time that, as president of the CLC, he was taking on an adversarial role on behalf of his colleagues, he was, as a composer and commentator, dependent on positive interactions with the CBC. That same year he was invited to host a program, *The Entertainment Section*, on CBC's FM Network and offered $600 for this service along with $100 travel allowance to reach the Ottawa studio from which the program originated. Harry ignored the threat to his personal relationship with the CBC and continued his role as a critic.

By the end of 1976, the B.C. Committee for CBC Reform had created a newsletter, and Harry was asked to contribute his views to that publication, yet early in 1977 he was invited to cohost a CBC Radio program in a series, *Music of the Twentieth Century*, that would focus on the works of his colleagues in the CLC. Balancing both roles created tension that stretched Harry's patience and restraint.

As president of the CLC in the mid-1970s he felt he had a crucial role — making Canadian music a more visible phenomenon in the Western world. He drew heavily on the impressions that Mary had brought back from her trip to the contemporary music festivals in Europe in 1968. She had been staggered by how little was known of Canadian music and composers. As soon as he was elected, Harry was ready to use the "old" technology of air flight to visit the major centres of cultural action and use his position to secure some attention. He decided to attend the International Society of Contemporary Music (ISCM) meeting in Paris in September 1975. There he carried the Canadian flag and spoke on every occasion about the expanding number of Canadian composers and compositions. It went well, and the fact that Mary and the Lyric Arts Trio were performing in Paris at the same time meant that a warm reunion of busy husband and wife was made possible.

Mary, on her return in 1968 had challenged the Canadian League of Composers and the Canadian Music Centre and all the other music umbrella organizations to join in an effort to change the situation that allowed the world to ignore Canadian composers and their music. But her efforts were limited by the energy and resources of Canadian agencies and the minimal interest on the part of the arts operations in Europe.

Harry made a major effort to bring at least the CMC and the CLC together to find common projects that would extend the reach of Canadian music, even offering a seat on the CLC board to the CMC membership, an invitation that could then be reciprocated by the CMC. One matter continued to haunt Harry, and he felt that both these organizations could confront it: commissions and first performances of contemporary works were given support by granting agencies, particularly the Canada Council and provincial arts councils, but there was little assistance for second and third performances of these works. It seemed to Harry that unless there were repeated performances Canadian audiences would never come to appreciate these compositions and these works would never enter the regular repertoire of Canadian ensembles. It seemed a lost cause, but one worth fighting for. It remains a continuing debate among granting agencies, arts councils in particular, inevitably faced with inadequate funding.

However, the ISCM and more regional conferences and conventions of contemporary music contributors and supporters were less prestigious in Harry's eyes than the Warsaw Autumn Festival. In his grant application to the Department of External Affairs he referred to this gathering as "the most famous festival of contemporary music in the world." Once again Harry played the salesman for his colleagues. He was able to report to David Aniedo, the assistant director of cultural affairs in the External Affairs Department, that though musically the Warsaw Autumn Festival was "most stimulating," what was most encouraging to him was "the realization that a program of Canadian music could stand up to most of the twenty-two programs" he had heard at that event. As well, things had obviously changed since Mary's visits to European festivals in 1968. Perhaps in part because of her efforts, Harry discovered that the Committee of the Warsaw Autumn Festival knew him and his work, as well as that of several other Canadian composers. Happily, Canadian compositions were now becoming a known presence in the minds of the more sophisticated European contemporary music lovers.

Conversations with European composers in Warsaw reminded Harry of another issue involving technology that he kept in the forefront of the CLC agenda during his tenure. His hosts had asked about why there were so few recordings of Canadian music available. "I was ashamed to have to explain that the Canadian recording industry is a typical example of our branch plant economy: that American companies which dominate the industry and control the distribution of records are not the slightest bit interested in promoting Canadian music." It was a situation Harry determined to change. It was another lost cause that he pursued relentlessly throughout his career as a promoter of Canadian music and its composers.

Of these two pioneers, it was Mary who made the initial breakthrough in the recording field. She had by 1967 participated in the most prestigious production of Canadian contemporary music recordings that had ever been envisaged. It was the major recording giant, RCA Victor, with considerable co-operation from the CBC, that allowed the project to be launched; indeed, it was the music from tape recordings of performances over the CBC network that had formed the artistic centre of the project. It was Centennial Year, and it was assumed that both the CBC and RCA Victor stood to gain from the wave of patriotism that would surely sweep across the country and create a lively market. The *Globe and Mail*'s Blaik Kirby called it "the biggest recording project ever undertaken — and the biggest of its kind in the world." In his view it had "bowled over leading U.S. critics and brought Canadian music a new and glittering reputation south of the border." It included what one report called a gathering of "the latest and hairiest and most contemporary music by 32 Canadian composers, 5 Canadian orchestras, 2 choruses, 20 soloists and chamber groups."

This sudden emergence of interest did exactly what Harry had claimed that the Canadian recording industry could do if it would only put its attention to Canadian musical composition and promote and market the result. Most surprising, the project received enormous attention from the American press, with the *Saturday Review*, the *Washington Star*, and the *New York Times* providing astounding coverage. As American journalists put it, "Musical Canada has come of age," and the recordings had "signalled the emergence of Canada as a power to be reckoned with in the musical cosmos." They went so far as to say the country was now "firmly on the musical map as a major power." It was entirely too exaggerated a claim, but it certainly focused attention on the presence of a considerable Canadian repertoire for a few days. Unfortunately it turned out to be a Centennial Year aberration, and the normal disinterest of the recording industry prevailed in 1968.

During these years, Mary was at the right place in Canada's broadcasting centre and at the right time in her career, with both the talent to perform contemporary music and the skill to bring these compositions forward most dramatically. She had been approached since her days at the Conservatory by a host of Canadian composers — including R. Murray Schafer, Harry Somers, and Serge Garant — who simply wanted to hear their music performed well. Mary became the most prolific performer in the RCA Victor–CBC series of recordings. She was described by a reviewer of the recording of Schafer's *La Testa d'Adriane* as "a most reliable performer — at the very least, sensational." She was the most consistently praised of all the performers on the released discs.

She sang Harry Somers's *Twelve Miniatures*, songs set to the words of Japanese haiku poems, Serge Garant's *Anerca*, Bruce Mather's *Orphée*, and Norma Beecroft's *From Dreams of Brass*. It was apparent that Mary was the Canadian interpreter of choice for recordings of Canadian music for solo soprano.

The entire enterprise was further evidence for Harry, who had conceded that the technology of the recording was the most effective mechanism for achieving public familiarity with the works of Canadian composers. He had been a supporter of a CBC dedicated not only to broadcasting but also recording Canadian artists and, most importantly, Canadian musical composition. He applauded the initiative of the Canadian Music Centre, which had become a major source of recordings of Canadian works. Nevertheless, in spite of his occasional enthusiastic encouragement for both CBC and CMC efforts, Harry continued to make the point that the major commercial recording companies still gave little commitment to Canadian music.

While celebrating Mary's success, one that had a major impact on the direction of her career, Harry was a relentless critic of the sell-off of Canadian control over the major sectors of the Canadian economy and could see how this general lack of national policy in a matter as central as its recording industry was affecting his own work and career along with those of his CLC colleagues. He worked assiduously to make the federal government aware of the serious disadvantage it was to every Canadian composer that there was no Canadian owned and operated recording company. There were promises of action from various federal government officials, even promises of direct subsidization — but nothing happened.

There was one area where Harry felt he could offer advice. He had been asked by foreign music critics why it was that Canadian music ensembles touring the United States, the United Kingdom, and Europe played little Canadian music. One prominent German composer had observed, "We get all the Brahms and Tchaikovsky and Dvorak we need from our *own* orchestras. What we'd like to hear from *your* orchestras is some of *your* music." Harry's suggestion to federal bureaucrat David Aniedo was simple. "The condition for any touring grant from External Affairs should be that Canadian music would be prominently featured in the programs of such recipients." Certainly the pressure was on, but the government was reluctant to be directive and thereby face the charge of interfering in the programming of an arts organization. Harry concluded that "there is a growing interest in Canadian music throughout the world" but could not resist the opportunity to contrast this interest with "the continued indifference of Canadian performers and performing organizations" to compositions by citizens of their own country.

The message of the need for Canadians to hear and appreciate the music of their own composers was a continuing theme as Harry spoke at countless meetings, conferences, workshops, and seminars — in short, wherever there was an audience, receptive or not. He was particularly popular on university campuses and meetings of music teachers in every province. In the 1970s alone Harry turned up at McMaster, the University of Windsor, the University of Western Ontario, Queen's, and York University in Ontario and the University of British Columbia and Brandon University in the West, purveying the same message — the desperate need to encourage and nurture the performance of Canadian music in a society obsessed with a populist consumerism that stressed pop selections. He emphasized the fact that the loss of an indigenous serious contemporary musical presence was at stake, and it threatened the development of a thoughtful and reflective nation.

During the 1960s and '70s, Harry was particularly active as an adjudicator. His experience in the classroom, his long role as a performer, and his continuing interest in the improvement of music performance made him a perfect choice, and his increasing public role on radio and television, and later the status of being the president of the CLC, gave him a presence that brought a certain prestige to these events. Once he was freed from TSO duties and able to travel extensively and before his CLC duties began in 1975, the CBC had hired Harry to adjudicate the winds at their 1972 festival back home in Winnipeg, and in the same year he adjudicated the Original Compositions Section of the Ottawa Music Festival Association. Two years later, he accompanied Victor Feldbrill in forming a jury to adjudicate a student composition competition sponsored by the TSO, and in 1976 he was asked to be a member of the jury for the National Competition for Young Composers that CBC producer David Jaeger was conducting. Through all these years he was involved with

Canada Council juries in a number of areas. The year 1977, his last year as CLC president, brought a seat on the jury of the Canada Council making grants in aid of the Publication and Promotion of Canadian Music, as well as on a Canada Council jury giving grants in a Community Musicians Program, both causes he had pushed in his leadership role.

These were years of maddening lack of confidence on the part of artists that they could be anything but second rate if they remained in Canada. Harry saw these competitions and festivals as opportunities to play a part in raising the standards of performance and strengthening the confidence of both performers and creators. He never stopped encouraging the sponsors of festivals to make use of Canadian works as test pieces in every category of performance that they were seeking excellence.

In spite of these years of defending the deserving qualities of his composer colleagues, the final year of his tenure as CLC president occasioned the most shocking example of Harry's sharp wit when he aimed it at the pretentiousness of some composers with a predilection to write totally unintelligible program notes when their compositions were being premiered. Susan Mertens of the *Vancouver Sun* put it succinctly in her review of Harry's 1977 premiere of *The Explainer*: "Freedman is saying and saying it in the tradition of the best satirists, with considerable wit and charm — *cut the crap*."

The Explainer was written for a small ensemble of five instruments, and both musical sound and written word were employed to give vent to the orchestral players' frustration with the contemporary composer. Mertens saw that "much of the humour comes from the discrepancy between the written word and the musical translation — a case of deflated reality, as it were." She also saw *The Explainer* as an example of "the composer as clown" and concluded that the piece "should be required playing once a season for every new music group — and required listening for all contemporary composers."

The technology of film was an even greater challenge facing Harry and his CLC. The fate of Canadian feature film production was largely in the hands of the corporations that controlled access to the screens in Canada and were a part of the conspiracy devised to protect the near-monopoly that Hollywood had achieved in the English-speaking feature film industry. Ironically, for the few small film producers in Canada, competing with the massive studios in the U.S.A. seemed to mean abandoning the proud traditions that had been developed initially at the National Film Board, such as turning to Canadian composers when soundtracks were in need of music.

In the light of the fact that the NFB, under the founding headship of John Grierson, had become a leading creator of the documentary film and had developed a phalanx of outstanding film track composers initially led by Louis Applebaum, there was a major issue at hand. Harry had already, as a citizen and composer, complained of the abandonment of this practice in the late 1960s and now suggested to film producers and government agencies responsible for subsidizing the film industry that the Canadian League of Composers should be represented on the Canadian Film Awards Committee where an influence on film music could be exerted.

In 1976, as president of the CLC, Harry was invited to join and bring his voice to the issue of encouraging the industry to seek out the best of the country's composing talent in producing the finest quality of feature film as well as continuing to lead the world in the production of the documentary film. From this vantage point, Harry was able to view the finest film work being produced by Canadians in the knowledge that little of these visual treasures were ever being seen by Canadian citizens in Canadian movie houses, which were nearly all controlled by American interests. It was another cause to which he gave decades of attention, resulting in seemingly countless speeches and endless written commentary.

While playing the role of critic of the film industry, Harry was also one of the most able and, in the 1950s, '60s, and '70s, most prolific writers for film destined for both the movie house and the television screen. It was, after all, the most lucrative source of income for composers in the first half of the twentieth century. Even internationally renowned composers like Shostakovich, Prokofiev, and Copland had written for film.

One would have thought that this form of music composition would have been perfect for Harry in the light of his visual arts route to musical composition. In an unexpected way, his respect for visual presentation and its capacity to inspire understanding was a deterrent. Harry never ceased to explain that, for him, a painting or indeed any visual experience could not be rendered musically. A composer could form and express an impression, but it was the overall impact of the visual reality that had to be conveyed by musical sound, not the details of the scene depicted. When in his composition *Images* he identified Lawren Harris's *Blue Mountain*, Kazuo Nakamura's *Structure at Dawn*, and Jean-Paul Riopelle's *Landscape*, he made no attempt to use a particular rhythm, harmony, or specific instrumentation to conjure a certain depiction in the minds of listeners. Rather, the music conveyed the power, the beauty, or the despair evoked by each work of art. This was the baggage that Harry brought to the writing of background music for film, and though he became involved in this genre early in his career, it dominated his work for only a short time.

It was Harry's strong commitment to music as an art form that demanded his full concentration. He stated constantly that the greatest threat to the composition of serious modern music was the presence of unending musical sound on car radios and in stores, elevators, and other public spaces. Its pervasive reach vied for the partial attention of people everywhere, thereby assuring that music achieved automatic trivialization. Film music, by definition, is very much in the background; indeed, if it is conspicuous it loses its essential purpose and diverts attention from the narrative and the image. That dichotomy was never fully resolved in Harry's mind and was another reason for his lack of full commitment to this form of music making.

While still working as a full-time member of the TSO, Harry had come to realize that in spite of these reservations he would have to come to terms with the role of being a composer for film. When, in 1956, he was approached by former Winnipegger John Hirsch to write the incidental music for a TV documentary called *Shadow of the City*, he succumbed. It worked well. He found that he could write to the time segments that were specified quite efficiently, and his enormous experience with the sounds of instruments as well as his broad knowledge of virtually every aspect of musical form resulted in work that was both professionally and personally satisfying. In particular, the value of his eclectic contact with every form of musical expression paid off. A year later, he wrote a jazz score for a feature film, *The Bloody Brood*, and it too satisfied his creative expectations, particularly his delight in delving into his jazz and popular music past.

The year 1958 concluded with Harry writing the incidental music for a documentary by Douglas Leiterman on the Doukhabours, a religious community that a westerner like Harry knew well. In 1959 Harry wrote for a series of TV documentaries — Patrick Watson's *Where Will They Go* and *Kingston Pen*, then Leiterman's *The United Nations* and *Election*, and finally Ross McLean's *India*. These were all produced by distinguished filmmakers and were all commissioned by the CBC. In fact, this prodigious collection of documentaries represents Harry's entire repertoire in 1959. Never again did he allow his energies to be so focused on writing background music for film. He continued to make a few forays into the world of film for TV broadcast during nearly each year of the 1960s, and although his greatest success came in that decade, he ensured that he would never be perceived as an incidental music composer.

Although Vincent Tovell's *Micheline*, a TV portrait of Micheline Beauchemin, captured Harry's interest in 1961, as did Douglas Leiterman and Beryl Fox's *20 Million Shoes* in 1962, both CBC productions, Harry was pulling back from this form of composition despite his excitement with the outcomes of this collaboration. Yet even as his enthusiasm for film music composition cooled, his contribution to a 1963 CBC-TV drama, *Pale Horse, Pale Rider*, produced by Eric Till, was another high point in this genre of composition.

In 1963, Harry met the one filmmaker who came to demand his very best effort. Paul Almond asked him to write the music for a CBC documentary called *The Dark Did Not Conquer*. Both men realized that they had similar views on the nature of film art. Paul Almond had ambitions to go far beyond the documentary and to find a future in the highly competitive but professionally satisfying world of the feature film. Almond had already achieved an enviable reputation, having found a niche in producing films that one critic called "visual poems about the spiritual turmoil of beautiful young women … studies of fear and the confronting of one's past." He was to bring Harry to new levels of accomplishment, and the mid-1960s were the pinnacle of his success as a screen music writer. Although their relationship continued with

Almond's CBC drama *Journey to the Centre*, followed that same year by *A Spring Song*, and a year later by *Romeo and Jeannette* and *Let Me Count the Ways*, these were but steps toward the two films that Almond was planning to complete with Genevieve Bujold, *Isabel* in 1967 and *Act of the Heart* in 1968.

These two films represent Harry's most effective scores. For *Act of the Heart* he wrote a complete cantata that was to have a life of its own as a concert piece. The highest award that is given by the industry was the Etrog Award for the Best Musical Score (later renamed the Genie by the Academy of Canadian Cinema and Television), and it was to Harry that it was presented in 1970. He was to write the incidental music for a number of television dramas, almost entirely for CBC and some directed by Paul Almond, but *Act of the Heart* was the mountaintop. There were other great moments. An outstanding documentary by Vincent Tovell on Vincent Massey commanded his finest efforts, as did Beryl Fox's documentary *The Mills of the Gods*, a film on Vietnam that was described as having "caught with searing accuracy the overwhelming tragedy" of the conflict in that unhappy country. It was commended for its "raw and gut-wrenching quality" by Jim Bawden in the *Sunday Sun*. Little wonder that it won the CBC's Wilderness Award, as well as the George Polk Memorial Award as an outstanding television documentary of 1965, the first such award won by the CBC in its eighteen years of producing such films.

The Etrog recognition, certainly the most prestigious award he'd received in almost a quarter-century of work as a composer, was important for many conflicting reasons. Harry had proved that he could compose for film and television with the best of his colleagues in Canada and the United States, but now he had to make a career decision of some gravity: Should he devote his life to the more remunerative but less satisfying genre called incidental or background music, or should he put his attention to the writing of concert and ballet music, with the financial restraints and unsure pattern of commission payments such a commitment would represent? It was a serious question that had to be confronted, as Harry was about to sever his relationship with the TSO, the only source of regular income that he had ever been able to count on.

A difficult shift in his priorities took place. Rather than making a break with film composition, he continued to write background music on a limited scale, perhaps one film a year. As John Beckwith recorded in the *Encyclopedia of Canadian Music*, "By the mid-1970s he had provided the background music for some 15 films and TV productions." Most importantly, all of the films he worked on had serious themes. Harry, with his concentration on social, economic, and political issues, was not prepared to write either advertising jingles or background music for silly and insignificant sitcoms. He sought out films concerned with important events and philosophical matters and the finest work of outstanding directors and producers.

The shift from film music writing came, as well, as a result of Harry's reluctance to accept the distasteful changes that were taking place in the process of making film and video. He had always enjoyed working with other people in a collaborative style, so the experience of doing this kind of work was personally satisfying. His life in music had mainly involved playing in ensembles, from dance bands and jazz groups to military bands and symphony orchestras. Intimate collaboration on creative projects gave delight to his life as a composer, particularly after he lost the intimacy of constant human interaction as an orchestral player. At its best, film art was the result of the meshing of a phalanx of creative minds whose inspiration came as much from each other as, in the case of feature film, from the script. Harry, a congenial individual, enjoyed such interaction.

However, inexorable changes were taking place in filmmaking as early as the 1950s. New patterns of film production influenced by the Hollywood example were changing the process from a round table repartee approach to a top-down style of production management that emphasized particular specializations. Though Canada had developed its own expert niche in the area of documentary rather than feature film, the shift in the mechanics of providing music for film was affecting all genres. The impact on the composer was considerable. Too often composers were the last to become involved and had little to do with the production decisions that affected their contribution. For most directors and producers, the music became an industrial rather than an artistic function, and Harry began to lose interest.

An example from Harry's own experience demonstrates the change. While working on a 1966 film about China being produced for the CBC by a private production company, Harry received letters from Mel Stewart, vice-president of Wolper Productions, that outlined his needs for specific cues (fragments of music). "I definitely can use the following: … I need a 45-second cue of despair. This music should emphasize the sorrow of the people, their loss of faith and hope in any type of governmental order. It would be used over the misery of the Chinese in 1920 under the warlord regimes." And again: "A one and half minute cue of the mystery of China. This should be very similar to the opening you had in the CBC film [*The Mills of the Gods*] when the script talked about the mists and myths of the seasons, etc." Further: "I could use a one minute cue of turbulence, student agitation, uprising, unrest. This should be on the fast side. I want to use it for all the bubbling desire of students to reform China, the riots they carried on, peasant insurrection, etc." The first letter concluded with a swipe at flexibility. "If you want to give me a minute, 22 seconds instead of a minute, 15 seconds, don't hold yourself down." *China: The Roots of Madness* was a major success described in the trade magazine *Variety* as "a fascinating mixed blessing of blood-and-thunder drama and a zooming blur of five years of history, all wrapped up neatly in a narrative of fancy *Life* Magazine prose." For Harry, who sought freedom of expression, this experience was an indication that the role of a film composer was not one that accorded with his deeply held beliefs that honoured the preciousness of the creative process.

Even during his transition year as composer-in-residence with the TSO he worked on *Night*, set in the Arctic but actually videotaped in the Lake Simcoe Ice Company refrigeration plant in Toronto. It was another film produced by the CBC that starred the full panoply of great Canadian actors, including Robert Christie, Gerard Parkes, Budd Knapp, Eric House, Gillie Fenwick, Chris Wiggins, and Frank Perry. Harry's music flowed from his own experience of the Arctic, and he felt a great sense of accomplishment. It revived his hope that there might be a return to a more congenial method of producing film. It was not to be.

In 1971, the year after his role as composer-in-residence effectively terminated his contract with the TSO, Harry wrote to Jan Kadar, an American filmmaker who was planning a film for Kino Productions in Montreal. Harry introduced himself and listed the range of his compositions, including the Etrog-winning film by the Paul Almond–Genevieve Bujold team. The offer came to nothing — an indication of the fact that writing for film could not provide any level of expectation and of the extent to which music composers were at the very bottom of the creative pole in prestige and recognition.

Eventually, Harry was to reject any further work of this kind, in spite of the fact that he had no compunction about making use of his film compositions for concert and recital presentation. The cantata *The Flame Within*, from the film *Act of the Heart*, was later sung in concert and recorded by the Festival Singers. Many years later, in an interview with Helen Dahlstrom, he pointed out that he had left the film music scene for a very good reason. That world had become filled with "music illiterates," producers and directors whose only interest was filling the soundtrack with music that was virtually invisible. There was no commitment to musical quality; indeed, there was no commitment to original music at all. Sounds could be gathered from the recorded repertoire of the old masters at great financial savings and with little criticism from paying customers.

In recent years, film composers such as John Williams and Elmer Bernstein have made breakthroughs, and today major feature films are planned as a total production with an array of outcomes that include a CD of the music that is as inevitable as the DVD version of the film, both for sale or rental. Though a very few commissions for CBC drama and documentary film came to Harry in the 1970s (including the National Film Board's *Tilt* and *November*), there were not many opportunities that commanded his interest.

One notable exception to the rule was the *Hand and Eye* series of the early 1980s. The goal of distinguished executive producer Vincent Tovell was "to stimulate curiosity about how for thousands of years man has created human culture by transforming natural materials for his daily use." The segments "All that Glistens," on the making of jewellery, and "Against Oblivion," on stone and metal sculpture, were produced by Catherine Smalley and had music provided by Harry Freedman. No composer could have been a more appropriate choice. He brought all his visual arts enthusiasm to a series that was an outstanding tribute to the surge of new interest in the Canadian craft movement.

The Etrog had proclaimed both Harry's genius and his predictable rejection of this form of musical composition as a major component of his career. He could feel proud that, in an industry saturated by triviality and commercial values, he had kept his own integrity unsullied. It was no mean task when the economic advantages of such composition beckoned.

The technologies that had promised to provide access to the greatest music by contemporary composers had conspired simply, in the case of recording, to ignore Canadian music makers, and in the case of film and video, to prostitute its use and bury it as essentially an insignificant aspect of the art form. Harry was a man who saw the opportunities that the recording and broadcast industries could open but was made aware of the degree to which these forms of technology had been captured by the commercial interests whose commitment to the broader educational and cultural purposes was seemingly nonexistent.

CHAPTER 11
The Performer as Professor

"Teach! Me, teach? Don't be silly!"

In the late 1960s, Harry and Mary had just arrived at a neighbourhood party. The hostess commented on Mary's frantic pace and how difficult any social life must be. Mary replied that a singer must perform as long as her voice holds out. Another guest joined in the discussion: "You can always teach!" To this suggestion, Mary's animated disagreement is recorded above.

Ironically, just as the 1960s saw Mary move from the opera stage to the recital and concert hall and from a repertoire that emphasized the great vocal masterpieces of past centuries to one that celebrated contemporary music, the 1970s witnessed another major transition — from performer to professor. In fact, the process was not as completely unexpected or unplanned as her negative reaction appeared to indicate. Many would say that there is an urge to teach others buried in each of us, begging to be released. As we mature we come to recognize and value the mastery of a particular skill or of a particular body of knowledge, and we inherit with this realization a universal enthusiasm for telling others, and, if the circumstances combine auspiciously, a great teacher is born.

Certain vocations are best enjoyed in youth and middle age. Certainly, exploiting a soprano voice is one of these. Every quality of sound production has a shelf life, and every human being experiences a waning of the energy that is necessary for all the travel, rehearsal, and performance expectation that the vocalist must face. Indeed, being an active professional performer demands the commitment, persistence, and conditioning of a marathon runner. For Mary, with loyalty to her concert and recital obligations as well as her Lyric Arts Trio responsibilities, there was little evidence of any fading of her youthful vigour. Her schedule was (and is today) a staggering feat of mental and physical activity, and her stamina is the envy of her colleagues. But the fact remains that in the career of a singer there is a time when it becomes evident that the voice's quality is about to decline.

The question of wisdom and courage arises, as in mid-life the artist must find another road to self-fulfilment that has meaning and integrity. Mary, to her sorrow, had witnessed colleagues who had simply stayed on the stage too long. The tired sound, the strained intonation, the slightly off-key entrance — all are phenomena that she had observed in the diminishing voices of colleagues who had preceded her. She was confident in her own capacity to discern the time when she should leave the world of performance. She was determined that she would retire at a time when she was one of the most celebrated soprano soloists in Canada, when the accolades were still deserved and accurate in their enthusiasm and when through her choice of demanding repertoire she could be sure she was still making a real difference to the musical scene of her community and country. Her friends and professional associates found no erosion of sound quality, no absence of dramatic presence. However, she began to feel it was time to move perceptibly but undramatically from one collection of artistic activities to another that was equally significant, if not as obviously exciting and publicly recognized.

There are singers for whom performance is life itself. The excitement of the stage lights, the knowledge of a host of admirers beyond, the thrill of the ovation, and the joy of reading enthusiastic accolades in newspaper reviews are as powerful motivations for a vocal soloist as for a star hockey player. Both forms of employment make physical and psychological demands that are comparable. But there are no old-timers games for sopranos in which different expectations in repertoire can allow continued performance. The pressure of an undetermined future on arts performers such as singers and ballet dancers is as real and ever present as it is for the aging hero on ice.

Mary, from the beginning of her career, had unconsciously prepared herself for the world of academe. Fortunately, she had addressed the broadest spectrum of repertoire and performing experience in a host of genres, from pop, musical theatre, operetta, and folk to the more serious side of the music world — baroque, romantic and contemporary vocal music, and both traditional and more contemporary opera. Most importantly, she had acquired a singular reputation for performing twentieth-century compositions by living Canadian composers. Indeed, her solo recitals and performances with the Lyric Arts Trio had included informal mini-lectures that were often seen as obligatory if full audience appreciation was to be achieved. In terms of content, there could not have been a more extensive preparation for a career as a vocal coach, instructor, expert, and professor!

She also had the advantage of learning from Harry much about the formal classroom at the elementary, secondary, and post-secondary levels during the many years he had spent in the classroom and at the Courtenay Music Camp. She herself had engaged in school programs, particularly with the Lyric Arts Trio, which gave concerts and interactive question periods in the school auditoriums that offered a place to perform. It was also the Lyric Arts Trio that moved Mary into the artist-in-residence phase of her career. It began with Simon Fraser University in British Columbia, but soon other universities perceived the advantage of having three extraordinary artists with a penchant for contemporary repertoire on the campus for weeks at a time. Mary quickly discovered the extra delight that came from extended contact with mature students who really cared about the music of the twentieth century and were prepared to accept what more traditional audiences called dissonance and formlessness with new understanding. She found it could be fun to lecture, but even more enjoyable was the opportunity to exchange ideas, understandings, and perceptions with members of her audience.

These moments reminded her of the positive time that her own schooling in Winnipeg represented in her life. She remembered how she had found her musical ability supported and developed by her teachers. It made the prospect of returning to the classroom warmly attractive.

Her time at the Royal Conservatory had also been happy. As she had moved to a more contemporary repertoire, she had found that it was much more than singing for an audience for a couple of hours; she was bringing insight and understanding as well as enjoyment. Indeed, that extension became the determining factor in arousing her enthusiasm for this repertoire, but it also led her to a more thoughtful, analytical, intellectual attitude towards performance.

Also, Mary had developed an interest in young people that came naturally from observing her own three daughters, who had attended a variety of Toronto schools. Huron Public School, for example, had "wonderful teachers," and for Lori, Whitney Public School had been equally satisfying. The teachers had provided the kind of support and encouragement that all parents crave for their children. All her children had attended Jarvis Collegiate, a secondary school with an excellent music program. There is no doubt that Mary's experience of strong family ties provided a base for extending affection to all children and youth and cannot be discounted in assessing the reasons for Mary's developing realization that she could find a place in the learning institutions of Ontario.

The breadth of her experience of associating with young people of all ages during her performing years had led her to the view that she could make her greatest contribution to students who were on the cusp of choosing a professional artist's career. For these students her own life was an example from which she could draw. She could make use of a rich and varied array of experiences that could inspire the more mature student in a college or university. The idea of moving from being an artist-in-residence to a full-time faculty member came to have an attraction that was simply waiting to be nurtured.

The 1970s had opened with a major triumph associated with the learning process. Mary and a close colleague, Patricia Rideout, were engaged to do a program on the music of John Beckwith and other composers as a segment of a series being produced by CBC's school broadcasting department. It went extremely well, and Mary found that she was able to reach out to children she would never meet but who would come to know her and her voice. The program received an award for broadcast excellence in an annual competition sponsored by Ohio

State University, one that was "considered prestigious in the field of public affairs, cultural and educational broadcasting." Mary was delighted, and the experience became yet another reason to perceive the 1970s as a transition decade in a performing career that had brought enormous joy but was now coming to a natural conclusion. When in 1978 the Lyric Arts Trio disbanded after fourteen years of performing across North America, Europe, and Asia, Mary had already moved into the Ontario university system.

Her first experience at the post-secondary level came by chance in the early 1970s. An instructor and old friend, Gladys Whitehead, at McMaster University, was taken ill and asked Mary to take over her class. It was a trial by fire experience, but Mary found it exhilarating. The students responded to her with evident delight and she found their open-mindedness refreshing. She could now face the prospect of teaching young people with the same intense commitment she had given to performing.

However, there was soon a longer-term commitment in the offing. A close friend from Harry's years at the Courtenay Music Camp, Robert Creech, had moved east. Even at the camp Bob had recognized Mary's gift, and while Harry was coming year after year, he had attempted to hire Mary as an instructor, hoping she would come and perform at a concert *The Four Last Songs* of Richard Strauss. The fact that there was a splendid French horn part that Bob wanted to play was no small part of his enthusiasm for having her presence at Courtenay. It never happened, but the negotiations strengthened Robert's interest in Mary's talent. Soon she, along with Robert Aitken and Marion Ross of the Trio, were being courted as potential Courtenay instructors.

By the mid-1970s, Creech had taken a position at the University of Western Ontario and was responsible for the section of the Faculty of Music designated as "Voice Training." In the fall of 1976, Mary was invited "to begin some voice training for us." In 1978 she was still at Western, still as a part-time instructor, but Hugh McLean (another Winnipegger!) was the dean of the Faculty of Music and expressed the hope that "this may blossom into something more permanent." The reputation she achieved in these few months had made her indispensable. As McLean put it, "Your pupils, to say the least, are enthusiastic." By

1979, McLean was aware he had found a treasure: "Bob Creech and I are more than delighted with your commitment to Western and your teaching is a great strength in the voice division."

Mary had now been accepted as a faculty member at two major Ontario universities. However, both institutions were some distance from St. Andrews Gardens, and a drive on the truck-laden Highway 401 or the Queen Elizabeth Way was not a pleasurable experience even in good weather. In winter, it was simply hell!

When a university in the centre of her own city of Toronto exhibited an interest in her talents in the late 1970s, she was ready to accept. With no experience of the occasionally demonic attitudes of some academics towards the performing arts, many of which remain intact even into the new century, Mary arrived with naive expectations of appropriate behaviour on the part of post-secondary administrations. She found that the university, with all its centuries of championing the things of the mind and spirit, could exhibit a narrow view of both the arts and the well-being of the physical — including those skills of the voice and the body that create the sounds that please and inspire. There is sometimes the attitude that such activity is not "intellectual" enough to deserve the attention of a university. Thus, the performance division of a faculty of music is too often subject to blatant disinterest or even vivid hostility. Although there may be some concession that great minds are at work in music history and theory, the view remains that there surely cannot be much to challenge the intellect in teaching young people to sing or play an instrument!

There are those who would say that in the Canadian context these activities should take place in a conservatory. Faculties of music, thus burdened with inappropriate activities associated with the world of entertainment rather than scholarly enterprise, are too often at the bottom of the academic totem pole in terms of university interest (and budgetary priority). Those who labour in the studio are made to realize that they stand well below those who inhabit the lecture halls and laboratories in the faculties of arts and sciences, to say nothing of the heady heights of business, medicine, or nuclear physics. Those instructors engaged in performance are too often part-time rather than full-time, temporary rather than long-term, adjunct rather than tenured.

Certainly more generous treatment could not be expected in the lean years of the late 1970s and '80s, as Ontario's universities sank to the bottom of the ranking in terms of per student support compared to that provided by provincial governments across Canada.

Obviously, the place for Mary to be was at a university that had voice studies and served the city in which she lived. In 1979 she made it clear to the University of Toronto that she was interested in such an appointment. However, the best that Dean Gustav Ciamaga could do was to secure a promise from Mary that "in the event students requested you as a teacher, you would be available to teach at the Faculty of Music during the 1979–80 academic session."

There followed a pathetically inadequate process whereby Mary was informed that no students had requested her as a teacher. Mary informed Ciamaga that the reason for the lack of student response was the fact that scanty information had been made available and that students had not been told, on registering, that she was available. Ciamaga replied that the lack of response might have been because her stated fee had been too high. That problem was soon rectified in typical fashion — instead of $35 per studio lesson, she would receive $28.

In the fall of 1980, Mary's availability was not even listed in the university calendar, virtually the only source of information that students had about choices they could make. This quibbling over fees and recognition between a dean of one of Canada's major post-secondary institutions and one of Canada's icons in the field of vocal performance says more about the status of music and the arts as a whole in the realm of higher education than any treatise on the nature of knowledge ever could.

In the light of her reluctance to continue the frightening trip on Ontario's most congested expressways, Mary finally confronted the University of Toronto's Dean Ciamaga with the question, "Should I finally consider a permanent teaching position at Western?" He reacted immediately. She was given a part-time appointment at the University of Toronto. Then, in 1983, a major budget cut forced the dean to tell Mary that he regretted that "we must freeze hourly teaching rates." The Applied Music Department had been identified as the culprit and was being blamed for the deficits the Faculty of Music had incurred.

It was no better a year later when Ciamaga informed Mary, "It is unlikely that an appointment [that is, a full-time, tenured position] will be made in the Performance Division during the next few years." In fact, a lessening of financial pressure and a greater realization of Mary's outstanding reputation and capability finally resulted in a more generous hourly rate for her teaching, and in 1986 a new dean, Carl Morey, made her an Adjunct Professor of Voice in the Faculty of Music, University of Toronto, for a three-year period. (It was made clear that "adjunct professor" was only a title and did not include any contractual obligations.) It was not an extravagant stipend — $21,600 for vocal teaching, and for days of auditioning applicants and adjudicating recital performances. Nor could she expect any place in the generous University of Toronto pension system for retired faculty. Presumably, individuals employed in the performance sector could continue to teach until they dropped!

Mary's involvement with the University of Toronto was eventually to become a long-term arrangement, and two decades later, Mary continues to cherish her relationship with the Faculty of Music and each year witnesses increasing evidence of the enormous contribution she has made in that now highly honoured segment of the university's work. She remains central to the success of the faculty and its Voice and Opera Division in achieving an international reputation as a place for students who are serious about a professional career on the world's concert stages.

The head of Voice Studies, Professor Lorna MacDonald, is aware that Mary came to teaching, not through any program of academic preparation, but through the trials of personal experience. For MacDonald, Mary's "pioneering" is a major reason for admiration — particularly her courage and self-sacrifice in pursuing the challenges of the advocacy and performance of contemporary vocal music. In spite of this background, "Mary understands that a good singer is much more than simply the result of having a splendid voice. It has to do with musicianship of the highest order along with a capacity for hard work." In short, it is the intellectual and spiritual qualities that accompany a great instrument that produce the great performer.

Another characteristic that rouses Professor MacDonald and her colleagues' esteem is the fact that Mary never interrupts her struggle to learn more. "If there is a master class being conducted by an internationally renowned figure, Mary will be there, no matter how busy she may be." MacDonald finds assurance in Mary's endless confidence and integrity. "If she believes another faculty colleague can assist her student she has no hesitation in seeking a transfer … she realizes that every student has differing needs and there may be some she cannot fulfil … she knows her strengths and limitations." MacDonald's veneration of Mary's contribution comes from the understanding that empowering students is the essential function. "We teach singers as well as singing!" is MacDonald's succinct description of Mary's genius.

Throughout most of the twentieth century, it was considered virtually mandatory to send Canadian vocal students to American universities and music schools, but today Julliard and Curtis are no longer perceived as necessary in the preparation of the increasing number of outstanding Canadian artists to be found on the world's concert and opera stages. Today, ironically, not only Canadian but also many talented young American and European singers apply for Voice Studies in the Faculty of Music at the University of Toronto as their preferred choice for training to bring out their potential as a performing artist.

However, although no academic appointment in the university sector of the educational system could be considered idyllic given the cutback years of the 1980s and '90s, the impact on Mary was less traumatic than that on most of the colleagues she encountered in the halls of the Edward Johnson Building on the Toronto campus. She had not been present during the halcyon days of the 1960s when there had been adequate funding. She had long been used to institutional penury — the arts sector had never been generously funded even when public resources abounded. As well, even part-time appointments gave a sense of personal security when compared to the gig-to-gig stipend that has ever been the expectation of the solo artist in our society. For Mary, there were moments to celebrate as she moved easily from studio to studio, from institution to institution, from one outstanding student of voice to another.

But her days were not free of angst and frustration. Within the first years of her arrival at the University of Toronto she found herself unexpectedly proclaimed the expert witness for the Faculty of Music, which found itself in a dispute with an undergraduate student who, though she had received over 80 percent in her final grade, was disputing the low 70s mark she had received for the performance fraction of her total mark. This altercation had gone before the Academic Appeals Board and the appeal had been rejected. Mary's reputation as a performer was brought to the fore when an appeal of this board's decision came before the Governing Council. Mary's defence of the adjudication process and those involved was stellar, and the second appeal hearing concluded there was no evidence of bias against the student, nor was there a lack of qualification on the part of those judging the performance. Any charge of misjudgement was found to be unsupportable. Mary had been able to express the reality of performance quality as a variable in the day-to-day work of any singing student or, indeed, any professional performer with such compelling realism that the Faculty of Music's reputation remained undiminished. It was a triumph of quiet common sense and reflective argument.

By 1989, Mary had also been invited to coach at the Atelier lyrique de l'Opéra de Montréal when her university schedule allowed it. In a few years she had established herself as a major force in the voice training community in Canada.

Achieving prominence in the University of Toronto's Music Faculty (and even more, later, at the Banff Centre) was a gateway to another phase in her life work — the promotion of stellar Canadian music performance from coast to coast. She became a familiar figure at the dozens of competitive music festivals that began to take shape in a country yearning for some recognition as a music community. There are many music enthusiasts who question this linkage of artistic expression with the competitive format and believe that it demeans the art form to a mere contest. However, the reality is that these events give focus to the ambitions of young people and provide experiences in confronting the pressures of public performance.

Mary, whose career had received a dramatic boost from such events in Winnipeg and Western Canada, had no hesitation in making herself available to appear at a broad representation of such festivals across Canada. She was perceived as "perfection" in her role as an adjudicator. Her own experiences of such competitions were positive, and she brought to her work a warm personality that was a boon to festival officials always wary of retaliatory threats from disappointed participants, their families, and their advocates. Her own extraordinary career gave Mary a prominence that brooked no question of her competence, and her broad exposure to virtually the entire rainbow of vocal manifestation made it possible for her to judge with integrity any number of categories of repertoire designation. Most of all, her understanding of, and sympathy for, what it was like for a young person to endure the pressure of public performance in a context of tough appraisal and inevitable criticism made her one of the busiest adjudicators in the country during the 1980s and '90s.

In spite of the tiring travel, the impossible expectations of listening to the same piece of music sung twenty or thirty times, and the exhausting schedule — perhaps seven or eight hours of judging in a single day — she carried this role off with amazing grace and distinction. She had, and still has, the determined energy of a Wimbledon tennis champion. Her commitment was such that she was, through compelling negotiation with festival officials, able to ameliorate some of the worst abuses of the competitive format. She was determined that every contestant with whom she interacted would come away with a clearer understanding of how to improve his or her skills and, most of all, the realization that singing should be sheer joy. Through all these festivals she never lost her capacity to provide thoughtful, helpful, practical advice along with softened criticism and a hearty sense of humour that inspired countless young people to make music central to their lives.

This role took her across Canada many times. She had actually started this trek in the early 1970s when the CBC invited her to judge the National Radio Competition for young singers. Later in that decade it was to be the CBC Talent Competition that captured her attention. Even before the CBC took advantage of her prominence as an artist, she had brought her expertise to bear upon a special festival of Gaelic music in Ontario followed every other year by similar festivals in other regions of the country. By the mid-1970s she was adjudicating at the London, Ontario, Kiwanis Festival, followed by other such festivals in Kingston and Niagara Falls. Then she was engaged by the Senior Voice Sections of the Saskatchewan Festival Association in both Regina and Saskatoon. In the late 1970s, she was off to the Trinity-Conception Music Festival in Newfoundland, then the following year back west to Calgary and its

Kiwanis Festival. A year later, she was invited to adjudicate the Edward Johnson Music Competition, which was held in conjunction with the Guelph Spring Festival, and it became the first of several such appearances at that festival. In 1986 and again in 1987 she adjudicated the Voice Section of the Contemporary Music Showcase, a competition that she found particularly appealing in the light of the later stages of her singing career. Adjudicating young singers, with all its tiring travel and discomfort, became a major element in her crusade to have Canada's creators and performers of music appropriately nurtured and recognized.

Although she had begun her consulting work with the Canada Council on advisory arts panels back in the 1960s and served on a number of their juries, no granting body took more of her time and talent in the last decades of the century than the granting body in her own province, the Ontario Arts Council. She was in constant demand, acting as an advisor to music officers who needed some assessment of the quality of clients and their work each year. In 1980 she was a member of the OAC's Music Commissioning Jury, and a year later she was viewing and assessing the production of the *Threepenny Opera* by a Toronto light opera company. By the mid-1980s she was part of a panel deciding which provincial choirs deserved project assistance, and a few years later she was judging applications for OAC support to music festivals.

The 1990s saw her as a member of the jury deciding on OAC support for a new genre that was developing — music theatre. It was a new venture in funding a type of musical and theatrical expression that, with her Lyric Arts Trio background, drew her particular interest. A Special Project jury determining the comparative quality of applicants for funding of exciting "on the edge" musical productions came a few years later, and as the century ended Mary was a member of a jury deciding on who should receive resources under a recording program for classical music, an area in which she and Harry had been both critics and participants over many decades. Mary was ever a popular and valued figure in the OAC's offices and halls over an extraordinary expansion of musical activity in the province of Ontario.

In November 1978, shortly after the Lyric Arts Trio had dissolved and she had begun her teaching at McMaster and later at the University of Western Ontario, Mary was approached by the Banff

Centre to spend part of her summer as a member of the staff of the
Academy of Singing, presenting "a five week period of intensive study
for young singers" mostly from the United States and Canada. She was
invited as well to offer a concert on site as an integral element of her
role as an instructor. The first year was something of a problem, as she
had contracted to adjudicate the CBC Talent Festival during the same
weeks in the summer of 1979 and had to be absent for a few days, but
throughout the 1980s and most of the '90s she was able to clear her
schedule for the full period of the academy's operation. It became a
major aspect of her new career. Indeed, teaching the most talented and
committed students in this glorious setting of the Canadian Rockies
along with staff drawn from around the world became the major reason for her international recognition as an illustrious teacher and
vocal coach. Foreign students and teaching colleagues from universities and coaches from opera companies around the world came to
appreciate the extraordinary reputation that Mary had achieved in
just the first few years of her new career.

She found these Banff summers an energizing and inspiring experience that prepared her for the challenge of the fall university teaching
session. There were no diversions in the Banff program. It was about
assisting ambitious young singers who had clearly achieved distinction
in their academic work and had reached a high level of technical skill in
their vocal studies. They came to the centre knowing that they lacked
the final touches in performance technique especially on the opera
stage, and the central focus of the program was the major production of
a great operatic work.

By 1983 she had extended her commitment and, along with colleagues, was conducting the Banff Academy of Singing auditions in
Toronto. Auditions were crucial to the work at Banff. The bringing together of a group of first-class singers who would benefit from the program
and could mount an operatic production of the finest quality became her
major task each winter and spring before the Banff summer session began.

In 1991 Mary was appointed assistant program director of the
Academy of Singing, and her most important task was to be the auditioning process that began in February, and which, by 1993, took place
in Winnipeg, Regina, Calgary, and Vancouver in Canada's West as well

as extending to Toronto, Montreal, and New York. By 1994, Paris, France, and London, England, had been added to the audition schedule. It was becoming clear that, for Canada, Banff was a major factor in the preparation of the nation's singers for a career, and by the early 1990s there was a considerable bevy of them who had come through the Banff experience in opera and concert, including Jean Stilwell, Tracy Dahl, Richard Margison, Gordon Gietz, Monica Whicher, and Wendy Nielsen, to mention only a representative handful of those now launching themselves on the music scene of every continent. Mary, along with Martin Isepp, Michael McMahon, Colin Graham, Stephen Lord, and John Hess, was to ensure that the very best possible potential vocal performers with the quality of voice, the intelligence, and the toughness to succeed were aware of the opportunity. The promotion process was at the very heart of Banff's success.

In the early 1990s reorganization at Banff became a continuing phenomenon, demanded in part by the diminishing resources available to its programs. The solution to the budgetary pressures was to combine the various Banff program components, Opera Banff, the Academy of Singing, and Banff Music Theatre, into a single singing experience for every participating student. The combined forces of the entire music community would be "dedicated to the continued development of 20th century singing theatre." There were tensions around this new program, which would be devoted to the needs of a more mature opera student. Colin Graham, an internationally renowned producer of opera, resigned. He found that the new flock of students attracted to this higher level of preparation were not sufficiently interested in the classroom and the instructional function. They performed in their operatic roles but showed disinterest in everything else associated with the program.

Yet, on the whole, the Banff Centre thrived. In fact, through these years, there was considerable jealousy in Eastern Canada that no "Banff East" emerged with the success that had attended this development in Alberta. Mary added to her Banff experience invitational weeks of instruction at the Britten-Pears School for Advanced Musical Studies, an international institution established at Aldeburgh in the United Kingdom, the very height of superb voice training across the Atlantic. Mary was now among the very elite voice teachers in the world.

These were years of extraordinary pressure and exhilaration for Mary. She suffered none of the withdrawal symptoms that so often characterize the latter years of a singing career. She was busy engaged in doing what she now realized she loved as much as performing. She was still singing publicly; indeed, her "farewell" performance was not until 1985, at a faculty recital open to the public in Walter Hall at the University of Toronto. It was no sad leave-taking — she was among her family, teaching colleagues, close friends, and adoring students. In her typical fashion, she ensured it was not a dramatic retirement occasion — rather it was a celebration of a glorious singing career and the transition to an academic role that she had found to be equally satisfying. Mary performed a selection of her favourite repertoire to the enthusiastic delight of those who loved her voice and her public persona.

Tracy Dahl, a successful soprano student of Mary's, now a recognized artist, in a personal note to Mary described her teacher's state of mind and body most sensitively: "You move with ease and confidence of a woman who has achieved all her desires in life — with more to come, I'm sure." However, it was also a time of sadness. Mary's mother, Louise, who had lived past ninety, died in the midst of all this positive activity.

The Banff Centre's reorganization, in spite of those who resented the change in focus, was going well. Realizing the danger that Mary might decide to leave, the administration had assured her at the time of the new program announcement that her participation would be critical to its success. In every way, the emphasis on contemporary music made Mary's involvement crucial. There was, for example, no one else on the Banff staff who had actually worked with Igor Stravinsky, as Mary had done, both as a soloist and as a member of Elmer Iseler's ensemble. This announcement made it clear that contemporary music was to reign supreme as the focus for the future. "The new integrated program is to be dedicated to the continued development of 20th century singing theatre through ... advanced training for professional singers, in the preparation, interpretation and performance of 20th century dramatic and song repertoire and new works." No program description could have exposed the central threads of Mary's musical interests more accurately. However, she knew that her success had been based on her command of the standard vocal music literature that had come down the centuries and she made her point clearly on this issue. The administration conceded in a note to Mary that "this does not exclude using other repertoire" and, indeed, "these 'calls' are to be made between you and your individual students." At the same time she was warned, "There is no doubt that the program is about contemporary music and all resources must be dedicated to that end." Mary was also informed that the singers would be "at the same or more advanced level than have come in the summers in the past." It was a further challenge for her as the major figure devoted to the auditioning exercise on which the quality of students depended.

Unfortunately, there was a lack of balance in Banff's determination to concentrate so exclusively on contemporary music. As a result, there was a loss of an audience for its productions. There was also a lack of judgement in selecting the composers who were stressed, with Banff sometimes tending to attach itself to trendy American composers who were associates of faculty drawn from south of the border. For a time the institution simply lost contact with the expectations of the music community, even though some of the outstanding faculty continued to come.

Being a part of all this disruption and refocusing gave Mary a unique opportunity to examine her own teaching style. She had not been drawn to any particular school of instructional practice. Rather, she had drawn on the many decades of her personal experience that included the techniques that, one by one, her various instructors had employed and that had brought her to the level of confident artistry that had defined her career. She never considered that she had been self-taught and she constantly accorded Dr. Vinci, Emmy Heim, Greta Kraus, and her other teachers appropriate accolades for their contribution to her success. But throughout her active performance life she had been highly reflective about the factors that had led to her extraordinarily rich and varied experiences.

She knew that in working with voice students there was no room for trial and error — a precious voice could be destroyed in the process. All in all, there is no more fragile and threatened figure in the entire population of young people preparing themselves for a professional career than a young vocal student. Throughout their period of schooling, they must face the reality that many are called but few are chosen, that, indeed, only a handful of the host of performance graduates emerging from faculties of music and conservatories across the country will actually make it as recognized performers and most will find their way into employment as teachers or in the many support roles that can be found in the spectrum of activities referred to as "cultural industries." There are so many expectations to fulfill — the strength, quality, and control of the voice, the capacity to acquire the extensive range that both the traditional and contemporary repertoire demand, the attributes of physical attractiveness that may unfairly determine the direction of a career, and most of all the extreme intellectual and expressive challenge that every important piece of music presents.

Walter Homburger, the extraordinary impresario who had such a part in the success of the Toronto Symphony over so many years, in a conversation with the author made the observation that there are dozens of tenors with the voice and personality of Pavarotti out there, but Luciano was "lucky enough to be in the right place at the right time." He would have willingly conceded that part of the luck was in having received the right preparation to make the best of opportunities that "luckily" came along. In no other area of preparation is the role of the instructor so crucial. A poor teacher can ruin the splendid natural quality of the finest vocal instrument by pushing the voice student too far and too fast or by setting a developing voice off on an inappropriate repertoire, thereby straining that fragile combination of membranes and muscles. Just as brutal can be making interpretative demands on a naive, inexperienced student that bring cruel criticism from all sides, devastatingly undermining the confidence of a new talent. A good teacher is to be valued in any corner of the learning society, but nowhere is that role as crucial as in preparing a singer for a performing career.

Mary's focus in the 1980s and '90s, with her own performing career now less demanding, was to become an outstanding teacher. She achieved that ambition beyond what could have been in her mind as the years sped by. In 2002, at a gala dinner at the Granite Club in Toronto, she was presented with the Opera Canada Educator Award, a "Rubie" (named after Ruby Mercer, Canada's first "opera lady" who had made monumental contributions to the art form, including the founding the country's major opera publication, *Opera Canada*). It was the highest honour her colleagues could have bestowed on her. Mary was accompanied on that festive evening by Leopold Simoneau and Pierrette Alarie, who had achieved great international careers as a tenor and soprano duo and on this occasion received Creative Artist Awards. The incomparable Nicholas Goldschmidt was presented with the Opera Builder Award, and as one of Mary's earliest mentors, there could not have been a more appropriate companion at this extraordinary affair. She received her Rubie from one of the great artists of the twentieth century, Marilyn Horne, who recognized the role Mary had played in her life and the role she was still playing in the amazing development of Canadian opera stars on the international stage.

There are countless books and articles on the subject of the great teacher in virtually every phase of a student's life. In music performance, as in any other genre, there are many theories and practices that are considered by some to be "the way." Mary has little patience with any formula. On the occasion of her Educator Award, Joseph So wrote an article about her in a celebratory issue of *Opera Canada*. In reply to his question, Mary stated categorically, "I don't have a method — not really. Every student is different and what works for one may not work for another." Her student Colleen Skull corroborated for So the success of this non-method. "I had a brilliant top and a huge chest voice, but a weak middle. Mary was instrumental in helping me line up the voice, in helping me solidify my technique and be comfortable as an artist with something to say. I wouldn't be nearly where I am today if it weren't for Mary."

There was no revolutionary moment of insight that brought Mary to this style of instruction — it had come from her own life experience. She believed every individual voice was a distinctive phenomenon with different qualities. That was the place to start — make each student aware of the process. Her secret was to "work with whatever they come with." Every sound and every physical expression that accompanied the sound was unique. Mary was determined, in every case, to encourage them to find their own voice and never to emulate someone else's. In short, there was only one strategy — listening with such intense care that she could then draw on her own knowledge of the array of methodologies that she had encountered, all developed in the effort to assess and care for the attributes of voice and presentation that might bring success and vocal freedom to that student — the sound and sight that could be used to create beauty, extend understanding, and ultimately bring pleasure and, on occasion, the inspiration that changes lives.

One characteristic of a great teacher that Mary brought to the role was confidence — the knowledge that she had confronted many vocal challenges, every imaginable height of repertoire expectation, and had succeeded. It was this quiet faith in her own capacity that she was able to transmit to her students. With singing, it is a frightening responsibility. Not every student arrives at the studio with a voice that can fill a huge auditorium, or one whose timbre will expand to present the variety of song and aria that can make each performance a memorable occasion. But success can have many faces. A singer can become an outstanding instructor, a fine arts administrator, or an arts manager; indeed, singing is a valuable preparation for any work that demands public presentation of virtually any kind. The thin line one treads in seeking to provide confidence without creating unrealistic expectations places severe pressure on every instructor. Mary excelled in this careful balance. Alison, a student at the University of Toronto, recognized this streak of genius: "I have never felt more indebted to a teacher in my life. Your lessons have benefited my voice greatly … and my confidence in my own ability has expanded as well. Your constant advice, concern and caring in times of trouble or confusion is truly inspiring to a student eventually interested in teaching some day."

Perhaps the most complex challenge for a teacher is to establish confidence while at the same time stretching the bounds of a student's understanding and performance capacity to a higher level. "It's about building a voice," Mary explains. The soft pressure that must be employed in order to elevate the quality of singing day by day, without bringing on a feeling of failure and a fit of depression, is a constant dilemma. One of Mary's strengths is her tolerant willingness to give students the time to absorb, to internalize, the lessons she is conveying. It was a student graduating at the end of the 1980s, Rayanne, who recognized that quality in Mary's teaching style: "I will miss you, your patience (with young and over-zealous singers), your sense of humour and your wisdom. I have a feeling that I'll be carrying a part of Mary with me wherever I go in life."

A teacher's intervention in the undergraduate life of a university student is short-term, at most a four-year phenomenon. A student's career is long-term. A great teacher is one who knows how to learn and how important continuing education will be. The singer's learning is never complete; indeed, many of Mary's most famous students return years after they have graduated for a "tuning up" of their voices. Mary is constantly contacted by graduates who have discovered, later in their careers, just how good she was! Often former students who had gone off to other institutions and renowned teachers recognized that they had been in the hands of a unique "Mary" and wanted to tell their new instructors about her. One student discovered that her new music program in Europe involved a mentor who was using one of Mary's teaching tricks. "Her teaching technique is so close to yours!" she wrote to Mary. "She is constantly looking for pure vowels — spinning, open sound." The result was that she was asked by her new instructor to show her other "tricks" that Mary had used. The student had become the teacher — the teacher, the student.

Mary's most appealing characteristic throughout has career has been a fire in the belly, a passion for what she was doing that could not be defeated or diverted. She had spent some four decades promoting Canadian contemporary music and her students came to share that enthusiasm. Every Morrison student gained some respect for the music of the nation's composers and many became missionaries in their own right. Jennifer, now studying in Boston, demonstrated this commitment. "I was also so angry that so little respect is shown our young Canadian composers," she wrote. She set about the task of revealing the wonders of her own country's compositions by singing a selection in a program but found that there was little time for rehearsal of the orchestra and ultimately "they were practically sight-reading the score." She had been well taught to gauge that this lack of rehearsal reflected the minimal commitment of foreign musicians to contemporary music and, in particular, the Canadian variety. Another student, Cheryl, while studying in New York, brought new music to her classes, Beckwith and Somers, as examples. "It amazes and frightens me that teachers here remain ignorant of compositions by Canadian composers. I'm trying, Mary…" she wrote.

The truly great teacher knows that the process of learning is more about providing inspiration than it is about conveying information. Jane, a student in the late 1990s, was as much thrilled by Mary's lifestyle as by her formal instruction. "I wish you all the best of health, happiness in every respect of your insanely busy, yet incredibly meaningful, generous and loving way of living and giving to all you meet…. I often am inspired by the spirit and wisdom you imparted to me during those years at the U. of T. opera school … you are a great woman and a wonderful teacher." Kelly, Mary's student in the 1990s, wrote to tell her that she set the example of bringing out the best in her students and that it was "inspirational … I walked in with a hammer and you gave me so many of the other tools in the tool box."

It is a well-known fact that a teacher who cares, even a teacher whose methods are dominated by constant efforts to judge and punish, rather than to celebrate and reward, is more effective than a teacher who is simply disinterested. Of the attributes one can find in Mary's array of teaching talents, it is the passion she shows for the total well-being of her students and graduates that sets her apart. In the case of a voice teacher, where so much of the instruction is on a one-on-one basis, the opportunity to deeply engage, or totally outrage, is palpable. For Mary, a studio lesson is an opportunity to bring into play a set of strategies: first to put the student at ease, then to move gradually into a format of exercises, and eventually to address the particular music being studied, a process that culminates in a revelation that a plateau has been reached, a breakthrough has been achieved.

Mary found at the outset of her teaching career that this process worked only if the student was assured that her concern extended far beyond an interest in her singing technique. She sought to discover all the factors that could possibly affect the student's learning life. Sometimes it was family tensions or, even more often at this age, a shattered relationship with a lover that made the lesson less valuable than it could have been. There is a tragic irony that the high point of a young woman's voice quality comes just when she is ready to achieve a lifetime relationship that will bring the fulfilment of bearing children into her life. For young women scarcely out of adolescence and facing such dilemmas, Mary became a mentor, an older sister, and a surrogate mother. "I cannot begin to tell you what differences you have made in my life," wrote Suzanne, a student who was going through a difficult time in her personal life.

Another graduate, Julia, joined Suzanne in expressing the fact that the studio sessions were more than just music lessons: "I have learned so much from you not only in music, but in your approach to people. I have so much more direction and I very much appreciate your candour and positive support." Mary was obviously one who understood that creative artistic life takes place in the context of confidence and well-being and that advice on how to cope with a boyfriend who resents such concentration on singing may be the most important contribution to that student's success.

For Mary, the love of music was central, but it was not everything that brought happiness and satisfaction. The observation that "there is a difference between having a career and having a life" was one that Mary had lived by throughout her life. Mary herself had chosen to have a loving husband, three devoted children, a home, and a phalanx of friends who were close and "counted." These values were conveyed to her students as well as instruction on singing technique and taking care of the voice. It was this extraordinary quality of character that inspired generations of students and made her a legend in the world of teaching, one that continues to influence the lives of students who will dominate the Canadian and international stages in the decades ahead.

Joseph So wrote in *Opera Canada*, "The students who have been through Morrison's studio read like a 'Who's Who' of Canadian singing: Adrianne Pieczonka, Nancy Argenta, Tracy Dahl, Kathleen Brett, Valdene Anderson, Wendy Nielsen, Ingrid Attrot, Barbara Hannigan, Anita Kraus, Tamara Hummel, Lynn McMurtry, Shannon Mercer, Joni Henson and Karen Wierzba." And there were men who fell under her influence, Ben Heppner, Robert Pomakov, Gordon Gietz, John Tessier, and Gregory Dahl, for example. But these names represent only a fraction of the people she has touched. Even her magnificent years on stage and in radio pale before the sheer magnitude of her cultural impact in the teaching studio.

One final example of Mary's influence on a voice student could be considered a template for effective teaching. At the middle of the first decade of a new century, there appears to be a host of outstanding

Canadian sopranos aspiring to achieve a major international performing career. None outshine the future prospects of Measha Brüggergosman. Her voice is magnificent and she has a commanding presence on stage that is truly electric. As a teenager she had already achieved recognition in her native Fredericton, perfectly reflecting the youthful Mary Morrison's prominence in Winnipeg. Fortunately for Measha, Wendy Nielson, a former Morrison student enjoying a successful singing career, lived nearby and offered to give the young singer the initial lessons she craved. Nielson realized that she had discovered an enormous talent and informed Mary of her find. Mary came as soon as possible to Fredericton to hear Measha and was thrilled by the quality and power of her singing. Then it was Mary's turn to "audition" for Measha's family. Both parents were prominent leaders in Fredericton's Baptist community and were quite aware of their daughter's potential. With her own experience as a guide, Mary convinced the family that coming to an institution with a high reputation in voice studies, in this case the University of Toronto's Faculty of Music, was the obvious direction for Measha to follow in pursuit of a significant singing career.

Measha came to Toronto and for four undergraduate years worked in Mary's studio, emerging as a prize graduate and outstanding soloist. Measha is unrelenting in her praise of Mary's role in her development. She emphasizes the importance of Mary's unwavering commitment to a work ethic that pushed her as far as she could go. She is also aware of Mary's wisdom in selecting, at every stage, the repertoire that suited Measha's voice development, building on her strength but forcing her to reach out to more demanding music that would stretch both her intellect and her technique. Without any maudlin babying, Mary was always there for her, from her beginnings as a fragile Maritime talent to her attainment of an appreciative response wherever she appeared. For Measha, "Mary understood the journey."

Perhaps even more assuring was the fact that Mary had taught her "to want the normal things in life — including marriage, family and loving relationships." Whenever there is a defining moment in her career, Mary is indeed "always there." In the fall of 2004 Measha made her Carnegie Hall debut, and Mary flew down to New York to be with her, to give support and share her triumph. Replacing the student-teacher relationship with one that exudes mutual admiration has become the hall-mark of the journey.

There was one lesson that was never formally taught but was the legacy left with every Morrison vocal student. It revolved around the word *respect*. Throughout her career, Mary exhibited an enormous reverence for the work of every composer whose work she sang, along with a similar admiration for the audiences for whom she performed. But even more, she constantly expressed her appreciation to all the musicians — fellow singers, accompanists, orchestral players, even backstage crew — who had any part of her success. This is not the trademark of every artist. There are those whose arrogance and selfishness are the source of outrage among colleagues in every musical genre and in every performing space. However, this attitude of respect for fellow travellers in the world of the performing arts has been conveyed as the only appropriate behaviour to every student Mary has taught.

By the turn of the century, Mary was quite conscious of what was necessary if Canada was to become a country whose culture would be enriched by the presence of opera and concert expression of the highest quality. She was called upon to assess the quality of the apprenticeship programs for opera singers in Canada. In reports to Canada's heritage ministry Mary examined the apprenticeship programs at the Atelier lyrique de l'Opéra de Montréal and the Vancouver Opera Company's programs, Opera in the Schools and Studio Ensemble. She opened her study with the confident statement that Canada is "producing more and better singer/musicians from university and conservatories." However, Mary explained, a must for future development were apprenticeship programs that would serve an interim period between formal education and "the next big step — the real world of opera," and significantly as "the time not only to develop their voices, musical and theatrical skills, but also to learn about the business of music and opera in particular." She noted that in Britain there is the National Opera Studio, which, though not affiliated to any professional company, was performing the same function as a large number of apprenticeship programs associated with American companies such as the Met, Chicago, Houston, and the San Francisco opera companies.

The point was made: If Canada was to continue its amazing progress of the past decades and become an even more dominant country with a fabric of good opera facilities as an important aspect of its arts expression, then it too must create even more programs like the Toronto's Canadian Opera Company, Montreal's Atelier lyrique, and Vancouver's Opera Company had done.

Mary was prepared to be critical. For the Atelier lyrique, the circumstances were not perfect. The young singers were rehearsing their operatic roles before they knew the notes. Mary was impressed by the efforts she witnessed but recognized the need to add classical theatre coaching to their stage experience. She also found the rehearsal hall "barely adequate." It all came down to a lack of resources and leadership, exhibiting the importance of placing a head music coach at the top of the crucial needs list. She could not leave her report without advising the administration of the Atelier lyrique to add to its repertoire by commissioning new Canadian works.

Unfortunately, her trip to assess the Vancouver Opera Company's Studio and Opera in the School ensembles came at a time of "internal upheaval between the general director, the music director and the Board." It was not a propitious moment to assess either operation. Yet, even with all this administrative havoc resulting in the obvious burnout of key figures, "the show does go on." With all the organizational difficulties, it was apparent that the ensembles were producing good work and that young people were enjoying a positive learning experience. Once again, space for the ensemble members to meet and develop some sense of collegiality was totally absent. Mary could not assure herself and the heritage ministry that a quality program could survive with such uproar in the administration, a fact that bothered her greatly, as Vancouver was so isolated from the rest of Canada, and especially at a time when the Banff Centre had just cancelled its opera and song summer training altogether. Thus, there would be no apprenticeship opportunity for young singers west of Toronto, in Mary's view a tragic way for Canada to meet the new century.

Despite all the problems she found, Mary expressed her optimism that the extraordinary development in opera, the success of Canadians on the concert and recital stages, was not an aberration. Canada, with its diverse but comparatively small population, has of late produced more fine writers, composers, visual artists, and performers than the most optimistic could have predicted. But as with all great commitments, continued success demands ongoing investment. Mary's advice was a call to governments at all levels for a mature response to this new era — an age that would be intolerable if not devoted to things of the mind and spirit that could only be guaranteed through the determination of its creators, artists and performers.

When Canada's place in the world is established in this millennium and its position of "soft" leadership by example is assured as the planet moves from a preoccupation with military and economic domination to a cultural focus, the importance of this country's half-century of artistic struggle from the 1950s will be perceived in its true light. It will not just be about a new opera house in Toronto or the seeming army of outstanding singers and musicians who have emerged from all this musical expansion; it will be about this nation's capacity to express itself as a cultural force, indeed, as a place with lessons to teach about multi-cultural respect and outreach that can change the world. That has been the Mary Morrison vineyard — first as a performer, and then as a teacher, mentor, consultant, and, most important of all, a source of inspiration to audiences, colleagues, and students.

CHAPTER 12

The Stream of Music

By the 1980s Harry had completed a sizeable repertoire that was played and sung by orchestras, choirs, individual musicians, and chamber music groups around the world. There was virtually no genre that he could be accused of ignoring; indeed, he had one of the most eclectic lists of compositions of any living Canadian composer. Ironically, for a composer who claimed to have little interest in sung text, his music for vocalists and choral groups was particularly popular.

In 1979, his place in Canadian music was assured when he was proclaimed Canada's Composer of the Year. There was no doubt that he now stood amongst the handful of Canadian composers of serious music whose works could be heard with some consistency both live and, at least for his smaller works, on records, tapes, and discs. Part of his time over the next decades was devoted to the task of seeing that there was more opportunity for his music to be performed and appreciated.

His exploits as a broadcaster and educator and his role as a promoter of Canadian music were also acknowledged, and in 1984 his contribution to the nation was recognized when he was appointed an Officer of the Order of Canada. Equally satisfying was the fact that the year before Mary had also been appointed an Officer of the Order in recognition of her career as an outstanding vocal artist. The honour acknowledged Mary's remarkable commitment to the performance of Canadian contemporary music as well as the early stages of her teaching career. It was apparent that the 1980s and '90s, for both Harry and Mary, would be decades of celebration of past contributions but also of continued additions to the classical musical expression of the day and an opportunity to build a nation's cultural future as a new millennium opened.

For Harry, the most dramatic continuing reminder of the aging process throughout the 1970s had been a back pain that made sitting for long periods quite uncomfortable and made it difficult to pursue the pleasures of golf. Indeed, in 1975 he underwent an operation that resulted in a fusion of three vertebrae in his neck. Finally, he found some relief, mainly as a result of his commitment to the Alexander Technique. But it was not the end of his discomfort, and in 1993 he returned to the hospital and endured an acute herniated disc operation. Once again, as nearly twenty years before, his travel was severely limited for many months.

Harry's health problems were not over. In the late 1990s he was plagued by hip problems and was forced to have both replaced. By that time, the inevitable prostate problem was also besetting his daily routine. Yet through all these health challenges, including pain, loss of sleep, and restriction of movement, Harry never stopped writing music, never reduced his public appearances at premieres and performances of his work, never sloughed off the mountain of correspondence with artists who sought his help, and never reduced his attention to the public issues that mattered to him.

Nor was Mary slowing down. Her life was characterized by the same frantic commitment to work that had always been her style. Indeed, if anything, both Harry and Mary were even more aware from travel abroad and across Canada of just how much needed to be done if Canadian music was to be seen as a central element of the nation's artistic expression. The challenge was to see contemporary Canadian compositions played in concerts both large and small in urban centres — cities, towns, and villages — from Atlantic to Pacific. But there also needed to be easy access through frequent radio performances at a time when the CBC was becoming less committed to the broadcast of such music. Indeed, at one point, in his frustration with the nation's broadcaster, Harry entered into negotiation with the American Public

Broadcasting Station emanating from Buffalo. This station, realizing the number of Ontarians who were listeners, had indicated that it had an interest in featuring Canadian classical music. Harry asked the Canadian Music Centre to make tapes available. For Harry, the avid nationalist, to engage an American radio station, even one devoted to public broadcasting, to feature the work of Canadian composers could be seen as the ultimate retreat.

In this regard it is ironic that it was in the late 1990s that an event took place that proved all that Harry believed, given appropriate resources, the role of the nation's broadcaster, the CBC, could be. His musician colleague Lawrence Cherney had become a major entrepreneurial arts producer. Through a company called Soundstreams, devoted to Canadian music performance, arts education, and the development of the country's composers, Cherney had established a project, Northern Encounters, dedicated to bringing artists and arts organizations from nations around the Arctic Circle to engage in a Toronto music festival that would explore their cultural similarities and differences. It was, and still is, an exciting interaction that draws significant attention.

Northern Encounters was a co-operative venture with the CBC, and one presentation was to take place in the new CBC building constructed around a magnificent atrium that had a performance venue on the main floor and balconies that reached up several stories. The acoustics were splendid. Music could float down from the balconies as a part of the performance dynamic. Harry was commissioned by the CBC to write a piece for full orchestra (players from the TSO conducted by Jukka-Pekka Saraste) and for four choirs (the Danish and Swedish National Radio Choirs, the Elmer Iseler Singers, and the Toronto Children's Chorus), all of whom would be strategically placed in the balconies.

The plans excited both Harry and a close colleague, CBC's David Jaeger, who toured the site and worked with him to see that the sound of his composition would be as close to perfection as possible. The result, *Borealis*, was a piece that was enthusiastically received. *Toronto Star* critic William Littler wrote of the "exciting bursts of sound, bringing together instrumental and vocal forces" producing a work that "sounded northern in mood and atmosphere." Music critic and theatre director Urjo Kareda wrote of the "lush, generous panorama of sounds" that "explores the north of the imagination in a spirit of awe and mystery" and declared it "a stirring work of festival proportions." Harry saw *Borealis* as the culmination of the previous twenty years of his life's work, and audience members approached him with tears of appreciation streaming down their faces.

Jaeger had the foresight to realize that he could submit this composition to an international competition committee of the International Rostrum of Composers taking place in Paris. Harry's *Borealis* placed fourth out of sixty compositions submitted from thirty-two countries. It was a triumph. As Harry put it, "It was like being short listed for the Booker literary prize … even if you don't win, it's something just to be nominated." Jaeger reported that the delegates to the Rostrum were impressed with the "freshness of ideas and the beauty of the sound."

Harry felt that this experience revealed that the lack of commissioning opportunities for Canadian composers compared to other jurisdictions was undoubtedly depriving them of similar successes on the international scene. His delight was tempered with the realization that he and his colleagues had many barriers to level before their work could be adequately recognized. A CBC radio network devoted to the task of commissioning works, arranging performances, and making use of its international connections to present the works abroad would be a major advantage in any process of positive cultural development. What had begun as an attempt to engage the interest of an American public broadcasting company had now become a twenty-first-century campaign to arouse the national broadcaster, the CBC.

Mary, who had been working full-time at the University of Toronto, cut back her workload in the 1990s, but she continued to be invited to Aldeburgh and its music school made famous by Benjamin Britten and Peter Pears. In the summer of 2000, for example, she finished her work at Toronto in April and took off almost immediately for Aldeburgh for ten days of teaching. Harry commented to a friend, "The older she gets, the more of a work junkie she becomes." Mary's many years on the stage and the road had been training tough enough to prepare a mountain climber, but even she could not escape unscathed the savage fall that came as a result of a malfunctioning elevator at the Faculty of Music's Edward Johnson Building in 2003. The accident resulted in a gash on her right leg that took twenty-six stitches to close. She was also badly shaken, and the shock laid her up for a couple of weeks. However, with her recovery came the demands that pushed her once again into a full-steam-ahead schedule.

In the late 1990s, Mary and Harry realized that they must think of their future. With all three daughters grown and out on their own, and with Harry's hip replacements an ongoing trial only exacerbated by climbing stairs, they decided that they no longer needed the large house on St. Andrews Gardens. They sold their home of some four decades and moved into an apartment in Don Mills. It was an unfortunate choice. It was distant from the University of Toronto, and Mary had to struggle daily with inconvenient bus and subway transportation. As well, Harry needed to be close to the artistic centre of the city. They remained there less than two years and then purchased a condominium on Avenue Road, close to Upper Canada College and a ten-minute bus ride to the University of Toronto. It turned out to be just the right place. But the challenge of two moves, involving the disposal of many years' accumulation of furniture, books, and papers, all while Harry coped with bouts of ill health and both were working frantically, took its toll. It was an exhausting period for both of them.

Harry had early realized that for Canadian citizens in the 1980s, particularly those in remote areas, the availability of music of their nation's composers came through the purchase of records and tapes, and, later, CDs and DVDs. For Harry, with his concern over equal access for all citizens to the "commons" of the nation's cultural achievements, this became a source of increasing tension. Harry felt some personal satisfaction when the Canadian Music Centre produced a disc filled with selections from the works of Beckwith, Ridout, Somers, and Weinzweig and included Harry's *Scenario*, written for solo alto sax and bass guitar with orchestra, and *Passacaglia*, the piece commissioned by CJRT for jazz band and full symphony orchestra. However, even with these occasional contributions, almost aberrations on the Canadian recording scene, Canadians simply could not become familiar with the works that expressed their own thoughts and feelings.

Little wonder that in the 1980s, which brought reasons to both celebrate and grieve, Harry sought professional help and underwent an extensive period of analysis. There was no problem with his confidence in his ability to write music and write it well. His output continued to be prodigious and varied. Rather there was a nagging dissatisfaction and a sense that, for a highly experienced professional, the process of composing should be more relaxed and satisfying. Also, he was sharing some of the angst of older composers that the field was being overpopulated with music makers, many of whom were more at home amid the new technologies of music promotion and distribution and much better at creating the hype that sold their talent. One could say that Harry was so articulate, curious, and laid-back about his search for personal help and advice on keeping a balanced mind that the professional analyst who took him as a patient knew she was essentially overseeing a process of self-analysis. She was as much the observer as the analyst. He was as much the probing physician as the curious patient.

Thus, for three years in the early and mid-1980s, he visited this psychiatrist four times a week. They spoke of many things but finally centred on the matter that Harry knew would emerge — the lifelong impact of a very dominant mother. It had been his mother who had made all the decisions that had guided his childhood, his teens, and his early manhood. Though he had been generous in crediting her with his success, he also harboured resentment for her strategy and motivations that he had never confronted. Week after week in analysis his troubled mind played two roles: one a kind of scholarly assessor of what this analysis was really all about, and the other, more importantly, a man confronting the demons of his conflicting emotions.

At the end of three years, the sessions ended. Was Harry "cured"? Had he ever really been "ill"? Both are valid questions. The process came to an end when Harry felt he had learned all he could about himself and the techniques that had revealed the pressures of the past that he had failed to fully understand and overcome. His mental crisis had done nothing to bottle up his creative activity, though when he reviewed the music he had composed during the period of analysis he was deeply dissatisfied. Indeed, years of work was destroyed and never brought to publication or performance.

From that point in the mid-1980s he came to feel better about the compositions that poured forth. The job of composing became more rewarding and he felt that he was producing some of the best work of a lifetime of music making. As well, his behaviour towards his friends and colleagues became warmer, less intense and aggressive. Even his voice on the telephone changed, becoming less strident and severe. The time had been well spent. It was a journey that had at times strained his optimism, but it had produced a different person. Harry was more reflective and contemplative and was willing to make use of new understandings in analyzing the profession of making music. He was still gloomy about the fact that his music was not being played as often as he felt it deserved, but he realized it was an opinion shared by most of his colleagues.

Harry's examination of his role of composer became even more intense. He had always understood the strong impact of the visual as his strength in expressing musical ideas. Conductor Victor Feldbrill believes to this day that his commitment to visual arts was the secret of the power and vitality of Harry's music. John Fraser, writing in the Toronto *Globe and Mail* in 1974, quoted Harry: "I find myself trying to translate something I see, either from reality or in my imagination." For Harry, music was "simply sonic design." At the lowest point of his dissatisfaction Harry suggested to William Littler that he might well abandon music for visual arts, and late in the 1990s he learned as much as he could about the secrets of film production with the idea that he might make use of his painting and composing to bring forth a form of animation devoted to the images of his visual creativity accompanied by the exciting sounds of original music that would create a new form of artistic expression. He had never forgotten what he experienced upon seeing Disney's *Fantasia* in 1941, with the music of Bach enhanced by moving images before his young and observant eyes. He thought he could take this memory to another level.

Harry recognized that there was a conflict in his position that he wrote only what he wanted to write and yet also composed only on commission. It placed a great deal of the focus of inspiration at the point of negotiating the commission. Harry developed a close relationship with the conductors and musicians who were the commissioning agents, in a sense, the co-composers. He was careful to commit to provide compositions only for arts organizations, conductors, musicians, and singers he could respect and trust. Thus, a good part of Harry's inspiration and motivation came from the knowledge of the sound that the individual or group could produce, as well as an appreciation of the circumstances surrounding the reason to play new music in a particular place at a particular time.

In speaking to Helen Dahlstrom in 1988 he stated very candidly, "I begin with the sound, that is the important thing … the notes are the last thing I think about…. Textures, rhythms and moods are as important as the notes." Harry had an enormous loyalty to the commission commitment. At the outset, he was not writing a piece for the ages but for a particular ensemble or individual musician and for a specific occasion.

Obviously, for aesthetic as well remunerative reasons, Harry hoped the composition would have a life beyond the first performance, and many of his works were played again and again. As one would expect he became an even stronger vocal supporter for second and subsequent performances. At the same time, he was the most severe critic of his own work, and no composer spent more time meticulously rewriting compositions that, in performance, displayed flaws that demanded correction. Few composers have withdrawn more works from a repertoire on the grounds that they no longer met their standard for public performance.

There was one genre of musical composition Harry was hesitant about writing — the opera. Except for the light and jocular *Abracadabra*, written in collaboration with Mavor Moore initially for a Courtenay Camp concert, he avoided commissions for such a composition. Indeed, he made it clear on several public occasions and on national television that he would accept a commission, not for one, but for three or more operas over a five-year period. He made the point that established operatic composers (Mozart, Verdi, Puccini were prime examples) wrote at least two operas that were complete failures before they made a successful breakthrough. Harry believed the opera form was so complex and challenging that one could learn to compose in this genre only on the job and benefit from the mistakes that would be inevitable in the initial efforts.

Harry went even further. He maintained that his preference would be to write a television opera, as opposed to a traditionally staged work. Menotti's *Amahl and the Night Visitors*, a Christmas season television production that has been seen by more people than any other opera in history, provided a format for such a work, though its essentially romantic nature would not have suited Harry's chosen compositional style. The debate was pointless in any case, as Canada had no funding body, private or public, that would commit to support a composer for several years to produce some three extensive works of music drama.

In that same year, 1988, Harry analyzed his own journey through the styles of twentieth-century music making. He had been drawn initially to the twelve-tone technique but, though there was a degree of liberation from a constricted romantic past, he had found it contained "too much formula." Instead, he found he was very much interested in the tone-row, a series of notes he could draw on, repeat, and revise throughout an entire composition. It gave him access to new levels of varied and exciting expression along with some comfort of familiarity as the composition developed. Shortly into his career as a composer he had lost all confidence in pure serialism. Harry explained in an interview, "It put too much emphasis on notes and not enough on music. It was a classic case of the tail wagging the dog." However, he found that by stringing together tone-rows he could produce a kind of "strangeness that it made atonality listenable."

In the 1980s and '90s, Harry, almost as an afterthought, did spend some time in the university setting, where he was able to reflect more profoundly on the nature of his work and on the question of the preparation of the next generation of composers. In the summer of 1989 Harry was asked to teach a course in composition at the University of Western Ontario in the spring of 1990. He succumbed, but before he had completed that assignment he was asked by the University of Toronto's dean of music, Carl Morey, if he would accept an appointment for the following year. His positive response resulted in a letter informing him that he had been appointed Jean Chalmers Visiting Professor for the 1990–91 academic year.

Harry's views on post-secondary strategies to prepare composers were little different from the elementary and secondary school methods that had served him so well in the 1960s and '70s. First must come an emphasis on *listening*, not just hearing but concentrated, goal-oriented listening. Second, he was convinced that "learning was doing." In an article written in December 2000, repeating the simple adage he had expressed for decades, he wrote, "The more you write, the more you learn." He conceded the value of a grasp of the fundamentals, that is, harmony and counterpoint, and was convinced that a great deal of attention to orchestration was important, but the main process of learning to compose could not be completed in four years of attendance at a university. It could come only through a commitment to the constant writing of music on a rigorous schedule. Composing, Harry believed, was the result of practice and demanded disciplined application, and creative success came as a result of work represented in his mind by a ratio of some 99 percent perspiration and 1 percent inspiration. His expectation of his students that they should turn up with compositions week after week was not always a popular methodology.

In particular, he was determined that budding composers should hear what they had written. He had memories of the postwar years at the Conservatory, when performance students were expected to assist hopeful composers by offering to play their efforts informally and at no cost. This was no longer the style of the 1980s, and Harry found himself raging against a program that failed to provide listening opportunities for would-be composers — what Harry thought to be the essence of understanding for any music maker. His views were not welcomed, and after a single academic year Harry was pleased to return to his studio. Happily, the end of his visiting professorship coincided with a Canada Council Senior Composer grant that allowed him time to carry out a number of tasks he was salivating to complete, including among other possibilities the revision of his Concerto for Orchestra, a re-orchestration of *Anerca* to include piano, vibraphone, and harp, and a new version of *Graphic II*.

The university may have regarded Harry's presence as something of a coup. He was popular among students and colleagues. However, he had by this time come to some conclusions about the lack of popularity of contemporary classical music that were particularly unacceptable to the community as a whole. To Harry, it was painfully evident as the twentieth century came to a close that serious music was not drawing new audiences to concert and recital halls — and certainly not younger audiences. He had witnessed the impact of the enormous hype that pushed popular forms of music to dizzying heights of popularity that could not be matched by contemporary classical music. As well, he was conscious of the lack of commitment on the part of the music industry to market CDs of serious music but he was courageous enough to put some of the blame for the state of music composition on the composing community itself. It concerned him that the younger generation of composers "learned about music at university and they are turning out reams of what one perceptive critic calls 'university music' — the kind of music that is more interesting to analyze than to listen to." In so stating the case he had the support of a most respected intellectual observer of the international music scene, Milton Babbitt, who had proclaimed that such music had no more place in a concert hall than a lecture on higher mathematics.

Harry saw no conspiracy, but he commented with some passion that, with the number of university composers on juries and positions of influence in commissioning and programming, "it's hardly surprising the audiences for new music are so small. They are hearing the wrong kind of contemporary music — the academic kind." He may have been right, but it was not a message that professors in faculties of music particularly wanted to hear. For those outside the halls of academe, it explained why many of the managements of symphony orchestras were scheduling fewer performances of Canadian contemporary music. It was a disconcerting debate at a time when Canadian symphony orchestra conductors and players were faced with dwindling audiences even for the eighteenth- and nineteenth-century repertoire.

Although he devalued time spent in post-secondary classrooms, Harry did not believe that composing good music was a matter of downplaying the intellect and the aesthetic. He considered his years at art school, not as a diversion or a delay, but as the very stuff of his preparation to become a composer. In an unpublished article entitled "Composing," he credited his colleague R. Murray Schafer's "enormous fund of ideas" to the fact that he read extensively, painted, worked in the theatre, and even wrote books. His success was based on the fact that Schafer was "a real renaissance man." It was these influences, not an academic understanding of how to put notes on paper, that were the basic building blocks of musical construction. He believed that to be a contemporary composer demanded the courage to "write to please yourself," to express "what is within yourself," and to be willing to be unpopular in doing so.

For Harry, the early 1980s had produced a new source of inspiration in the form of a prestigious group of authors, composers, and painters who came to call themselves "The Loons." It was an amazing collection of elite artists: writers and poets Margaret Laurence, James Reaney, Adele Wiseman, Timothy Findley, Earl Birney, Miriam Waddington, and Sylvia Fraser were active members. As impressive was the gathering of composers, who came to include John Beckwith, Murray Schafer, Harry Somers, Raymond Pannell, Alexina Louie, Alex Pauk, and, on occasion, John Weinzweig. Efforts to reach out to painters and sculptors resulted in members like Joyce Wieland, Ronald Bloore, and Vera Frenkel. Attempts were made to include filmmakers and dancers, but they were not successful.

Harry was there from the beginning. It was meant to be "a loosely-knit club which will serve mainly as a social club for an alliance of artists from several disciplines." The interaction between artists from varied disciplines was the central raison d'être; "exploring of the similarities and differences between artists working in different mediums" was the objective that fuelled Harry's interest. The initial planning group had gathered at Adele Wiseman's place, but Harry hosted the second gathering and the subsequent planning meetings in his own home.

It was decided that though there would be no formal organization and no committee structure, there would be a regular late afternoon meeting at a bar or restaurant each month. The first meeting took place in The Dell, an eatery popular with musicians very close to University Avenue and College Street in downtown Toronto. However, both the muzak over the sound system and the uninspired artwork on the walls met the strong disapproval of Harry and visual artist Ron Bloore. Anesty's, a bar-diner on Church Street, was the next venue experiment before the perfect place was discovered — the top floor of the Park Plaza Hotel at the corner of Bloor Street and University Avenue, just north of the University of Toronto, where there was not only a public bar but an unused dining room that could be an exclusive refuge for the expression of the most outrageous proposals for saving the world.

Composers perhaps more than any other creative artists are engaged in a lonely activity, and Harry Somers immediately questioned the reason for such a club. It is something of a mystery to understand what would have encouraged Harry Freedman, who revelled in silence and loneliness in his composing practices, to become involved in a regular discussion group that almost immediately seized on the name "The Loons." It was a designation that encouraged a discussion that went on good-humouredly for several months on the excuse that the debate on the group's name "protects us from the larger lunacy of petitioning government for funds for concerts, readings, art exhibits or ... worse ... hold concerts, readings, art exhibits for funds to petition governments."

The group became an intimate gathering of artistic minds determined to range over a broad collection of subjects of mutual interest but always in a state of high spirits. The minutes of the meetings were nothing but accounts of the hilarious bons mots of those present, with emphasis on the incredible madness of the society they found around them. The idiocy of the tax rules for self-supporting artists drew Loon attention, as did the invasion of technology in every aspect of life. (At one point, Margaret Laurence used a calculator to determine her share of a "looncheon" and it turned out to be $33 million.) These and other "loonacies" were all objects of Loon disbelief, ridicule, and general frivolity.

But there was a serious side to the discussion that certainly influenced Harry. The very presence of such a wide array of artists from every discipline sharing their concerns diminished the reaction to every frustration and outrage that had been exaggerated by Harry's isolation. As well, it strengthened his resolve to seek paths of artistic integration in areas of visual arts, film, and video. However, on the lighter side, for Harry, seeking to understand himself and his past, the experience of being a member of this group and thoroughly enjoying the boisterous interaction was a salvation. It gave him not only pleasure but increased self-understanding to spend time with such a range of creative people, all facing their own demons and finding their own measure of success.

John Fraser saw this need for ironic analysis in Harry's music and easily connected Harry's music with his persona. "Freedman's music is like the man himself — immediately approachable, lively, often humorous, and always questioning. This last quality is one of his most attractive and leads him along a number of controversial roads." Perhaps no composer saluted the reality of laughter and intense pleasure more assiduously. Professor Gail Dixon, the pre-eminent student of Harry's work, concluded in her book, *The Music of Harry Freedman*, that "affable, approachable, and eminently likeable, Freedman is the antithesis of the image many people have of the contemporary composer as a stodgy, isolated figure." Indeed, "naturally gregarious, Freedman is endowed with a rich sense of humour." The monthly meetings of the Loons lasted only three years, reaching their demise in the mid-1980s, but they gave Harry a sense of intimate contact with minds that counted. Even more important, in a period of some personal questioning of his life role, these moments of verbal interplay gave Harry a reason to laugh uproariously and place both his triumphs and disappointments in perspective.

Drawing on his own experience, Harry cautioned any student hoping to be a composer that penury would be the likely financial outcome of a musical vocation. He pointed out that although he had lived in a large house in Rosedale, certainly the most prestigious old neighbourhood in Toronto, he had struggled financially throughout his career. He was quite open about the reason for his seeming affluence — Mary's income as a performer, then a teacher, had made it possible for them to have a comfortable home that could, at one point, accommodate three teenage daughters.

The insecurity of the composer's income was a constant drain on Harry's morale, particularly during the years from the late 1970s to early '90s when his back condition affected his work schedule or the funding process worked to the disadvantage of the composer. In 1979, he estimated that he had lost $10,000 of expected revenue when the Canada Council was prepared to give only 60 percent of a requested commission to the Vancouver Symphony for a piece that would include the Purcell String Quartet (admittedly in some state of disruption). The performance as planned had to be cancelled when the rest of the cost of the commission could not be raised. Harry had already worked for two months on the project, and finally the piece became *Blue*, a work for string quartet. However, while all the funding issues were being sorted out, Harry had turned down several other commissions. Indeed, at this very time, when the Bach-Elgar Choir in Hamilton requested that he make himself available in the spring of 1980 to do a celebratory work, he was forced to refuse on the basis that he might receive a commission that would, in the remaining months of 1979, extend into the new decade.

It was also in 1979 that he complained bitterly that the policy of the Ontario Arts Council, in a period of constrained funds, had placed a limit of $4,000 on every applicant composer for commissioning funds in any year. It was blatantly discriminatory. That amount could cover the cost of composing only a short selection, and if a longer piece was required, the client organization, like the Vancouver Symphony, might be unable to raise the rest of the money and thus withdraw from the commissioning obligation altogether. It was a risk that Harry thought unfair. Such a limit undermined the OAC's commitment to excellence in that it penalized the best and most prolific composers in its effort to spread the largesse over a larger number of applications. This policy might be politically advantageous but it brought into question OAC's contention that grants were based solely on considerations of quality and excellence. Needless to say, it would make being a full-time composer virtually impossible if such policies were adopted by other granting agencies, both public and private.

As well, at a time when the OAC was being forced through lack of funds to reduce the levels of commissioning grants, Harry discovered that it was providing grants to orchestras, choral groups, chamber ensembles, and individual musicians who were commissioning works from composers residing in other provinces. Harry asked pointedly, "Why should Ontario composers have to compete for Ontario taxpayers' money with composers from other provinces?" He found that other provincial funding bodies restricted their commission recipients entirely to their own resident composers. Harry's concern was not assuaged by the response that the OAC's contribution to out-of-province composers was less than 2 percent of the annual sum for commissioning music. Harry's point was that a principle was being breached.

In spite of these hurdles, during the last decades of the century, when Harry was in his sixties and seventies, the normal retirement age, he was at his most prolific. Even though in the 1990s his number of compositions began to lessen, the quality of his work was perceived to be improving. A larger percentage became a part of the regular repertoire of musical organizations. Though his music received considerable attention, in his mind it was not enough. He was conscious of the substantial rise in the number of young composers with whom he was now competing. His and his older composing colleagues' successful instruction of the next generations had created a competitive hell that, in spite of the dramatic increase in performing arts groups, resulted in a smaller segment of the market for each. On top of that was the sense that in the creation of a single performing rights organization in Canada, SOCAN, serious composers had lost ground to the pop sector in the amount of royalties their works brought in. All in all, it was tougher to make a living by making music.

In spite of his dissatisfaction with the music industry, Harry continued to make the music flow. He had begun his *Epitaph for Igor Stravinsky* in the late 1970s, dedicated to a composer he had admired and whose death he mourned. The CBC initiated a program in honour of Stravinsky that would include the master's *Epitaph for Dylan Thomas*, and Harry was invited to compose a piece using the same instrumental and vocal forces — a tenor, a string quartet, and four trombones — an extraordinary combination that allowed a direct reference to the impact of the sounds that Stravinsky added to the store of musical literature. Harry included in his work a poem by his close friend John Reeves.

Harry's commitment to the revolutionary spirit, found both in his personal reaction to political and social situations and in his response to artistic assaults on the status quo, led him to compose with the music and the visual art of his contemporaries very much in mind, whether it was an Emily Carr, a Harold Town, an Igor Stravinsky, or a Harry Somers he wished to salute. An aspect of Harry's music is surely the democratic egalitarianism that led him to honour, not corporate leaders or political figures, but the genius of ordinary people. There are no "Graphics" to celebrate prime ministers, great generals, or even outstanding athletes. Instead, the humble figure with a cause or the beloved literary artist was the subject of his musical adoration. On their deaths, Harry wrote pieces in honour of both Terry Fox and Margaret Laurence. By the end of the millennium, he was delighted to be writing music celebrating his own musician daughter, Lori, very much alive and performing magnificently.

One of the reasons that Harry was disappointed in the reception his music received from many people was the perception that his works were inaccessible, whereas his whole background had been in jazz and popular music and so much of his inspiration came from that source.

An example is his treatment, in 1981, of *Royal Flush*, a Concerto Grosso for Brass Quintet and Orchestra, commissioned by Charles Dutoit for the brass section of the Montreal Symphony Orchestra. Writing in the Montreal *Gazette* after the premiere performance, Eric McLean commented, "It is a particularly effective piece by a man with a special gift for instrumentation…. He has employed the medium with humour and a fine ear for colour. Although it uses jazz elements, they are not hauled in by the hair of the head, but meld naturally with more conventional rhythms." Symphony orchestras with excellent brass sections have seized on this piece as an opportunity to surface a section of the symphony orchestra that, in some cases, receives little opportunity to do more than provide massive sound.

By the 1980s, Harry had lost his inhibitions about making use of his long association with jazz music. Ellington was now a god in music circles. Darius Milhaud, a celebrated classical composer, had presented the jazz idiom in his ballet music *La création du monde, op. 81*, as early as 1923, George Gershwin had broken into the concert repertoire of North American and European symphony orchestras in the 1920s and '30s, and now Harry had no hesitation in celebrating the jazz influence in his own music writing.

In 1982, his old orchestra, the TSO, commissioned a piece for its first season in the new Roy Thomson Hall, which was to replace Massey Hall, its home through the twentieth century. The composition was to celebrate the quality of a great symphony orchestra, much as Bartok's famous Concerto for Orchestra had done some decades earlier. As a great scholar of Bartok and an admirer of his work, Harry used the same designation, but his Concerto for Orchestra was much more aligned with the new sounds of the twentieth century and included unusual effects that Bartok had never thought of addressing. Periods of silence and a surprising use of temple bowls and a referee's whistle "played" by the conductor shocked the audience but also gained their attention and appreciation.

Basically, as John Beckwith reports in his *Encyclopedia of Canadian Music* contribution on Harry Freedman, "The Concerto justifies its title in a series of characteristic solo segments separated by slow orchestral refrains." Ronald Hambleton, writing in the *Toronto Star*, perceived the concerto as an exploration of orchestral timbres, and proclaimed

Freedman "a more imaginative explorer than most," indicating his appreciation of "bursts of symphonic fervour, alternating with splendid brass choir noises, and long elegant phrases on clarinet and bassoon." However, he saw this commitment to exploration as the "eventual downfall" of the piece. "Freedman is not nearly as adroit with strings, which are given a mechanical supporting role, and his final section was all too evidently a dutiful rolling out of parts to the battery of drums." John Kraglund, commenting in the *Globe and Mail*, thought "the Concerto made agreeable listening" but felt it was too long. Nevertheless, he said, "Balance seemed excellent, as the themes were projected clearly."

Harry was delighted that his Concerto would be the first piece of Canadian contemporary music played in Toronto's new concert venue, Roy Thomson Hall. He told William Littler, "The piece is a bit of a departure … I've been very naughty: I've been having fun … one part will break up the audience [the referee whistle]. It's not avant-garde…. But it's not like any concerto for orchestra I've heard." Part of that "naughtiness" might very well have arisen from a personal reaction to the irony of having Toronto's symphony hall named after a newspaper tycoon who had evidenced little interest in music of any kind throughout a lifetime but whose family was prepared to contribute millions of dollars towards building a new venue that would carry his name down the corridors of time. However, Harry felt his later works were accessible in every meaning of the word and drew their accessibility from a background on the bandstand or in the ballroom rather than the studios of the university or conservatory — yet they carried the disadvantage of being termed "serious" music.

However, in addressing the most complex and highly developed genre, the orchestral symphonic work, Harry drew on impressions of folk themes and particularly on the instruments used in the street and around the campfire. These elements were apparent in 1983, when Harry launched another major work, a Third Symphony, commissioned by his close friend Simon Streatfeild, conductor of the Regina Symphony. It was a success with the audience and critics and was nominated as an orchestral work in the Netherlands for a festival in Hilversum, Holland. John Miller at the Canadian Music Centre worked hard to find the resources to fly Harry to the first performance but with little success. Finally his flight was provided by the Dutch air carrier KLM, and he was able to hear his work played by a fine European orchestra. Harry described the first movement as an exploration of musical space and the second as an evocation of Canada's Northwest Coast Indians, not through native themes but through musical form and the use of an Indian rattle playing beside a solo piccolo. Again, the images of Emily Carr were brought to mind. The final movement features a middle section based on a Ghanaian drum song and requires two drummers playing four drums each. Harry was five decades from his first contact with native people, but his music continued to celebrate that warm memory of Canada's past.

In 1984, Harry returned to an old love affair with dance. But it was also a return to his love of the folk music of ordinary people. In the 1960s and '70s choreographer Brian Macdonald and Harry had collaborated on a number of works, and in the 1980s Macdonald made use of Harry's suite of Eastern Canadian folk songs, *Green... Blue... White*, for choir as the score for a ballet. Now he was presented with a different task: the use of Venezuelan folk song material for dance. This time it was Constantin Patsalas, the resident choreographer for the National Ballet of Canada (NBC), who contacted Harry about writing a score for a ballet. Patsalas, while on a trip to South America, had become impressed by Venezuela's "rich, colourful folkloric music ... that manifested Spanish, Indian and African influences."

These songs became the resource for Harry, though he made it clear that he would be exerting his own musical creativity on the material. The result was the score for *Oiseaux Exotiques* (Exotic Birds), the most popular of all his ballet scores, played in the form of an orchestral suite and recorded by the CBC. The NBC's performance of the ballet was quite sensational, characterized by a dazzling display of bright colour and sensuous movement. William Littler, writing his review in the *Toronto Star*, startled some readers by observing, "The National Ballet uncovers sin and knows how to enjoy it," giving much of the credit for the success of the ballet to "Freedman's skilful transformation of Latin American folk music." Freedman himself described it as "all fast and loud and has so many notes. It's wonderful, the Latin American rhythms are infectious." It was not the last ballet that Harry produced in the

1980s. The dance company Encore commissioned a work, *Heroes of Our Time*, for Expo '86 in Vancouver.

Certainly the continued success in writing music for dance was a matter of mystery to its composer. He told John Fraser, who reported his amazement in the *Globe and Mail*, "I don't write music with dancers or choreographers in mind. It's just the way it works out." He thought it might be his roots in jazz that emerged in his dance music. Fraser's conclusion was quite simple: "Freedman likes people, that is the reason he writes for ballet," quoting Harry's observation that "there is real involvement that I find satisfying. The music is working with people and people are working with music in a very physical way … you have to get involved. I like that."

A commission that received more popular attention than perhaps any other musical expression in the 1980s came in 1985, when the Victoria Symphony Orchestra asked Harry to write a piece that would honour Terry Fox. *A Garland for Terry* was born. The work was to accompany a narrative by Miriam Waddington and was written in honour of a Canadian hero like none other. Terry, a young man who had already had one of his cancerous legs partially amputated and whose life ultimately ended when that cancer reached his lungs, attempted in 1980 to run across Canada to raise money for research into the cause of the disease that was ravaging his body. His courage and determination moved Canadians as no other individual feat of physical endurance had ever done. Harry attempted to give a musical description that exposed Fox's quiet humility in all the pain and discomfort of running what was essentially a marathon every day and then touched on the despair of his final hours as he collapsed near Thunder Bay, Ontario, after thousands of miles of tormented effort. Even in 2004, a questionable CBC program called *The Greatest Canadian*, which invited viewers to vote on who they thought was deserving of that title, was given integrity by the surfacing of Terry Fox, who came second to Tommy Douglas, with many more votes than the prime ministers, military heroes, inventors, and popular performers who were nominated. For Harry, it was the recognition of the courage of an ordinary young man who could rise above discomfort and suffering to inspire a nation.

In 1986, as part of the Year of Canadian Music festivities, Harry was commissioned by the Chamber Players of Toronto to write what was essentially a work for fifteen solo strings. Calling his piece *Contrasts*, with a subtitle *The Web and the Wind*, Harry adopted a new technique, what he called "textural melodies," consisting of "several instruments playing very busy lines, all within the same small interval, and this busy texture moves up and down to create a melodic contour." It was not a device that captured every listener. Robert Everett-Green, writing about a performance three years later by the Esprit Orchestra, found the textural melody "either too indistinct or too subtle for these ears." However, in the second movement he found "a striking melody in the four lead strings." The work has received many performances by other ensembles, including one at the annual conference of the Society of Composers held in 1987 at Northwestern University in the United States, where it was judged one of the highlights of the event.

Again in the 1980s it was to his visual arts past that he turned in his effort to give musical expression to the life and work of the controversial Toronto artist Harold Town, who had captured Harry's interest and that of the Windsor Symphony Orchestra. Harry had met Town and had spent many hours reviewing his canvases, prints, and sketches. Harry found his creativity overwhelming. Town could take a particular theme and fill a gallery with expressions of his imagination. For example, one truly extraordinary exhibition in the 1980s was a collection of works using the children's rocking horse as its theme. A large presentation space was filled with dozens of images that explored every possible element of this piece of furniture that is be found in many nurseries and drew conclusions about the human condition along the way. In *Graphic VI: Town*, Harry provided musical impressions of four of Town's paintings. Harry understood Town's mind, indeed felt it reflected his own desire to extend both observation and philosophic ideas through many transitional compositions, often over many years, to bring insights that a single work could never capture. For example, Harry worked on several compositions that revolved around the *Alice in Wonderland* theme expressing a variety of moods and meanings.

In 1991, when the Esprit Orchestra wanted a composition simply called *Town*, Harry has pleased to oblige, and a work he described as "an orchestral impression" was presented. It revealed much about an artist who gave leadership and inspiration to a generation of artists in Toronto during the 1960s, '70s, and early '80s. In a sense, Harry was writing music to honour those whose political and social views mirrored his own, and the iconoclastic Town was on the other side of every cause that pitted poor against rich or "tree huggers" against loggers. Harry felt both musically and psychologically at home.

Harry had a love for young people that flowed into his works. By the late 1980s he had more than memories of the classroom. His daughter Lori had taken up the bass clarinet and was becoming most proficient. Not only was she a player in various ensembles, she was also moving in the direction of being a composer — not of classical music in the pattern of Harry Freedman but of the spontaneous music of her own generation. With all these influences it is little wonder that he was delighted when, in 1988, Catherine Glaser-Climie, the artistic director of the Mount Royal Jr. Children's Choir, wrote to describe her reaction to a Choral Conductor's Workshop given by the Toronto Children's Chorus (TCC) and its director Jean Ashworth Bartle. Glaser-Climie effused, "One piece which WE ALL fell in love with was a composition which you had written for the TCC which I believe is entitled 'Songs from the Nursery.'" (The correct title was *Rhymes for the Nursery*, and it had been commissioned by the TCC in 1986.) "What a marvellous work," she said of the composition that had been used to exhibit the techniques of rehearsing children in the performance of contemporary works. Unfortunately, the composition had not been published and was thus unavailable for performance. "It is so important for those of us who work with children to provide them with opportunities to learn about and sing the music of our great Canadian composers. You, sir, are one of them." Harry made sure that copies of his work were soon in the hands of the Mount Royal Jr. Children's Choir and its conductor.

Rhymes was not the only commission that Harry received from Jean Ashworth Bartle and the TCC. In 2001, the TCC commissioned *Aqsaqniq*. When Harry reached the age of eighty in the new century, it was significant that the most enthusiastic celebration in his honour came at a TCC concert devoted to his music, at which *Aqsaqniq* was premiered. That piece, along with *Rhymes for the Nursery* and *Keewaydin* (though the latter was not commissioned by the TCC it had become a choir hallmark composition), had led to a close relationship of composer and performers. Bartle, the TCC's founding conductor, believed that children were artists and should be so treated. In a letter to Harry, she expressed her appreciation: "Thank you for your superb writing and for enabling children's voices to take their rightful place in the musical world as artists."

Jean Ashworth Bartle believed that the quality of the music her choristers sang had significance both for the development of the children and for the transformation of the audience. On this basis, the reputation of the choir had soared. She realized that Harry's serious and concentrated efforts to challenge these children with demanding scores indicated his respect for their talent and commitment. Harry's extended work in the classrooms of the province had convinced him that writing music for children was a serious responsibility and could not be trivialized. Harry's belief in the commissioning process that took into account the sound possibilities of the client led to pieces that were exciting and worth singing whether they were commissioned for adult or children's performances.

There was sadness in the 1980s and '90s that accompanied Harry's realization that his closest colleagues were passing away. Margaret Laurence shared Harry's love of the West, his respect for the native people, and his left-wing activism. She also shared his delight in young people and had been seriously hurt by the attacks on her books by those who felt students in public schools should read only expurgated editions that excluded the very words and ideas found on any playground. After Margaret's death in 1987 Harry accepted a commission from the Thunder Bay Symphony that he called *A Dance on the Earth*, the title of her biography. Once again he was able to make use of his familiarity with dances from Venezuela, Ghana, and America. She had "danced" with turns of phrase and generous compassion for every person she met. The work was Margaret's in every way.

The death of Harry Somers in 1999 brought to an end a close relationship that Harry had treasured. No other person understood his music as intimately as did this other Harry. A millennium program largely funded by the federal government, Music Canada 2000, devised by Nicholas Goldschmidt to encourage Canadian composers to recognize the coming of the new millennium, would result in the creation of some sixty new works. One of these was a commission by the Canadian Chamber Academy that Harry called *Graphic IX: For Harry Somers*. It was written for sixteen solo strings and revealed the intense respect and intimacy that had been a part of Harry's life with Somers over many years. It was premiered, disastrously as it turned out, in front of the Stratford Art Gallery, with the traffic noise on a major city street completely obscuring the qualitative interweaving of the strings. Nevertheless, it was a composition that was destined to be played in the future, not only in memory of the work of the man to whom it was dedicated but also because it exposed the highly developed techniques that had come to characterize Harry's treatment of the string orchestra.

Eric Booth, arts educator and author of *The Everyday Work of Art*, speaking at the Chorus America Annual Conference in June 2003, stated, "Art is not about standing back or judging, having lots of intellectual things to say, and requiring lots of education to appreciate its difficulty and complexity. Rather, it is about engagement, about pouring yourself into it and knowing what it feels like to be a part of the arts." Harry could not have put it better. His compositions, as the old century ended and the new one began, illustrated that philosophy of artistic creation and invited every listener to share his respect for Canadians he believed had made his country a better place.

CHAPTER 13
Completing the Circle

As the twentieth century matured, Harry Freedman was faced with the dilemma that haunted all Canadian composers. He had written a wide repertoire of compositions, but access to many of his works was severely limited. He had always regarded himself as primarily an orchestral composer, yet there were few opportunities to program contemporary classical works for full orchestra. There simply were not enough Canadian orchestras. It was little wonder that Canadian music makers had established an enviable reputation internationally as choral composers. The country was filled with fine choirs led by capable, in some cases splendid, Canadian born and trained conductors.

For Harry, the popular compositions that had already attracted much attention at home, like *Keewaydin*, had significant performance records. As could have been expected, compositions that demanded attention to text, such as *Songs from Shakespeare* and *Green... Blue... White*, were also to be found on the programs of choral ensembles across the ocean and below the border. Harry's original enthusiasm for orchestral sound had produced in mid-century *Tangents*, *Images*, *Graphic I*, and, for the world of dance, *Rose Latulippe*, but unfortunately there were even fewer performances of the orchestral works of Canadian composers as the 1980s opened than had been mounted in the previous decade.

The largest symphonic works that had received an initial playing in earlier years were receiving virtually no attention. Harry's Symphony no. 1 and Symphony no. 3 and the Concerto for Orchestra were major compositions. One of the reasons for this state of affairs through these final decades of the century was the lack of any champions for Canadian music on orchestral podiums across the nation. Victor Feldbrill had led the Winnipeg Symphony for several years and that city had become a centre for the performance of Canadian contemporary music. But he had moved on. As well, Mario Bernardi and Simon Streatfeild, both supporters of contemporary Canadian composers, had stepped down from the NAC Orchestra and the Regina Symphony Orchestra respectively.

It was during these years of moving toward the new millennium that senior Canadian composers saw a major shift in the environment they had known in past years. It seemed that the juries of the Canada Council and the provincial arts councils tended to favour the works of new young composers, a seemingly reasonable choice if the long-term health of Canadian music was to be encouraged. Pioneers like Weinzweig, Beckwith, and Freedman understood the rationale for this shift; with limited funds available, the needs of high-quality young composers had to be a priority. However, it meant that older composers tended to be overlooked by commissioning juries, even if the experience and musical wisdom of these icons was essential to the ongoing perception of Canadian compositional excellence that had permeated international circles in the 1960s, '70s, and '80s.

The irony of the situation was emphasized as the century turned. In 1998 Harry was the winner of the Lynch-Staunton Award, which the Canada Council gave out to three artists who were designated "senior" or "established" and were engaged in music or visual arts. But essentially the announcement of this award surfaced the pathetically inadequate support there was in Canada for those whom other countries regard as national treasures and support as a matter of course in order that their contributions could be assured throughout their lifetime.

It was and still is a dark hole in our arts support system that Elizabeth Bihl, the director of the Canadian Music Centre, would like to fill with a heritage program focused not on saving buildings but on supporting great minds and creative forces housed in more mature bodies, those like Harry, whom William Littler, one of Toronto's pre-eminent music critics, referred to as the "cultivated composer." At a moment in time when the cultural well-being of established composers should be at the pinnacle of public concern, the financial health of self-employed artists with limited investment and pension income is very much at risk. The courageous decision to become a full-time composer can turn into a nightmare of embarrassing penury as age overcomes the advantages of both artistic experience and recognized talent.

As Harry observed, a good example of distressing disinterest on the part of the Canadian music industry, both live and technologically presented, was the composition *Images*. It was consistently the most frequently performed Canadian orchestral selection in the overseas concert repertoire. Yet for fifteen years, there had been no recording available. Such extended compositions needed the commitment of a major recording label and a strong marketing effort to promote these recordings. As for live performance that might lead to recording sessions, there was in Canada a dearth of heavily populated cities providing a wide range of orchestras competing for audiences and seeking a more varied repertoire for the more discriminating listener.

The main problem, though, was the fact that there were no Canadian commercial enterprises able and willing to carry the expense of recording large-scale orchestral works with such a relatively small market of purchasers. The CBC certainly made efforts, and the CMC introduced its label to general applause, but neither could compare with the advantages of having large-scale commercial labels that could produce, promote, market, and distribute Canadian music globally in the mainstream of the international music industry. Successive governments at the federal level had made it plain that funding for such a marketplace activity was simply not on, and Harry and his colleagues were unable to argue successfully that creating a body of familiar, expressive music that celebrated Canadian themes and personages through this process was necessary for cultural nation-building and positioning.

In the 1980s and '90s, Harry set about to change that situation. He found little succour from a CBC that had shifted its emphasis from recording Canadian works to recording Canadian artists performing international classics. The CMC was committed to Canadian composition but had no budget for orchestral selections. Harry found that two hours of recording with a Canadian symphonic ensemble cost $300,000 in Canada but less than $60,000 in the U.S.S.R. Victor Feldbrill, a Canadian conductor who was familiar with the recording scene in Japan, corroborated Harry's sense that there was a solution to this problem, and a letter from the manager of the New Japan Philharmonic convinced him that there was another direction he should take. Obviously, it was a matter of recording his orchestral repertoire beyond North American shores. At one point, Harry enlisted a friend, Terry Sheard, who had connections with the J.P. Bickell Foundation, but to no avail. The Department of External Affairs also informed Harry there was no program to support the making of recordings abroad. The money could not be found and Harry's major orchestral works remained technologically silent.

Harry could gain some satisfaction from the fact that the name "Freedman" was recognized by all composers and musicians associated with professional performance and in the halls of conservatories and faculties of music across the country. As well, his full-time commitment to music composition was an inspiration to younger composers. Though they might be unable to follow his example in regarding composing music as a single preoccupation, they nonetheless perceived his career choice as the ultimate goal in the struggle to build a Canadian sound that expressed the beliefs and feelings of its citizens. He remained in constant contact with dozens of former high school and university students, former Courtenay campers, and the thousands he had addressed at festivals, workshops, and conferences.

In the late 1980s, Harry's presence as a composer was further enhanced when he hosted the CBC-TV program *Music on a Sunday Afternoon*, an exploration of outstanding musical performances across a wide spectrum that included both the orchestral and the operatic repertoire. Harry brought the confidence of a seasoned composer to the introductions he prepared, and he expressed his views in a language and with a style of rhetoric that delighted his audience. After only two years, however, the program shifted to emphasize a more popular selection of artistic activities that no longer required a host of Harry's background and musical expertise, and he was replaced by former ballerina Veronica Tennant. It was fine choice of host, but a letter from a listener complained of this "dumbing down" and expressed appreciation for Harry's controversial commentary: "I did not agree with everything Mr. Freedman said but he was unfailingly informative and/or provocative." It was an assessment that mirrored the enthusiastic agreement of other viewers.

Another difficulty in making the work of Canadian composers better known was having written works published, and once published, given active promotion. Only in that way would the musical composition fall into the hands of the conductors and artistic directors who decided the programming of musical organizations in cities and smaller communities from coast to coast and particularly abroad. The Canadian Music Centre continued to be the most effective distributor of the scores of Canadian composers but had no resources to promote music, particularly in less populated Canadian communities and more obscure countries overseas.

Once again, it was Harry's experience that there was little capacity, even by the last years of the twentieth century, for the large or small music publishing enterprises to find the resources to produce a representative body of his work, and most certainly there were none that could provide adequate promotion of his works to choirs and orchestras either in Canada or abroad. His solution, as he entered the 1980s, was to found his own publishing company, Anerca, named after a piece that he had written early in his career. He would operate his business from his own home on St. Andrews Gardens.

Initially, it seemed as though it might work out. Harry advertised in music periodicals, putting particular emphasis on his choral works that were already in the repertoires of a number of ensembles. The first years of operation brought an enormous flow of requests for catalogues, complementary copies of music, and advice, all demanding much of his time but providing little income. He could not even afford to hire secretarial help or to provide representation at the countless festivals and gatherings of musicians across the continent. He soon tired of the task. The problem was one shared by all composers. They wanted to write music, but that left them with little time for the drudgery of replying to correspondence and ensuring that proper accounting procedures were observed, along with all the management decisions that such an enterprise, no matter how small, entailed.

Very soon other publishers saw an opportunity to "assist," and the first serious interest came from the Thomas House of Publications in California. But these companies wanted to take responsibility for only the popular titles, such as *Keewaydin* and *Rhymes for the Nursery*. There was no commitment to the cause of broadening the Canadian experience with the more challenging material for adult audiences, particularly those attending symphonic concerts and willing to approach less well known works.

There was yet another problem besetting the composer and indeed all those seeking to make a living out of the music industry. It was to come to a head in the twenty-first century when the technologies of reproduction in both print and sound made profit from creative work immeasurably more difficult to achieve. For reasons beyond explanation, people who would never steal a chocolate bar in a corner store see nothing illegal or unethical about copying the work of writers and composers for wide consumption. The complexities of copyright are beyond common understanding and acceptance, particularly if the basic tenet that words and musical notes are the property of the creator is not understood and accepted as a general proposition.

In 1985, Harry appeared in Ottawa before the government's Standing Committee on Communications and Culture. The question of illegal copying of films, television programs, and recordings by the illegal use of audio and videocassette was on the agenda. It was, in Harry's view, his particular problem in the print media as a publisher. He was now involved with the role of a distributor and promoter and saw the need to protect that element of the music industry.

Harry was prescient on this occasion. His proposal reeked of practicality. In the matter of illegal recording of music the solution was simple — make it legal to reproduce such material for personal use but place a surtax on the retail sale of all the technological equipment associated with such reproduction and assign the money collected to performing rights organizations, like CAPAC, dedicated to ensuring that authors and composers and their publishers were adequately recompensed for their efforts. In the light of the inexcusable and uncontrollable march of technological progress, Harry's solution deserved more attention than it received. Essentially the issue was destined to remain on the agenda of both the music industry and lawmakers long after Harry's appearance before the committee. Indeed, Internet downloading became a central issue of the new century.

As for Harry's efforts as a publisher, Thomas House of Publications in California took over the publishing and distribution of Harry's works everywhere in the world but in Canada, the one jurisdiction that Harry felt he could look after himself. It was not a solution. The lack of a viable Canadian music publishing industry remained a stumbling block to the wider distribution of his music and that of his colleague composers.

Nevertheless, even this foray into the marketplace had increased Harry's public presence and he had become even more the cultural guru giving counsel to every imaginable information seeker, some of his advice disregarded but much of it valued. Being one of a handful of composers who, even in the 1980s, could live off the commissions he received, he became an informal source of information on how to be successful in doing just that — securing commissions from arts councils and private foundations. "Grantsmanship" became just another area of expertise, along with the full rainbow of composing skills he had acquired.

His intense commitment to the Canadian League of Composers led Harry into another fray. The CLC was, in every way, an arts service organization. In the era that had witnessed the dramatic growth of the arts, such agencies were to be found in every corner of the arts disciplines devoted to performance and display, providing specific services to singers, actors, dancers, visual artists, and composers. By definition, the vast majority of the members of these agencies, such as the Canadian Association of Symphony Orchestras and, provincially, the Ontario Choral Federation, had insufficient annual income to be charged adequate fees to support the agency's work. Nor were these agencies visible enough to command private largesse. Nor, in fact, did they want to compete with their constituent members in hounding the few foundations, corporations, and more wealthy arts supporters who could be attracted. At the same time, one of the primary roles of, for example, the Canadian League of Composers was to harass governmental arts councils and cultural ministries to provide a basic level of support to their particular art form and to the country's culture as a whole. The arts community could argue, with some validity, that without organizations to give voice to the concerns of individual artists as well as a presence to all the orchestras, choirs, and ballet, dance, and theatre companies, there would be no supportive structure in place even to inform and educate. Certainly, there would be little likelihood of influencing the values of a society obsessed by the acquisition of material things to shift more and more in the direction of becoming arts performance devotees.

As the economy cooled, governments were quite willing to reduce support to these service organizations, even though they knew they had little chance of making up the loss in the private sector, where visibility was the expected advantage in making a donation. Harry, on behalf of the CLC, expressed the not-too-popular position that such arm's-length service organizations were essential to the health and well-being of the arts and that allowing these supports to diminish would ultimately hamper every aspect of a strong cultural expression. He went so far as to point out that the money that was being spent on commissions and the support of organizations like the Toronto Symphony, the Canadian Opera Company, the Mendelssohn Choir, and the Stratford and Shaw festivals would be wasted without the presence of a strong and viable infrastructure, such as, in this case, the Canadian League of Composers. It was not an argument that pleased even CLC members, as they saw such organizations draining away money that could otherwise go directly to themselves in their role as creative artists. Once again, Harry had discovered an unpopular cause to promote.

The Canada Council, a body Harry respected, became a major drain on his time and energy. He served on numerous advisory panels and discipline juries, sometimes replacing the other Harry (Harry Somers) when he was otherwise engaged. Harry was constantly writing and speaking on behalf of the country's major source of arts funding. It was difficult in the early 1980s, as these were the Trudeau years, dominated by a Canadian prime minister who had a reputation as a cultivated traveller, a serious writer, and an arts enthusiast, and the assumption was made that the federal government was onside both spiritually and financially. With Trudeau's friend and colleague Tim Porteous as the director of the Council and with such chairs as Maureen Forrester and Mavor Moore, it was thought that money would rain down on the arts. It was not to be. There were other priorities, and the arts slipped into a quiet backwater of federal disinterest.

Harry not only had to raise his voice in public support of the Canada Council but also had to take on unpopular issues that threatened to lose him the confidence of his colleagues. One program that had little support across the arts community was the funding of foreign artists to visit and work in Canada. When there was little money for Canadian artists, such a program came under direct fire. However, Harry realized that artistic isolation had held Canadian culture back for at least a half a century in the past and that providing modest funds to bring in significant artists with a valuable message was a wise investment for the future. A perfect example of how important a visiting artist from another country could be was the role that Tyrone Guthrie played in the establishment of the Stratford Festival. Richard Rutherford, the Canada Council awards officer, realized the value of having Harry, openly a Canadian nationalist, onside in terms of both the validity of the concept and the selection of the individuals who were to be assisted. "I cannot thank you enough for all the effort and thought you put into helping us to adjudicate the Visiting Artists applications…. I know it was difficult but you were superb," Rutherford commented.

It is rare that artists, almost all of whom have been turned down at some point in their careers, will openly defend government funding agencies, such as the Canada Council, in the public forum of the letters to the editor of a major newspaper. In the summer of 1985, Patrick O'Flaherty wrote a scathing attack on the Council in the *Globe and Mail*. It was very difficult for such agencies to defend themselves, both for political and diplomatic reasons. In August of that year, Harry penned a letter to the same newspaper in which he answered O'Flaherty's criticisms. First on the list was the charge that Central

Canada received more support than other regions. Harry replied that "the obvious reason that Central Canada gets the lion's share is that an overwhelming proportion of the country's artistic activity takes place there. Or does Mr Flaherty believe that 'equal access' to the Council's programs means equal apportionment, on a regional basis, of the Council's funds?"

O'Flaherty had charged that because most of the jurors came from Central Canada, they inevitably favoured applicants from that region. Harry pointed out that there was no "inevitability," that, indeed, there were jurors from every region, and when the process to determine the successful applicants was changed to a blind system where evidence to determine artistic quality was not attached to any identifiable applicant, it had virtually no effect on the outcome of past years when all names of applicants were known.

Harry's final thrust was in answer to the charge that certain artists were favoured and others discriminated against. Harry referred to his own experience. "There are some composers who were almost invariably granted awards. They are still being granted awards. There are some composers who were never granted awards and who, again, are still not being granted awards. I know several in this group. They are all from Central Canada." It was an important intervention from a respected artist who was prepared to defend a system that favoured excellence over both persistence and geographical location and who had over some forty-five years not always had his way with Canada Council juries. It carried weight and influence.

There were individuals who engaged Harry for advice that was much more interesting, even if frivolous. Christopher Ondaatje, the publisher of Pagurian Press, was doing a follow-up to the *Canadian Book of Lists*, which had first appeared in 1978. For a future publication Ondaatje wanted Harry to supply him with the names of the ten most sensual pieces of Canadian music and the ten most sensual Canadian singers. Mary certainly appeared in Harry's latter list, a choice that would have received wide agreement, but no other responses have been recorded or remembered.

In 1986 Harry became a member of the Toronto Arts Council (TAC). His interest in that body had been aroused in 1985 when the mayor of Toronto, Art Eggleton, wished to convince the federal government that funding for the arts was important to Toronto, now a cultural centre of some distinction. A small delegation, including Harry, was sent to Ottawa to wait upon the ministers of the Crown, members of Parliament, and senators. Until the 1980s, it had not been apparent to municipalities the extent to which a vibrant civic life was based on the presence of an active artistic community developing in its midst. Harry had witnessed the cultural desert of Toronto in the mid-1940s blossom into the exciting scene of the 1980s and '90s. He also knew that artists, like himself, depended on a general understanding that in a country with a relatively small population, with fewer cities, with private sources of support less abundant, governments at all levels must be made aware of their responsibilities to provide appropriate support.

Previously, the emphasis on municipal arts funding had been on the extent to which the arts provided jobs, incomes, and tax revenue and, even more importantly, drew tourists from other countries, particularly the United States, who would spend money in those centres that had theatres, galleries, and concert halls. Harry's life in the arts had little to do with these aspects of the argument for a well-funded arts scene. However, whether it was because of his Winnipeg roots, the fact that he had been the child of a family on welfare in that city's streets, or because he had learned through experience the horizontal nature of any attainment of a dynamic city filled with the artistic expression and learning opportunities that encourage civil behaviour, Harry knew he had to contribute his understanding.

In accepting a seat on the TAC Board he was replacing Mary, who had given years of service early in the existence of this funding body when it had few resources but heralded high expectations. She had served the TAC well, making her own vast experience a well of knowledge from which younger members could draw. She had preceded Harry in signalling the fact that the funding of Toronto's arts activities was not just about bringing in tourists but also about nurturing a human environment. In short, it was about building a civilization. Mary brought her knowledge of the problems of individual performing artists to the TAC's attention.

When, after Harry's arrival, Dixon House, a community service that provided music lessons to poor kids, asked for support, it was more than just a request to address basic needs — it was a cry for help for the arts as a healing force among the dispossessed. While he realized that arts funding bodies could not be social service agencies, Harry could hear that call and, recognizing the splendid artistic quality of Dixon House's work, did not hesitate to influence his colleagues on the Council. With his feet on the ground of human need and his head in the clouds of artistic idealism, he was the perfect replacement for Mary but a splendid candidate for the TAC Board in his own right.

Harry spent several years with the TAC. He played a special role — ensuring that arts organizations devoted to serving the less wealthy received proper attention and appropriate funding. Unfortunately, his time on TAC came to an unhappy end in 1991. His resignation came over the fact that, without consultation, the nominating committee had rejected a particular candidate on the basis, it seemed, of his lack of popularity with TAC clients compared to that of an alternative nominee. Harry had no time for such machinations and took his leave. Months later in 1992 he received the same recognition for his contribution that Mary had received a few years earlier — a Medal of Service from the City of Toronto. The Freedman household now contained a matching pair of presentations from the city they had both come to love.

However, it was the Canadian Music Centre that received Harry's most intensive concentration. In 1979, he had been advising that organization's Standing Committee on Education of the possibility of setting up a program that would emulate one that the Canadian League of Poets had created some years before. It involved composers visiting schools, playing examples of their music, and then discussing the works with students in the hope that some would decide to become composers themselves. All of Harry's historical determinants for classroom success — careful listening, thoughtful reaction, and the possibility of having music made by the students themselves — were present. It was a program that Harry could enthusiastically support.

In 1986, Harry was named a director of the CMC and given the task of offering advice and suggestions of an artistic nature "on any project which involved Canadian performances where the Music

Centre is itself encouraging presentations." The feeling of mutual admiration shared by the CMC and one of its respected composers was illustrated by John Miller, then director of the CMC, who took it upon himself in that same year to ask Andrew Davis, the conductor of the Toronto Symphony, why, when Oscar Morawetz's seventieth birthday was being celebrated by the TSO's playing his music, similar treatment was not forthcoming on Harry Freedman's sixty-fifth. That intervention seemed "too restrained and too late" but did something to ensure that Harry's subsequent birthdays were indeed suitably celebrated by the music community.

Whenever Harry received news about the playing of his compositions from ensembles across Canada, he tried to be present at the performance, and occasionally his advice was sought at rehearsals. One of the developments that gave Harry great joy was the increasing willingness to connect various arts disciplines, in the case of many of his works, quite fittingly. It pleased him that when, in 1985, for example, the National Arts Centre Orchestra scheduled *Images* on its program, the National Gallery, then just across the street from the NAC, exhibited the paintings of Harris, Nakamura, and Riopelle. Indeed, the NAC, in its promotion of a special showing of Emily Carr's paintings, included *Klee Wyck* as the musical reference. When in 1988 the Windsor Symphony commissioned *Graphic VI: Town*, dedicated to the visual artist Harold Town, the Windsor Art Gallery close by displayed his works.

It was not unexpected that, in a decade in which Harry's music for *Oiseaux Exotique* had excited National Ballet of Canada patrons, when Dance in Canada, an umbrella organization that served its discipline, organized a conference on the "The Future of Dance" it would call on Harry to express his views. The topic was "Creative Thought and Expression," with a subtitle, "The Role of Dance in Society, Its Responsibilities and Influence." These concerns were at the very core of Harry's interest in any art form. It enabled him to make the point that if dance was nothing but beautifully executed movement, it would never have any influence on the world around. He was able to express his philosophy that it was the interconnected power of the arts that a hurting society demanded and that an arts-integrated response could represent a valuable social movement.

By the mid-1980s it was painfully apparent that Western society was moving towards a different set of values, one that had more focus on technology and efficiency, on globalization of the marketplace as the larger solution to planetary economic problems — all directions that Harry had identified and criticized earlier than most observers. In his mind, the devotion to the "team" demands of the ballet or dance corps should counter this obsession with the concept of individual rights that had overcome Western society. Every example of ensemble behaviour that resulted in trust and dependence and emphasized the importance of partnership and collaboration was a lesson for the world out there.

Harry was determined that Canadian composers should focus on Canadian themes. In a North America dominated by the elephantine influence of the United States, it was easy to go in other directions — at great profit. Sometimes the hope of collaboration was doomed by conflicting values. One project that proved to be impossible and yet so attractive was the creation of an opera on a western Canadian theme. In the 1980s, the idea for a Canadian opera that would rank with Somers's *Louis Riel* attracted Floyd Chalmers, still a most generous contributor to the artistic life of the country. Rudy Wiebe, a prolific literary figure, had in 1973 published a book called *The Temptations of Big Bear*, whose hero was a chieftain of Cree and Ojibway ancestry. There was some talk of turning the novel into an opera, but although Chalmers was interested in aboriginal heroes, unfortunately he felt Big Bear was not well known enough to attract audiences to opera houses south of the border. Instead, he saw enormous potential in using the more famous Sioux chief Sitting Bull as the subject of an opera. Conveniently, in Chalmers's view, Sitting Bull had played a minor role in the affairs of the Canadian West.

Wiebe, whose book had initiated the process, gave up on the idea of writing the libretto but handed the possible commission over to an academic colleague who was equally reluctant to trade Big Bear for Sitting Bull. Harry, though still filled with reservations about the demands of operatic composition, wanted to try his hand at an opera on such a theme. The story of Big Bear would have placed in direct contrast the treatment of Native people in America's Wild West with the more civilized relationship that had been characteristic of the development of Canada's West. But the effort came to naught. After many months of negotiations it was clear that Floyd Chalmers was convinced that only a figure as prominent in American history as Sitting Bull could be sold in the United States and make the mounting of such an opera financially viable. Harry's main disappointment lay in the fact that a Canadian Native leader was not given the attention he deserved.

One of the great triumphs of Harry's life was the contribution he made to the musical learning of thousands of young people in the 1950s, '60s, and '70s. Although he was no longer prepared to spend weeks of his time teaching, he was determined not to lose contact with the wondrous openness he found in youth and accepted the invitation in the mid-1980s to be composer-in-residence at the Ontario Federation of Symphony Orchestras (OFSO) Youth Orchestra Festival in London, Ontario. Betty Webster, the OFSO executive director, wrote to express her delight: "Your participation provided the students with a unique opportunity to be directly involved with one of the creators of Canadian contemporary music … it made a lasting impression."

It can be seen only as the ultimate triumph that Harry's devotion to young people should result in the most popular of all his compositions being one that children sing, *Keewaydin*. Though commissioned in the 1970s by Bill and Mary Heintzman for the Bishop Strachan School in Toronto, by the 1980s it had become the most requested selection in the Toronto Children's Chorus's vast repertoire. It was recorded by this ensemble and appeared regularly in its concert programs. Harry stated, "The text is taken from the map of Ontario, place names taken from Cree and Ojibway nations." He had no idea what any of the names meant in their original context; he was interested only in the sounds. However, the music and these sounds depict the Canadian North perhaps as no other piece in the choral repertoire. On the last page of the *Keewaydin* score there are a few seconds when the soaring call of the loon is heard. It brings a shudder of pride to every listening Canadian.

The impact of the composition across Canada is quite surprising. Sailboats have been named after it. An afternoon CBC Radio program was hosted by Bob Kerr, who played it so often that it achieved a unique familiarity with his listeners and became an anticipated staple offering. In 2003, the conductor of the Toronto Children's Chorus, Jean Ashworth Bartle, was invited to adjudicate children's choirs at the Choir Olympics in Bremen, Germany, and was thrilled to discover that three ensembles from China sang *Keewaydin* as the test piece. One of the performances was choreographed for appropriate movement. Jean was homesick for the sight of the Canadian North but even more delighted that a Canadian composition had achieved such international attention.

When later in the 1970s Harry was commissioned to compose another choral work, he chose Eastern Canadian folk songs and produced *Green... Blue... White.* In these decades, it too became popular, particularly as it included a song based on Dennis Lee's poem "1838." One American listener compared this excerpt to his own country's *Battle Hymn of the Republic,* as it "spoke for Canada" and the nation's democratic, populist leanings in just the same way.

In the late winter of 1985, Harry was invited to participate in the school music festival at the Collins Bay Public School. It was a glorious experience, bringing back all the delight and excitement of earlier decades. The principal, John R. Macdonald, wrote to him, "You dove into the Festival with patience, enthusiasm and your usual good humour ... all the richer for your personal and musical involvement. I think Canadian music was well served." Harry's periodic involvement in arts education continued unabated into the new millennium.

Harry also kept up his active role in the political life of his city, province, and nation. Although he pressed on local issues such as the preservation of the Brickworks in Toronto, an extraordinary area in the Don Valley that had both historical and geological significance, and he approached successive provincial governments over the move to market value assessment that he believed was savaging the ability of older Toronto citizens on limited income to keep their homes, his interest was focused more intensely on the national and international scenes.

Harry had a particular interest in the remote areas of his nation, including the Canadian park system, and was outraged when, in 1991, the decision was made to destroy some four thousand diseased bison in

Wood Buffalo National Park. His advice to the minister of the environment, the Honourable Robert de Cotret, was that it was unwarranted and was, ironically, in violation of the Free Trade Agreement with the United States. A few months later he received a reply from Prime Minister Jean Chrétien that the government was now "examining the recommendations of native people that an approach focusing on the elimination of the disease rather than healthy bison be adopted." In 1998, he was equally irritated by a proposal that he believed would allow the killing of the wolf population in the Northwest Territories and informed the minister of the environment of his opposition.

When the story broke about the horrific sanitary conditions endured by the Mushuau Innu people of Davis Inlet, Harry complained to Minister of Health Allan Rock and was assured that the community would be moved to a site that would allow a modern technical response to the problem. He was constant in his financial support of the Lubicon people in their efforts to secure justice in their land claims, but the issue remained unresolved year after year. Knowing with some intimacy the beauty of the west coast and its islands from his many years at the Courtenay Camp, he was a determined opponent of commercial interests who wished to log Salt Spring Island, and in 2000 he wrote to the federal minister of the environment, David Anderson, who replied that the land proposed for logging was in private hands and all he could do was to seek co-operation from these interests. It was not good enough for Harry, and it was one of the reasons he became disenchanted with the Liberal government that took Canada into the new century.

It was the Goods and Services Tax (GST) imposed by the Mulroney Government that particularly upset Harry. In his view, it was a regressive sales tax that failed to differentiate the resources of the rich and poor, and he felt it should be abandoned by Jean Chrétien's Liberal Government in the 1990s. Harry advised the prime minister to cancel the GST, as he had promised to do in his election campaign, but to no avail.

By far his greatest concern throughout the late 1980s and the '90s was the Free Trade Agreement (FTA) with the United States, which was later broadened to include Mexico in the North American Free Trade Agreement (NAFTA). He felt that such an agreement with the U.S.

would mean the end of an independent Canada. In 1987, he wrote to the Honourable Flora MacDonald, enclosing an article from a fiercely left-wing periodical, *This Magazine*, titled "Losing it in the Lobby." MacDonald's special assistant replied, seeking to allay Harry's fears that there would be unpleasant consequences from the agreement. The main point of the letter was, "The Prime Minister has stated repeatedly that Canada's cultural sovereignty is not at stake in the negotiations." This statement did nothing to reduce Harry's suspicions, as he recognized that one could not disconnect the cultural from the increasing dominance of American economic power and control over Canadian energy and water resources.

In the midst of the free trade negotiations, Harry had been critical of the Conservative Mulroney Government's cuts to the cultural sector, primarily borne by the Canada Council but also having deleterious effects on such federal agencies as the CBC. He had written to New Democratic Party (NDP) Leader Ed Broadbent, asking why the New Democrats had been "so silent." Harry was convinced that these cuts to the arts, education, and social welfare sectors had been unnecessary, in spite of the need to restrain the national debt. He believed this debt was the result of many years of deficit financing and that a turnaround could have been planned over a comparable period with considerably less impact on ordinary people — and on the artistic community. In the immediate situation, he found in the budget papers that there had been some $18 billion in tax concessions to corporations and that there was some $30 billion in back taxes owed by that same sector. These were the people a former NDP leader, David Lewis, had identified as "corporate welfare bums." Harry saw a pattern in the policies of almost all Western governments, one that was borne out by subsequent events: massive deficits were reduced by cutting social programs and, in particular, arts funding. At the same time, taxes on corporations and the well-to-do were reduced dramatically and loaded on the middle class. He expressed disappointment that the NDP had failed to provide adequate opposition to these fiscal shifts that were changing the social landscape of his country.

In September 1989, he wrote to the NDP recommending the creation of a coalition with the Liberals to stop the implementation of the Free

Trade Agreement. The federal secretary of the NDP replied, "While it is true that opposition parties were opposed to the Free Trade Agreement, there are plenty of items with which our Party is in sharp disagreement with the Liberal Party. Generally speaking, the Liberal Party has more in common with the PCP [Progressive Conservative Party] than ourselves." For Harry, philosophy and particular issues were more important than party labels and historic allegiances. Within a year, Harry was focusing on the fact that the Mulroney Government had won the election with only a minority of the votes cast. He was outraged that this election victory was perceived to have given Mulroney a mandate to move ahead on a fundamental Conservative policy shift — initiating free trade negotiations with the United States. His opposition to the Free Trade Agreement and the process by which it had become reality became the major plank in his campaign to reform the Canadian electoral system.

Harry was relentless in his determination to place electoral reform on the agenda of the nation and every province. In 1993 he warned the editor of the *Globe and Mail* there was "lots of anger out there" that could be contained only by getting rid of "an archaic election system" and proposed as a solution some form of proportional representation. He recognized the desire of electors to vote for specific candidates who would represent them and their interests in particular constituencies. However, after a certain number of individual members had been elected constituency by constituency, Harry saw a second voting day when electors could place their support behind a second flight of candidates whose political party connection was stressed and whose election would automatically ensure a closer relationship between the support political parties received and the number of seats they would hold in the legislature. The problem of a multitude of political parties appearing on the scene would be restrained by a limitation demanding 5 percent of the votes for constituency candidates on the first ballot before that party's candidates could participate in the second electoral process. It was a form of proportional representation that would ensure the system no longer produced inappropriate party majorities that did not reflect of the views of the electorate.

In 2000, Harry confronted John Ibbitson, a political columnist for the *Globe and Mail* who had dragged out the spectre of a plethora of splinter parties under proportional representation. He pointed out that Ibbitson had based his assessment on the record of Italy when, in fact, Germany was a better example and there were other Scandinavian examples that belied this argument that automatically linked political instability and proportional representation. Indeed, Harry pointed out, there were only four democracies wedded to the first-past-the-post system, and all these nations but Canada were engaged in some form of electoral reform. When a year later an organization calling itself Fair Vote Canada, with Doris Anderson at its head, came on the Canadian political scene, Harry was one of its first adherents. Soon he was actively recruiting others to the cause: prominent Canadians Max Ferguson, Peter Herrndorf, Brian Macdonald, Richard Bradshaw, Oscar Peterson, and Patrick Watson were all recipients of his letters inviting them to join the cause.

Although the Free Trade Agreement was now irreversible, Harry saw the entire process that resulted in its acceptance as the negation of democratic decision-making. He was distressed over the number of cynical and disinterested young people who were not even prepared to become voters. He had come to agree with a host of Canadians who believed that the reason for this disdain was that the existing system was flawed and political parties were receiving many more seats in the House of Commons than the number of votes they received justified. Some modification that aligned the number of seats more closely to the overall percentage of votes any party had gathered across the electoral jurisdiction was essential to the strengthening of Canadian democracy.

His public preoccupations were an expression of the same nationalism that led him to compose music about his fellow Canadians and the land in which they lived. He was confident that there was a definable, recognizable sound that characterized his work and that of his colleagues. It came not from forming a "school" that would follow certain rules of composition but rather from the individual Canadian composer's experiences of daily life in a special country. So often his music came from the rocks and the soil, very often transmitted through one or another of its visual artists. By the 1980s, and ever since, one of his most popular compositions was *Klee Wyck*. It had been composed in 1971 for a Victoria Symphony Orchestra concert celebrating British Columbia's centennial year and was inspired by the art of Emily Carr. For Harry it depicted the "favourite theme of her paintings: subjects that rise to great heights, e.g., trees, mountains, church steeples, totem poles." The piece also drew on West Coast Indian music. A review of the first presentation called it "baffling" and "brilliant" and described it as a work that "deserves to be heard again during this season. It is musically successful and definitely satisfying."

And heard again it was! When *Klee Wyck* was played by the Montreal Symphony in the late 1970s, critic and arts broadcaster Karen Keiser commented that Freedman's work "draws on the sombre colours, brooding quality and latent energy of Emily Carr's paintings" and observed that the piece "gets right to the guts of what the artist was all about ... and had conceived a dark angular theme as a unifying basis.... At one point, the violins interact pianissimo, evoking the rustling of a rain forest and the twitter of birds." It was never Harry's intention to evoke such obvious sounds of the forest, but he was delighted that his *Klee Wyck* found its way into the orchestral repertoire of several orchestras, including the Toronto Symphony Youth Orchestra.

William Littler, in surveying the repertoire that Harry had produced, declared that he had given Canada a distinctive musical voice. This was a perception that had a long history. Canadian composer and music critic Udo Kasemets, who had reviewed Harry's works in the 1950s, at the time of his writing of *Tableau* and *Images*, commented, "He has all the makings of becoming a prominent figure on the Canadian scene, especially since he has captured in his music much of the spiritual atmosphere of this country. If we ask, what is Canadianism in music? a great part of the answer may lie in Freedman's work and personality.... Here is a man whose ethnic origin is neither English nor French and whose birthplace was outside this country, yet whose upbringing and education took place in Canada and whose artistic fights are fought in the atmosphere of the land of his parents' adoption." The last fifty years of the twentieth century proved the accuracy of this prediction.

Edward Said in his book *The Public Role of Writers and Intellectuals* quotes a colleague's observation that "modern music can never be reconciled with the society that produced it, but in its intensely and often despairingly crafted form and content, music can act as a silent witness to the inhumanity all around." Harry wrote music, not propaganda, but he was unwilling to concede there could never be any reconciliation of his music and his beliefs. In his passion for a country and a people represented so often by its painters, writers, poets, filmmakers, and choreographers, there was a commitment to a Canada capable of leadership in creating a better world. He knew there was a clear relationship between his music and that commitment and explored the connection assiduously. In his public life he had no intention of being a silent witness to the events around him, nor could he accept any distance that would allow his music to be seen as anything but an extension of his philosophy and his values.

CHAPTER 14

Celebration

Harry and Mary's lives were defined not by calendar years but by performing arts seasons. In 2000–01, the musical community expressed its appreciation to them for over 120 years of combined contribution to the cultural life of the nation. These celebratory occasions included Mary's seventy-fifth birthday, Harry's eightieth, and the fiftieth anniversary of their marriage. It was a time to look forward with anticipation to further times of contribution and triumph, but these particular years invited their friends and colleagues to peer back with nostalgic delight on lives that had given so much joy and satisfaction to others.

One could not avoid remembering that in the late 1940s and '50s they might well have travelled south to greater riches and an international celebrity status but had chosen to remain in Canada at a time when colleagues were finding the prosperous postwar American entertainment industry a seductive opportunity that seemed to have no limits. Now, at the beginning of the twenty-first century, Mary and Harry knew they had made the right choice. They had sensed an excitement in the air while at the Royal Conservatory that promised a new Canada emerging. They had realized that for those who remained this unprecedented dynamic could hold the thrill of participating in the moulding of exciting artistic initiatives that would lay the foundations of a unique

Canadian culture. These two Winnipeggers would be among the pioneers who would suffer indifference and humiliation but who would also experience the thrill of knowing they had played a role in changing Canadian society. Both would be a part of the explosion of music, theatre, and dance that had dramatically altered Canada from the frontier land to which their parents had come to one whose artistic expression would be the envy of many more mature jurisdictions around the world.

On November 9, 2000, Mary celebrated her seventy-fifth birthday, and the CBC chose the occasion to provide an extended tribute to her life in music, both as performer and teacher, on the national network's Saturday afternoon opera broadcast. Though much of the emphasis of host Howard Dyck's commentary was directed towards Mary's extraordinary role as a professor at the University of Toronto's Faculty of Music, it was in every way a tribute to one of Canada's national treasures and featured the comments of Jon Vickers, Niki Goldschmidt, Adrianne Pieczonka, Measha Brüggergosman, Stuart Hamilton, and Carl Morey, who extolled her enormous contributions as a magnificent soprano soloist and outstanding member of notable ensembles and particularly her genius as a great teacher.

On February 6, 2001, Alex Pauk and the Esprit Orchestra, an ensemble dedicated to the music of Canadian composers that Harry and Mary had both been associated with since its beginnings, celebrated their careers at a concert that included the playing of Harry's *Graphic IX*, dedicated to the memory of his colleague, Harry Somers, who had died but two years before. The concert had been the initiative of Mary's student and close friend Barbara Hannigan, who after an unsuccessful attempt to secure the University of Toronto Faculty of Music's support for an appropriate event was able to insert these moments of celebration into the program of the Esprit Orchestra. She sang the music that Harry had composed for Mary and then movingly spoke on stage of her mentor's contribution to the musical life of an extraordinary number of vocalists like herself who had been influenced by her commitment to the art of singing.

On April 5, 2001, the CBC's Sunday evening program of contemporary music, *Two New Hours*, hosted by composer Larry Lake and produced by composer David Jaeger, was completely given over to Harry's remembrances of his life and works, with a playing of his *Toccata, Spirit Song, Dances from Rose Latulippe, Tableau*, and *Graphic IX*. For many listeners it was the first time they had heard such a spectrum of his composition. It was a revelation of what extraordinary quality and variety of musical expression had emanated from his pen over so many decades and gave evidence for the introduction of Harry as a "great composer," a description that Larry Lake had thoughtfully conferred in the light of this extraordinarily extensive repertoire.

On May 4, 2001, the Toronto Children's Chorus celebrated Harry's eightieth birthday by featuring his music in concert. Somehow the children's voices singing his works, including a new commission, *Aqsaqniq*, and, of course, *Keewaydin*, made it truly a birthday party. The concert was performed at the George Weston Recital Hall in North York and was followed by a celebratory reception in the foyer to which Harry and Mary's family and friends came to listen, enjoy, and drink a toast on this glorious occasion.

However, it was September 15, 2001, when Harry and Mary rejoiced on their fiftieth anniversary, that a second significant decision of their lives came into focus. It was a happy occasion with family and friends gathered in a modest suite at the Inn-on-the-Park, a hotel in northeast Toronto beside one of the city's most beautiful parks. It was in every way a reminder of a very significant choice. Was a marriage and family a possibility for two musicians and artists who had so much music making to accomplish if their lives were to be satisfying and complete? They had decided that it was possible, while fully aware of all the tensions and difficulties that lay ahead.

The anniversary party was an appropriately intimate affair, with Phil and Noreen Nimmons and Gordon Kushner from Conservatory times, Walter and Emmy Homburger, Nick Kilbourne, Eugene Rittick from Toronto Symphony days, Don and Jean Bartle from the Toronto Children's Chorus, composers John Reeves and John Beckwith (with his partner, Kathleen McMorrow), and Rosedale neighbour and CBC Radio legend Max Ferguson, along with dozens more of those who had travelled the long road with them.

The occasion was hosted by three very strong, confident daughters, Karen, or Kim, as her family knew her; Cyndie, now carrying the surname of her husband, Moe Jacobs; and Lori, the youngest, who had become a respected artist and musician in her own right. They had each followed a separate path and had made the choices that would establish their contribution to the world about them. They moved through the crowded apartment dispensing food and drink with grace and purpose, sharing the delight of their parents surrounded by those who loved them.

Kim had experienced the full impact of the frantic nature of the Freedman-Morrison union, particularly during the first years of seeking the balance of career and family life that would provide adequate income but also assure the intimacy of sufficient time together to give content and meaning to their relationship. Kim had faced the moves in the 1960s from Richmond Hill to Lowther Avenue and to St. Andrews Gardens in Rosedale, with all the disruption of a settled life and the loss of friends and changing of schools and teachers that is seen as such a tragedy at that stage of life.

Kim, more than the others, was aware of the dichotomy of family roots symbolized by the continued presence of Harry's mother, Rose, the aging matriarch who still spoke Yiddish and made magnificent chicken soup and on family occasions happily conversed with Mary's Gaelic-speaking mother, Louise. For her, in particular, these roots were strengthened by the frequent presence of Harry's brother, Doc, happily married to Mac, a woman of Russian Jewish extraction, both making her aware of the rich cultural heritage that was largely ignored day by day in her immediate family but drawn upon when decisions had to be made about important causes to support and significant actions to be taken.

Kim was aware that her parents' lifestyle was very different from that of her friends' parents. "Mom" was nearly always home for lunch but, unlike her friends' mothers, was out to rehearsals and performances in the evening. "Dad" did not leave after breakfast carrying a briefcase but took a musical instrument off with him for most of the day and often into the evening. When he was at home, he was making notations on lined paper and expecting silence as he worked. Both of them were often away in the evening, but there was always someone there, either an older lady from next door or Judy, a young woman who lived at their house, almost becoming an older sister to the Freedman girls.

Kim had no sense of being abandoned. In fact, she was rather proud of the fact that she, unlike her friends, knew what an oboe was and had a father who turned up in her school on occasion to make music with her classmates and even wrote music for them to play. As for her own musical education, she had been enrolled in Orff classes before elementary school and had taken up the clarinet in the early grades when she arrived in the formal system. At Jarvis Collegiate, which she and all her sisters attended after the family had finally settled in Rosedale, she joined the orchestra and band and revelled in the level of technical skill she had already achieved.

Kim had no difficulty graduating from secondary school but decided to take a year off before going off to McMaster University in Hamilton — far away enough to assist her move toward greater independence but not too far from a home that provided warm support. Romance languages rather than romantic music commanded her attention, but she did play in the "Mac" band and sing in the McMaster Choir conducted by Professor Thorolfson in the three years she was on campus. However, by her third year she was pursuing a program in French-language studies that took her all the way to France. This country was to be her focus for the next ten years, though she did return to complete her BA at the Hamilton campus before returning to France for her master's degree.

A love affair intervened and she married Patrick, had a daughter, Melanie, and prepared to remain in her newly chosen country amid the intense culture she had come to love. Her plans went awry. She had married a dominant male, and both Lori and her parents, who visited when one or the other was on tour, found her unable to deal with that aspect of Patrick's character. Mary and Harry were horrified at the erosion of confidence and inner strength that they saw in their daughter. Despite all the pain it represented, they were pleased when Kim left Patrick and filed for divorce. They were even more pleased when she took a job at Ontario House in Paris in the Ministry of Industry and Trade section at a time when Adrienne Clarkson was agent general for the province there. During these years, Kim led a small choir of English-speaking friends that sang a largely English repertoire that included even madrigals and found time to be a member in other choral ensembles. Finally, she returned to Canada and Toronto, attended a Faculty of Education that assured her a teaching certificate, and began a new career in the Ontario education system. Ironically, in the light of Harry's political leanings, she teaches at Dr. Norman Bethune Collegiate Institute in Toronto. Her musical performance needs are satisfied by her active presence in Lydia Adams's Amadeus Choir, a major Toronto choral ensemble.

Cyndie was to take a path as contrasted as Kim's in its rejection of the musical studies trail her parents had followed. Though there were obviously strong parental influences, she had worked hard to assure herself that her life was in total opposition to the intense but unpredictable world that Mary and Harry had chosen. She, too, had been offered and had accepted the Orff preschool experience, and her time in elementary school and Jarvis Collegiate had been satisfying, both socially and academically. She had come to the opinion that she did not have the same passion for music as her parents. Yet, coming from a family so immersed in orchestral and vocal sound, she fell into the musical life of the classroom quite easily. She played the flute but shifted to the French horn at Jarvis. While at the Courtenay Music Camp, a summer experience she came to love over the several years she accompanied Harry, she acquired a cello and a capacity to perform on strings. But she had no desire to be a professional musician. On her graduation from Jarvis, her love of being with children easily overcame her musical prowess and she went off to the University of Waterloo, the one institution that offered a degree in early childhood education.

Though she rejected the seemingly disorganized, frenetic life of the artist her parents led, she came to realize later that they had provided the warmth, support, and attention that she thought was missing as a result of their frequent absences and their devotion to their music making. It was not for her or, indeed, for any family she might parent. Yet, in discarding their lifestyle, Cyndie chose a direction that had been an important aspect of both of their careers — a commitment to teaching children and youth, in her case, first at the elementary level for four years and then in the secondary school for over a decade.

The genes were at work even in her choice of subjects: mathematics, a discipline that had attracted Harry in his high school years, and, surprisingly in the light of her negative feelings, instrumental music. She excelled. At this point she discovered something of the passion that had enveloped Mary and Harry. The young people about her caught the magic of her skill and commitment. When she decided she needed a change of career, she left the classroom to pursue the issue of justice in the education system of the province of Ontario. Teachers were at war with the Conservative Ontario government in the 1990s, and she went from giving political leadership to her union local in the jurisdiction of York County to working with the Ontario Secondary School Teachers' Federation at head office and, finally, at the Ontario Teachers' Federation (OTF), the organization that served all the teachers in the province.

Cyndie recognizes that she went through rebellious teenage years in a strangely dichotomous state of resentment and pride. She was angry that her family was not like others on the block, with the regular hours and definable roles that could be explained to her friends. Yet somehow she had come to realize that what her parents were doing was important and was being celebrated by a cultural community that was somewhat in awe. The positive memories included the excitement of the regular after-concert parties in their home, especially when they lived on Lowther Avenue so close to the Faculty of Music and the Conservatory. Even in the context of day-to-day survival there was this divided perception that, on the one hand, she hated her mother being off in Europe and Asia with the Lyric Arts Trio, but at the same time she enjoyed the relaxed rules about household duties that reigned when Harry was looking after the ship and was trying to complete a commission. Of course, warm nostalgia surrounded the summers at Courtenay with joy, even though Mary was sometimes absent, either at Banff or in Europe or the U.K. She also remembered the summer trips to the Freedman Creemore countryside property and the camping expeditions to one seacoast or another that involved the whole family. For Cyndie, Christmas was a time of magic once the pre-season's musical feast was over, with the house colourfully decorated, including the presence of a Christmas tree, which was not a part of Harry's past but was the centre of attention at St. Andrews Gardens.

As a director of the curriculum and assessment activities of the OTF, the "super-union," Cyndie has a special claim on Harry's influence — the maintenance of a continuing sense of outrage, in this case about the neglect of children's needs in an affluent society obsessed with private consumerism while the "commons" of public education continues to fray. Cyndie now lives in Uxbridge, a burgeoning community just north and east of Toronto, with the two daughters that she and her husband Moe have brought into the world. Perhaps most understandably of all, Cyndie's greatest delight is conducting the pit orchestra and the chorus for the town's annual variety show that is mounted both to raise money for charity and to remind the local inhabitants that music and drama are part of the community's cultural life.

It was left to Lori to emulate most closely the direction and lifestyle of her parents. She too had experienced Orff before elementary school. She exhibited extraordinary proficiency at a number of instruments — piano, guitar, and trombone — along with a delight in various percussion instruments. However, at the Courtenay Music Camp she had settled on her father's original choice, the clarinet. In both elementary and secondary school, music dominated her learning. She played in the school orchestra at Jarvis and any other ensembles that were available to her. She skipped academic classes to practise her chosen instrument. She seemed destined for a musician's career from the outset.

Graduating from high school, Lori went a few blocks west from Jarvis Collegiate to the Faculty of Music at the University of Toronto, graduating with a bachelor's degree in music performance. On a study grant, she continued her education in Chicago for a further two years, then moved back to Toronto to attend the Orchestral Training Program at the Royal Conservatory, a perfect fit for an instrumentalist with an interest in ensemble work. By this point she was focusing on the bass clarinet, an instrument with a combination of flexibility and sonority that she found thrilling. After a short stint in the symphony orchestra of Grand Rapids, Michigan, she went off to Amsterdam for further studies but also broadened her practical experience by playing in a sextet involving both instrumentalists and singers. She found that she enjoyed being a member of a group creating and developing a piece of opera theatre, touring extensively in Holland and Belgium to accolades each night. Yet, in spite of this professional delight, she yearned to return to Canada.

She came back to the very city where her parents' careers had been launched — Winnipeg. As a member of the Winnipeg Symphony Orchestra, she had now "arrived," but after two years, in 1988, an invitation to join the Vancouver Symphony Orchestra reminded her of the climatic and scenic delights of the West Coast she had so enjoyed at the Courtenay Music Camp. The Vancouver job turned out to be a disappointment, but she remained in that city until 1993 pursuing a freelance career that included commissioning works for her role as a solo performer as well as for small ensembles of musicians with whom she played. During that period of four years she also travelled about Canada and the United States and even back to Amsterdam pursuing a genre that included the mixing of contemporary and improvisational music. She was finding her way to a form of musical expression that gave great artistic satisfaction — both in terms of her instrumental skill and her creativity, a form of musical activity that was separate from the world of classical music but not covered by the term "jazz," either. It included both spontaneous composition and creative performance — demands and challenges that met her needs in every way. She returned to Winnipeg in 1993 and stayed there until 2001, when she moved to Montreal, where she now resides.

Harry and Mary were proud of Lori's achievements despite their concern that financial security would not likely be found on this edge of musical expression. Although she was impatient with the process of composition, the results of her work pleased Harry immensely. It was more than a fatherly delight in having an offspring following in his footsteps and doing well. He had an "I wish I had written that" response to her work. He himself composed works (for example, in 1988, *Little Girl Blew*) and dedicated them to her. Mary is pleased with her daughter's career but expresses anxiety for the loneliness and exhaustion that she knows to be part of a solo career, particularly one that demands a commitment to performing all around the world.

Lori's take on Mary and Harry's roles as parents and partners is even more positive than that of her older sisters. How did they keep a marriage together? Lori's response is unequivocal: "They were the King and Queen of that challenge … each imparted a huge mass of love for each other…. They were able to cope with the lack of time together because they were confident in that love and were basically happy people. They have an inspiring blend of essentiality (a kind of non-ambitious drive) and a sense of fulfilment in their music making … it creates a focused base in their lives as individuals and as partners."

Lori recognizes how much she learned from both their professional and personal lives. "The creative life is relentless," she acknowledges, but her parents survived and thrived in that life. Her commitment to a performing and composing career is a distinct Freedman-Morrison creation. "Being a musician and performer is who I am," she says. Tamara Bernstein, a Toronto critic, in a review of a celebratory concert for Mary and Harry that did not even include Lori's presence, expressed the opinion that in the genre of music she was pursuing she was "Canada's finest clarinettist."

On this, their fiftieth wedding anniversary, it could not have been clearer that Mary and Harry had succeeded as parents, advisors, mentors, and now friends of three attractive, intelligent young women who were making the kind of contribution to their society that one would expect from offspring of the Freedman-Morrison union.

What significant difference had Harry made to Canadian music creation? William Littler considers Harry's special role as defining in qualitative terms what it means to follow the profession of a composer in this country. There were years of physical challenge — a sore back and painful hips that took their toll. There was a continuing sense that his efforts received less attention than they deserve — a feeling that he shared with both older and younger composer colleagues. From the 1970s, he was on the cusp of monetary difficulty and aware that only with two incomes could they sustain the family responsibilities and the lifestyle that they enjoyed. But as a result of his efforts there is a repertoire of some two hundred compositions, from full symphonies to short solo offerings, a life's work that would impress even the most casual contemporary classical music lover.

But it was not only looking back to the past that made the celebratory season a satisfying experience. With all the accolades, the music continued to flow. In one year, 2003, New Music Concerts, with the Laidlaw Foundation's help, commissioned a new string quartet called *Phoenix* that made particular use of Harry's jazz background. That same year Harry's music was part of another Brian Macdonald dance work, *Breaks*, at the Banff Centre. Robert Cram, a superb Ottawa flutist, premiered Harry's *Romp and Reverie* ("A really fine piece," proclaimed the prestigious instrumentalist) in Montreal on a musical evening that included a performance by his daughter Lori on her bass clarinet. Harry's response to the occasion was to ask, "How often in Canadian history has a father and daughter appeared on the same musical program?"

The excitement of a fiftieth anniversary had made it even clearer to both Mary and Harry that their careers, though lived individually with complete artistic integrity, had been complementary. They had never been a song-and-dance team; rather, they had followed separate paths that led to the same destination, had covered much of the same ground, and had achieved common objectives beyond both their expectations. Their combined careers are unique to the musical history of the country.

Harry and Mary had believed Canada was a land deserving of a musical voice. Mary's decision to concentrate on the work of the nation's contemporary composers was as much the outcome of the same search to find an original Canadian expression as Harry's works, which had emerged from a landscape that overwhelmed his senses along with an admiration for the creative individuals who were its citizens. Mary was never more relaxed than when she sang of the glorious lakes and glens of Scotland with an emotional tug that emphasized to her audience that she was really expressing her love of the land her parents had chosen rather than the one they had departed.

There was an infectious sense of humour to be found in their work that was typically Canadian in its moderation and self-deprecation. Harry sought to deflate the self-consciousness that surrounded contemporary music and Mary was prepared to play the role of comic in her performance of serious classical works that cried out for laughter rather than tears. A Canadian musical comment seems to demand a greater breadth of cross-disciplinary opportunities, and Harry's willingness to include jazz and the folk traditions of a host of peoples, and to bring the visual arts into some interaction with his music, illustrates that search for a special multi-disciplinary Canadian sound. Mary, too, in her enthusiasm for the theatrical that went far beyond traditional opera, seemed to be on that same track. However, neither was on a determined mission to unearth a recognizably Canadian music that would satisfy some common denominator. They simply shared a strongly held belief that the inclusion and integration of the various arts disciplines could make an insightful statement about the nature of their society, just as the words *multicultural* and *tolerance* resound as a Canadian social focus. R. Murray Schafer, in his book *On Canadian Music*, points out, "It is not the arts themselves but the *relationship between the arts* that will characterize most of the creative thinking of the immediate future." That was a central commitment that both Mary and Harry nurtured. In so doing they expressed the hope that the country whose citizenship they proudly bore will seek a comparable creative objective of building a nation that will be an example of such attributes on a planet that seeks the elusive but challenging goals of universal peace and justice.

Both Mary and Harry demanded community in their music making. Their closeness to the organizations that supported artists, to the learning institutions that honed the skills and extended the knowledge of its students, to the individuals with whom they shared a stage, a production, or a moment of triumph as the "hurrahs" resounded reflected that love of others engaged in a common purpose. For Harry it revealed itself in the determination to work with teams in film and the theatre and even more directly his success in writing for the dance stage. For Mary, that sense of community surrounded the work of the Lyric Arts Trio as it crossed Canada and flew to Europe and Asia as well as the many hours spent with the Festival Singers and the COC soloists and chorus. An ultimate irony exists in the fact that for both the lonely soloist and the isolated composer the making of music was a communal experience.

Only after becoming Canada's paramount singer of contemporary repertoire did Mary realize what a dangerous and slippery slope she had traversed through all those years of addressing the unpopular but significant sounds made by her country's composers. It came most dramatically after she had begun teaching and discovered that she was almost unique in her insistence that her students know there was now a qualitative repertoire of Canadian work available for performance, selections that deserved a place in her students' recital programs.

Harry never had a moment's hesitation about one aspect of his contribution — carrying his initial love of jazz to the making of contemporary classical music. That it would express his interests in the land and people of his homeland he had no doubt. Neither Harry nor Mary had any interest in the triumphalism of empire represented by the music of Elgar or Holst, music already destined to be the last gasp of a dying hegemony. Both were conscious that they were living through an aggressive stage of the American Empire, whose values, including the tentacles of ephemeral but materially rewarding success, they had eschewed from the outset. They had decided to bring up their family in Canada, a country that, increasingly, in spite of economic ties, was following contrasting values of tolerance, justice, and diversity and thus ironically becoming less and less like its trading partner to the south.

Both were educators in the widest sense of the term. Harry's efforts not only to instruct but also to provide a musical curriculum for every instrument were ambitious and exceeded the bounds of resources available. That his works composed for children became favourites of adult audiences indicated his determination that children were not to be marginalized and trivialized. That Mary, the mentor and instructor of a phalanx of successful young artists, discovered that her most valued contribution came as a teacher is sufficient indication of her love of young people and the way they learn. Indeed, her daughter Cyndie would observe that since the three children have left home, Mary has acquired another family — the students who idolize her willingness to reach out to them with understanding and love. Harry even became a surrogate father in that second family as Mary's students saw in him a figure who understood the life they wished to build for themselves.

To have known Mary and Harry is to recognize lives well lived. They expressed their ultimate philosophy in decades of service to a country that faces a unique opportunity to be seen as a model of persistent but non-aggressive "soft" diplomatic leadership, which its long history of tolerance in diversity has prepared it to provide. The making of music that reveals the strength and beauty of such a land and such a people has been the contribution of these two extraordinary figures. It is a reason to celebrate!

POSTSCRIPT

As I completed the manuscript of this work and submitted it to the publisher, Harry's health was deteriorating. By April 2005 he was constantly tired and found it difficult to eat properly. But there was work to do. He completed a commission from the Esprit Orchestra creating an orchestral suite from Harry Somers's music for the opera *Mario the Magician*. A commission from the Gryphon Trio was left unfinished.

Harry wanted to be present for the spring 2005 recording of his choral works by the Elmer Iseler Singers and the Amadeus Chamber Singers (in which his daughter Kim sang) — both ensembles conducted by Lydia Adams. He always wanted to attend performances of his music, and the playing in April of *Duke*, his celebration of the music of Duke Ellington, at the River Run Centre in Guelph, conducted by his good friend Simon Streatfeild, was not to be an exception. A high point earlier in the spring had been the revival of Harry Somers's *Louis Riel* in Montreal, to which all the members of the 1967 cast had been invited, including Mary. Although exhausted, Harry went and enjoyed himself enormously.

Mary had agreed to teach at Orford in the last days of June and early July. She had wanted to cancel and had found a replacement to teach her students, but Harry was adamant — she must go. Kim could stay at the condo and other members of the family were close by.

As it turned out, the main challenge was in securing an appointment with a medical specialist. (How ironic that the lack of immediate medical attention should be a factor in Harry's effort to recover in the light of his lifelong crusade against the continued erosion of public sector services!) The earliest appointment available was six weeks away, in mid-July. Fortunately, Harry's nephew, a medical practitioner in Detroit, was able to find a colleague at St. Michael's Hospital in downtown Toronto, and an earlier appointment was secured.

June and early July 2005 were marked by a series of efforts on the part of urologists, nephrologists, and oncologists to alleviate Harry's discomfort. Prostate cancer had been present since the 1990s but had been kept at bay through radiation and hormone treatments. Sunnybrook Hospital, with an excellent Cancer Centre and a special role for serving Canada's veterans, became the venue for Harry's treatment, and all the work of this array of specialists was pulled together by Dr. Yoo-Joung Ko. It was agreed that aggressive chemotherapy from August 8 to 10 was the only course.

However, when Mary took Harry to Sunnybrook, Dr. Ko determined that Harry was not strong enough to bear the scheduled chemotherapy and he was simply admitted as a patient. A brief visit home a few days later was a mistake; Harry collapsed and had to be returned to his hospital bed. Dr. Ko spoke frankly and openly to both Harry and Mary: it was time to seek comfort from pain and let nature take its course. Harry's response was typical: "I think I have written enough music. Two hundred compositions isn't a bad record." He was admitted to the veterans' section of the palliative care centre at Sunnybrook.

Even though his health deteriorated daily, Harry continued to hold court with the many friends who visited and brought him flowers, cards, pictures, and CDs. Mary and his three daughters were at his bedside every day, providing care and support during the few weeks before his death in mid-September.

A private cremation was followed on September 23 by a memorial tribute. Musicians, composers, conductors, performers, relatives, and family friends gathered to reflect, weep, and, yes, laugh heartily. Patricia Wynne, a dear friend; David Jaeger, his collaborator at the CBC; Annette Av Paul, a dancer who had performed his *Rose Latulippe* and subsequent ballets; and lifelong colleague Phil Nimmons all spoke with warmth and intimacy. However, it was the words of his daughters that moved the gathering. Kim, Cyndie, and Lori recounted what it was to know Harry as a father and a special friend — and there were few dry eyes in the room. Throughout the afternoon, the spoken word alternated with selections of Harry's music. And Mary was there, gracious and beautifully composed, guiding the celebration of a life that had been so entwined with her own.

Canada had lost a man who saw music as a transformational force in his country and world — and one who loved his family deeply and cared profoundly about the people he knew. It was in every way another celebration!

APPENDIX
Harry Freedman
Selected Discography

(Discs still available through the Canadian Music Centre)

Compositions (Chronologically Arranged)	Year of Composition	Recording
Tableau (for string orchestra)	1952	Centrediscs CMCCD 8402 *Canadian Composers Portraits: Harry Freedman* (2002)
Two Vocalises (for soprano, clarinet, piano)	1954	Centrediscs CMCCD 6700 *Spirit Song* (2000)
Quintette for Winds	1962	Centrediscs CMCCD 5595 *Quintette* (1995)
Trois Poèmes de Jacques Pervert (for soprano and strings)	1962	Centrediscs CMCCD 6700 *Spirit Song* (2000)
Rose Latulippe (ballet score)	1966 (revised 1976)	CBC Records PSCD 2026-5 *Ovation, Volume 1* (2002)
Anerca (for soprano and piano)	1966	Centrediscs CMCCD 6700 *Spirit Song* (2000)

Tangents (for orchestra)	1967	Centrediscs CMCCD 8402 *Canadian Composer's Portraits:* *Harry Freedman* (2002)
Toccata (for flute and clarinet)	1968	CanSona Arts Media CAM 9502 *Playing Tribute* (1995)
Toccata (for soprano and flute)	1968	Naxos NAXOS 855017 *Introduction to Canadian* *Music* (1997) (with Mary Morrison, soprano) Centrediscs CMCCD 6700 *Spirit Song* (2000)
Soliloqoy (for flute and piano)	1970	Independent CML CD 101 *Canadian Music for Flute and* *Piano* (2005)
Tikki Tikki Tembo (for narrator and woodwind quintet)	1971	CBC Records PSCD 2026-5 *Ovation, Volume 1* (2002)
Keewaydin (for SSA Choir)	1971	Marquis Classics ERAD 199 *My Heart Soars – A Canadian* *Celebration of Life* (1996)
Celebration (concerto for baritone saxophone and orchestra)	1977	CBC Records PSCD 2026-2 *Ovation, Volume 1* (2002)
Pastorale (for SATB Choir and solo French horn)	1977	Centrediscs CMCCD 6599 *Elmer Iseler Conducts Canadian* *Music* (1999) CBC Records PSCD 2026-5 *Ovation, Volume 1* (2002)
Epitaph for Igor Stravinsky (for tenor, string quartet, and four trombones)	1979	Centrediscs CMCCD 6700 *Spirit Song* (2000)

Appendix

Chalumeau (for clarinet and string quartet or string orchestra)	1981	CBC Records PSCD 2026-5 *Ovation, Volume 1* (2002)
Graphic VI: Town (for orchestra)	1986	Centrediscs CMCCD 8402 *Canadian Composers Portraits: Harry Freedman* (2002)
		CBC Records SMCD 5132 *Irridescense* (1993)
Bones (marimba solo)	1989	Centrediscs CMCCD 4592 *Alternate Currents* (1992)
Touchings (concerto for percussion and orchestra)	1989	Centrediscs CMCCD 8402 *Canadian Composers Portraits: Harry Freedman* (2002)
Spirit Song (for soprano and string quartet)	1993	CENTREDISC CMCCD 6700 *Spirit Song* (2000)
Touchpoints	1994	HARBORD STREET TRIO LYRA ODR 9315 *Harbord Street* (1999)
Bright Angels	2001	Centrediscs CMCCD 6700 *Spirit Song* (2002)

To be released by Centrediscs in 2006: *The Choral Music of Harry Freedman.* Compositions to include: *1838* (1983), *Songs from Shakespeare* (1974), *TheTokaido* (1962), *Voices* (1999), *Valleys* (2002), and *Keewaydin* (1971).

BIBLIOGRAPHY

Abella, Irving. *Coat of Many Colours: Two Centuries of Jewish Life.* Toronto: Lester and Orpen Dennys, 1990.

Adaskin, Harry. *Fiddler's World: Memoirs to 1938.* Vancouver: November House, 1977.

Adaskin, Harry. *A Fiddler's Choice: Memoirs, 1938 to 1980.* Vancouver: November House, 1982.

Axworthy, Thomas S., and Pierre Trudeau. *Towards a Just Society: The Trudeau Years.* Markham, ON: Viking Press, 1990.

Barnouw, Eric. *Documentary: A History of Non-Fiction Film.* New York: Oxford University Press, 1983.

Beckwith, John. *Music at Toronto: A Personal View.* Toronto: University of Toronto Press, 1994.

Beckwith, John, and Udo Kasemets. *The Modern Composer and His World.* Toronto: University of Toronto Press, 1961.

Beckwith, John. *Music Papers: Articles and Talks By a Canadian Composer, 1961–1994.* Ottawa: The Golden Dog Press, 1997.

Berton, Pierre. *1967: The Last Good Year.* Toronto: Doubleday Canada Limited, 1997.

Bradley, Ian. *Twentieth Century Canadian Composers, Vol. 1.* Agincourt, ON: GLC Publishers, 1977.

Cherney, Brian. *Harry Somers.* Toronto: University of Toronto Press, 1975.

Clarke, F.R.C. *Healey Willan:Life and Music*. Toronto: University of Toronto Press, 1983.

Dixon, Gail. *The Music of Harry Freedman*. Toronto: University of Toronto Press, 2004.

Ford, Clifford. *Canada's Music: An Historical Survey*. Agincourt, ON: GLC Publishers Limited, 1982.

Fraser, Matthew. *Free-for-All: The Struggle for Dominance on the Digital Frontier*. Toronto: Stoddart Publishing Co. Limited, 1999.

Galbraith, John Kenneth. *The Culture of Contentment*. Boston: Houghton Mifflin Company, 1994.

Granatstein, J.L. *Canada, 1957–67: The Years of Uncertainty and Innovation*. Toronto: McClelland and Stewart Limited, 1986.

Green, J. Paul, and Nancy F. Vogan. *Music Education in Canada: A Historical Account*. Toronto: University of Toronto Press, 1991.

Hanley, Betty, ed. *Leadership, Advocacy, Communication: A Vision for Arts Education in Canada, Summary of Proceedings, National Symposium on Arts Education*. Victoria, BC: National Symposium on Arts Education, 1998.

Henighan, Tom. *Ideas of North: A Guide to Canadian Arts and Culture*. Vancouver: Raincoast Books, 1997.

Henighan, Tom. *The Presumption of Culture: Structure, Strategy, and Survival in the Canadian Cultural Landscape*. Vancouver: Raincoast Books, 1996.

Ibbitson, John. *Loyal No More: Ontario's Stuggle for a Separate Identity*. Toronto: HarperCollins Publishers Ltd., 2001.

Kallman, Helmut, Gilles Potvin, and Kenneth Winters, eds. *Encyclopedia of Music in Canada*. Toronto: University of Toronto Press, 1992.

Kallman, Helmut. *Music for Orchestra I*. Ottawa: Canadian Music Heritage Society, 1990.

Keillor, Elaine. *John Weinzweig and His Music: The Radical Romantic of Canada*. Metuchen, New Jersey: The Scarecrow Press Inc., 1994.

Kennedy, Paul. *Preparing for the Twenty-first Century*. Toronto: HarperCollins Publishers Limited, 1993.

MacMillan, Sir Ernest. *Music in Canada*. Toronto: University of Toronto Press, 1955.

Bibliography

MacMillan, Keith, and John Beckwith. *Contemporary Canadian Composers*. Toronto: Oxford University Press, 1975.

MacSkimming, Roy. *For Art's Sake: A History of the Ontario Arts Council, 1963–1983*. Toronto: Ontario Arts Council, 1983.

Manchester, William. *The Glory and the Dream: A Narrative History of America, 1932-72*. Boston: Little, Brown and Co., 1973.

Manera, Tony. *A Dream Betrayed: The Battle for the CBC*. Toronto: Stoddart Publishing Company Ltd., 1996.

Nash, Knowlton. *The National Dream*. Toronto: CBC Publications, 1972.

Nash, Knowlton. *The Swashbucklers: The Story of Canada's Battling Broadcasters*. Toronto: McClelland and Stewart Ltd., 2001.

Neufeld, James. *Power to Rise: The Story of the National Ballet*. Toronto: University of Toronto Press Inc., 1996.

Pettigrew, John, and Jamie Portman. *Stratford: The First Thirty Years*. Toronto: MacMillan of Canada, 1985.

Peers, Frank W. *The Politics of Canadian Broadcasting*. Toronto: University of Toronto Press, 1969.

Peers, Frank W. *The Public Eye: Television and the Politics of Canadian Broadcasting, 1952 – 1968*. Toronto: University of Toronto Press, 1979.

Pitman, Walter. *Louis Applebaum: A Passion for Culture*. Toronto: Dundurn Press, 2002.

Pitman, Walter. *Learning the Arts in an Age of Uncertainty*. Toronto: Arts Education Council of Ontario, 1998.

Proctor, George A. *Canadian Music of the Twentieth Century*. Toronto: University of Toronto Press, 1980.

Rosenberg, Stuart E. *The Jewish Community in Canada, Vol. I*. Toronto: McClelland and Stewart, 1971.

Saul, John Ralston. *Reflections of a Siamese Twin: Canada at the End of the Twentieth Century*. Toronto: Viking Press, 1997.

Saul, John Ralston. *The Unconscious Civilization*. Concord, ON: House of Anansi Press, 1995.

Schabas, Ezra. *There's Music in These Walls: A History of the Royal Conservatory of Music*. Toronto: Dundurn Press, 2006.

Schabas, Ezra. *Sir Ernest MacMillan: The Importance of Being Canadian*. Toronto: University of Toronto Press, 1994.

Schabas, Ezra, and Carl Morey. *Opera Viva: The Canadian Opera Company: The First Fifty Years.* Toronto: Dundurn Press, 2000.

Schafer, D. Paul, and André Fortier. *Review of Federal Policies for the Arts in Canada, 1944-1988.* Ottawa: Canadian Conference of the Arts, 1989.

Schafer, D. Paul. *Culture: Beacon of the Future.* Westport, CT: Praeger Publishers, 1998.

Schafer, D. Paul. *Culture and Politics in Canada: Towards a Culture for All Canadians.* Markham, ON: World Culture Project, 1998.

Schafer, R. Murray. *On Canadian Music.* Bancroft: Arcana Editions, 1984.

Schafer, R. Murray. *The Tuning of the World.* Toronto: University of Toronto Press, 1977.

Setterfield, Gwen. *Niki Goldschmidt: A Life in Canadian Music.* Toronto: University of Toronto Press, 2003.

Sharp, Rosalie, Irving Abella, and Edwin Goodman, eds. *Growing Up Jewish: Canadians Tell Their Own Stories.* Toronto: McClelland and Stewart, 1997.

Skene, Wayne. *Fade to Black: A Requiem for the CBC.* Vancouver: Douglas and McIntyre, 1993.

Tulchinsky, Gerald. *Taking Root: The Origins of the Canadian Jewish Community.* Toronto: Lester Publishing Limited, 1992.

Walter, Arnold, ed. *Aspects of Music in Canada.* Toronto: University of Toronto Press, 1969.

Wright, Ronald. *A Short History of Progress.* Toronto: House of Anansi Press Inc., 2004.

Wyman, Max. *The Defiant Imagination: Why Culture Matters.* Vancouver: Douglas and McIntyre, 2004.

INDEX

(Unattributed musical selections listed below are Harry Freedman compositions; operatic roles listed below were sung by Mary Morrison)

Index

Index

Index

Index